WETWARE

Books

by

C R A I G

N O V A

WETWARE

a novel by

CRAIG
NOVA

Shaye
Areheart
Books

NEW YORK

Published by Shaye Areheart Books, New York, New York. Member of the Crown Publishing Group.

Random House, Inc. New York, Toronto, London, Sydney, Auckland
www.randomhouse.com

Shaye Areheart Books and colophon are trademarks of Random House, Inc.

Printed in the United States of America

DESIGN BY LYNNE AMFT

Library of Congress Cataloging-in-Publication Data
Nova, Craig.
    Wetware : a novel / by Craig Nova.
    1. Genetic engineering—Fiction.   2. Human genetics—Fiction.   3. Androids—
Fiction.   I. Title.
    PS3564.O86 W48   2001
    813'.54—dc21   2001049043

ISBN 0-609-60595-X

10 9 8 7 6 5 4 3 2 1

First Edition

For Richard Szalwinski

WETWARE, n. , a living thing, whether natural or artificial, separate from a program or a machine. See Hardware, Software.

WETWARE

BOOK

March 26, 2026

T H E   L O G O for Galapagos Wetware was an enormous turtle which smelled of iodine, salt, and seaweed. It hung above the door like a shoe above a cobbler's shop. The geometric pattern of the shell showed in dark greens and yellow, and the turtle's leatherlike flippers squeaked as they moved. Galapagos Wetware was in a building that had originally been a mill, and the architecture of the place still suggested the height of the machine age. What had been made here? Transformers? Electric motors? Generators? When Briggs worked late, he thought he could smell something that lingered from the time a small factory had been operated here. What was it? The scent that came from a spark in an electric engine or from the copper brushes in a generator? Even now he could feel the lingering, almost erotic quality of this scent that had been the essential perfume of that previous industrial age.

Briggs's first project, which he had started five years before, had been to design workers who would do jobs that no one else wanted: people who cleaned up in hospital rooms after patients had died from new, virulent diseases, or who worked in nursing homes where people died alone in the usual messes. And people were needed for jobs that still required the efficiency of the human hand. For instance, coal was mined and used in making plastics, but the automated cutter at the face sometimes got jammed, and someone had to go down into the hot depths, to the coal face, and reach into the machine's stainless-steel blades. A lot of people had tried to come up with an automated human hand, but everyone confronted the fact that nothing was as good as the opposable thumb. Briggs's boss, Mashita, was proud that he had been clearheaded enough to start making these creatures when other people were still worrying about whether or not such a thing should be done at all.

Of course, there were many emergencies. That was one of the things about all of this: everything was learned the hard way. One night the technicians had looked into the glass-covered platforms where the prototypes had been growing and discovered that the skin of the models was turning black, like plants touched by the first hard frost. Except, of course, these weren't plants. They had the shapes of humans, or the advanced ones did. There had been some speculation about how the room had been infected with weapons-grade smallpox. A pinprick in the tubes that circulated the growing medium, for instance, or maybe the virus had gotten in through some breach of procedures for maintaining a sterile room. The rules were rewritten and enforced more strictly.

When the skin turned black from smallpox, the technicians had looked through the glass canopy, where a creature's face had an expression of confused horror and a suspicion of events just beyond its ability to comprehend. The first thing, of course, would have been the sensation, only partially realized, of being almost alive. Briggs tried to imagine what it would be like to exist as an inanimate object feeling the first blush of life. The first sensation must have been increasing warmth. And along with that, an apprehension of the first odors, which here would probably be iodine, but perhaps the novelty of them would have made them pleasant, like the scent of apple pie in an oven. In this moment, though, the creature had been trying to make sense of the effect of the smallpox. It went through the growing medium like acid, like some starved thing that had finally found the feast it had always dreamed of. The prototypes had turned black from the toes up, from the lungs in. It took about twenty minutes. And this, of course, was just enough time to feel how the smallpox worked and to wonder about what it meant. IQs just sufficient to ask the hard questions, but not high enough to be able to answer them.

The technicians sat against the wall, hands in fists, bawling. It had surprised management how attached to the first prototypes the technicians had gotten, and how they had stayed extra hours to watch them grow. In an unguarded moment, the technicians said it had been reassuring and beautiful to see the extra-long polymers at work: the organs revealed themselves in magenta and gray, from which blue veins emerged, the pattern of the blood vessels like a tree in the fall without leaves. The bones got hard, and the eyes focused on a light for the first time. The technicians had found it hard to explain why they were certain that these creatures had been delighted by a sense of increasing life, by vitality that grew each day, but all were convinced that this was the case. You could see the delight in a creature's partially formed brow, raised in surprise, in obvious and joyful anticipation of what was happening. This keen thanksgiving for being alive, or almost alive, acted as a tonic on the people who saw it, and afterward these people looked at small things with a renewed pleasure, such as the pistachio-ice-cream tint of leaves in the springtime. These early technicians all learned something from the creatures beneath the glass. This was something that the technicians didn't talk about (for fear of getting fired), but it was one of the things that made them work long hours for little pay, just as it was the reason that they often came in on their own time to make sure everything was all right.

The bad thing had been the cleanup, the black shreds, the wilted bones, the pools of fluid, but the technicians had done it. In fact, they hadn't wanted anyone else to do it. They had all shown a fierce proprietorship, like members of a family who didn't want strangers to handle and bury their dead.

Well, those early technicians didn't work here anymore. There wasn't time now for such considerations, and of course it could cause trouble. What the personnel section was looking for were professionals. Cool. Certain. Who didn't give a damn about the first cry of surprise or terror that came from one of the growing platforms.

Briggs had watched the effect of the smallpox like the rest of them. Then he'd gone back to work, redoing the code for the first models, improving their immune systems, but as he worked he felt the first desire to add something that was not in the specifications. He thought about it at night, when he was on his way home, and then first thing in the morning. What he kept coming back to was this: since he was the basic designer for this project, he was allowing these creatures to be sentient, but not allowing them the ability to make sense out of those moments when a sentient or conscious creature had to confront mortality. Or just exquisite pain. How could they make sense out of that? All they felt was a kind of black terror. And, of course, these creatures would certainly confront the obvious fact of mortality, not through an accident, like the smallpox, but in their ordinary work. These creatures would be used until they were worn out or killed.

These new creatures were, as Briggs began more and more to believe, pornographic, which is to say they would exist as people to be used. And yet, in the places where they were allowed to be almost human, they had nothing but a few obsequious gestures and words. There was nothing intricate in their makeup, nothing beautiful or passionate, nothing that would respond to music or would allow them the freedom to investigate, with a thrill, the onset of the enormous and mysterious attraction to another human being. Their psychology was perfect. They were too practical for such concerns as the mystery of being alive. They were gray-skinned, dull-eyed, with hair like an indoor-outdoor carpet.

Briggs added a cue for the first models. He wanted them to have a capacity for visionary experience, however brief, that would give them peace and allow them to perceive their difficulties, even in extreme circumstances, as something beautiful. Briggs had studied the lives of the saints, looking for descriptions of the most beatific moments, and then he had worked long hours to find a way to include this ability in these blunt, gray creatures. In those days he had been uncertain about doing such a thing, and so he had included a cue, a word that activated this ability. He didn't tell anyone that he had done this, just as he didn't tell anyone what word triggered this ability.

Of course, when these creatures were put into production, he would see them from time to time, working on the garbage truck, for instance, that came through his neighborhood. They were plodding, uninspired, uncurious, going about their business with a brutal frankness. The men had short haircuts and heavy beards, and they wore baggy clothes that were gray, and looked as if they were cut from rags that had been used to clean a floor. If a button fell off, or if a hole was worn into a shoe, the creatures did the only thing they knew how to do, which was to endure. They pulled their coats together and persisted. Maybe they stuck a piece of paper into a shoe or tied the coat together with a piece of twine, but that was it. They had thick hands and undefined but large muscles. They tended to be dumpy. Briggs noticed that their noses were often running, and he made a note to himself to look into the sections of the creatures' code that controlled their immune systems and their allergic reactions.

Briggs saw these early creatures in other places too, in the alleys behind restaurants where they worked as busboys and dishwashers. Once he looked into the window of a greasy spoon and saw one of them working at the side of a gray dishwasher, which looked like an armored car in a cloud of steam. The man (or at least that was what he looked like) seemed an extension of the machine: the same gray color, the same sluggish insistence, and a repetitive movement of elbows, as abrupt as the push rods on the side of an old steam locomotive. Briggs was mesmerized as he watched the gray shapes in the steam.

The inside of the window was covered with rills of condensed water, the bead at the head of each one giving them the look of transparent and very small snakes, and as Briggs watched, the lines of moisture obscured what was going on inside. He went on looking, his heart pounding, his head aching. He rolled his shoulders and looked around and tried to walk away. The night was clear and cold, and he took a step up the street, but turned back at the sound of a hiss.

Through the window he saw that the creature had been tugging at a black tube, jerking it one way and then another, and that it had come loose and had started spraying a white jet of steam. It swept over the creature's face, almost like water coming out of a hose. Then the black tube fell to the ground and swung back and forth, spraying steam, bumping into the legs of the dishwashing machine.

The creature made a low, doglike howl, a two-tone wail that was repeated over and over, since the only way the intensity of it could be increased was through the sheer number of cries. His face had been scalded, and as he sat down, shocked by the sudden sensation, he let his apron fall into the mechanized works of the machine. He was dragged into the stainless-steel works of the tanklike thing, where the levers, gears, and chains worked in the damp. By the time that Briggs had got-ten inside and called to a cook to turn the thing off, the creature had been mangled.

"Ah, Jesus," said the cook. "What a mess. Shit."

Briggs leaned down, under the machine, and held the creature's head. His hair was wet and his skin had an unnatural heat, although the skin wasn't really red yet. His eyes looked up at Briggs and blinked, and then he howled that same two-toned cry, which seemed to be un-informed by anything aside from the rankest, unrelieved misery, like that of a child who has just lost a leg in a stupid accident. The crea-ture took Briggs's hand and pulled him down into the greasy hot space under the machine, but all the creature could do was say, "It hurts. It hurts."

Briggs put his lips close to the creature's ears and whispered the word, the cue.

The creature looked up at Briggs, his stare sharpening, everything about him quickened, more alert, more penetrating. The howling stopped, and for an instant the creature looked around the room, at the clouds of steam, which appeared cloudlike and soft, and out of it he must have seen Briggs's face in a nimbus of steam and light. Briggs looked down, desperately wanting to comfort, to do anything to make up for this, which seemed so like that moment when the smallpox had done its worst. The creature closed his eyes. When he opened them, he said to Briggs, "Oh, if you could only see."

Briggs sat there while the creature trembled, eyes closed, concentrat-ing on a moment of illumination. Soon, though, it passed, and when it did, the man looked at Briggs and said, "You did that. I know you did. It was so . . . " He grasped Briggs's hand and looked at him. "Oh, please, mister. It was so . . . If I could just tell you." He closed his eyes and trem-bled with concentration. "Beautiful," he said. "Is that a word?" Then he went back to the two-toned, unrelieved howling, although every now and then he looked at Briggs and said, "Mister, oh, please, oh, mister . . . won't you help me?"

Briggs sat in the alley when it was over, looking up to the end of it where the avenue began. He could still feel the grip of the creature's hand on his forearm, the desperate, imploring touch, just as he could remember in the creature's eyes that terrifying and soothing instant of illumination.

Briggs went to work the next day and the day after, trying to tell himself one thing and then another, trying to explain, to let himself off the hook, but never really able to do so. In fact, while he wanted to get away from the entire thing, from encoding biology into digital form, the project went into the next stage, and in a way Briggs couldn't quite explain, he was almost exhilarated by having a chance to do more of what was causing him such terror. Maybe, he thought, I can find a way to put some of this to rights.

The next stage for Galapagos was to produce creatures more like humans than the originals were. The imperatives of the market for these new models seemed to be working like natural selection, and often Briggs wondered whether he was in charge or merely encoding the markets. Surely, though, some of the nasty jobs the next, more advanced versions would be required to do would involve violence. These were the worst jobs, the ones that most people didn't want to do. For instance, the new creatures were going to have to be good with handguns, just as they were going to be required to understand more complicated orders. And there were other items that the market seemed to want: the ability to deceive, to bide one's time, to do all the morally suspect things that people have always had to do, but which made them feel dirty. The creatures had to be versatile, able to understand the way to do often mischievous work—whisper campaigns, say—or to pose as something they weren't. Law enforcement was interested in using them to buy illegal drugs, of which there were many these days. Too many police officers were getting killed with traditional methods. Of course, the company knew there would be a black market in these creatures, too, but the truth was that this just meant the profit margin would be greater. Far greater.

Many things had changed at Galapagos since the first models. Now the technicians kept regular hours, and worked with information that was gathered not by their own observations but from instruments, and even the instruments were removed from the technicians, because they were read by software, and then the software reported to the technicians, who, frankly, liked it this way. And, anyway, all they did now really was to monitor things that Briggs had planned and written a long time before. The technicians were in their rooms, which were outside of the shop where the growing platforms were. At least they were out of the way. They filled out the forms, signed them, completed the work that was done by methods discovered through the exquisite misery of those times in the past when things had gone sour. Everything was labeled, validated, stamped. Most people were numb to the scale of the work that was being done.

And as far as Briggs was concerned, the beginning of this next stage was the most satisfying. Maybe he would get a chance to compensate for the things he had done. He wasn't sure in the beginning what it would be, but he knew he was looking for it.

His first task, when he actually went to work, was to come up with names for them. He had never liked the generic names, the ones that came out of the abbreviations of the titles: ALM-1, or COM-L-2, which always had the air of the bureaucratic, which by definition was obscure. After all, what, really, was an ALM-1?

Briggs had gone through the phone books, but there hadn't been anything good there. He saw in the newspaper that a bank was getting ready to close some accounts of people who hadn't done any transactions in a couple of years, or who had moved without leaving forwarding addresses. Often people just left. Then the banks went to work, and Briggs knew, too, that a crew went to clean up in the apartments of people who had taken off. Perhaps "taken off" was the polite way of putting it: exiled or terrified into fleeing was probably better, although sometimes it got rougher than that.

He wondered how the crew divided the things in an abandoned apartment. Maybe it was done by seniority, or maybe by force of personality. Or just by force. In any case, Briggs knew what the slang for the usable stuff was: *mungo.* It could be anything really, an indoor plant, some clean sheets. Maybe a little souvenir, some wetware junk that had been bought in Arizona or New Mexico. Originally, cleaning up these apartments where people no longer lived had been done by men, but like a lot of other jobs, washing dishes, digging graves, cleaning up in a mortuary, this was now done by the first models that Galapagos had produced.

Briggs had made some of these living souvenirs himself when he was between jobs, before he got lucky and landed a job at Galapagos. He had done the usual things, such as a living cactus that grew in such a way as to show, on its skin, a changing picture of the mountains in New Mexico: snow-covered peaks in the winter, flowers in the spring, the coming of fall. He had also worked on mice that were able to speak a few words: "Miami is the Fun Capital of the World," or "I met you at the Seattle World's Fair." Cute items, badgers, small bears, little deer: all of them could be used in a living pitch for one product or another. Biological versions of matchbooks. A beaver sang a little song about toothpaste: the kids loved it.

He hadn't liked doing it because of the shoddiness of the things he produced, a cheapening of life that showed up not only in the garish colors and in the materials that he had used, but in the fact that none of it was supposed to last very long. It had been built to die.

As he looked for the names, he tried to find something else too, a way to make up for something. He wasn't quite sure what it was, but he knew that his desire for it increased. And as he worked and felt the pressure grow, he thought about beauty. Or perhaps it is safe to say that this is where he started. Previously he had tried to keep beauty out of the code for wetware. Beauty was old-hat. Practicality was in. The engineered, techno look. Ugly as homemade sin. And what did he mean by beauty anyway, the merely physical, or something more elusive? What was really attractive? A spirit, an attitude, an instinct for understanding, weren't these the qualities that mattered? Friendly spunk and an ability to love? And what about courage and trustworthiness, or desire? Weren't these beautiful?

And as Briggs brooded this way, he found that he thought of other items, such as the sheen of a blue sky, say, on the bare legs of a young woman. Or the expression in the eyes of a human being who is doing what is necessary and right, and who is brave. He also thought of the scalded dishwasher's two-toned cry, its plea for help. He couldn't bear to remember the cry, but he couldn't forget it, either.

He named the female Kay Remilard. Kay. He said the name to himself when he first came across it. Surely it was right for the first woman ever to be produced this way. He could even imagine how she moved (perhaps her earlobes were the color of barely ripe raspberries, the light, almost invisible fuzz on them silver, or more elusive than that, filament-like). Kay. He thought of the shadow under her arms where she had shaved, the new-moon shape of the tips of her toenails . . . Kay sounded frank and sweet, which, of course, would be nice as a matter of contrast.

Jack Portman was what he decided for the male, since he wanted a name that suggested the solid, unflinching dependability of someone who knew what he had to do and when he had to do it.

Once a month or so, Briggs was called into the executive offices to explain what he had been doing. Krupp was the division's head of future development, Briggs's boss's boss, and Krupp showed up in his rumpled jacket, his short haircut, his small round glasses, his chin and jowls needing a shave. He sat behind a borrowed desk in a corner office, the river out the window behind him looking lead-colored and as though only mechanical fish could swim in it. Krupp had scars around his eyes from a bad automobile accident, and these looked a little white when he was exhausted and had just gotten off a plane from Taiwan or Bangkok. When Krupp spoke, he reached up and squeezed the sides of his nose as though he had a headache that was so bad he had to do something, just a small gesture, to acknowledge the constant throb.

Krupp said, "So, what's this on the time sheet about names? We've got a couple of names, don't we? What are you wasting time for?"

At night, the sensibility of Krupp's voice came back to Briggs, and he thought, *Cook the books for the time sheets.* Once he had crossed that barrier, the one where he hid what he was doing, it was easier. In fact, he realized he was free if he was willing to do the work in such a way as not to get caught. Late at night he looked up and saw the blue glow of monitors through the glass walls of his office. At these hours the office had the light of twilight in a dream—soft, but with a little something lurking in the shadows. It was during these hours that he had started to add the personal stuff: a sense of humor, gentleness, an instinct for the beautiful. A delight in the vital. The love of music. And, of course, he had paid attention to the specifications, such as the handgun stuff.

To add the personal details, he had started with blood-cell-sized robots, small scanning devices that he injected into his own arm and then used them to record the brain from the inside. He was able to get a little time with the big computers to decipher the noise of this into discrete elements: he isolated specific sensations or specific talents, and then encoded them to be able to convey them to Kay. And Jack. One of the beauties of the microscopic robots was that they were biodegradable, and all he had was a bad headache each time he did it. He had access, too, although no one knew it, to the recordings that had been done this way of musicians and mathematicians. Briggs took a certain amount of pride in the fact that he had been the one to produce artificial versions of these talents.

Mashita had hired someone else to keep an eye on Briggs, a woman named Leslie Carr. She was twenty-nine years old, a little younger than Briggs. She had studied biologic algorithms at Stanford, and had worked in advertising and in digital entertainment before coming to Galapagos. Carr had red hair and blue eyes, and her skin was lightly freckled on the shoulders. She liked to wear nylon stockings and short skirts with blouses that accentuated her broad shoulders and long neck. Her expression was one of sultry disapproval.

From the beginning, Briggs knew she was wasn't paying much attention to the details of what he was doing, although every now and then, when he had been working so hard he had gotten shaky, he thought this might be her way of testing him, of giving him just enough freedom to make a real mistake. Then he considered it again and was certain that that was not her style. Mostly she got what she wanted by withholding approval, and through a mixture of brutality and delicacy, she hinted that if Briggs (and other people she kept an eye on, too) could just discover what she really wanted, she could be enthusiastic and even warm. It was obvious that she thought this was enough to keep people in line, and that she didn't even have to look that closely at what Briggs had done.

He realized this was the case when he first began to add things. He gave this work to Carr and she sent it back with a pro forma comment, such as "Looks good," or "Keep on with this," or "I want to see more."

She never included a specific comment. His impulse hadn't been to deceive her, but to try to make up for his sense of having done something wrong, not only in the first project, but more generally. Passion, beauty, love—weren't these the antidotes to the worst and most infuriating limits of being human? They were the best of what Briggs had. Anyway, that's how he had begun. Not with a plan, but with an impulse.

WENDELL BLAINE, the director of the Central Bank of North America, lived in a building that was solid but not ostentatious. It had twelve floors, and his apartment was on the top. He liked the vista, the conglomeration of lights, which in their reds and greens, in their radiant aggregate, suggested wealth, blue tinted diamonds, gold, rubies, and wet-looking emeralds. He often stood by the window, hands behind his back, thinking things over. The furniture in his apartment was dark but comfortable. He had a housekeeper who prepared his meals and put them on the table. Blaine liked well-cooked, simple food: a roast of pork with spinach and mashed potatoes and an endive salad with vinaigrette, and perhaps, if he was feeling that he had done something clever, something that would have an impact without leaving any signs of just what was going on, he would allow himself a small fruit tart.

Blaine was tall. The overall impression he gave was the essence of gray power. Limousine doors were opened for him and he seemed to exist in a world of office buildings with polished marble floors. His suits were perfectly tailored, his custom shirts were cut from Egyptian linen, and his ties were made of silk. He was capable of making billions of dollars disappear simply by raising an eyebrow at the right moment.

His routine was as regular as the ticking of a grandfather clock. Blaine came home, had his drink, read the papers, looked over some journals, opened his mail with an ivory opener, which he often used to hold a letter, spearing it by one corner, like a butterfly under a pin.

When he was done with his mail, he liked to have his housekeeper announce that his dinner was ready. He came into the dining room, which was not bright but not dark, just golden and comforting, and when he had served himself and taken a bite of just about everything, the housekeeper came back and asked him if everything was all right. Invariably, almost like liturgy, he said, "Yes. Thanks." The housekeeper waited behind the door in the kitchen until she heard the final scrape of his knife on his plate, and then she came in and asked if he would have dessert. He said yes or no. When it was yes, she put a pear tart on the table and he ate it, listening to her putting the few dishes in the washer, the squeak of her shoes on the floor, and then the diminutive click of the front door as she let herself out. The silence increased, like a room cooling when the fire burned down to ashes.

Often Blaine went into the library, where there was a piano, and he sat in a chair, by the shiny gloom of the instrument. He listened to some recorded music.

Blaine had always prided himself on one thing. It was not something he was born with, although he often acted as though it were, but a discipline he had learned over the years. It had cost him a great deal to learn it. He prided himself on the fact that he never allowed himself to be swayed by any feelings at all, and that when he had to make a decision, he did so with all the weight that a keen mind, untroubled by emotion, could bring to any problem. He faced up to everything: hard choices, hard decisions, the appalling implications of his actions. He had learned to do this by years of restraint, perfected by decades of discipline, like the exercises that Zen priests subjected themselves to, and at times he liked to think that this quality of mind was "tectonic." He smiled when he thought this way, but underneath it all he was quite proud that he could make decisions that were so demanding.

The ability to make hard decisions had cost him more than he could admit. He had found that it was difficult to give in to the chaos of family life, to the messiness that went into having children and the uncertainty of his wife's moods; so he had given up his family, or, more to the point, his family had given up on him, although he still saw his wife a couple of times a year for lunch at an elegant restaurant. She sat opposite him, despising him in her quiet, unmistakable way, accepting his advice about the markets, giving him monosyllabic answers to his questions about the children, who were now grown up. He may have been formed by years of exercise, by the practice of making decisions on the basis of what was best for the most people, but he was not stupid, and surely, given the passions that lay just beneath the surface and with which he struggled so continually, he was not unfeeling, either. So he knew, as he sat there and his wife looked across the table at him, the wine in her glass the color of the distilled sunshine of southern France, she was counting the days until he died, praying that she would have the exquisite luxury of being there to watch him lowered into the ground. He knew this and accepted it, but he woke at night, seeing that expression in her eyes. It always shocked him, whether he experienced it firsthand or just remembered it in the middle of the night, and the shock of it was like hitting a wall, just walking into a wall without knowing it was there. The emotional shock, the endless impact of it, required the discipline he had so carefully learned.

On one occasion when he and his wife were having lunch, he had reached across the linen tablecloth, over the organized shine of the silver, which was lined up like instruments for a medical procedure. He took her hand and she flinched, as though she had been struck. She put her hand in her lap, as though to wipe it on the napkin. He had wanted to say he had missed her and he was sorry about the way things had turned out, but he said nothing. Instead he cleared his throat and said, "The bass is quite good here. I think I will have the striped bass and the broccoli soufflé. And for you? Would you like something to start? Those small fish sausages are wonderful, really. Would you like some?"

She sat there, giving him that look.

He hadn't realized, in the beginning anyway, that he had turned to music as a way of staying alive. After all, it would have been easier for him if he had just felt nothing, but he wanted to have a private life—one that, while lonely, was nevertheless full and intricate, and that allowed him an understanding of those aspects of being human that could only be felt.

So he had started going to concerts. Slowly he became a member of the various boards that oversaw orchestras and contests, too, competitions of one kind and another. Everyone was glad to have his expertise in financial matters and, of course, to receive his outright gifts, which were much larger than anyone could explain. The philistines on the committees he joined never gave a second thought to Blaine's taste in music—he was "just a money man, for crying out loud"—but the musicians who served on it began to give him some grudging respect, which, in a way the musicians found hard to explain, segued into admiration and finally to a fond devotion, not only for the man but for his opinions, so much so that after a long association most musicians were more certain of the value of Blaine's opinions than of their own. Blaine appeared to take such devotion as his due, but secretly he watched with pleasure the slow, inevitable advancement of the admiration the musicians showed him, seducing them by a raised brow, a smile that only a musician would understand, a slight sniff at something that was merely fashionable and empty. This respect was more important to him than he could say, but even this he refused to allow to interfere with what he considered his reason for existence: making hard financial decisions. He had never made a mistake. One of the ways he knew this to be true, or one of the ways he measured it, was by the personal, emotional cost of his efforts.

He had dinner once a year with his son. They ate silently, saying almost nothing, and then made a date for the next year.

Each morning he went downstairs and stood under the green canvas awning of his building, where his limousine was waiting at the curb. The driver usually stood against the wall, and when Blaine emerged, the driver opened the door of the car so that Blaine was able to get in without breaking stride: the door opened, and Blaine slipped in, folding up his legs like a drafting compass that was going into a box. The interior of the limousine smelled of the vacuum cleaner that had been used on it earlier in the day.

Often Blaine's driver, Jimmy, had some sheets from Blaine's secretary.

"You're supposed to take a look at this," Jimmy said.

"Yes?" said Blaine. "What?"

Then he would look down at the sheets to see what mischief there was to consider. For instance, a group of investors in India had been trying to manipulate silver futures, and now that they had been exposed, one had to consider how the world stock exchanges were going to react, and what to do about it if they reacted badly. How far was it going to spread? How big a bump was there going to be? Shares would fall. And what would people do as they tried to find a safe haven, as greed morphed into panic? At one point Blaine had done some work with models for the markets, and he knew what the difficulty was. The equations for the markets had to include, for example, nonlinear items, the financial version of friction, and it was these things that always caused trouble. There was always some infinitely small thing, hidden at first, that revealed itself later.

In fact, though, this was what he lived for: a disruption in the market, a panic, a need for liquidity, for reassurance. He was at his best in those moments. He liked to make hard decisions. In the beginning he had been aware that many people had this knack, but he knew, too, that it was usually good for only one business cycle. He didn't want to be one of those who only lasted a single cycle. He had stayed up-to-date. But even though he had done so, he was careful about new ideas, since he didn't want to confuse the merely clever with knowledge. Fads, novelties—these were the kinds of things that he had spent his life resisting. Knowledge, as far as he was concerned, was something you could depend upon, and while it was sometimes accidentally discovered, it had the quality of not being diminished by time.

The car stopped in front of the building where he worked. Jimmy pulled open the door and Blaine got out and went into the lobby. The floor was marble, and the shine of it was still maintained the old way, with buffing machines at night, and above it was a domed ceiling on which was painted sky and clouds with angels moving through them, stern ones to be sure. They reached out to touch one another, each of their fingers perfectly suffused with the roseate glory of God. Around the dome was a gilt edge. At regular intervals, chairs were arranged in the hall just far enough from one another so that anyone who sat in one of them couldn't talk to someone else in another without shouting.

Inside, people went about their business, carrying papers, briefcases, murmuring to one another, although when Blaine came in, they all instantly hesitated. They seemed to say, in that momentary hesitation, *This is the man who knows what to do. Thank God he is here.* He nodded to one or two of them, and walked over the polished floor. The elevator waited. He went up to his office at the top of the building.

December 2026

LESLIE CARR had a dream of who she wanted to be, and she dedicated herself to trying to live up to it. Of course, she had the anxiety of someone who is trying to manufacture a sense of self from the things she had seen in movies, magazines, and advertisements, and from what she could learn from the occasionally attractive and powerful women she ran across. Carr didn't really understand these women, and when she tried to model herself on them, she did so with the exaggerations of ignorance. This didn't show in her sense of style, but in her carefully maintained aloofness, which, she erroneously believed, was what a successful woman needed.

Her father had owned a junkyard in Connecticut. Carr had disliked his bluntness, his vulgarity, and his insistence on the futility of just about everything. He wiped his nose on his sleeve and ate sardines from the can, forking out the silver fish with his fingers. When Carr had been twelve years old she'd stood at the part of the dump where used computers were kept, and there she'd taken a hammer to the piles of motherboards and mounds of printed circuitry and broken these things into bits, glad that she was able to smash the mysterious order of these objects into something she understood, which was the finality of broken junk, ragged edges, and shards of plastic bound together with electric cables with frayed ends, looking like whitish snakes with copper fangs. Sometimes her father took a turn, too, getting as much pleasure as she did out of the sudden fury that both of them barely understood. Then they stood there, sweating, breathing hard, over the machines they had broken. Her father winked at her. They understood each other perfectly. They had been angry together and had had fun. This understanding was bound up, in Carr's mind, with the odor of her father's wholesome sweat and the strength of his arms. She clung to this memory with the fierceness of someone who has told many lies, but is able to continue because she has made an effort to remember one hard, precious truth.

She had gotten a scholarship to Stanford, and she had learned how to behave and how to dress, how to use a knife and fork and pronounce the names of French wines. She noticed just how it was that people impressed one another. But almost always, when things weren't going right, when she felt a little false and unsure of herself, she longed for those afternoons when she and her father had stood in the pale, smoky sunlight and worked until they were both short of breath. "That's the beauty of this stuff, Les," her father had said. "It breaks."

The first meeting for the project at Galapagos had taken place in the conference room on the second floor. Mashita, the project director, had stood at the head of the table there, his hair brush-cut, his eyes showing pleasure in his ability to put these people together, his confidence filling the room like a gas. Everyone there was reassured by the fact that this man had personally picked each one of them, and that he had done so—or so his attitude seemed to imply—with the conviction that each of them was perfect for the job. Mashita's handshake was firm and dry (at least it had been in the beginning), his clothes gray and well cut, and he wore a black shirt and a white tie, like a gangster, but he did it in such a way as to appear cool. No one at the meeting looked twice at the people who were cleaning out their desks to make room for the new team.

Until Leslie Carr met Wendell Blaine, she hadn't worried about much aside from where was she going to be in two years, in five years, in a decade. But as things progressed, she found that she was easily bored, and while she thought she had made her peace with boredom, this was only one stage in a metamorphosis that progressed as smoothly as light seeping into a room at dawn. She didn't want to admit that her boredom had turned into loneliness. Her plans reassured her, and each new position, each advancement, had a wonderful quality, a glow that had a romantic component, as though everything were possible after all. She clung to this sensation, although from previous experience she knew that it drained away, not suddenly, which she could have accepted more easily, but with a constant, unstoppable progression until one day what had seemed grounds for self-congratulation and pleasure was just another confinement. Secretly she longed for an ally.

Carr walked along the avenues at night. The windows in the office buildings above her were filled with a blue, almost starlike light, as though the power of the people who worked there lingered as a sidereal tint. Her sense of romance increased when she saw the upper floors of the buildings in an island of clouds, and then, in the blue haze of vapor, the light in the windows seemed even more illusory. One night she looked down from the blue, diffuse lights above her to the window of Tiffany's. Behind the glass, diamond bracelets were hung from the limbs of a leafless tree to suggest glittering fruit. Then the scene changed, and the tree sprouted green leaves as the jewelry morphed into crystalline flowers. Still, she liked the diamonds the best, like some fruit harvested in the depths of winter.

After six months at Galapagos, Carr often woke up in the middle of the night and sat listening to the silence of her bedroom. Then she told herself there was nothing wrong. She was being silly. She had a new job. She knew precisely what to do with it. She had often felt this way, and she had always been able to define herself as someone who did not give in to momentary fear. Yet in the morning she decided that something was wrong with the coffee she was drinking, that it was too hot, or too bitter, or too cold. Clothes that she had always liked seemed too dowdy, the skirts too long or too short, or somehow they had stains that were hard to see, but that she was convinced had ruined them. The way she looked in them, or the style of her apartment (brown leather chairs, green window shades, blood-colored carpets), or the touch of the sheets in her bedroom left her with a strong but only dimly understood claustrophobia. Sometimes when she was in this mood, she took a bath, but the water turned cold and led to that moment when she heard the harsh gurgle as it spun around the drain and disappeared like finality itself. Then she would look in the mirror to see if there were any lines around her eyes. Not yet.

A friend gave her a ticket to the Philharmonic and she went, not really caring much about music, but hoping for an evening in which she would be distracted. She had never really liked crowds, since they made her feel somehow diminished, and yet the ones at the concert hall were different, not like the claustrophobic press of people at an amusement park, where the cries of people on a roller coaster, the sweet fragrance of cotton candy, and the buzz of old-fashioned neon lights left her on the verge of panic. At the symphony, men and women wore evening clothes and drank champagne, the glasses bright in the light from the chandelier. Carr stood in her black dress at the side of the lobby, where she drank her champagne quickly and then stood there with her empty glass.

Her seat was not far away from Wendell Blaine's, who came here regularly and who was a member of the Philharmonic's board. He arrived at the last moment, and a frisson rippled through the crowd as he went down the aisle. People turned to look at him with a combination of exquisite curiosity perfectly combined with fear of being caught gawking. The whispers spread out from his wake with a hissing, almost hallucinatory sound in which some words or phrases could be heard. *Wendell Blaine, that's Wendell Blaine. Is that Blaine, yes, that's Blaine . . .* Then he sat down and the conductor tapped his music stand with his baton, the small noise hitting Carr as though she were a hypnotist's subject who had suddenly awakened at the snap of fingers. She recalled the thrill of those voices, and as Blaine folded himself into his seat, she thought, *Well, look at that, would you?*

The music came to an end. The audience filed out, still glancing at Blaine, who was oblivious to it. He got up and walked out to the lobby, where the chandeliers glittered and people drank champagne in the hard, thundering echo of their voices on the marble of the floor and walls. Carr went down to the place where Blaine had sat and saw the seat number, 6L, engraved on an oval brass tab on the seat back. She sat down and put her hand onto the armrest where Blaine had put his hand. Her skin in her black dress looked white, and as she sat there, close to the deserted stage, she appeared exhausted. Her dark hair, the black material of her dress, her expression as she closed her eyes, all left an impression of someone desperately isolated, an impression so strong as to change the space around her, which, before she sat down, had been merely empty, but now had the electric quality of disordered feelings. As she sat there, mystified that she should be doing such a thing, she thought, *What am I doing here?* and almost instantly, answered, *Oh, you know.*

At home, when she played a recording of the music she had heard at the concert, she imagined the audience, the mass of people, their dark clothes pierced here and there by the flash of a diamond. She thought of the space that had been enlivened by his presence, and as she did, she told herself that she was behaving this way because she was restless and that if she ever got a chance to meet Blaine, she would despise him. Didn't that make her feel better? No, she would not feel better if she met him only to find out she detested him. She told herself that she was interested in novelty, which, after all, usually distracted her at other times when she felt like this. Why should this occasion be any different?

She called the box office and bought a ticket next to seat 6L. She would have to wait a few weeks to use it, but at least she had it. She found that it was hard to concentrate on her job, and out of sheer anxiety she thought that perhaps she should be checking Briggs's work more closely, but when she tried, she found that she could only glance here and there.

Her seat was on Blaine's right. He came in just before the last call and brushed by her, apologizing quietly, trailing the usual wake of murmurs in the crowd. Carr and Blaine sat together in the dim light of the hall, which was relieved only by the pool of luminescence on the conductor's podium and the cones of light on each musician's sheet music. The tuxedos, starched shirts, and shiny ties of the musicians appeared as a conglomeration of black and white, among which one saw the sheen of instruments, and all of it was imbued with an anticipatory rustle of sheet music. In that moment, which was similar to one in which something was about to happen (a first kiss was what came uncomfortably to Carr's mind), she put her hand next to his on the seat's armrest. It was dry in the auditorium, and a blue spark of static electricity jumped from her finger to his hand. Blaine looked down at the almost invisible fleck of voltage.

As she glanced at Blaine, her eyes had small points of light from the conductor's podium. Her dress rustled as she sat back, her hands folding in her lap. He hesitated, glancing at her, and then said, "Excuse me."

"It was my fault," she said.

"What can fault possibly have to do with a spark?"

She blushed. "I meant I didn't mean to . . . "

"To shock me?" he said.

"That's right," she said. "I didn't want to shock you."

"Between the two of us," he said, "I'm not easily shocked." He offered his hand. "Wendell Blaine," he said.

"Leslie Carr," she said.

There was another spark, a small *fit,* when she took his hand.

"I guess we've got to be careful or we'll get electrocuted."

"Well," she said, "it's nice to meet you. Whatever the voltage."

Blaine made a noise that might have been contempt, but then it might have been pleasure. The orchestra played Schumann's First Symphony, and as they listened, Carr felt the lingering, diminishing buzz on the back of her hand from the touch of his fingers. What could she say when the music was over? Something about the markets? Surely that would be a mistake. Of course, the best thing would be a comment that would make him laugh, or at least smile. Or perhaps she could tell him a piece of trivia—for instance, that Mozart had never owned a piano. Did he know this? Would he be interested to hear it?

She sat there, feeling his starched, crisp presence. He nodded as though he knew the score by heart and might be turning the pages of it and letting the orchestra read it aloud to him. As she sat next to him, she thought that everything about her was just a handful of tricks, a couple of gestures, a few phrases, and all of it added up to what she felt herself to be at this moment, a rude young woman, or not-so-young woman, sitting next to a man who really understood the way things were.

The music ended. The applause began. She sat there. Blaine turned toward her.

"Excuse me," he said.

She stood up too, and stepped into the aisle.

"I wonder what you thought of it," she said.

"The question is," he said, "what did you think of it?"

She looked him in the eyes and said, "I thought that it was more form than substance."

"Precisely," he said. "It was his first symphony. How could it be otherwise, no matter what the critics say?" He looked at the shape of her lips, the heated, fervid intensity of her eyes, which had more to do with the fear of embarrassment than anything else. "Would you like to have a glass of champagne? Leslie Carr, isn't that it?"

They went up the red carpet toward the door at the back of the auditorium, through which came the loud, almost hysterical sound of people in the lobby.

A mass of people stood at the bar, but one of the barmen stepped to the side and said, "Mr. Blaine. How nice to see you. What can I get you?"

"Two glasses of champagne. The Cliquot," said Blaine. He took a bill from his pocket, a new one that looked as though it had been ironed by his housekeeper before he put it in his pocket.

"Did you know that Mozart never owned a piano?" she said.

"No," he said. "I didn't. Why not?"

"He couldn't afford one," she said.

"Yes," he said. "I suppose that's right. Here."

He pressed a glass of champagne against her fingers.

"Thank you," she said. "But, you know, that's one of the things about money. You can see its beauty sometimes not by its presence, but by its absence."

"Not its beauty," said Blaine. "Its power." He smiled. "Let's step out of the mob. Over there, where we can look out the window."

She saw Blaine against the chandeliers, which were shaped like toy tops, constructed in circles of light. Blaine said, "I always like to look out this window. You know, glass isn't firm, not really, but plastic, although it takes a long time to collect at the bottom of a frame. In a couple of hundred years, it is thicker at the bottom than the top."

Carr looked up at the dark squares of night sky, on which there was a film of light from the chandeliers, and as she stepped up, the heel of her shoe snapped off.

"Oh, no," she said, blushing, putting a hand to her lips.

"May I confess something to you?" said Blaine.

"Yes," she said.

They were both looking down at her shoe.

"I have always wanted to walk on the marble of this floor in my stocking feet. Would you mind if I took off my shoes?"

He then reached down and undid his laces and stepped out of his shoes.

"Just as I thought," he said. "It feels wonderful. Would you like to try too? Let me hold your glass."

She took off her shoes and they both stood on the marble floor.

"I wonder if you would like to have dinner with me," he said.

She laughed and said, "Yes. But how are we going to get out of here?"

"We are going to walk," said Blaine. He took his shoes in one hand as though he had picked them up from the floor of a closet. "I always thought it would feel good, but I never imagined anything like this. Don't you agree?"

Outside, Blaine's driver opened the door, the car appearing in the crowded street like an object of certainty, almost like a monument, a black, sleek monolith. The pavement was cool and damp, its texture rough against her feet. The car was instantly silent after the driver closed the door, which shut like an expensive refrigerator.

"Armor," said Blaine. "It makes the car quiet."

His driver got in.

"Jimmy, we'd like to go home," said Blaine.

The car slid up to the building like a long shadow. Blaine got out first, looking one way and then the other, and reached in and took her by the tips of her fingers, as though they were at dancing school. They went in, under the green canopy, past the doorman in his blue uniform with the gold trim, across the black and white order of the tiles of the lobby, and into the elevator, which was paneled with dark wood and had a mirror, in which Carr glanced at herself. She looked at her skin, her eyes, her hair, the somewhat disordered appearance of herself, which made her look as though she were in the midst of a fall, rather than rising in the cool elevation of the machine. It was all so smooth and easy, and she still felt that sense of almost lubricated movement when in the morning she left the apartment and found that the housekeeper had fixed her shoe and left it by the door, just as she found the car waiting for her, as though the driver had never gone home, but had been waiting there for her.

At work, she told herself that she had to get a grip on herself, that this was wonderful, but she still had a job to do. She started going through Briggs's code more carefully.

CHAPTER 4

January 15, 2027

AT 8:00 A.M., Blaine walked through the marble lobby of the building where he worked, carrying nothing at all, not a piece of paper, not a briefcase, nothing. As he passed under the dome, he glanced up at the stern angels. He went through the swirling hush of people, nodding here and there to people he liked, only raising a brow to people he tolerated, and ignoring a fair number of people altogether. Upstairs, he came into the room where staff meetings were held. These morning assemblies were known, by the people who attended them, as the Hit Parade. The room where they were held was just a little too small, and some people who came late had to stand. The others sat around a dull gray table.

The head of each section (Currency, Trade, World Interest Rates, Stock, Futures) named one item that was cause for concern. Bad loans in Russia, an attempt to corner the futures market in copper in Brazil, erratic and seemingly chaotic movement in the Asian stock exchanges, the fact that some currency speculators had started to move against the UAD (United Asian Dollar, a currency modeled on the euro). Sometimes, when a section head was worried, the speech went on too long. And when they were close to panic, they tried to be cool, but this only made matters worse, since subdued hysteria only accentuated it. At these moments it was as though someone had released a rattlesnake on the floor and everyone tried to ignore it. When a department head went on too long, Blaine raised his fingers in a small gesture of dismissal and said, "I understand. Next."

At the end of the day, he asked his secretary if Leslie Carr had called, and he was told that she had and that he could reach her at home. He dialed her on his private phone, where he had put her number in its memory, idly wondering, as he did so, how long it would stay there. Blaine was not used to casual affairs, and so his curiosity was more a matter of ignorance than experience. It went without saying that the schedule of his life—the meetings, the time spent waiting for news of the markets, the execution of his strategies (talk or action)—established the hours in which he was able to see Carr.

When they agreed to have dinner, she came to his apartment and kissed him at the door. He took her coat. They went into the library and sat in the comforting browns and greens, in the glow of the lights, beyond which the gilt titles of books gleamed. They heard the domestic clatter as the housekeeper worked in the kitchen, and as they sat together, Carr having a brandy and swirling the fluid around and watching the film of it on the crystal glass Blaine pressed into her hand, she found that she began to relax, and there, in that comfortable room, she realized how brittle and tense she had been during the day. Her relaxation came in a series of steps, the first one being his call. Then she went home and bathed and came to his apartment, getting a little relief at each ritualized moment. It built as she came into the lobby and then increased as she rose up to the twelfth floor, and continued through the drink and was amplified at dinner, a meal that they found set for them in the dining room. White china, delicate glasses, the roast beef, or pheasant, or venison on a silver platter, and the creamed spinach or roast potatoes or Yorkshire pudding in a silver bowl with a silver lid.

After dinner, with the taste of a chocolate soufflé in her mouth and the tickle of champagne in her nose, they went into his room with its enormous bed, and out the window she saw that blue light from distant office buildings. She removed her dress and her bland, black underwear and stood there with her skin awash in the blue tint from the distant light. The sheets were Egyptian linen, and they were tinted blue in that romantic light. He sat down next to her, the enormous bed creaking with a piercing intimacy. It was the small, private sound she had been waiting for all her life. On the first night there, she started with what she thought of as her tricks, which she did with the intensity of someone beginning a long sprint, but after a few minutes Blaine said, "Shhh. Don't worry. I just like being with you. Here. Let me put my arm around you." She sat back and looked at the lights, concentrated on letting him hold her or whisper in her ear, all the while feeling that relaxation turn into a warmth and a slowly building intensity that left her mystified. When she fell asleep it was in the fading rustle of the Egyptian linen and in that blue tint from the light outside.

From time to time, when she came home from work, she found a box of roses with the doorman of her building, and while she tried to dismiss this as nothing more than sentimentality, she took them upstairs and put them in a vase. She walked by the flowers, at first touched that Blaine thought of her in such a way, and that he had been discreet enough to send them to her apartment rather than her office, but as much as she tried to dismiss them, she still got up and walked over to look at the yellow dust at the tips of the pistils, the sharp-edged red petals, their moist texture giving off an aroma that was indistinguishable from that relaxation and certainty which seemed to be part of those evenings she spent with Blaine. The transformation from cynic to heart-sick woman was sudden and complete, and while she tried to deny it, she enjoyed the frame of mind that allowed popular songs to seem profound, or that left her inhaling the fragrance of these flowers with such wistful pleasure.

She was almost disoriented by the changes she had to make. In order to love him (and she finally had to admit that that was what it was), she had to abandon the methods by which she was accustomed to doing things, such as withholding approval, or not getting involved, or seeing people as creatures who were like life-sized photographs of themselves. More and more at work, she found that she couldn't handle people the way she had in the past. She was desperate to keep people from knowing how vulnerable she was, but just when she needed the tools that had gotten her where she was, she was least able to use them. More and more she wanted Blaine's advice, his affection, his crisp, even charming approval when she said something keen or clever.

They went to concerts in the evenings. She noticed that Blaine was following a young Russian woman named Tatyana Barokova, who played the violin. She performed with precision, and yet she nevertheless had a sultry desirability. On a couple of occasions they had gone back-stage and into the young woman's dressing room, where she sat with her short blond hair and her lacy black top. Her blue eyes had an Asiatic quality. Carr had never seen a woman who so perfectly suggested "the other," the distant and the exotic. Blaine spoke to this young woman in a way that he had never spoken to Carr, and Carr waited, her face flushed, while he did so (mentioning, in passing, that Mozart had never owned a piano, although Tatyana knew this). Tatyana appeared to dismiss Carr as a needy woman of no particular importance, and this left Carr with a jealous fear that was indistinguishable from nausea.

Later, she and Blaine walked along an avenue where the buildings stretched away like walls bespeckled with lights, and in the fog, the lights from the shop windows made a golden haze. In one window, Carr saw diamonds and platinum, bracelets and necklaces, the impossibly bright gems suggesting everything she loved about being with Blaine, and while she wasn't able to be precise about what this was, she knew that part of it was the affection of a powerful man. Just looking at the diamonds soothed her, as though, if she had them, they would reassure her anxious brooding.

The next evening she found a courier with a package waiting for her at her apartment, and in the carton she signed for, buried in masses of rustling pink paper, she found a hinged box. She took a bracelet from it, which swung back and forth as it hung from her fingers. The sparkle made her skin white, and the tug of it on her wrist gave her the sensation of being part of a world that soothed her and filled her with a profound sense of ease. It wasn't the expense or the value of the bracelet that she admired, so much as its suggestion of dependable affection. When she was afraid of what had happened to her, she looked at the bracelet. Blaine had known that she wanted a gesture, and had given it to her.

At work, a couple of assistants took one glance at the slight bounce in the way she moved, the glow in her skin, and hearing the lilt in her voice, one of them said to another, "What do you think Carr has been smoking?"

February 15, 2027

CARR SPENT a lot of evenings waiting for Blaine. She worked harder, since it was obvious that her job made her more interesting to Blaine; when she made plans, she thought of how she would appear to Blaine in a year or two when she had Mashita's job. Then Krupp's. She was more careful than before and more uneasy that her supervision of Briggs had been *pro forma*. She started to go through Briggs's work in earnest.

At first she had nothing more than suspicions, a collection of details that she thought were unnecessary, such as Kay's eye movements, which were established in such a way as to give an almost infinite variety of expressions. In particular, Kay had the ability to mimic, not in parody, but in understanding, the glance of someone she was speaking to. At first, Carr supposed this was a refinement of the specifications, but when she checked the appendices, she found that there had been almost nothing about eye movement, or about the muscles of the face surrounding the eyes. The original plan called for a "pleasant visage," but that was all. It was hard to say where "pleasant visage" ended and the expressions of intimacy began, but she was sure there was a threshold.

When she thought about this, she considered the evenings she spent with Blaine. Often, when they were sitting together, in the library or in that enormous bed, she was able to convey by a glance, by the movement of her eyes, just how much such moments meant to her. Just a look. It was better than words. It was like two people who had lived through the same cataclysmic event, and had developed out of this experience a private understanding that was perfectly revealed in their expressions. As she looked at the details of Briggs's work, it was like opening a book at random and finding a line of prose or a fragment of a poem that seemed preternaturally to apply to one's own circumstances. The details she saw, given her current state of mind, suggested intimacy and the beauty of articulating something that was almost impossible to express. How could she object to that? When she found a new detail, the economy and precision of it thrilled her like a haiku that perfectly invoked love and desire. She was infatuated with these details, since they illuminated her own experience, which even now seemed somewhat mysterious to her, but when she saw something in Briggs's work that she understood perfectly, she felt the self-righteousness of the newly reformed. She became strident in defense of her own new feelings.

She kept a diary of these intimate details, and when she made a notation of what she thought each one was, she saw that her entries made a fractal pattern that was repeated almost everywhere, although it was completely submerged in the structure of the elements she looked at (the membrane on the ganglions, the hair follicles, the reticulations of the brain's surface, the color of a fingernail). What she saw in Kay's ability to play music alone reminded Carr of her own most private and satisfying experiences with Blaine, such as those evenings in bed when the lingering effect of music blended with the warmth of his affection and the promise of it, too. To see these moments described and encoded, not as something that was mechanical, but more as a matter of possibility and longing, left Carr trembling and thinking, *Yes, I have felt that. Yes.*

There were occasions when she recognized something she hadn't really known she had felt, and in the instant when she did so, she fell that much more in love. She was able to articulate a reason that she had only been hazy about before. It left her sighing with relief mixed with fear. This wasn't so much a matter of having her experience summed up, as of exploring parts of it she hadn't previously understood. It was a matter of increasing her sense of scale. And underneath Kay's ability and talent, her steadfastness and intelligence, her beauty, Carr detected an unstoppable vitality, and this left her reassured by the power of women.

Late at night, when she was noticing these details, she knew that she was making a mistake. It didn't matter that the mistake was beautiful or attractive, or that it reflected on her own personal circumstances. Her job was to make sure Briggs was doing what he was supposed to be doing and nothing else. That was what she was paid to do, and she justified her pleasure in what she saw by telling herself that she still had plenty of time before her inaction would pass into complicity. Even though she thought she had time, she knew the moment of complicity would arrive, as it did, when she found the forms in her mailbox for a quarterly review of Briggs's work.

She wanted to think clearly about it, and she cleaned off her desk at home, putting the list of suspicious details on one side and the forms on the other. The forms were printed on heavy paper that had the Galapagos logo at the top and, underneath it, the slogan, LIFE. IN ALL ITS FORMS. She went down the boxes on it, and the scales for each element of performance. At the end there was a place to add extra sheets if she needed to expand on any "events unexplained by the checked boxes and the standard scales." Well, the time had come.

In the morning she still hadn't filled it out. She wondered if Briggs had any idea of the jeopardy he was in. Surely it was no secret what happened to people who tampered with Artificial Life, or the intricacies of the Gaming Patents. The only good thing was that the project was still in the architectural or planning stage and they were a long way from spending money on putting the code into production. But no matter which way she looked at it, she knew that it was her goodwill that stood between Briggs and the street, the loss of his license, and the rest.

At Galapagos, she stopped at the door of Briggs's office.

"Hi, Leslie," he said. "Come in."

"Do you mind if I close the door?"

"All right," he said. "If that's what you'd like."

She pushed the door shut, the enormous glass slab swinging around to the metal latch. The glass walls trembled.

"I was just filling out the performance reviews for this quarter," she said. "I'm doing yours first. I've been going through your work pretty carefully."

"Have you?" he said.

Beyond the glass walls of his office she saw other such walls. The place looked like an insurance office or news room. Here and there someone had taped up a poster or a photograph on one of the walls, and these appeared suspended, as though the entire place were in free fall and some of the things in it were floating. She glanced back at him and saw that he was sweating.

"Did you find anything?" he said.

"Well, I wanted to talk to you about that," she said.

"No time like the present," he said.

"You think so?" she said.

"Yes," he said. "I guess I do."

"I've found your work to be economical and precise," she said.

"Thank you," he said. But he went right on looking at her. "Is there something else you want to tell me?"

"I wonder how closely you read the specifications," she said.

"I've read them," he said. "I don't think I've missed much."

"So, then, if you made a mistake, you'd know what you were doing?"

"I'm paid to be informed," he said.

"That's not what I asked," she said. "I'm asking about a matter of intention. Did you know what you were doing?"

He dropped his eyes.

"Yes," he said.

"And why did you do it?" she said.

"There are some things it's hard to give up."

"Like what?" she said.

"Oh, I don't know," he said.

"Sure you do," she said. "Come on." She gave him the smile that she had given many other people over the years when she had been trying to get them to rat on themselves. Then she dropped that. "Look. I need some help here. What's hard to give up?"

"Being attached to another human being," he said. He looked right at her. "The idea of it. The sense of it."

"You mean love, don't you?" she said.

"You could call it that," he said.

"You remember the business about how Kay perceives love as that moment when the ordinarily beautiful becomes ominous. Do you remember?" she said.

"Yes," he said.

"Tell me. What should I do?"

The form between her fingers started to shake. She hadn't seen it until now, but, yes, her entire life with Blaine was lived in that region where beauty kept rising into the realm of the ominous. This was at the heart of the thrill she felt when she stood with Blaine and looked out the window of his bedroom and saw that the lights of the city had been transformed in a way that was at once so delicate and yet so appallingly large. She swallowed. The form went on trembling in her fingers.

"You've helped me see what is happening to me. That's the way I feel about someone now," she said.

They both got up and Briggs opened the door. Carr seemed exhausted. She walked out, although she hesitated and glanced into his face once.

"I guess we're in the same boat," he said.

"No," she said. "We aren't. What you are asking me to do is to get in the same boat with you."

She walked a few steps down the hall that was made out of glass and where those pictures and slips of paper had been hung so as to suggest free fall.

"Leslie," he said.

She stopped and turned back.

"What?" she said. "What do you have to say to me?"

"Good luck," he said.

She went down the hall, the paper still shaking in her hand, and in her office she checked off the boxes, marked the scales for imagination, dedication, effort, precision, innovation, all at 99 percent (no one ever got a hundred), and then signed her name and put it in the out box. She thought, *Well, what am I going to do now? I have just signed off on work I should have reported.*

She wanted to talk to Blaine about it, but he resisted her. They had established rules of behavior with each other, and those rules had been created without any discussion. She would never ask for anything overt, and he would never offer it; they existed in an epic of the tacit, of the unspoken. Now, though, with a sense of complicity that left her at once amazed and sick (how, after all, had she gotten herself into this?), she needed to change the rules. She was certain that she had been seduced, but by whom and what?

At dinner, as they sat among the glint and shine of the silver, eating fish ravioli, endive salad, sea bass with a garlic crust, she looked up and said, "Would you risk everything for me?"

"Risk?" he said. "I'm not sure I'm a big believer in risk."

"You know what I mean," she said.

"Do I?" he asked. "Would you like some more wine?"

She sat there in the noisy gurgle of it being poured into her glass.

"Let's put it another way," she said. "I'd like you to tell me you love me."

"My dear," he said, "I thought we understood one another."

"We did," she said. "But there are times when understanding needs to be precise."

"You mean like a contract?" he said. "Is that what you are asking?"

"No," she said. "Not like a contract."

She sat there, realizing that the conversation had turned from what she wanted. She closed her eyes. Maybe later.

He was affectionate to her in the enormous bed, and in the warmth of it, she almost felt better, but she still wanted to speak, to explain. And what was there to say, really? She thought, *A hell of a lot.* For instance, now that she was so vulnerable, she didn't get such a thrill when she noticed the lights had changed from the beautiful to the ominous. In fact, now they didn't seem beautifully ominous so much as just plain scary. It was obvious that the mistake she had made at work was a reflection of being utterly besotted. And yet, the notion of going back to her own life before Blaine filled her with panic. With a change this big, she had to have things clear: Blaine had to love her, too.

She was scared. She whispered in the dark, trying to explain the metamorphosis of the lights. Ominously beautiful and then just frightening. Of course, she knew it wasn't really the lights so much as her state of mind. She needed something. Her words came out in small, damp, insistent puffs on his shoulder. He listened quietly. She hoped he wasn't going to send her another bracelet, which, as she thought about it, was undergoing a transformation, too, just like the lights. Not ominously beautiful anymore, but just frightening.

She stayed in the warmth between them, or tried to, and as she lay there, Blaine reached up and turned on the light. He had never done this before, and then she heard the rustle of some papers as he began to read. Reviews of concerts that the Russian violinist had given in other cities. Carr saw a picture of the young woman's face lost in the bouquets of roses that had been thrown on the stage, and even in this stock photo, the musician had that manner of sultry assurance, as though the erotic and the music she played were somehow intertwined. How could Carr compete with that? And then she thought with horror, *Am I competing? Is that what has happened?* He read carefully, as though trying to remember the sound of the music that the critics were writing about.

March 15, 2027

THE MEETING of Blaine's board of directors took place on the first Tuesday of the month in a brownstone on a public commons. Downstairs the building had a library and a restaurant, and upstairs it had bedrooms for directors who came to these meetings from out of town. On the second floor was a conference room with green cloth wallpaper, a table with a green felt top, like a billiard table, and a window through which the trees on the commons could be seen. This was where Blaine faced his board of directors. Outside, the new leaves were the color of crème de menthe mixed with milk. As Blaine waited, he was fully aware of the way he would lose his job: in the midst of some difficulty, the board would release a statement of complete support, and then, in the space of an afternoon, they would panic and he would be asked to resign. This was the way his predecessor had been removed.

He stood in front of them, thinking about Carr's desire to be told that he loved her. What, after all, did love have to do with what he would face here? He had trouble putting the two together, since there was so much difference between the personal aspect of his life and the fact of his business. Then he turned to face the members of the board. They were men and women chosen for their understanding of economic and social difficulties, and for their ability not to lose their confidence when dealing with trying matters. Now he was confronted by their faces, all gray bags, with necks like gray accordions, their eyes not so much lizardlike as tempered by years of experience in exceedingly tough circumstances. When one of them made a joke, it was with a raised eyebrow or a subdued comment, and even the youngest one had the look of an itinerant executioner. They were not here to be lied to or trifled with, and Blaine had learned long ago that he should never tell anything but the truth. He gave his report, going through the list of items from the Hit Parade, explaining what each worry had been, and what had been done in each case. When he didn't know an answer, which was exceedingly rare, he said, "I don't know. But I will soon."

In this meeting, Blaine went through the list of items, although he and everyone else knew that at the end they would have to make a hard decision. But as far as Blaine was concerned, it was either hard medicine now or radical medicine later, and he was convinced that an adjustment in monetary policy was the best thing. He knew, and everyone else knew, that people would suffer. Unemployment would increase and businesses would fail, but there was nothing else to do. Blaine went through the list. He came to the difficult decision. The board listened. When he asked for the authority to do what had to be done, they voted by nodding: it was a gray, moving, quiet assent. They looked at him like vipers who have just injected a rat with venom. All but one.

This was an industrialist, Harold Warren, a relatively new member of the board, tall and thin, with blue eyes and a beautifully made suit. There was not much he hadn't seen, such as the strikes in South America in which thirty thousand people had been killed in one afternoon. He was one of the most ardent supporters of the action they had decided to take, and when it was approved, he said to Blaine, "Well. It's not going to be easy."

"That's not your worry," said Blaine.

"I know," said Warren. "But perhaps you would like some assistance."

Blaine stiffened.

"Assistance?" said Blaine. "No. I have my orders and, as I think you know, I am aware of what has to be done."

"But still," said Warren, "perhaps there is something we can do. Maybe we can help you take the heat."

"My job is to take the heat, as you say," said Blaine.

"But—" said Warren.

"For Christ's sake, Warren," said Evelyn Black, a woman who had made her money in the last dregs of coal. "He said he can take care of it. Why don't you listen to him?"

"Because, Evelyn, I think this is a hard decision."

"Don't you think he knows that? Don't we all?" she said.

"Well, I just wanted him to know we are here for him," Warren said.

Black made a dismissive gesture with her hand and turned to look out the window.

"Twaddle," she said. "Our job is not to be here for him. Our job is to stay the hell out of his way." The gray faces expanded and contracted with approval, as though their jowls were organs of respiration. "Now, if there is nothing else, let's get out of here. It's a beautiful day, for Christ's sake. What's done is done." She shrugged again, her bulk moving in her black clothes. She turned to Blaine. "Good luck and Godspeed."

The members of the board filed out, bent, angry, somehow still voracious after all the years they had lived, and then Blaine was left alone. He knew that the most important thing was the timing of the announcement he was going to make. He went back to his office, waiting for the elevator as he stood under the angels in the dome, who looked down at him with their usual lofty and cool, gilt-winged indifference. Blaine picked a date, a Friday, to make the announcement and he had his staff, or the communications part of it, begin to work on the release. He spoke to other department heads.

In the evening, Blaine went to a hotel, the Metropol, where he was going to meet Carr. A small fountain stood in the center of the lobby, surrounded by overstuffed leather chairs among some palm trees. At the rear of the room, musicians in black tie played music that was popular and yet old-fashioned, and Blaine sat there, on this evening, waiting for Carr and hearing, through the plash of the fountains, the sound of music from a hundred years before. A few more days and the announcement would be made, and that would be that.

Across the room, Blaine saw that Harold Warren was sitting with a man who was the financial editor of an international business paper. Warren looked overwrought and he spoke quickly, sighing from time to time, and then speaking again. Blaine watched, hearing "Fascination," a song he had always detested and that seemed to him to be somehow correct, as though this nightmare should have this music to go with it. He stood up and walked across the room. A number of people watched him as he went, their eyes following him as though they were seeing a wife or a husband with a secret lover.

"Harold," he said. "How nice to see you. And McCourt. Of the *Financial Times*. Well, well."

"Wendell," said Harold. He looked sick.

"Yes," said Blaine. "Would you like to explain yourself?"

"I've been having second thoughts," said Harold.

"Second thoughts," said Blaine. He looked around. "About what?"

Harold licked his lips.

"Policy," said Harold. "Like the announcement you are about to make."

"Announcement?" said Blaine.

"Fascination" continued to play, the violin rising to a yearning peak.

"Which one, in particular, are you talking about?" said Blaine. The colors in the room had a luminescence, a throbbing pulse, which Blaine supposed was a reflection of how the blood was moving through the veins in the backs of his eyes.

"Look," said the editor, "Harold has been telling me that you are about to make an announcement."

"Is that right?" said Blaine. "That was quite considerate of him, from your point of view, don't you think? Harold, it was pretty considerate, wasn't it?"

Blaine looked around. Ten, perhaps fifteen people in the lobby. He tried to see each of their faces, and he knew that any one of them could be someone who should not see Blaine, the member of the board, and a reporter from the financial papers looking sick in public. He turned back. Harold had tears in his eyes.

"I guess the pressure got to me," said Harold.

"Would you excuse me for a moment?" said Blaine.

He went across the heavy carpet and around the palms, putting his hands in his pockets, and when he came to the desk, he asked the clerk if he could have a room. He needed to discuss a couple of personal matters. The clerk gave him a card, which Blaine filled out.

"I'll take the key," said Blaine. "I can find it."

"Are you sure?" said the clerk.

"Yes," said Blaine.

He went back to the lobby and said to Harold and the reporter, "Let's go upstairs."

"Why?" said Harold.

"I think we could use a little privacy," said Blaine.

Blaine made a small gesture toward the room, the green palms, the white tablecloths, the dark furniture, around which people sat, each one of them glancing at Blaine when they had the chance.

"We can talk here," said McCourt.

Blaine smiled, although it wasn't very warm.

"I don't think so," he said.

"Oh," said Harold, looking around. "Yeah. I guess that's right, isn't it?"

They stood up and walked through the room, all of them with their shoulders square, and as they went, Blaine made a joke, a rare one, and as McCourt smiled, as much in shock as in recognition of something funny, the people in the room turned away. If they were smiling, it couldn't be that much. Not really. The elevator slid open and they stepped in, all staring into the distance, which was chopped off by the closed elevator door. The grain in the wood, which usually looked elegant, now appeared to Blaine like flames in hell. Warren took a handkerchief out of his pocket and blew his nose. "Christ," he said.

They went down the hall, Blaine leading the way and thinking that at least he had been able to get them out of the lobby. He pushed open the door and saw a sitting room with gray walls, a sofa in light blue, an easy chair, a coffee table. The lights were on. Blaine stood until the others sat down.

"Would you like something to drink?" said Blaine. "Something hot? A cup of tea?"

McCourt took out a notebook and put it on the table.

"That's all right," he said.

"I just got to thinking," said Warren.

"Did you?" said Blaine.

"It seems like a bad idea," said Warren. "A lot of people are going to be hurt, and then I thought that there had been no public discussion, and so I called McCourt."

Warren looked even worse up here, his skin pale and greasy, his shirt dirty.

"I think Harold is a little overwrought," said Blaine. "But, yes, we are going to make an announcement. He has told you that, hasn't he? And the details, too."

"It's not the details that bother me," said McCourt. "It's the chaos. What's going on? How come Warren is calling the papers?"

"So that's the way you would print it? That we don't know what we're doing?" said Blaine.

"Well," said McCourt. "How would you put it?"

He picked up his notebook.

"You're missing what is happening," said Blaine. "I know precisely what I'm doing. Have you ever known me to make a mistake about a thing like this?"

McCourt shrugged. He glanced at Warren. "What's gotten into you people?"

"I told you," said Blaine. "Nothing. I know precisely what we are doing. Warren here is overwrought."

"Is that all you've got to say?" said McCourt.

"No," said Blaine. "Obviously you want some proof. Isn't that right?"

"Well, yeah," said McCourt.

"And if I give you some, will you forget this"—Blaine looked at Warren—"unfortunate display? There is no need to start a panic. Surely you can see that if you ran a story that said we were in disarray, why . . . "

"What's the proof?" said McCourt.

"Your word," said Blaine. "That you will forget this."

The reporter looked around.

"All right," he said. "What's the proof?"

"I will pick three indices," said Blaine. "Markets, stock prices, futures. I will tell you what they will be for the next three days, give or take a half-percent. If they are what I say, you will forget this. In fact, if I were you, I'd try to come up with some money to take advantage of what I tell you."

"No kidding?" said McCourt.

"No kidding," said Blaine.

"Okay," said McCourt, "you've got yourself a deal. What are they going to be?"

Blaine told him.

"Well, well," said McCourt. "And what's with him?"

He made a gesture to Warren.

"As I said, he's overwrought," said Blaine. "That's all. It happens to everyone from time to time."

Blaine smiled. Then he sat back and put the tips of his fingers together and thought, *Is he going for it?*

"Okay," said McCourt. "If the markets aren't the way you say, you'll be hearing from me."

"I expect we will never speak again," said Blaine. He stood up. "Good night, Mr. McCourt."

They walked to the door, and the reporter went out into the hall, which stretched away like a nightmare, the doors regularly spaced and diminishing in size, the hall getting smaller and smaller as it stretched into the distance. Blaine closed the door and turned back to the room.

"Do you know what you have done?" said Blaine.

"I was just worried," said Warren.

"Worried," said Blaine. "Worried?"

He closed his eyes.

"Maybe I can get on the phone to the other members of the board," said Warren.

"The decision has been made," said Blaine. "But that is not the issue here. The issue is what you have done to me. There is a good chance McCourt will never think that I am in charge. Ever. He will talk to other people, and the next time a hard decision is made, they won't believe me. They will start calling members of the board. Panic is built into such an arrangement."

Warren looked up at him.

"I hadn't thought . . . " he said.

"No," said Blaine.

"I'm sorry," said Warren. "I really am. My God, what have I done?"

Blaine stood there, seeing the gray walls as they seemed to throb.

"But," said Warren, "the way you handled it made it all right. That was pretty good."

"You think *I knew?*" said Blaine. "I was guessing. And what happens if I made the wrong guess? I don't know what those numbers are going to be any more than anyone else. *I guessed.*"

"Oh," said Warren. "Well."

"Go home," said Blaine. "Keep your mouth shut. Can you do that?"

Warren nodded.

"Yeah," he said. "I can do that."

Blaine went out the door and into the hall. In the elevator he buttoned his coat and took out his handkerchief and wiped his forehead, and when he came into the lobby he saw Carr's reddish hair, her pale skin, her arm with a diamond bracelet on it under the fan of a palm tree. The band had stopped playing "Fascination." Blaine sat down next to her and said, "Would you like a glass of champagne?"

"Is something wrong?" said Carr.

"No," said Blaine. He got a waiter's attention and ordered a bottle of champagne.

"I missed you today," said Carr.

He was thinking about the indices and guessed that he had a chance, but then it was possible that he hadn't seen the latest report. Had he looked at them before he left the office, or had he only seen the ones in the early afternoon? He didn't know. The champagne arrived and they each took a glass. He put his on the small table between them.

"Well?" she said.

"Excuse me," he said.

"You don't even know I'm here," she said.

"Please," he said. "Let's just sit here for a moment."

His glass sat on the table, and she saw the room distorted there, bent into a shape like that reflected on the surface of a shiny spoon. *That's perfect,* she thought, *everything here is distorted.*

"You are trying to tell me to be quiet," she said. "Aren't you?"

"No," he said. "I'm trying to say I want a moment to relax. That's all. Nothing more. Nothing less."

He closed his eyes.

"I want to talk to you," she said.

"This may not be the best time," he said.

She shrugged.

"There's nothing I can do about that," she said.

"Yes, there is," he said. "You can wait."

"Why won't you look at me?" she said.

He turned his pale green eyes on her, the expression in them seeming as crisp and shiny as a scientific instrument, like the lens of a microscope. The glance seemed extremely bright, almost as though a light were being shined in his eyes, and she supposed that this was a matter of his remoteness, his refusal to be intimate.

"Is that better?" he said.

"Yes," she said. "This way I can see what you are thinking."

"Can you?" he said. "And what would that be?"

She looked away.

"Not about me," she said.

"And is that a crime?" he said.

"Right now it is," she said.

"Leslie," he said. "I'm trying to decide whether or not I have made a mistake. If I have, why, then I have to do something."

"Oh," she said. "You've made a mistake, all right. You've had many opportunities to discuss this with me, but you haven't taken them. So if this is a bad time, it is your fault. Your mistake is thinking you can put me off. Well, sometimes there are people who will not be put off. Are you listening?"

"Don't," he said. "Please."

"I want you to tell me you love me," she said. "I want to know if you would risk everything for me."

He closed his eyes.

"Risk," he said. He opened his eyes and looked at her with that same bright glance, which was almost mesmerizing in its intensity. "And what do you know about risk?"

"Plenty," she said. "Tell me. I want to hear it."

"I love you," he said.

He trembled with the effort.

"Say it like you mean it," she said.

"Please," he said. "I am asking you to wait just a few minutes. That doesn't seem like too much."

"I bet you are going to a concert tonight to watch that Russian woman. Is she in town?"

"Yes," he said.

"Well, well," she said. "Say it like you mean it."

Beyond the palms, which opened with a fan of green fronds, the musicians picked up their instruments. Everything about them was so crisp and starched that it was almost possible to hear the scrape of their white collars against the skin of their necks. They looked at one another, each nodding his head, counting, One, Two, Three . . .

"I think this has gone far enough," said Blaine.

"What has gone far enough?" she said. "This discussion? Let me tell you that this discussion has just gotten started."

"No," he said. "Not this discussion."

"What do you mean?" she said.

Perhaps one of the guesses he had made was wrong. He looked around, seeing the fans of palms, the green blades that looked so sharp. If he only had someone he could talk with about it. The light pulsed here, too, and he looked around the room for a dark recess where the throbbing might be less. Maybe he had picked the wrong indices. But then, he hadn't had any time. Didn't this matter? No, it didn't matter at all. He was in the position of being right or wrong.

He looked back at her.

"I'm sorry," he said.

"What are you sorry about?" she said, raising her voice one shade above the conversational. The other people in the room turned toward her with all the speed of a reflex, but after they saw her, their expressions changed again, from mild alarm to a subdued smirk of amusement.

"Leslie," he said. "We don't have to do this here. Not like this."

"That's what you've got to say?" she said. "Great. Do you think I give a shit what these people think?"

She stood up.

"Do you?"

"No," he said. "I guess you don't."

She pushed the small table in front of her out of her way and it fell over and lay there on its back, like a dead animal in a cartoon. The waiters who stood in a small group by the kitchen door had the sense to stay out of the way. Then she dropped her glass into the absolute silence of the room. She put a hand to her face, and when he tried to take her arm, she jerked away from him.

"Don't you dare," she said.

She went across the soft carpet, through the gazes of other people, even raising her arm once as though these glances were so palpable as to feel like spiderwebs. Blaine picked up the table and put it back up, right where it had been. Its legs had made little indentations in the carpet, and Blaine was careful to make sure that the table was placed so that the small metal caster, about the size of a nickel on each leg, went right back into the indentations. As though everything was put back precisely the way it had been. He thought about the indices. Then he picked up her glass from the floor and put it on the table with his. He signaled for the check. A couple of people still stared at him, but he avoided them. Maybe, he hoped, it would just look like a lovers' quarrel.

Outside, she noticed that the lights above her now seemed ugly. The bracelet on her wrist looked that way too, and she took it off and carried it like some dead thing. She couldn't bring herself just to drop it into the gutter, but when she came to a cross street, she struck the bracelet against the corner of a building, the diamonds not breaking, but coming out of the setting and falling onto the street like flecks of ice.

Then she stood there, her back against the wall, where she felt the cool pressure of the stone through her dress and against her shoulder blades. Blaine had often told her what a beautiful back she had and how, when he saw the movement of her defined muscles under the white skin, he was reminded of the movement of wings, not of a bird, but of an angel. She had thought this was idiotic, but with the cold caress of the building behind her, she remembered it with a mixture of fury and the desire to have him say something like that again. And as she stood there, she looked up the avenue, feeling the cool air. Then she looked down at the diamonds, which were spread out around her shoes.

She realized that only a fool would walk away from them, and while she had the impulse to do so, she found that she was frozen like someone at the edge of a precipice. Too scared to move. She looked down, telling herself that if she could just leave the diamonds here, she could walk away from Blaine too, and never look back. She took a step up the side-walk, but as she did so she knew she was bluffing and that such postur-ing was for no one aside from herself. And what was the good of that? To try to outsmart herself? Well, she had done that well enough, thank you. Even as she reached down and picked up each one, pinching it between her fingernails to get it off the sidewalk, she had the sensation that these shards of light were evidence of how she was bound to him. The effect of his charm overwhelmed her even now like the scent of a flower, honey-suckle, for instance, that is associated with some piercing intimacy. He had power, and he had put it to use in his understanding of her, and this combination had been the essence of his charm.

She refused to get down on her hands and knees (which, she realized, was a desperate gesture to her somewhat tattered dignity), and as she squat-ted in her high heels, she heard a *hush, hush, hush.* The street sweeper came along, pushing his broom with three quick shoves and then stopping, set-ting his feet and getting ready to do it again. He had short, thick, ugly hair and a pug nose, like some Irish prizefighter who should never have gotten into the ring. His clothes hung around him as though they had been cut from a tattered tent, and his gait was brutish, a kind of side-to-side swaying, as though he were a little unsteady on his feet but nonetheless unstoppable. One of Briggs's early models. He halted just in front of her and said, "Hey. Look. See?" When she followed the direction of his finger, which had knuckles the size and shape of walnuts, she saw the one she had missed. "You don't want to miss that, hey? That's worth something, hey?"

"Yes," she said. "I guess it is."

In the morning she woke and sat at the side of the bed, where she was instantly alert to the silence of her apartment, which had a new, stark quality. It wasn't just the bad scene with Blaine, but the presence of a ter-rifying isolation. In the mirror that was hung on the inside of the closet door she saw the freckles on her shoulders and arms which made her look younger than she was. The corners of her eyes had a few almost invisible wrinkles, and she was amazed that she should have them at all. The silence, the wrinkles, the sight of the diamonds on her dressing table, like disorder itself, made her think that her anger of the previous night had been a mistake, but not necessarily one she couldn't handle. *Least said, soonest mended,* she thought. *That's the way to handle this.*

She called Blaine, but she didn't even get past the first secretary, who was new. A lot of people thought they wanted to work for Blaine, but the pressure got to them, and soon they looked for something else. Carr hung up and thought nothing of it, although she noticed a deepening of the silence in the room where she sat. If nothing else she would be able to find him at night, since she knew that he was going to a concert. Her plan was to run into him as though they had planned to meet, and to tell him that she'd had a headache the night before. She would act as though nothing had happened at all. If he had any lingering resentment, he would feel that he was making a mountain out of a molehill. After all, she wouldn't appear to make much of it. No abject apologies, no begging for forgiveness, and this would throw him off balance. Was he going to be peevish or spiteful? She would use his best qualities against him. He hated being unreasonable, and her lack of concern would leave him no place to go. The diamonds lay on her dressing table, winking at her with a cold light as she moved around the room.

At the theater, she didn't have a ticket, and when she tried to walk past an usher, she was stopped. It made her uneasy, not just for the momentary embarrassment, but through the sense of having a guard, like an angel at the gates of paradise, telling her that she was no longer allowed. She had begun to think she belonged here as much as Blaine. She went across the street to a polite café and had a drink, and then another, and when she saw Blaine's car pull up in front of the theater, she paid her check and went out, running a little, glad to have the cool air on her face and to see the lights of the theater. She heard the voices of an after-theater crowd, a laugh or two, a shout of recognition, and then a general wash of sound made up of rustling skirts, the click of high-heeled shoes, the sound of satin liners hissing over a dress, and through it all she could smell the perfume and the lingering whiff of champagne. Carr saw Blaine and the Russian musician coming across the sidewalk. Jimmy got out of the car and moved toward the rear door and opened it. Just as the young woman got to the curb, she looked up at Blaine, her eyes filled with light, like diamonds, and before she slipped into the car she put her lips together and gave him a kiss, the intensity of which was somewhere between a suggestion and a promise. Carr stood at the edge of the crowd, wanting to speak, or to shout, but she did neither. She heard the heavy, armored door close. This sound had changed too, like everything else around her. Whereas before it had been a sign of powerful elegance, it was now just a thud, a signal that she was no longer wanted.

At home, she took a bottle of wine from the refrigerator and held it against her eyes, which were swollen. The cork broke when she tried to get it out, and then she was reduced to pushing it into the bottle. This just showed how inept she had become. She poured the wine, flecked with pieces of cork, into a glass as she came into the living room and sat down in front of the TV. After flipping back and forth, she found a channel that showed nothing but storms. A big one was moving across Central America, and she watched as brown water washed down a hill, slowly undermining the shacks with corrugated tin roofs that stood on the bank. Palm trees swayed back and forth in the gales, and at the height of the hurricane the debris from the disappearing roofs of buildings looked like black birds, like bats, like shreds of funeral bunting blowing in the wind. Dead creatures, all black in the current, were being carried down to the ocean. She listened to the sound of the hurricane and thought, *Yes. Listen.*

She looked out the window at the city. It had changed too, no longer the impossibly romantic collection of lights, but just the rankest physical phenomena. Electrons in a void, absolutely indifferent to her or to anyone else. She had an overwhelming desire to go back to those afternoons when she and her father had broken computers into bits, when they had worked until they were out of breath. Her father was long dead, but she now realized that he had been trying to warn her. He had resisted hope, and now she wondered if he had had a night like this one, and in a moment of recognition that came with a sense of weight, she was certain that he had. Of course, in her innocent beliefs she hadn't been able to understand him, or to do anything but disapprove of his brutality. Her innocence had shown everywhere, and in particular she now saw that it had been in her notion, which she had just accepted at face value without a moment's thought, that if she just worked hard enough, hid who she really was long enough, spent enough time alone, did without, at least in any part of her existence that could have been warm and delicious, she would turn into someone admirable and even grand. She sat there and thought, *And look at me now. Just look.*

The odd thing was how flimsy this entire construction of herself seemed now, just a bunch of fraudulent habits and gestures that had probably fooled no one. She had built herself up, bit by careful bit, and now this analog of a person, this thing made by years of blinding effort, seemed like a dress that had at one time seemed fashionable but was now obviously just a knock-off of the real thing. She hated what she had been and yet didn't have a clue of where to go, of what to do.

She closed her eyes now and realized her father had been telling her a secret, the kind of thing no one wanted to admit, at least not out loud. Chaos has its own charms. It grows, it advances, it seeks out weakness, it lives for revenge. Then she thought that Blaine was really at the center of her grief. How in God's name could he have come into her life, changed her, and then discarded her in such a manner and still think that he was immune?

And what did darkness have to offer? As she considered this, she remembered with a thrill her father's wink of understanding. She felt the attraction of the darkness through the seductiveness of it, as though she were looking at a woman in black, shiny underwear, who put out her hands to be tied, her eyes filled with an expression of subdued, even languid, but still definite pleasure. Carr considered this not with understanding, but with a delicious impulsiveness about the shadows' possibilities. Now she saw darkness, like malice, as a stain on the light, its promise so perfect and so much more reliable than innocent delusion. And Blaine, of course, loved the light, the force of reason, the power of music, the beauty of discipline. All she wanted, in the moment, was to be close to her father. After she had stood at the window, imagining the winking out of each light, she went to a market and bought a can of sardines and ate them with her fingers, picking the silvery fish out of the olive oil they came in and sprinkling them with hot sauce, just like her father. It burned her mouth. The heat felt like happiness.

The next morning she went to work, and she tried to go through a new section that Briggs had done, but just the sight of the blue case it came in left her feeling seasick. It was like seeing stains on the sheets on the bed in Blaine's apartment, or some other evidence of what a fool she had made of herself. It reminded her of finding a book of poetry that had made sense at one time, but was now just another incomprehensible book. She found herself dialing the number of a headhunter who often called her, and she agreed to accept what he had to offer, the phone call made with the air of floating, of just surrendering to an impulse she had tried to deny, but which had finally taken over. She went down the hall, turned in her resignation, and cleaned out her desk, although, as she picked the papers up, she decided she couldn't bear to look at them, either, since they were just reminders of what she had lost. She slammed a drawer shut, but it didn't close, and she slammed it again and again. As she walked out, one of her assistants said to the other, "Well, whatever she was smoking, she isn't smoking it anymore."

IN THREE days the markets were just as Blaine had guessed, within a half-percent. He sat in his office and thought about the meeting of the board of overseers. The first order of business was to get rid of Warren, which, he guessed, wasn't going to be much of a problem. McCourt sent him a book, a copy of Marcus Aurelius's *Meditations,* with a card that said, "Funds for my retirement have been established. Never been happier. Retiring soon. McCourt."

CHAPTER 7

2027—project continuing

BRIGGS THOUGHT the entire thing had probably gotten too hot for Carr to handle; at least it had gotten that way when she recognized part of what he had been doing. Briggs was inclined to think that she hadn't turned him in; her quitting was a way for her to resolve the difference between what she knew she should do and what she wanted to do. Get out before the project corrupted her. It was better to be far away when things went south. Anyway, he guessed that was what had happened. She had been smart enough to get out.

He was still thinking about this in the evening, when Mashita came in to see him and said, "You know, you take someone from nothing and build them up to something in this business, and what do they do? They up and quit on you."

Briggs shrugged. "What can I say?"

Mashita stood in the door of the office.

"We didn't need Carr anyway, did we?" Mashita said.

Briggs looked through the glass walls of his office, where he saw the blue glow from the monitors that were on in here and there.

"Well?" said Mashita.

"I think we can get along from here all right," said Briggs. "We're about half done with this stage of it. All the basics are complete."

"All right," said Mashita. "It's yours, then. I'm not hiring anyone to replace her."

Still, Briggs was careful, since he thought things could change and that Mashita would decide to hire someone after all. He was even more cautious than when Carr had been there, but slowly he started again, taking bigger chances now, or at least more obvious ones. The days combined into weeks, and the weeks into months. The architectural part of the project was finished, and Galapagos started to put the work that Briggs had done into production.

When he needed an emotional lift, especially at night when the building wasn't crowded, he went to look at Kay and Jack. At the end of the hall, Briggs came to a metal door that had lines of rivets along the top and bottom, the pattern of them implying the strength and order of an earlier age. In the stairwell he put one hand on the red banister that switched back and forth from landing to landing. His feet echoed in the air of the concrete hall. That was the thing about concrete. Always damp.

At the bottom he opened the door to the cellar, and instantly the odor of dry ice came up to him from below. It made him think of a skating rink. Here, the lighting had a deep blue tint. One of the company's concerns was infection, and they had done a lot with lights to kill bacteria. The door closed behind him, the pressurized air whooshing out: dust could be blown out, but it could never make it in, not past the outward flow of five feet per second. And in an emergency, it could be increased. In the basement, where the growing platforms were, the air was filled with the mixture of iodine, antibiotics, the odor of a newborn child, and the sweetness of spilled intravenous fluids.

During certain cycles, when the order of operations had to be carefully observed, and when the pace was slowed down by lowering the temperature, the room was filled with snow. The humidity, which came in at a pretty high rate, froze and fell in straight, windless lines, the individual flakes white with a little blue cast to them, each one having a pattern that reminded Briggs of the feathery shape of a carrot top. The snow had a particular odor, too, which was of roses and iodine.

When he had first seen Kay, her face emerging from the vapor, he was reminded again that he had done the one thing that could get him killed, no questions asked. That is, if anyone found out. Briggs supposed that he had been drawn to it because fertility, as far as he was concerned, was bound up with beauty and a damp sultriness. Well, he wasn't sure why he had added it, aside from the thrill, but whatever the reason, he had made it possible for her to have a child.

He wondered if she wanted to have a child. He had made it possible, but that didn't mean it was something she necessarily desired. What he had done was forbidden for good reasons, since the other items he had written in, not just her beauty and her capacity for love, but those qualities that had been required by the specifications for the project, such as cunning and hostility to humanity, her coldness, her profound ability to think that only one thing was important (her current, mostly violent task), all of these, and some other nasty items, could cross into the human gene pool if she had a child. Delight in killing, pleasure in doing the thing that really hurts, indifference to a plea for mercy.

Briggs always did his examination in the same order, to be sure he missed nothing. He started at the bottom of the platform where her feet were, and went through the checklist: color of skin, rate of oxygenation, which he knew by the scale which was inside the platform. As he did so, he moved along the side of the transparent steel. He looked at the shape of her toenails, the flesh under them as pink as a rose petal.

Her feet were longish, and the tendons in them radiated outward from a band just beneath the ankle, like the spokes of a closed umbrella. As he stood there, she flexed her toes. Was she dreaming? And if so, was it of a detail that she thought of as beautiful, such as the blue tint in a dragonfly's wing, the membrane colored by a sky on a clear day in summer? Or the oily luminescence in a hawk's eye as it hunted for movement in a field below. Of course, she would like the speed as the bird dropped, the beating of its wings after the kill, as it lifted what it had caught back into the sky. Maybe she dreamed of childbirth, the panting, the shivering, the first sucking tug at her breast.

Or, he thought, was she dreaming of him, of their mutual slippery movement, the gleam of sweat, of the creamy expulsion of semen, the fluid heat of it and wetness seeming right, too, and necessary? He stood there, his hands sweating, thinking that he would go back upstairs and delete the code, but then he realized that it had already been validated, compiled and checked, and that if he did anything like that, it would call attention to himself.

He had added more than her ability to have a child. He had set it up so that when Kay saw him, she'd feel as though she knew him. She'd be delighted to see him. She'd trust him. She'd smile. She'd speak to him as though she had seen him once and had always wanted to get to know him better. "Hi, Briggs," she'd say, taking a step closer and smiling, putting out her hand to take his with a warm and friendly touch. "It's good to see you," she'd say. Then she would wait for a moment, just looking at him. She would feel this as a combination of warmth and sweetness, almost as though her attitude were palpable, like the scent of cinnamon and sugar in a bakery. What could be wrong with that?

It took a while, but the next step came, even though he told himself that he would never take it. He had approached the technical problem as though he were writing music, and he went about establishing a common, unstated understanding between the two of them, an attitude that was known to both: they would recognize a similar sensibility in each other. This, of course, increased the intensity with which they would meet. She would be far more than just friendly. The warmth would still be there, and that sweetness, too, though suffused with a more tactile sensation, as though the scent of cinnamon and sugar had gotten under her clothes. It wouldn't be untoward, not kinky or convoluted, but just the opposite—frank, innocent. Her hand would take his a little more firmly, but without a hint of shame or discomfort of any kind. It was all right. She might blush with pleasure.

Of course, he hadn't stopped there. It was harmless, he told himself, like writing poetry or some other pursuit that one should keep to oneself. It was a vision of the best of what people felt sometimes, an invocation of . . . well, of those times when someone felt only the warmth that came from a common sensibility and the most loving aspect of another human being. In fact, he was trying to allow himself the exquisite pleasure of love, which was that he could be, in Kay's presence, someone he liked to be. And as he did this, he realized that more and more she determined who he was. What could be wrong with that? He and she would laugh at the same things and have a language that no one else could understand so well as the two of them. He thought that before Kay was released, he would add a cue to control these things.

He took a step along the side of the platform, toward her head. Her calves had a slight curve to them, but it started pretty far up the leg. She would look good in stockings and heels, although he didn't think she would ever get the chance to wear them. Pale skin. Not a mark on it.

She had never nicked herself with a razor as a teenager, trying to look grown-up. The shape of her kneecaps had come out all right. No chronic knee problems, nothing like that. Long thighs, powerful, slender. Hip bone a little prominent. Ribs just barely visible beneath her breasts, which had a pattern of small blue veins, just beneath the skin. Nipples the color of raspberries. Long neck, prominent shoulder bones, fingers of the hand long and graceful, perfect for playing the piano. Light down on her neck that made a swirling pattern as it disappeared into her hair.

He had drifted down a long cascade, one detail flowing into the next, and with each forbidden detail he had added, the more infatuated he had become. And then, too, he didn't even know precisely what he had done, fertility included, because the code went through many *in silica* generations before actually being produced, and although he had set up the rules by which this was done, he was afraid of what he didn't know.

When he had been working on the code at home, he had listened to Mozart. The code was almost an echo of the music, since often he had the sensation of a piece of music going through his mind over and over in a way he couldn't shake, and this had been so prominent that he had begun to try to encode the harmonies, the notes, the way in which the music was put together. It wasn't so hard to do for Mozart, since the music bore a relationship to mathematics, but the difficulty came as he tried to invoke her ability to play and write music. He had lingered over the Requiem, adding the details of it and trying to suggest, as he did, the longing that had gone into it. The longing was twofold: for the loss of life and the devotion to something larger. Here, of course, he thought that Kay would respond to the presence of life, the approach of it, with all its tragic consequences. What increased a sense of beauty more than one's own sense of being ephemeral?

He had painstakingly encoded Beethoven, Stravinsky, Mozart, Bach, Schubert, Puccini, Bizet, and had set Kay's talent up as a problem to be solved by the *in silica* natural selection: What was at the heart of this music, and how could one use it as a tool to take the next unexpected step in composition? He added the coordination, strength, balance, and tactile precision that had been uncovered in years of studies of concert musicians. Just as he had set up another problem for the code to work through *in silica:* how these tools could give expression to enormous emotion and the most profound longings.

As he stood next to Kay's stainless-steel bed, he closed his eyes to concentrate. He bent his head, too, his face just over the transparent cover that went from the head to the foot of the bed. When he opened his eyes, he saw that his breath had turned white on his side of the transparent steel. Kay raised herself up to get close, her lips just on the other side of the glass from his, her breath condensing too, on the inside, a mirror image of his, just a fraction of an inch away from the white mist of his breath.

As he stood next to her, by the platform, he put his fingers into the condensation and rubbed it away. She raised an arm, the muscles taut and yet fluid under the skin, as she reached out and put one finger into the condensation on her side. Impatiently she rubbed it away. Then she stared at him through the spot she had cleared. She lifted her head a little and came closer, her eyes on his: she looked into every corner of his consternation. Their lips were separated by just a fraction of an inch, just back from the clouded glass. Even from here, he felt her loving forgiveness.

Briggs went over to the next platform, where the growing medium swirled around Jack. He had started to add things with Jack too, and these, he guessed, were in addition to those he had given Kay, but then they might both receive something that had been added to the other, since they shared some of the basic code. Briggs had no idea how this would work. He guessed it would be sorted out, but he wasn't sure how. Certainly, he had added defiance.

Briggs had started in with Jack to compensate for all those things he had wanted when he was young, and for that matter still wanted, although less strenuously. Briggs had started with his own talents. Jack was going to be good with math, much better than Briggs, because Briggs had been able to build on what he knew with the information in the world's libraries. Jack would like the order, the forces that are illuminated by mathematical descriptions, and he would like, too, the sense of proportion that math brought to perception. But Briggs hadn't stopped there. He had wanted someone he could trust. A real friend.

Briggs's feet left tracks, perfectly impressed in the snow, as he went across to the growing platform where Jack was emerging from the swirl of the growing medium. The examination routine was the same. He started at the feet, which, like Kay's, were long, and had high arches. In fact, as Briggs looked at the calves, the muscles in them defined like those of a good 440 man, he remembered the anatomy he had studied, the autopsy pictures he had gone through of runners who had died in their prime. The muscles of Jack's thighs stretched upward in defined ridges. Power and grace. Light pubic hair that ran up his stomach a little, toward the navel, which existed in the neat segmentation of muscles that appeared to be tightly confined by his skin.

Briggs moved toward Jack's head. Along the rib cage the muscles had the pattern that receding water leaves in the sand, like strands woven together. Chest like a breastplate. Prominent larynx. Small ears. Bushy hair. Still, Briggs worried about the interior surfaces, the lining of the esophagus, the stomach, the lungs. It didn't take much. Of course, this knowledge had been acquired the hard way, but what knowledge hadn't?

Jack's eyes, the set of the jaw, the brow furrowed with effort, showed the qualities that Briggs had been concerned with and that were now obvious. If, for instance, Jack ended up as an infantry officer, cut off from his battalion with a handful of men, short on ammunition, short on water, he would know what to do: establish lines of fire, take inventory, count the ammunition, decide on the right rationing for the water, cut losses, try to establish communication, treat the wounded. Of course he would be afraid, but these actions would be a matter of a discipline, and a reflection of his certainty that the discipline, while difficult, was still all that he had. Jack lived, or would live, for those moments when everything was most frightening. Danger and difficulty would be like oxygen to him.

As Briggs came to the top of the platform, Jack turned to look at him. Jack moved his lips as though unsure of the language, and although Briggs couldn't hear him, he made out the words: "Don't worry."

Briggs stood there until the snow covered the canopy, each flake touching the surface with an almost infinite gentleness. As it piled up, he suspected that he had managed to trap himself, and that with each new attempt to escape, he would probably make the trap that much more intricate and that much harder to get out of. Yes, he thought, that is the trouble: I can't tell whether I am getting out, or only getting in deeper. The snow fell around him. He suspected that he was in the midst of all the unseen aspects of himself, all the hidden desires and wishes that usually existed as shadows and distant shades, but that one saw clearly in a disaster of one's own making.

Still, as the blue-tinted snow fell around him, he confronted the central fact that his understanding of the mechanism of life did nothing for him beyond the mechanics of it, and all he had done was to extend the old mysteries into new realms. The only thing he was certain of was that he disliked a lot of what had been done with his work.

For instance, in the early days, when people cloned themselves to produce organs for transplant, the clones had been used for their hearts, kidneys, livers, thyroids, pituitaries, and anything else that came in handy (the way an Eskimo cut up a walrus). This crude use had been troubling, but in the end practicality took over; this entire process had been reduced to one of ownership, and if you owned yourself, you owned what was grown from it. You took what you needed and discarded (at first) and then sold (later, to defray the costs) what you didn't need. Briggs had simply folded his discomfort with this, and other items too, like the cry of the dishwasher, into a general sense of numbness, although at times he could still feel the squirming of some unnamed but enormous fury in the depths; it was like putting his hand on an eel in dark water.

It occurred to him that his fascination with Kay's ability to have a child was one of those things in the depths: it was possible that Kay's sultry fertility was a matter of his resistance to the current brutal state of affairs, at least where artificial life was concerned. If he and Kay could have a baby, then could one treat the child as an item to be sold by the pound—or by the piece—like auto parts?

He had suppressed the desire to resist, pushed it into a shadowy part of the mind, but he hoped, with a wild vanity, that this impulse was still alive. Did a bird ever forget how to fly south in the winter, even after years of being kept in a cage? He clung to this notion with a fierce hope, as though knowing what was right and what was wrong and being able to act on it was a matter of his own resurrection. If you killed the moral impulse, you killed the man. And as he considered this, he thought of Kay dropping her clothes, of the almost inaudible sound of the skin of one leg slipping over the skin of the other as she crossed them. Perhaps she would do this when she sat at the side of the bed so as to consider him before running a hand along his chest, over his stomach, all the while looking him in the eyes.

Briggs stood where the blue light washed over Kay. She put her lips together, not so much trying to give him a kiss as making him a promise.

BOOK  II

KAY DISCOVERED that there were many words to choose from, but she found it hard to get used to this, particularly when she was looking for one that did the job better than any other. She and Jack stood in an alley, each of them wearing a jumpsuit with a zipper that ran from the crotch to the neck. Kay's lips were blue.

"I'm getting . . . cold," she said to Jack.

The lines of rain were tinted crimson by a red neon sign that ran from the top story of the building across the street to the ground floor,

H
O
T
E
L

one letter for each floor.

"I know what that sign means. It is a place to get an . . . accommodation," said Kay.

"Oh? Is that right? Okay," said Jack.

The hotel had been built a couple of hundred years before, and the iron of the fire escape suggested some antiquated and yet still dangerous object, like a bear trap. As Jack and Kay stood in the rain, they heard the buzzing of the neon tubes. Every now and then a woman in a clingy dress and fishnet stockings led a man up to the door of the place. Kay looked at these couples and said, "What are they . . . doing?"

"F-f-f- . . . " said Jack. "Sex."

"You think so?" she said.

He shrugged.

"I don't know. Maybe," he said.

They crossed the street in the red and silver lines of rain, their feet disrupting the surface of the puddles tinted red by the neon.

"You think you can do the talking?" she said.

"I don't know," he said. "I'll try."

"Be careful," she said.

"I said I was going to try, all right? What more can I do than that?"

She tried to speak, but her teeth chattered, and then she started shuddering. What she thought was that this would be fun, or could be fun, putting a word on everything, giving names to everything they saw, if she hadn't been so cold.

The desk clerk seemed to speak a language that Jack didn't understand completely. What was an hourly rate? What was a daily rate? A checkout time? Jack had two hundred dollars in his pocket, although he hadn't known exactly what the bills were. Funny paper with a little hologram in the corner.

"That's more like it," said the clerk. "Why didn't you tell me you had cash? That makes it easier. Here."

He pushed a card across the counter.

"Fill this out," said the clerk.

They stood there for a moment. Kay was still shivering.

"What's wrong with her?" said the clerk. "The jones?"

Jack shrugged.

"She needs a blanket," he said. "You know. Something to get her . . . heat."

"Oh, yeah?" said the clerk. "Hey, sister, are you all right? You miss a shot?"

Kay shook her head.

"Here's a pen," said the clerk to Jack.

Jack reached out for the pen. What the hell was this, anyway? The flashing of the sign came in the window of the lobby, where a man sat with a wine bottle in a paper bag, taking a sip every ten flashes. Just like clockwork. Then Kay reached over and took the pen and the card and started writing. The script she made looked like something out of a penmanship book, each letter formed almost as though it had been printed. She wrote, *Kay Remilard. Jack Portman.* No address. No telephone number.

The clerk looked from one to the other.

"We want it for the . . . " She looked out the window at the darkness. Storm? No. The opposite of light. "Night. Until . . . morning."

"Okay," said the clerk. "You're the boss."

He pushed the piece of plastic across the counter, like a credit card but used a lot, cracked. It had a little piece of adhesive tape on one side, and someone had written a number on the tape with a ballpoint pen.

They took the elevator, which lurched on the way up, and Kay took Jack's arm and hugged it, saying, "Why is it doing that?" Jack thought for a moment: it was a matter of the difference between fear and anxiety, right? Then he thought, *What is fear?* He tried to imagine the way this car worked: the cables dropping down in the dark, a system of pulleys. He guessed there was some mechanical advantage involved, if, as he suspected, work was equal to force times the distance over which it was applied.

The hall was empty. Jack looked at the number on the first door and then the next. Yes. That's the way they went. One to 100. Just keep adding zeros. It was easy. By the time they were at the end of the hall, Jack had thought of a way to solve quadratic equations by using a formula. It was pretty simple. If you put it in the basic form of a squared plus $2ab$ plus b squared, it was pretty easy.

They opened the door. Mismatched curtains over the windows, but at least they were both white if not made of the same material. The red sign flashed on and off, and the curtains and the room were bathed in the crimson light. Kay shivered. She took off her clothes and got under the covers, pulling them up to her chin. Jack undressed too, and took her clothes and his and put them over the radiator. It was still warm. He guessed that there was some way of describing, with equations, the way in which heat was transferred from one object to another, or even to the air, but he wouldn't worry about it until tomorrow. What he was concerned about was finding a damn . . . what was it called? A list of words with their meanings?

He got into bed too, and lay down next to Kay. How nice to feel her hip against the small of his back. After a while she stopped shivering. Then he guessed that he wouldn't be able to describe the way heat moved from one object to another with the quadratics, but something else, an estimate of the space under a curve. A calculus. He guessed it was possible if you started with a graph and worked from there. The thing would be to estimate the area under the graph, but to do so in a particular way.

KAY WOKE just at dawn. She closed her eyes again to concentrate on the warmth under the covers. It was almost fluid in the way it moved, caressing her skin, seeping into every crevice. At first she ran her hands over Jack's chest, and then down her stomach, lingering for a moment between her legs, and then going along her thighs. The touch on her fingertips was . . . she had the sensation of looking for a particular drop of water in a sea. *Smooth.* That was it.

She turned on her side and looked at Jack. He was sleeping on his back, hands at his side. The light of the morning made everything look as though it were confined in gray webs, but as the room got brighter Jack seemed to emerge from them. At first there was nothing more than his silhouette against the window, but soon she saw the texture of his hair, the shape of the muscles in his arms and chest. She slowly pulled back the sheet until he was exposed. Then she got close to him, putting her nose just behind his ear, which she sniffed. His chest rose and fell as he breathed. She put her ear against him and heard the steady *flub-dub, flub-dub* of his heart. She ran her hand farther down his stomach and then between his legs, where she looked at what she found, turning it one way and then another. Jack continued to sleep. Then she got up and looked out the window at the deserted street.

A taxi went by, its lights on. A man sat in the gutter, his head in his hands. Down the street was a gaming parlor, and young men and women were just coming out, into the first golden light of dawn. She watched the way the young women walked, and then she stood in front of the mirror and walked, swinging her naked hips a little. Well, she guessed she could do that. Was that what they wanted? What did she want? It might be fun, she thought, under the right circumstances.

She looked out the window again, seeing the street in grays and blacks, the mirrorlike puddles, the occasional couple. It all took on the color of her own feelings. And what were they? She raised a hand to make a gesture. What was the word? Incomplete. This word came with a physical sensation, as though something had been torn from her, deep within her chest. She swallowed and tried not to cry. What good would that do? It wouldn't help her find a specific person. A man. She knew that. It wasn't anything sexual, strictly speaking, although if she could do something more intense with him to add to the sensation of being closer, of being . . . together, she would do it in an instant. She knew that what she wanted was to see him approaching her, to recognize him, to smell his skin and hair, to see him smile. That would make her complete, or it would be the first step. *But even then,* she thought, *I have to be careful.*

In the drawer of the bureau she found a pair of fishnet stockings and a tube. It was a gold tube that was supposed to look like metal, but she was pretty sure it was something else. Plastic, she guessed. The top came off with a little sucking sound and inside was a bullet-shaped substance that was very red. It smelled a little like roses, and something else, too, not a flower but . . . pears. Of fruit. She opened it up again and raised her arms and put a streak of red under each one.

"I don't think it goes there," said Jack.

"No?" she said. "What do you know? You're a boy."

He shrugged.

"Try your lips," he said.

Jack reached over and picked up the tattered plastic screen on the floor, which was a cheap digital entertainment magazine that came with the room. He ran his finger along the menu: under his touch he saw such titles as *Teen Vixens, The Forbidden Zone, The Wild Side,* and when he scrolled through them he saw images of men and women. He looked at the pink tissue, the glistening images, and then flipped by, onto something called *Vogue.* He found a woman's face and held it out.

"Like that," he said.

She glanced at it once and put the lipstick on. As though she had done it for years.

"What do you think?" she said.

She sat down next to him and he took the bedsheet to clean her underarms. She pulled on the stockings and stood there, wearing nothing else. The sun rose enough for a light, like a golden film, to fill the room. They both sat in it, feeling it on their faces.

"Oh," he said. "Oh, it is so warm. Warm."

"It's the sun," she said.

"Like a . . . " he said. He closed his eyes. "A caress . . . "

She got up, still wearing only the stockings, and went over to the bureau where there was a black object the size and shape of a small briefcase. The top of it was burned where people had left cigarettes on it. Even cheap rooms like this had a small computer. Kay looked it over. She smelled it and then opened it up. Inside was a small screen and a keyboard, and after she had fumbled around with it, the power came on. The glow of the screen reminded her of the infinite amount of time before she had been alive, which she imagined as a blue light. It was reassuring to see that light on the screen, but frightening too, since it was a glow that suggested some bigger presence.

The instant she put her hands on the keys and felt the little bump under her fingers, she had the sense of . . .

Kay searched for the word, and in her frustration she found that while she didn't have the vocabulary she wanted, she nevertheless could swear. The words came out in a disconnected stream, the usual ones seen on a bathroom wall. Some of them worse than that. These words, she knew, arose in a part of the mind different from the one where ordinary vocabulary was kept. She said to Jack, over her shoulder, "What do you call it when you feel you have seen something before? When you know it?"

"Rec . . . recognize," he said.

"Yes," she said. "That's it."

"It's coming a little faster," he said. "The words are coming a little faster. But I wish I had a dictionary."

"A what?" she said.

"A list of all the words in a . . . " He sat up. In a what? "What we use when we talk . . . "

"A language," she said.

"Yes," he said.

He rolled over. She sat on the one chair in the room, her back nude, her legs in the stockings, her white skin reflected in the mirror in front of her as she looked at the screen. She typed a little. Hit a key, but nothing happened. Then she ran her finger across a device at the bottom of the screen, a little thing that moved an arrow, and then she hit a key. The screen changed. "Oh," she said.

"What?" he said.

"The machine," she said. "It's how . . . you know . . . it has an organization . . . "

She scrolled down the directories, and she found, too, that she knew some commands. This knowledge was familiar, just like remembering how to ride a bike. The code for a program came up, the functions called and labeled in slashes on one side, and as she went through the loops, the input/output programming, she said, "Yes. That's right. Oh. Of course. That's the way it works. Sure." After that, she typed now and then, nodding as though beating time or hearing music, and then recognizing the subdued and beautifully repeated theme.

What was it Jack wanted? A dictionary?

"What language?" she said.

"The one we are speaking now," he said.

"What is it called?" she said.

He licked his lips.

"Brit—" he said. "No. That's the place. Where it started. It's the thing that came from Britain. It has some other languages in it. Latin. Or is it Roman?"

"Latin," she said. "Here's a Latin dictionary."

"We don't want that one," he said.

He tried to imagine what the clerk would think if he came downstairs and asked for a towel in Latin.

"English," she said. "It's right here."

They looked at each page, their eyes moving from the top to the bottom, *"abnormous, abomination, abyss . . . "* Sometimes Jack scrolled to the next page before she was ready, and she said, "Hey, wait."

"What?" he said. "Can't you keep up?"

"I can keep up," she said. "Let me have the keyboard. We'll see who can keep up."

She started to control the pages and they both sat there, watching the flickering words, both hardly breathing: they stayed at it, increasing the pace, until Jack said, *"Dihedral, dihedral,* what a beautiful one. Hey, wait a minute."

"So," she said. "Who's giving me a hard time about going too fast?"

"It was beautiful," he said.

"Well, so what?" she said. But she knew he was right. She slowed down, and they both went at it more carefully.

"Sidereal," she said.

"Yes," he said. *"Sidereal."* He rolled it on his tongue. They both turned and looked out the window where there was a morning star that lingered.

The screen went through the pages to *zariba.*

"What is a zariba?" she said.

"A cattle enclosure in the Sudan," he said.

"Where is that?" she said.

He shrugged.

"I'm just getting started," he said.

"Oh, yeah?" she said. "Do you think you learned anything?"

"I picked up a few words," he said.

"All right," she said. She got up and stood in the middle of the room, still wearing the stockings, her lips red from the lipstick. He sat on the bed, his chest covered with a gold film from the dawn. She pointed at the bureau.

"A chest of drawers," he said.

"And this?" he said.

"A sheet, a pillow," she said.

He took her hand.

"And?" he said.

"Fingernail, knuckle, wrist, skin, vein, down . . . " she said.

"Down," he said.

She put her hand on his chest.

"Muscle, bone, skin, nipple," he said. "But I can't nurse. Can you?"

He touched her breast, the nipple.

"I don't know," she said, but then she blushed. She suspected that she could, although she didn't know how she thought she could. It was bound up with her wanting to be close to someone she loved, and of being as intimate with each other as possible. Wasn't that having a child together?

They stood at the window, applying the words, but the sensation was not of using the language so much as discovering it, of naming the objects they saw. As Kay worked at it, she said a word and then another to herself, putting her lips together as though the words had a taste or a texture that she could feel on her tongue or in the slight moisture of her mouth, or on her lips. Pear . . . this is a pear. This is a shoe. This is my . . . love. Love. As she chose a word, something definite coalesced out of the haze of almost infinite possibilities. This is my . . . love. For each word that gave definition to an ill-formed impulse, or to an object that seemed to exist in a conglomeration of things, the haze of possibilities lifted. Bit by bit she built up a sense of clarity, which had its own inertia, since it was exquisitely pleasurable to name something and to recognize it afterwards, each bit of pleasure driving the next. She was almost giddy, and then she came to some other words: my passion, my heart, the center of my existence, my sun. My stars. My darling. She shook her head, trying not to cry.

"Hey," he said. "What's wrong?"

"Nothing," she said.

"Didn't you like naming things?" he said.

"Yes," she said.

"Well, what's wrong?"

She shrugged.

"The words let you see what something really is," she said.

"What's wrong with that?" he said.

"It depends," she said. *Darling. Oh, my darling, why have you abandoned me?*

KAY SAT down at the machine. In addition to the familiarity of it, she was aware of something else too, and while she struggled to be precise, it was still difficult to articulate just what it was, even though she

had the vocabulary. In fact, the entire sensation was so odd that it frightened her. Large. Big. Overwhelming. But this didn't come close. Now,
when she sat down again, she had a variety of longing, or of what she
imagined someone might feel in a church. Or perhaps her state of mind
might be one that came from discipline and fasting, or spending time
without speaking, or any of the many other methods of trying to feel . . .
Again she faltered. Feel what? Connected to something that was enormous, that existed in such a way as to be at the essence of everything
there was, at once so large as to be frightening, and yet having a reassuring quality that she perceived as light and warmth perfectly colored by
an enormous scale and unimaginable distances. In fact, sitting there,
looking through the code, and then reaching out, into the deeper sections of distant machines in South America, Poland, Germany, in the
cities of London, New York, Evanston, Berkeley, she had the contradictory sensation of warmth and mystery that was perfectly combined with
the ominous.

She sat there for a moment and started to hum. Jack turned to listen.
She began to sing quietly.

"When you wake you shall have," she sang, "hushabye, don't you cry,
blacks and bays, dapples and grays, coach and six white horses . . . "

"What's that?" said Jack.

"Oh, just an old song," she said. "Do you like it?"

"Yes," he said. "I do."

She went over to the bed, where Jack had a little stub of pencil and a
scrap of paper, the wrapper from a candy bar that someone had thrown
in the wastebasket. He was drawing a graph, and there were some equations written along the bottom in a script that was like the one that
architects used. Neat, clear, precise. He had discovered that there was a
way to estimate the area under the curve . . .

Kay rolled her eyes up and sneezed.

"Oh," she said.

"God bless you," said Jack.

She put her hand to her head.

"Are you all right?" said Jack.

"Sure," she said. "A little headache. My eyes are itchy. Too much
excitement, I guess."

"I know what you mean," said Jack. He put his hand on her forehead.

Kay pulled back the covers and got into bed.

"I'm going to rest for a little," she said.

"Sure," said Jack. "That's the ticket."

She rustled in the covers.

"Jack," she said.

"What?" he said without looking up from his scrap of paper.

"Where are we going to get some money?" she said.

Jack looked out the window.

"We'll think of something," he said.

KAY SLEPT while the radiators in the room clinked like iron manacles, and when she sat up, alarmed at the sound, she saw that Jack was sitting at the screen of the cheap computer. Kay turned her head toward the radiators. The sound seemed coldly vibrant, and when she tried to think of what it reminded her of, she thought of visions she had only experienced in her dreams, the sound of a slave ship belowdecks, or the finality of steel bars being swung shut behind her. Jack was intent on a page he had found, and when she sat up, letting the sheet fall away from her, she saw that it was *The Single Man's Guide to Women*.

The *Guide* was divided into various sections, and Jack looked at one now that dealt with the correct way for men to move. It had clips of old actors, Cary Grant, Brad Pitt, and Miguel de Sorrento, and the narration pointed out the curiously fluid and keenly graceful locomotion of them all, not jumpy, not abrupt, but smooth. Jack watched for a while and then tried it out, walking across the room, head up, shoulders not noticeably squared, not braced, but still emphasizing, with a fluid movement, the way his shoulders hung. He looked good, and she thought that he would be terrific in evening clothes, although she had only seen pictures of this.

He caught her staring at him and said, "How do I look?"

"Oh, Jack," she said. "Don't be vain."

He smiled at her. It was obvious that he had read a section about smiling, and when he smiled now, he was irresistibly charming. Then he went back to the screen, where he scrolled through the possibilities before choosing Conversation, which gave him advice about what was amusing and pleasing and what was gloomy and oppressive. He went through the sample dialogues, showing his smile. Then he turned to a link labeled Sex. She saw him nodding, intrigued if not mildly surprised, but still pleased and happy.

"Kay," he said.

"What?" she said.

"Do you think a woman would like that?" he said, holding up the screen for her to see.

She blushed.

"Yes," she said. "Yes. I think that might be nice."

"That's what I think," he said.

He scrolled through more pages.

"Well, Jack," she said, "what are you planning?"

"Not much," said Jack.

CHAPTER 2

March 22, 2029, 3:30 A.M.

LET THE people at work try to come after me, Briggs thought. But he couldn't maintain this attitude very long, and after the short emotional lift of defiance, the warmth of it drifted away like a shot of liquor that elevated his mood, only to leave him a little more troubled than when he had first taken the drink. Liquor or something worse.

Briggs's apartment building was a brownstone with a stoop, and it had shutters over the windows, trees in the street, flower boxes from which a cascade of flowers fell. It was in a section of town that was charming and disreputable, where students lived. Briggs was on the tall side, and he had short hair and a small scar on one cheek, a little quarter-moon shape at the side of one eye. If he answered an ad in the paper for an apartment, the landlord would be glad to have him as a tenant. Briggs inspired confidence, but after having taken a deposit, the landlord would instantly wonder just what it was that Briggs really did. He seemed competent, but the question was always, competent at what?

The glass of the front doors of Briggs's building had beveled edges, and in the afternoon, when the sun was out, the hall was filled with bits of rainbow. The colored flecks reminded Briggs of an old dance hall with a globe covered with mirrored squares, where dancers clung to one another beneath the dappling light. When he saw these evanescent specks of light, he imagined the rustle of sequins on a dress like spectral confetti, the heavy brush of a woman's hair across his face . . .

When he came into his building from the street, he smelled the odor of fried steak and onions, cabbage soup. Not good, but still comforting.

The concierge had an apartment at the rear of the little hallway next to the stairs. Briggs saw her sitting on a chair in front of her open door. She wore blue jeans, and red eye shadow, and she treated her hair with a dye that made it glow in the dark. On a hook in the apartment behind her, she had hung a black leather jacket with a decal on it, but it was a little unfashionable, a little out-of-date, and people who wore those jackets were in that zone where the previously cool men and women had slipped back to being only moderately hip.

"Hey, Briggs," she said. "How are things?"

What could he say to that? He shrugged.

"Fine," he said.

He climbed the stairs to his apartment, hearing the sound of his feet and smelling the musk the young woman wore. Then he put his key into his lock, hearing the cold ratchet of the tumblers. He dropped his satchel on the sofa and sat down. What he wanted was to go to sleep, since he had been up all night and all day, too, not tired now so much as intoxicated by fatigue. Maybe he could stretch out here, but he didn't want to wake up in his clothes, feeling the grit of his beard.

His apartment had a kitchen, a bedroom, and a living room. A plant was in the corner of the living room next to the sofa, which was a comfortable one with big cushions. In the bookshelves there were some books and technical manuals: *The Principles of Artificial Life; DNA and Source Code for Professionals; Gene Sequencing for the Practical Man;* the Harvard Technical Series *(Viruses, The Varieties of Cytosil, Procedures for the Biological Engineer, Cost Estimates in Artificial Life).* Piled up on the floor were some catalogs from discount houses he had used when he had been working on a per-piece basis at home.

Next to the bed was the clock, which had the shape of a young, athletic woman dressed in Spandex. The Spandex was very tight, but somehow it made her seem generic, if only because it smoothed out the shape of her calves, the slight bulge of her stomach, the strength of her shoulders. She had freckles and short blond hair, a Midwestern, corn-fed way about her that made him think of Kansas, of Iowa. Rolling hills and green crops. Big blue skies and clouds dragging along, gray on the bottom, fluffy on top. The clock sat on a bench with her legs crossed, meditation-style, the GE logo on her arm. She could talk, but not move.

Briggs had spent some time hot-wiring the clock when he had first gotten it, but he hadn't been able to add much, not really, just the ability to
speak in platitudes, to offer the most conventional comments about
things. Briggs and the clock were polite to one another and they tried to
do their best, but it was like talking to a calendar that had a thought for
the month printed next to a picture of a dog. What could he expect? It
was just a GE clock, no matter what he had done to it. Sometimes the
clock trembled with frustration that she couldn't do more.

He sat down on the bed and fell asleep with the sense of warm darkness sweeping over him, not from the side or from his feet or head, but
all together, as though he had fallen into a tepid liquid. He liked sinking
into the warmth of it, and midway to the bottom, dreams started just at
the edge of his vision, and then they closed in. He slept in his clothes
with his feet on the floor.

At two-thirty in the morning he heard the clock say, out of the darkness of the room, "Briggs. You've got a message."

He sat up.

"Who's it from?" said Briggs.

"Work," she said. "You told me to wake you if something came from
work."

He had been sound asleep, and if it had been pleasant to slip into the
warmth of it before, he now had the sensation of having been under-
water, and that he had come up fast and had traveled a long way.
The quick ascent had left him nauseated. When he sat on the edge of
the bed, he was concerned about what had been in the green water
he had risen through, vague shadows like sharks or other creatures,
unknown, but just waiting to take a bite. He tried to shake off the ugly
memory, which left him feeling like someone who was universally
suspected.

"Some technician called," said the clock. "Something about growing
platforms."

"Oh," he said.

"You look worried," she said. "Is something wrong? Would you like
to talk about it?"

"It's hard to explain," he said.

"Try me," she said.

He knew right where it was going, just as she did. They would come up against the same blank wall as always. She would end up saying that there was no crying over spilled milk, that there was more than one way to skin a cat, and so on, and he would sit there in the onslaught of the conventional, nodding, yes, yes, that's true, but there is another element here . . .

He shrugged. "I don't know," he said.

"You don't know what?" she said.

"Where to begin," he said.

"How about at the beginning," she said. "That's the usual place, isn't it?"

"Yes," he said. "If I knew where the beginning really was."

"Take it one day at a time," she said. "Rome wasn't built in a day. So, what is it?"

He sat there blinking, running a hand across his face, hearing the staticlike sound of his beard. It wasn't so hard to get this far, to admit this much, but to go on from here, to put the rest of it into words, left him with a sense of futility. What good would it do to put it into words?

"Did they say what they wanted to see me about?" he said. "At two-thirty in the morning?"

"No," she said.

He sat there, trying to think. He suspected that at the heart of his mistake had been the fact that he had gone on feeling when he should have . . . what? When he should have cultivated the ability not to feel. To act dead. No, to be numb. Who got into trouble by feeling nothing? If you felt nothing, your armor was complete.

He tried to shake off the mild nausea that came from waking up too quickly. He thought of that sense of a rapid ascent from the bottom of a green sea where those shapes were concealed.

"Start at the beginning," the clock said. "See? What happened first?"

He got up and went into the bathroom and turned on the shower. The steam rose in filaments, like cigarette smoke.

"Briggs?" the clock called out after him. "Do you hear me? You've got to learn to listen better than you do. You've always got your head in a cloud. What was the first thing? It's as simple as one, two three . . . Isn't it?"

He looked in the mirror, at the salt-and-pepper color of his beard.

"So?" said the clock from the other room. "The first thing."

"Just a dream," said Briggs. "I guess that's it."

"I don't dream," said the clock. "So I wouldn't know about that."

"I don't mean a dream that you have when you're asleep. I mean one that you pursue."

He stood for a moment, looking into his own eyes. He hadn't done this for a while, and he guessed it was because he had gotten into the habit of avoiding things, particularly his habitual expression, which, as far as he was concerned, was that of a man who has cooked the books and is counting the days until it comes out. Still, as he stood here now, looking into his own green eyes, he tried to see a physical detail that betrayed the first hint of disaster. Could it be something as obvious as an expression in an eye? He guessed not, but one thing he knew for sure: you can pursue a dream only to have the unpleasant surprise of discovering that it is coming after you. That was the change he guessed he saw in his eyes: not the keen expression of the hunter, but the wary, quick glance of the hunted.

Maybe he was wrong about the beginnings of disaster. Maybe if you had an ounce of sense you could see trouble coming, like those scenes in the old movies where a steam locomotive appeared at the edge of a prairie. At first all you saw was a distant wisp, but soon it revealed itself as a column of black smoke made up of discrete pulses impelled upward with all the brute force of a machine. Then the engine itself arrived, as black as coal and gleaming like it too, releasing steam with a *husssh,* and of course with the engineer blowing the whistle.

Maybe he should start with the psychoactives again. They worked, in a way, but he had the feeling of something in his brain, funguslike and dreary, and yet with an interest of its own. That was the difficulty with the psychoactives, sweet as they could be at times. They didn't illuminate. Instead they damped everything down. He didn't notice the small weight they added the first day, but after the first week he began to feel the accumulation. Like water dripping into a bucket. And as the weight increased, as the sense of being smothered became stronger, as though he were under a blanket, he thought that the drugs were just a quiet method of telling him to shut up.

Briggs looked around for the toolkit he almost always carried. It had a couple of adapters, some Med-liner, protective gel, generic antibiotics. It all fit into a small leather case that he carried in his pocket. Then he went to the door and the clock said, "Good luck, huh? Is there anything I can do?"

"I'm afraid not," said Briggs. "I'll see you later. Take care."

"Yeah," she said. "Sure. Every cloud has a silver lining."

Briggs hesitated at the door, just about to say, *Don't bank on it,* but then he went over the threshold.

Briggs found a gypsy taxi. He sat in the backseat, beneath the torn headliner that hung like black pendants, and looked out the window as they went along the river. The water was the color of graphite, and the black swirls always formed in the same shape. The lights from the city on the other side of the river lay in streaks of yellow and red, but the reflection had a cold cheer, like the bright signs in a closed-up carnival.

"The high pressure is going to come in," said the driver. "A stationary high."

"It'll blow over," said Briggs.

"Naw," said the driver. "High pressure lingers, you know?"

The driver stopped in front of the Galapagos building and Briggs got out and smelled the scent of iodine and heard the slow, labored breathing of the logo above the door. The most important thing was not to anticipate anything, or to imagine the consequences of events that weren't going to happen. He believed that there was a difference between fear and anxiety. Anxiety was just a phantom, a fantasy that existed because of one's emotional state, but fear was another matter. Fear had an object, something real. The trick was to be able to tell what was anxiety and what was fear.

C H A P T E R ③ | *March 22, 2029, 3:30 A.M.*

BRIGGS STOOD at the door of Galapagos. He opened it and stepped into the cloud of cleaning mist. It was a fish-belly color, somewhere between white and sickly gray, about six inches thick, and it smelled like a combination of Clorox and wax. The cloud was laid down at 3 A.M., and it hung over the stone floor for about a half hour before it was sucked away by little vents in the bottom of the walls. It left the floor with a bright shine, like polished onyx.

Briggs went to the end of the lobby, his shoes making spirals in the mist and a noise too, a *tock, tock, tock* that reminded him of something. Chambering a round. That was it. Chambering a round and putting on the safety. Brass hulls, copper tips. It was funny the way things didn't work out sometimes. For instance, those high-speed rail guns had never come to anything, and people were still using gunpowder. After all these years.

A security guard sat at the black, horseshoe-shaped desk. His name was Jackson, and he was a retired military man who was glad to get the job to supplement his pension. The cleaning mist had a medical drawback, and a lot of the late-night guards complained about respiratory problems. The shine was good, though. No one could deny that. Jackson appeared to be floating on a cloud.

"The mist won't take but a minute more," said Jackson. "This new stuff works a little faster than the last muck they used. Stinks a little more, but, Jesus, talk about a shine."

When he spoke, he looked down at his hands, which were next to a blue diskette case that sat on the desk, the kind that held extra-dense

CDs, about the size and thickness of the wheel of a dolly. Briggs guessed that, like a lot of security guards, he was stealing software and selling it.

"Aren't you supposed to wear the respirator mask when the mist is out?" said Briggs.

"It's uncomfortable," said Jackson.

"Maybe it would be a good idea to wear it," said Briggs.

"Well, shit," said Jackson. "Have you ever tried to wear one? Jesus. It feels like I'm suffocating." He coughed.

Briggs stood in the mist. The stuff moved along the floor now with a tidal motion, a misty flow that reminded him of wisps of vapor on a river at dawn. They both stood there in the mist. It was withdrawing now. Briggs thought about that train coming: the trouble you could see from so far away. Briggs said, "You know, you've got to look for another job."

"This is pretty good," said Jackson.

"The mist makes you sick. See? You understand what I'm trying to tell you?" said Briggs.

"Come on, Briggs," said Jackson.

"Well, think it over," said Briggs.

"I'm just glad to be working," said Jackson. "You know? Anyway, you're supposed to go downstairs."

"What do you hear about that?" said Briggs.

"I hear all kinds of things," said Jackson. "Rumors."

"Like what?" said Briggs.

Jackson shrugged.

"You better go downstairs," he said.

"How bad is it?" said Briggs.

"You better go look for yourself," said Jackson.

He shrugged.

"You know how it is," Jackson said.

"If I were you, I wouldn't leave those diskettes around where everyone can see them," said Briggs.

"Oh, Christ," said Jackson. He reached out for the diskette case and put it in his pocket. "You won't say anything, will you?"

"No," said Briggs.

Briggs waited, hoping that Jackson would look up at him. Surely it was a bad sign that Jackson didn't want to look at him.

"Have you been here all night?" said Briggs.

"No," said Jackson. He licked his lips. "I had to go home for a while. I wasn't feeling so good."

"What was wrong?" said Briggs.

"I had to take some aspirin. Headache," said Jackson.

"Well, I hope you feel better," said Briggs. He turned and started walking toward the door at the back of the lobby, but after he had gone only a few steps, Jackson said, "Hey, Briggs."

"What?" said Briggs.

"You remember how you used to come in late at night and I'd tell you a joke? You remember the one about the lawyer and the polar bear?"

"Sure," said Briggs.

Jackson grunted. Then he looked right at Briggs and said, "We were always pretty good friends."

Were, thought Briggs.

"Yes," he said. "We were."

"Well, I just wanted to say good luck," said Jackson.

"Thanks," said Briggs.

"And to ask you one other thing. Since we were good friends," said Jackson.

"What's that?" said Briggs.

"Don't think badly of me," said Jackson.

"You mean in case the stink here gets you? Because you wouldn't wear the dumb respirator?" said Briggs.

"Yeah," said Jackson. "In case of that."

Briggs looked around.

"They're waiting for you," said Jackson.

Briggs's feet sounded in the stairwell as he went around and around, spiraling downward, passing the doors on each landing. In the hall he looked at the bulbs on the ceiling, which were in baskets. He had always thought that this was a military style, or the way the lighting was done in the halls of places where people were interrogated. He took a deep breath. What, after all, was the difference between anxiety and fear? Did he know it or didn't he?

The growing platforms were empty. The blue plastic tubes that carried the growing medium, the masses of red, yellow, and green wires that had been connected to the gauges and computers, the clear bags of nutrient, the pneumatics, with their wires still attached, the bright edges of the cutters, all looked like the objects in a ransacked apartment. The steel covers had been pushed back, and were off their runners, and the vapor from the platforms condensed at the edge and made a steady dripping sound as the drops fell. Light came from the ceiling, but now, in the disorder of the room, in the torn and broken materials, in the curdling of the vapor, the place was filled with a clutter of shadows, triangular and black shapes like pennants of ill intent. A little snow still fell, the lines of it erratic and slowly diminishing, like a storm in which the temperature rises and the flakes turn to rain.

A technician came in and stood there in his disposable clothes.

"They're gone," said the technician.

"That's what it looks like," said Briggs.

"This is a first," said the technician. He was scared, too. After all, it had happened on his watch.

Briggs sat down on a stainless-steel bench.

"Christ," he said.

"You know what everyone is asking," said the technician.

"What's that?" said Briggs.

"How did they know to escape?" said the technician.

"I don't know," said Briggs.

The technician stared at him.

"Uh-huh," the technician said. "And there's something else everyone is asking about. If they know how to escape, just what else do they know?"

Briggs got up and went over to what had been Kay's platform. Her shape was outlined in the soft material, which had the texture of a womb, although it was the color of aluminum foil. He ran his finger along the depression, which was still warm.

"I'm asking you a question," said the technician.

"You've got me there," said Briggs. Could anyone hear the quaver in his voice? He looked around the room. "What a mess."

"Well, that's not my lookout," said the technician. He looked around. "I've just got to keep my records straight."

Briggs looked at the platform that had been Kay's.

"You don't need me for anything, do you?" said the technician.

"No," said Briggs. "You better see to your records. They should be in order."

"That's what I've been thinking," he said.

"Go on," said Briggs.

"All right," said the technician. "I will. You don't have to get huffy."

"This isn't huffy," said Briggs. "You want to see what huffy is?"

"You don't have to talk to me that way," said the technician. "I don't have to take that. This wasn't my fault."

Briggs shrugged.

"Time will tell," he said.

The technician looked at Briggs for an instant.

"I guess that's right," the technician said.

He went out through the door.

Briggs heard a dripping sound and turned toward Kay's platform. Liquid collected in a crease and then dripped from it to the floor with a *tick, tick, tick.* It was clear, the basis of lymph fluid, sweat, secretions of one kind or another. Briggs looked at it and then took a glass tube from the rack on the stainless-steel bench and held it out to collect it, the drops filling the container slowly. It looked just like the fluid in a blister. He held it up to the light. It was clear, like liquid diamonds, nothing obviously wrong with it, but of course you couldn't tell just by looking. Briggs capped it and put it in his pocket.

Then he sat down on the floor next to the wall, and put his head in his hands. All right. He sat there, on the cool floor, thinking, *There's no going back now.*

In the clutter of the room, in the mess of broken equipment, in the shine of the stainless steel and in the dripping of fluids, he confronted what seemed to be obvious here, the perfidy of the human heart, but what drew him up short and made him even more troubled was his suspicion that the heart that had betrayed him was his own. After all, he had gotten himself into this.

Upstairs, Briggs went across the floor that looked like black ice.

"Well," said Jackson. "Finito, huh? Things aren't looking so good."

"No," said Briggs.

"How long, do you think, before you have to clean out your desk?"

"I don't know. I might be able to hang in here."

"You got a problem," said Jackson. "It's against the law to convey human desires to these creatures."

"No one knows that better than me," said Briggs.

Jackson gave him a long look.

"Come on," said Jackson. "Who do you think you're talking to? Some hick?"

Briggs thought all he really wanted now was to go home and sleep for a while. Maybe he could come up with something if he could just get a little sleep. He was still a little nauseated.

Briggs shrugged.

"I'll be upstairs for a while if someone wants me," said Briggs. "Then I'll be at home."

He walked across the black floor, thinking, *Can Jackson keep his suspicions to himself, or is that another worry?* No, not worry. Fear. After all, Jackson knew the number of times Briggs had made unnecessary visits downstairs. They had never talked about it, but Jackson knew that Briggs had gotten something out of those occasions in the middle of the night. Even at their best, those visits would make it look as though Briggs cared too much, just like those technicians who had become overwrought at the effect of smallpox. Maybe that was what was bothering Jackson: he was uncomfortable knowing things about Briggs that he wished he didn't. It made them accomplices.

Briggs went up the stairs with the steel mesh landings, and when he was at the second floor, he stopped to think for a moment. What he wanted was to be someplace between where he had been and where he was going, since each place he had been, or had yet to go, was filled with details that suggested questions he couldn't answer. He kept thinking that he had never actually written in anything about escaping. And if he hadn't, who had? The question was enough to make him close his eyes, but all he saw were explosions of color, swirling shapes that gave him no comfort at all. Even his eyes were playing tricks on him. And if someone else had been adding things, what had they been?

Upstairs, the walls of his office had just been cleaned, although this was done by running a charge through the glass that turned all the smudges, the fingerprints, the marks left by sticky fingers, into a fine dust that was collected by a vacuum at the base of each wall. The glass smelled like Windex, and Briggs guessed the odor of Windex had a way of suggesting a new beginning. He looked into the other offices, which were empty. He supposed his chances of starting over weren't good, and as he admitted this, he instantly longed for the clarity of innocence. For Briggs, innocence had disappeared slowly, like vapor condensing out of a clear summer evening and gradually obscuring the stars. He closed his eyes to recall some youthful memory that was reassuring, but this effort only enhanced his sense of innocence's elusiveness.

The port of the machine on his desk appeared like a dark rictus. He had some of his records, all on CDs as thick as bagels, and now he loaded them in, feeling the heavy mechanism inside take hold.

He wasn't sure there was going to be any evidence of . . . what should he call it? Sabotage? This, surely, was not the issue. He hoped. Manipulation, was that better? While sabotage was a possibility, it still didn't seem right. *Tampering* was the word he thought he could live with. Neutral, or less. Almost a prank. There it was again. He simply had to stop using the words to hide what was really happening. When would he learn? *Prank.* He felt ashamed that he had even tried to put it in those terms.

If anything had been done, where would it have happened? He supposed that tampering would be hard to detect, because whoever did it would have the common sense to use his style, which, to the untrained eye, might look indistinguishable from others, but in fact it was a lot like the touch on the key that Morse code operators used to have: each of them had an identifiable "voice" that was instantly recognizable to other operators.

He rarely considered the complexity of what he had done, since he often worried about details rather than an overall pattern. As far as coherence was concerned, he trusted to a general sensibility that allowed him to make changes in any particular section. He did this like a painter who lets each brushstroke be guided not only by the object it delineates, but by the intended effect of the finished painting. So Briggs scrolled through the miles of code, not sure what he was looking for. Something that just didn't look right. An ugly sensibility.

There was another matter too, which made it more difficult for him to determine whether anyone had tampered with what he had done.

Briggs had written the basics, which by any standard didn't have the delicacy of a living, breathing creature. To get the detail, the delicacy, and the beauty too, not to mention the stability of a living thing, Briggs had set up a method of amplification in which the code had been reproduced again and again. When spontaneous changes occurred (data could be corrupted by cosmic radiation, just like genes), they were retained, at least to the extent that this process enhanced his designs. If they worked to the design's disadvantage, such changes were discarded. But these variations took place at the most elemental levels, and as far as he could tell, there had been millions of small adjustments, maybe even billions. As he searched, he didn't know whether what he was looking at was a matter of the process he had set up, the artificial natural selection, or something that had been added by someone else. How could he tell the difference between a mutation that had been retained and something that had been added with the appearance of being harmonious with the original design?

He was bothered by another matter too, in that he hadn't done the code all at once, but by sections—for eye color, say, or skin texture or the ability to write music—and each of these had been enhanced on the basis of hundreds of thousands if not millions of reproductions, and so each section had possibilities for tampering. Would the sabotage have been done in some exceedingly unobtrusive way, such as adding something to the qualities of the hypothalamus or the lining of the lung, or to the covering of the spinal cord? Or would it be in some more obvious spot, as in the development of the frontal lobes? It was like trying to guess where a cancer might be found: a mole on the skin, or a tumor in the pancreas. And if the changes were hidden away like this, how did they work? He didn't know.

Mostly he flipped here and there aimlessly, and what gave him the creeps was that he wasn't going about this in an orderly fashion, with a method, but just taking a look here and there. What would he find in the mess?

Then he tried to come up with a method: Should he divide the code he had into discrete sections and look through each one, on the basis of anatomical systems, or should he start right at the bottom, at the feet, and work upward through everything—nerves, bone, blood vessels, lymph system, muscle, skin, even the light down on Kay's arms and on her thighs, and which could only be seen when the sun was on it? Could it possibly be something as small as a change in the code for a hair?

He realized it was hopeless. There was no way he would be able to tell by the finished code what was what or how it had come to be, since at this stage everything was seamless and looked so natural that all he could see was the endless complexity of a living thing. How was he going to pick out the one significant detail of that? What he needed, he realized, was not the details of the finished versions, but the log of how they were put together, the ongoing record of just how each detail came into being. The clue would be sudden appearances of traits that no one expected or wanted or that, according to his idea of things, suggested the ungraceful, the ugly, and the brutal.

He had always thought that one of his jobs was to make an estimate of the whole by the parts, and there was something in the escape that left him trying to be specific about what had been done to Kay. If he had added love and desire, mathematical brilliance, an instinct for music, why, then it would have been possible for someone else to add other qualities, like fury, a delight in power, or the worst possible instinct for doing injury, as though darkness were an irresistible and delicious way of knowledge. Whose ideas were dominant anyway, his or someone else's?

CHAPTER ④ | *March 22, 2029, 4:30 A.M.*

BRIGGS CAME out of the Galapagos building, hearing the squeak of the logo and smelling, too, the sea-stink of iodine. He turned down the avenue, walking with his hands in his coat. The last thing he wanted now was to go home and sit by the phone for the next call that was surely coming. His boss would tell him to come to a meeting. No. Not his boss. His boss's assistant would tell him to come to the meeting, and his voice would betray the slightest impatience, the first sign that Briggs was being diminished.

Briggs walked toward the lights up ahead, where there were some bars and diners with antiquated neon signs. He listened to the sounds of the street behind him, and from time to time he stepped into the doorway of a building and waited in the shadows. Well, he wasn't being followed yet, he supposed, but it wouldn't be too much longer before he was.

Then he turned and went up the street toward the cherry-colored neon of a gaming parlor, which looked like a combination of an arcade where kids used to play video games and a casino with cocktail waitresses in short skirts. The games were at one side of the room: these were set up in little booths with a clear membrane, like soft glass, that you could walk through when the game was available. Two cots were inside. It was on these slender beds that the people who played against each other stretched out in their full skin-suits, which were connected to the game's network. People gambled on the games, and this gave the fictional world of the games a sense of risk. It was like being in a movie that could affect your life.

The most important aspect of these games was that they couldn't be changed. They were tamper-proof. In fact, Briggs had done a lot of work to make sure of this: he had had a knack for it, and this job had been one of the things he had done right out of school. No one knew the complete key, but if anyone did, Briggs was close. It was inconceivable that anyone could obtain an advantage by changing a game. Billions of dollars were involved, and no one was going to be allowed to interfere with that by tampering with a machine. It wasn't a local business, but an international one. Every now and then you heard a story about someone who had penetrated the first protective shell of a game, and the next thing you knew he was gone. Just like that. No questions asked. Briggs stood just outside the gaming parlor, but he had no real interest in going in.

In the years when Briggs had smoked a lot of opium, the entire process had been ritualized, and part of the ritual had been the beginning, in which he began to build a case for letting go: he was working too hard, he had been successful, a little break would make everything easier, he worked better after a little relief. After all, he wasn't made of steel, was he? Anyway, he wasn't really going to do it. He was just out for a walk.

After a few minutes he stopped at the entrance of an alley.

Even from the entrance he could smell it, at once harsh and filled with promise. The alley had brick walls, fire escapes, trash cans fluted like Greek columns. Here and there a puddle of water was filled with light. Briggs remembered being here one night when the moon was reflected in the thin layer of water. He had often stood here, smelling the opium and telling himself that he wouldn't go back to the end of the alley.

Maybe he'd just have a "look around." He lightened his step, if only because he was sure that everything was under control. He had faced up to the temptation and was probably going to defeat it. Adversity did build character. Then he came to the end of the alley.

Just a little fun, wasn't that all he needed? Just think of how tense things were. He knew what was in the basement at the rear of the alley. The receptionist had dark hair, and she usually wore a jade-colored dress, the material of it clinging to her figure, the bones of her shoulders disappearing into the green fabric, the folds falling from her hips and swinging over her legs when she walked. She wore red lipstick and a string of pearls. Everything about her had the musky scent of opium.

Briggs had often stood here thinking about her, the shape of her lips when she saw him come in. Never a smile, just a look of keen understanding. It was all right, she seemed to say, she understood.

He went to the end of the alley and down the steps into the light below. He could smell it.

"Hey, Briggs," said the doorman at the bottom of the stairs. "Where you been? Haven't seen you for a long time."

"Here and there," said Briggs.

"Uh-huh," said the doorman.

Briggs went into the room. The golden light, the flowers in the vase, the woman who stood in the green dress, the clean walls were right there, as though he hadn't been away at all. "So, hey, good to see you, Briggs," said the woman.

He sat down on a chair by the door.

"I need to think for a minute," he said.

The woman smiled. Of course. He could think all he wanted. She knew what the outcome would be.

He closed his eyes and thought of Kay. He knew she was out there, but what was she doing? And why didn't she contact him? Maybe she was too smart for that. Then he thought of a dream he had had, of the blue sheen on Kay's legs from the sky. He had been with her in an apple orchard in bloom, under the snowlike fall of petals. She had said to him, "Can you cry from happiness?" In the dream, he had felt the slight heaving of her chest. She had wanted him to taste the tip of her finger, salty with tears: the taste of happiness. All bound up with other things she didn't understand, but still, would he taste it? It was the taste of childbirth, of passion, of everything that was so vital one cried in the face of it.

Now he opened his eyes.

"I just came in for a moment," he said.

"Sure. Any time," the receptionist said. "We're always here."

"I know," said Briggs.

He turned and went up the stairs, nodding to the doorman, who said, "Some other time, I guess."

"I guess," said Briggs.

At the mouth of the alley, where it opened into the street, Briggs heard a steady brushing sound, a *hush, hush, hush,* and when he looked up he saw a man, a dumpy one with short hair like indoor-outdoor carpet, who was sweeping the street. He had a wide push broom and he came down the street, propelling a growing moraine of dust and dirt. Every now and then he stopped to tap the broom a couple of times on the sidewalk. He put his hand to his head and rubbed it through his coarse hair, but he didn't look around, and he stood there, resting, eyes on the ground ahead of him. One of the early ones, Briggs thought. Brutish, short, but dependable. Then the man started sweeping again, the *hush, hush, hush* haunting Briggs as though it had been a cry.

A couple of young men came up the street, nineteen or twenty years old, one with an earring and the other with a black plastic coat that had been fashionable a couple of months before, and when they bumped into the sweeper, they stopped and looked back.

"Hey," said one of them, "what the fuck are you doing?"

"He's just a dummy," said the other. "Ain't that right. Yeah. You. I'm talking to you."

He stuck his finger into the sweeper's chest.

"Sorry," said the sweeper, keeping his eyes down.

"Sorry," said the other. "He doesn't know the meaning of the word."

"I didn't mean nothing," said the sweeper.

"Yeah?" said the first. "Well, you don't know anything about meaning, either."

"Come back in here," said the other. "I want to show you something."

"Is it a job?" said the sweeper.

"Sure," said the first. "It's a job."

"I've got to do all the way to the corner," said the sweeper.

"You won't have to worry about that," said the other one. "Come on."

"Leave him alone," said Briggs.

"Yeah?" said the first one.

"Yeah, leave him alone," said Briggs.

"What's it to you?" said the other.

Briggs turned and slowly looked at this one.

"Go home," he said.

They stood there for a while. The sweeper started to use his broom, pushing the dirt he had collected with short, brutal, yet efficient strokes.

His shoulders were somewhat dropping, and he kept his head down, working his way to the corner.

"Ah, shit," said the first one. He was the one in the black plastic coat. "Come on."

The two of them walked back into the alley, going toward the stairs to the room at the bottom. Briggs waited until they were gone, and then the sweeper came back and said, "Thanks, mister. They were going to hit me. They do that sometimes."

"I know," said Briggs. "Why don't you finish your sweeping?"

The sweeper looked up, his eyes dull under his hair.

"Okay," he said. "You're the boss."

Briggs considered going back to the end of the alley, into the clouds of opium smoke, but instead he found himself looking at the sweeper. The man shoved his broom, a little cloud of dust rising and turning white with each repetitive movement. The sweeper's insistence was a small echo of the one thing Briggs knew how to do, which was to persist. The sweeper limped up the street, his progress marked by the silver puff of dust, and everything about him, the sluggishness, the brutality, the single-mindedness of this drudgery, appeared to Briggs as an omen, since it left him considering the dangers of his own steadfastness. He had always depended on it, but now, as the figure limped up the street, so obviously doomed, Briggs wondered if his own perseverance was making things worse, getting him in deeper. He stood there, smelling the distant scent of opium and hearing the *hush, hush, hush* of the broom.

KAY AND JACK went down the street on which there were some signs in Ukrainian, and in the cafés and coffee shops, Kay saw people sitting at a counter where they ate pierogis, little dumpling-like items that were filled with potato or cheese. They passed an old man dressed in black, head down, carrying a book. The buildings had shops on the street level, and one window had been cracked and patched with transparent tape. Newspapers and wax wrappers formed a small drift in the recessed doorways, and people had written on the sidewalk with colored chalk. Awnings could be cranked down from the storefronts, and they gave the impression of a circus tent that is being used for its last season. A couple of bookstores were open, and in their windows were displayed volumes in many languages, some of them dead (Latin, Greek, Russian, and Polish). The entire neighborhood was at once impoverished and somewhat intellectual. An immigrant spirit imbued almost everything, the clothes people wore, the food they ate, and a hidden but still profound belief in progress perfectly mixed with a desire to hang on to everything familiar. Dead rabbits hung in the window, skinned, the membranes on them looking like ice.

Jack and Kay were sweating even though it was cool. Kay took a handkerchief out of her pocket and pressed it to her forehead. Thin rills of moisture ran out of Jack's hair and along the sides of his face, which he wiped with his sleeve.

He stopped in front of a building.

"This is the place," said Jack. "Doesn't look like much."

Kay shrugged.

"I don't know," she said. "It has a . . . well, a certain vitality."

"Vitality?" said Jack. "Don't make me laugh."

"Yes. Vitality," she said. "There's a difference between vitality and newness."

"Words," said Jack. "You are into words now. Jesus."

"Maybe I'm into accuracy," she said.

He shrugged.

"Come on," he said. "The place is on the second floor."

He had the newspaper turned back to the want ads, and he took one last look before dropping it into a trash can. Even now, people liked to read newspapers, and a few were still published. The paper fit perfectly in this part of town. Then Jack opened the door, and both of them looked up the stairs, which went up twenty steps or so and stopped at a landing, and then went up another twenty. Fluorescent lighting. More smells of cooking that is done on a hot plate. At the top, from the musty depths of the building, they heard a piano. The same piece, played again and again. Like two people going into the rain, they went into the sound and up the stairs. Kay shivered. Her nose was running. Her breathing had a wet, diminished wheeze. At least she had bought some Kleenex. She guessed that she had some allergies, but she hoped nothing else had gone wrong.

The door of the office they wanted was brown, although the paint was chipped and underneath it the metal of the door showed through. In the middle was a round brass peephole, over which Jack put his thumb.

"Frankly," he said, "I don't know why you want to do it this way."

"It seems like a good thing," she said.

"Okay," he said. Then he took his thumb away and knocked. Once and then again, harder the second time. From beyond the door they heard someone making a scurrying sound. The noise suggested a pile of paper on a desk, newspaper that had held fried food, pierogis from the coffee shop. The man inside was rolling the greasy sheets up, but he probably didn't have the energy to do more than stick the greasy paper in an overflowing trash can or, at worst, into the pocket of a jacket. The door opened.

The man who stood inside the doorway was about six feet tall, fat, and he wore half-glasses. He was bald, although he combed some strands over the top of his head, and his eyes, while small, were quite bright. They moved from Jack to Kay. He had crumbs on the front of his cardigan sweater, which he brushed in a slow, methodical, and yet absentminded way, as though he weren't so much trying to get rid of the crumbs as thinking over what the appearance of these two people at his door could possibly mean. He had a paper napkin, one that had been used more than once, and he wiped his lips. He had a mole on one cheek. His eyelids were red, and his sweater was dim green, but the combination of his inflamed eyes and the color of the sweater was somehow fertile.

"So," he said. "What can I do for you?"

"You put an ad in the paper?" said Jack.

"And since when has it been against the law to advertise?" said the man.

"He just wanted to know if we came to the right place," said Kay. She smiled. The man looked at her for a while, as though it had been a long time since a woman like Kay had smiled at him that way.

"Perhaps, perhaps," he said. "Come in."

The room was filled with bookshelves that sagged like old barns, and on the floor, books were stacked in columns that looked about to fall over. The cloth covers of many of them were an antiquated oatmeal color from an era in which books like these existed in libraries where there were leather chairs, green-shaded reading lamps, and long oak desks. Here, in this office, the light from a lamp came down in a golden cone on a book the man had been reading, and now one of the pages slowly rose from one side of the open book and flipped over to the other side, making a little *tick*.

He looked from one of them to the other and said, "So, have you got a cold?"

"It's nothing," said Jack.

The man didn't look convinced.

"Are you a musician?" the man said to Jack.

"This one," said Jack, gesturing to Kay. "She's got the talent in this group. But I play a little."

"Umm," said the man. "Talent. Uh, talent. A lot of people think they have talent. But, I don't see so much of it, not really. And I suppose you want rehearsal space?"

"Yes," said Kay.

"With a piano?" said the man. "We have them with pianos and without."

"With," she said. "Or, I think I would like to look at the piano and decide."

"Oh, so you know pianos?" he said. "She knows pianos." He said this last as though there was another person, invisible, in the room. "This is a good thing, because I have a good piano for you. If you know pianos, you will be able to tell."

By the door he had a set of keys hung on cup hooks, and he reached out for one now, his fingers picking out one and then taking it down. He turned back to Kay and said, "Come on. Come on. If you know pianos."

In the hall the landing creaked under his weight. For a moment he turned and looked up the stairs and listened to the sound of the playing. He nodded to himself, as though he had had a suspicion confirmed.

He turned to Kay.

"And so do you think that is talent?" he said.

Kay listened for an instant, the turning of her head, the lifting of her eyes, the judgment all happening with a speed that was almost like a nervous tic.

"No," she said.

"So, you make decisions fast. Is this a good thing, do you think?"

Then he started climbing, doing so with the slow, patient gait of a man who knew that the thing he was doing was going to kill him one day, but what else could he do?

"But between you and me," he said, panting. "That is not talent. No."

They got up to the next landing and the man put the key into the lock of a door and turned it.

He said to the door, "My name is Stone. What's yours?"

"Kay Remilard," she said.

"Ah, and where have you studied?" said Stone, pushing the door open, into the musty rehearsal room. Light slanted in through a dirty window, and on the floor, the shadows of pigeons moved as they fluttered up to the sill outside. "Kay Remilard?"

"Here and there," said Jack.

"Ah, many people have studied here and there," said Stone. "But, for instance, was it here and there in Europe or here and there here?"

"Europe," said Kay.

"Oh," he said. "Oh. So it's Europe. I wonder where? Somewhere near Salzburg? Or Vienna? Or was it a little farther north?"

"Farther north," said Jack. "Is this it?"

Stone went over to the piano. The pigeons on the sill flew up, marking the floor and the walls again with sudden shadows.

"Of course," said Stone. "They have pigeons in Europe, too. Did you notice?"

But by now Kay was looking at the piano. She sat down and worked the pedals. They made a little squeak. Stone shrugged. Jack went over to the window and looked out at the pigeons. The top of the piano was not open, and in front of Kay, on the surface, a layer of dust dulled the finish of the instrument. The dust was the color of the light that came in the window. Stone came over and opened the top of the piano, propping it up. Kay hit a note, just one, listening as it hung so definitely in the empty room as to seem as real as a clothesline stretched from one side to another. As it lingered, she looked up, almost as though she could see it. Then she hit another key and waited.

"So it needs to be tuned a little. What can I tell you? If it needs to be tuned, I will have it tuned," said Stone. "I am not a fraud. Do you think it is a good idea for a man to say he is one thing when he is really another? So, what do you think of the piano?"

"It's suitable," said Kay.

"Suitable, is it?" said Stone. "Unh. But is it enough for talent? That is the question." He turned to his imaginary companion. "You see, maybe my piano is not good enough for someone who has talent and studied in Europe. North of Salzburg."

Jack looked at Stone. The lack of movement as he stood there was a little odd, as though he were not himself but a photograph of himself. Absolutely still. Stone reached into his pocket, making some paper rustle there. Jack shrugged, as though he had made a decision that he didn't really like. Maybe later.

"Why don't you play?" said Jack. "Isn't that what we came for?"

"Yes," said Stone to Kay. "Play."

Stone took a chair from the wall and was about to sit down, but then thought better of it.

"Maybe I will just stand," he said. "I'm a busy man these days, and I may have to go back down to my office. So play. If you think you can play."

Jack looked out the window. Kay sat at the piano, her hands in her lap. Her hair was damp, and she pushed it away from her forehead. The only sound in the room was Stone's asthmatic breathing. He reached into his pocket and rustled the papers there, took out a napkin, and rubbed it between his fingers. It was as though the bits of paper he carried around were worry beads and that when he was thinking things over, he wanted to have them in his fingers to help him come to some decision. He was old enough now not to care if anyone saw him or if he was dismissed as dowdy. So, dowdy, they call me? So, and what are you? His eyes weren't dowdy, though, and he stood there, rustling around in his pockets and watching Kay's hands.

She straightened her shoulders, rested her hands in her lap. She stared across the room, although she didn't seem to notice the dirty, cream-colored wall in front of her. The wall had existed like a barrier for the musicians who spent time in this room, a fact that they could never get over, because even the best musicians, or particularly the best ones, repeatedly came up to a limit. Sometimes it was a technical matter, although the worst was one of feeling or lack of understanding. Sometimes they managed to push the barrier farther away than at other times, but it never disappeared.

"What are you waiting for?" said Jack. He was shivering now too, like Kay.

"I don't know," said Kay. "I guess I'm just thinking about things."

"What's to think about?" said Jack.

"We've come a long way," said Kay.

"So what?" said Jack. "You're not going to go soft on me now, are you?"

"No," said Kay.

"Glad to hear it," said Jack.

"It doesn't hurt to think about how far you've come and what it cost you to get here," said Kay. "Or about people you miss."

"You want to know what I think about missing people?" said Jack.

Kay shook her head.

"It's just that we came a long way," said Kay.

"Especially if it's from Europe," said Stone. "I wonder where it was. You don't have an accent, or not much of one."

"You can get farther away than Europe," said Jack.

"Oh, can you? Maybe you're talking about Australia?" said Stone.

Jack went on looking out the window. Over the piano lid, the shadows looked like pieces of black nylon that were slipping to the floor. Jack shrugged. Stone went on breathing with a heaving sound. Kay began to play.

She started with some easy pieces, just exercises really, and as she played, the shadows of the birds slid across the piano and the floor of the room with a silence that was like dark ghosts of the notes she played. She moved on to Chopin, and as she did, the room was filled with the audible intake of air as Stone gasped. He listened without moving, as though caught in amber. She played other pieces, going up the order of difficulty, and as she did, Stone took a seat on the chair. Jack looked out the window. There were other pieces she went to now, not only more intricate, but also allowing for more interpretation, and as she went through them, she concentrated on the phrasing, on the slow, lingering moments in which the approach of silence allowed the full access to emotion, just a hesitation here and there, which for her had to do with the most profound longing, the uncertainty that is at the heart of any real love, if only because of the risk such devotion involves. She tried to recall that blue light and saw not only snow, but Briggs's face. She had reached up to put her finger right against his, on the transparent material that had been between them. She tried to imagine what it would be like to touch him, without anything between them. When would that happen? Or when would she ever feel complete? The phrasing took on other shades, like the sensation of life making its tragic approach, right into her skin and muscles, into her bones, the ache and wonder of it leaving her with a keen, almost sexual excitement. How could this sensation be so filled with pleasure and promise, and yet have such a profound threat built into it, some accounting of time, some inexorable diminishing of everything that was precious?

She continued to play. Jack looked out the window. The shadows of the birds flitted around the room, across the wall, over her hair and hands, through the sounds that lingered in the dusty air. The bits of dust turned in the light and flashed now and then, just small flecks of gold in the otherwise dreary room, but which seemed to suggest the ephemeral and piercing quality of the notes she played.

She stopped. The sound of Stone's weeping filled the room.

"I am afraid," he said, looking up, shamelessly showing his face, "that I didn't recognize that last piece. Perhaps I'm getting old. Perhaps an old man forgets things, but I can't place it. Mozart, maybe, but too muscular for Mozart. So, can you tell an old man what it was?"

"It's just a little something I've been working on," she said.

"A little something you've been working on, my darling, my *liebchen*?" said Stone.

He reached into his pocket and took the used napkin and wiped his eyes and blew his nose. Then he started crying again.

"So," said Jack. "Do you want it or not?"

He gestured to the piano.

"It needs to be tuned," said Kay.

"Of course," said Stone. "I will have it tuned. Please. I will go downstairs and call the tuner. His name is Gotts. I owe him a little something, but I will fix that. I will call right now. A little something she has been working on?"

He blew his nose.

"Have you ever entered a competition?"

"No," said Kay.

"And why not?" he said.

"I never had the chance," she said.

"That's the long and short of it," said Jack.

Kay closed the cover over the keys.

"I don't know why that made me so tired," she said.

"I do," said Jack.

"Well, we have something to talk about," said Stone.

"We don't want to waste time," said Jack.

"No," said Stone. "Not a second." He blew his nose again. "I wonder if this is good for an old man? Well, that doesn't matter. Nothing else matters. What did you say your name was?"

"Kay Remilard," she said.

"Jack Portman," said Jack.

"Do you play too?" said Stone.

"A little," said Jack. "But she's got the talent." He looked out the window. "I have other things I like to do."

"Here," said Stone. He gave Kay the key to the room. "You'll need this. Take it."

She put out her hand and cupped her fingers around the key. The shadows of the pigeons flitted over the floor, the walls, and then disappeared into the black of the piano top, as a shadow being absorbed by a shadow. The popping sound of their wings came in through the dusty window.

"You'll have to trust me for the money," said Kay.

"Money," said Stone. "You want to talk to me about money when I have heard you play?" He made an impatient gesture with one hand. "Don't bother me about money." He took her hand in both of his.

"Thanks," she said.

"Yeah," said Jack. "We appreciate it."

"I'll get this room cleaned up," said Stone. "I can't imagine why I ever let it get this way. It is easy for an old man to get cynical, you know, and he does. But then something happens and you began to think maybe you have gotten mean-spirited. And old. But the important thing is to care again, don't you see? It is like waking up from a sleep."

Stone sat down and started crying again.

"I don't want to make a spectacle," he said. "Give me a moment."

"I'm glad you liked it," said Kay.

"*Liked* it?" said Stone. He spoke again to the imaginary person. "She says I *liked* it? Am I hearing right? Oh, my darling, 'liked' doesn't do it justice." He shook his head.

"Let's get some air," said Jack.

"Yes, of course," said Stone. "Get some air. Take care of yourselves. Rest. Get some juice. Tea."

"THEY'RE GOING to lock us out of our room," said Kay. "Unless we get some money."

"I've been thinking about that," said Jack.

The erratic descent of the elevator in the hotel was so predictable that it didn't worry Kay anymore. It was like the creaking of a floorboard in an old house. The cage itself was made of wrought iron with scrollwork along the top, and it had a worn green carpet on the floor. Usually the elevator was filled with the perfume that the women in fishnet stockings wore when they brought those silent men here. Kay thought of the cables in the shaft, the long, drooping shapes of them like creepers in a jungle. The elevator went down, stopping and starting in the shaft, the lights from each floor momentarily cutting into the darkness of the cage. Each of them had had two hundred dollars when they first found themselves in front of the hotel, and now only Kay had any money left, and it was just a few dollars.

The elevator stopped at the ground floor, and Jack pushed the bars of the gate aside. The lobby was deserted, although the ashtrays next to sofas were filled with sand that looked like the beach at the end of the Fourth of July. Cigarette butts, foil wrappers, half-eaten candy.

They stepped out of the elevator and Jack touched her arm and nodded toward the clerk, who sat at his desk. Blood dripped from the clerk's yellow, nicotine-stained fingers, which he had cupped under his nose. The suddenness of the nosebleed left the clerk absolutely still, as though he were trying to be invisible. His eyes moved toward Kay. The blood spilled over his fingers and began to drip onto the desk's green blotter.

"It's just a nosebleed," said the clerk. His hand was cupped as if he were trying to hold water to drink.

"What's a nosebleed?" said Kay.

"It's nothing," said the clerk. "You bleed from the nose."

"Does it happen a lot?" said Kay.

"No," said the clerk. "I never get nosebleeds."

"Here," said Jack. He took a handkerchief from his pocket. "Lean forward. That's the way."

"I don't know what causes it," said the clerk. "Just happens, I guess. There's a tenant here who has fits." The clerk shrugged.

"Why don't you go wash up?" said Jack. "Isn't that your apartment there?"

He pointed at a door behind the clerk.

"Yeah," said the clerk. "But what if someone comes in and wants a room?"

"I'll watch the desk for you," said Kay.

The clerk looked one way and another. No one else was around.

"Thanks," he said. He held the handkerchief to his nose and stood up and then looked around again, just to make sure. Kay had never seen a ferret or a mongoose in a trap, but she recognized the motion. An anxious movement from side to side.

The clerk went through his apartment door, closing it quickly so that Kay couldn't see his sad, mismatched furniture and the posters he had on the wall, large ones from a model airplane convention. With the door open just a crack, he said, "It won't be a minute." Then he closed it.

On the papers in front of Jack, and on the floor too, there were a series of red circles about the size of a coin. Jack looked at them with the particular interest a trapper or hunter would have in blood spoor. Outside, people walked past the glass door of the hotel, bent forward, pulling their coats together. The sky was clear, but it had gotten colder.

Kay watched a woman in fishnet stockings who was walking up and down in front of the hotel, looking one way and then pacing again, her movement, her gestures, all suggesting impatient hunger.

"Maybe you can stand out here and then we'd go to a hotel with some guy and we'd just take what he had." Jack looked out the window. "It's got possibilities."

"I don't want to do that," said Kay.

"Why not?" said Jack.

She shrugged.

"I just don't want to," she said. "All right?"

"Have you got something against killing one of these jackasses?" said Jack.

"And then what do we do?" said Kay.

The clerk came out and said, "Thanks," and Jack looked at him, thinking it over. Kay said, "Come on, Jack. Let's go."

Outside, the stars appeared in the sky like a couple of blue sequins on a black dress. At the horizon there was a smear of red from the crimson lights of the city. Kay reached over and took Jack's arm.

"Come on, Jack, we don't have to be that way, do we? Not to each other. That's the important thing."

"I'm just worried about the money," he said.

"No one is a friend to you like me," said Kay. She turned her face up to his and tried to catch his eyes, but he was too ashamed to return her gaze. Instead they walked along for a while with Kay holding his arm with both of hers.

"You know, Kay, if anyone tried to do anything to you, why, I'd . . ." He made an economical gesture, not violent so much as like a butterfly collector putting a specimen into the killing jar.

"I know," she said.

"No one is going to get by me where you're concerned," he said. "You can trust me about that. I'm here to make sure no one bothers you. So don't worry. You can really trust me. You know, I'm devoted to you. Like a brother."

They walked a couple of hundred yards before stopping in front of the gaming parlor. The place was filled with people who hung around looking for a sucker—usually a recreational player, or someone who hadn't spent the time to keep up with each new release of the current games. A really good game had the intricacy of life about it, not only the complexity but the brutality too. Winning was like being able to escape fate's most cherished and hidden details.

A brass bell that had come from a nineteenth-century sailing vessel was hung in the doorway of the place. It had been used to call out the first dog watch, the second dog watch, the morning watch, and now it had ended up here as a prop, just an antique. Jack stood under it, eyes on it, but still drawn to the bell as though seeing something he had always thought to be beautiful or romantic. He imagined the coast of Africa or South America, the creaking of a sailing ship in the light airs of a hot afternoon: What could be more attractive than a coast with peaks and dark vegetation visible through shreds of cloud?

"Hey," said Kay. "How about him?"

She smiled at a man who had short hair, a face scarred by acne, and who wore glasses like a student, although it was obvious he hadn't seen the inside of a classroom for a long time. Beautiful white teeth, which, Jack supposed, were false. Jack wondered how the man had lost the real ones.

"It's your funeral," said Jack.

The man came over like a fish rising through polluted water.

"Hey," said Kay. "Do you know how to play these games?"

"Oh, I've played a few of them," he said.

"They all look about the same," said Kay.

"Yeah," he said. "You know one, you know them all. Yeah. That about sums it up. What's your name?"

"Kay Remilard," she said. "This is Jack Portman."

"Where are you from?" said the man.

"Here and there," said Jack. "What's the difference?"

"No difference," said the man. He looked from one of them to the other. "Okay. My name is Hart. Do you want to play?"

"She does," said Jack.

Hart had a checklist he usually went through before playing with a stranger: age, experience, reflexes. Sometimes he'd drop something on the floor to see how fast a mark really was. Instead he just looked at Kay. As nearly as he could tell, she had a faintly academic quality, or the manner of a woman who had spent time in a convent. Or a conservatory.

Maybe she played the violin. Frankly, though, he didn't have much time to speculate about it, since he was playing on what was known as "deep margin"; he couldn't say why he had been losing recently, but he guessed it was part of the cyclical nature of gambling. Every player knew this aspect of the life. Hart was borrowing the money to play and paying a high interest rate, calculated not in weeks or even days, but hours. He dropped a key chain, a little promotional piece of junk that was being given out for a new game, and it hit the floor with a click. Kay bent down slowly. When she picked it up, she dropped it and then made a grab for it and missed. Hart reached down for it.

"You can get dressed right back there," he said.

"Thanks," said Kay.

"You're welcome," he said.

Kay walked through the smoke of the place, her hips swaying a little, like the woman she had seen on the street the first night she had looked out the window of the hotel. When Hart turned back, he found himself face-to-face with Jack. Hart said, "Nice night, huh?" but he was thinking, *Watch the bozo.*

An attendant sat near the door of the changing room, but otherwise the place was empty. A bench went along one side in front of some small black metal doors. Closets? No, Kay thought, but they had something to do with storage. Lockers. Yes, that's what they are. Sure.

Maybe, if she could get some money, she'd be able to control things a little better. For instance, she'd buy some clothes, new shoes, makeup, and then she could find out where Briggs lived. And yet she wanted to resist this; the obsessive impulse left her at once exhilarated and tired. Why couldn't she just forget about him? But even as she considered this, she felt the panic of being without the desire for him, which left her with such clarity of feeling and purpose. She stood in the room, looking around. The first thing was the money. But even so, she let herself have the momentary pleasure of imagining what she would do when she found him, got him alone somehow, or maybe even came into his apartment when he was already there, sleeping maybe, naked under the sheets. She thought of standing there watching him breathe, of how she would slide a hand under the sheets, along his stomach. Then she shook this off and went back to thinking about the money.

Four shower heads were lined up at the end of the room, all of them dripping in a different cadence. Kay dropped her jumpsuit in front of the lockers and then turned to the mirror opposite them, where she appeared in a silver and flecked darkness: pale skin, her damp face, the shape of her ribs, the indentation of the backs of her arms where the thin triceps were defined. She looked around and, as discipline, she named the objects in front of her: mirror, bench, shower. Drip. Drop. Odors. Like dirty socks. Then she looked back at herself and thought, *Am I attractive?*

A drop of sweat fell from her forehead and splashed on her leg, the silver track of it disappearing along her calf.

Oh, darling, she thought, *please.* As she stood there in the gloomy space, she was convinced that she could get relief from her desperation in only one way: in her lover's touch, or his odor, or that look in his eyes which came from the fact that he wanted to have a child with her, and that this desire came not out of his sense of duty but because he loved her so much that he wanted to mix his blood with hers. *Oh, darling,* she thought. *I want to believe that is the way it will be.*

"Which one are you going to use?" said the attendant, who came up with a small cart on which there were three suits. They all were of one piece and made of thin material, although two of them looked newer and were obviously better made. The better-made ones were actually uglier than the original models, since they were covered with long chaotic shapes and colors.

"The Burton, that's this one," said the attendant, "It's the cheapest. Twenty-buck deposit. It hasn't got the connections that the others have, like the Magnin, but if you don't have the dough, it's the best you can hope for."

The attendant was about thirty and had dirty hair.

"I'll take the Burton," said Kay.

"That's what I thought. You can't fool me, although some of them try. Where's the twenty?"

Kay's jumpsuit lay across the narrow bench in front of the lockers, and Kay reached down to take the last of her money out of the pocket of it. The bill was damp.

"Here," said the attendant. "One Burton."

Kay rolled up the first leg of the suit and put one foot in, pointing the toe to do so, and then she unrolled the thin material, about as thick as a film, really, pulling it up over her calf and knee, doing the first leg and then the second, the material fitting her perfectly, molding to her knees, her thighs, her stomach. She stuck her arms in, too. Pulled the suit up to her neck. Then she looked at herself in the mirror. The sleek material took the light so as to define her in luminescent smears on her shoulders, her arms, her legs. The attendant said, "Come here."

Kay stepped closer to him, and she took out a tube of clear electrolyte gel, which she put on the plug at the end of the belt of the suit.

"Sometimes the contact isn't good," said the attendant. "This helps. All right. There."

Kay heard the sound of the water dripping. She swallowed and took a deep breath.

"All right," said Kay. "Thanks."

Outside, Kay and Hart stepped into a cubicle in which stood a couch about the size of a double bed. It had a disposable cover, and while it was not of the best quality, it still smelled clean. Hart stretched out and plugged his belt into the receptacle on the wall at his side. Overhead a small light glowed. Then it turned green: all set on his side. Kay plugged in too, feeling a little of the gel on her hand, a moisture that seemed familiar. Smooth on the fingers. Damp. The light overhead on her side blinked, a little longer than it did above Hart, and then it turned green. She guessed her connection was slower than Hart's.

Her skin felt as though she had been sprayed with cologne and now stood in a slight breeze. This, she guessed, was the setup, the registration with skin chemistry. She and Hart lay side by side. His eyes were almost yellow, speckled like a butterfly's wing. She had never seen a butterfly, but she knew that she wanted to. His pupils expanded. The cool thrill on her skin grew more uniform. As she waited, as she looked into the eyes of the man who lay next to her, she tried to make the necessary changes in the code of the game.

Looking for a way to do it was like a dream of a room where she had grown up. As she reached out to the top of a dresser, a brush was right there where she had left it. She felt the familiar heft, the balance. The code spiraled open.

"Are you ready?" said Hart.

"Not quite," said Kay.

"Nervous?" said Hart.

"A little. I guess. Wait. Just wait a minute," she said.

"Well, okay," he said.

Kay knew that what was required was a particular playfulness just when things were at their most difficult, so as to be able to be inspired just when you were most distracted. She also knew there was an enormous difference between information and experience, and she wondered how to compensate for this. She had the theory, but what had she actually done with it? Nothing. She was looking for a pattern in the code, a key to it, like a dictionary, or the smallest detail, like a fractal, that would be repeated over and over again. She hoped that this would be a matter of recognition, a variety of empathy. Or maybe it was better to say that she would recognize it out of instinct. She would understand, but not through words or formulas or anything abstract. She would know it at first touch. Like putting on an old shirt.

She wished it were a little cooler in this room, and a little less smoky. It was getting hotter. Little drops of sweat, the color of mineral oil, formed on her lip.

Jack sat at the foot of the couch and looked out into the room where the other machines were. A woman went by in a tight red suit, her hips swinging in smoke and in the noise the players made as they came close to the breaking point. Jack watched the woman's hips, the light playing on the skin-tight material. The woman looked over her shoulder at him, and in a little while she came back, closer this time.

"So, how's it going?" he said to Kay.

"I'm working on it," she said.

"Well, all right," he said. He turned and looked into the room again, at the glitter through the clouds of smoke. "I've got things to do."

Kay looked into Hart's eyes.

"I'm ready," he said.

"Please," she said.

"How much are we going to bet?" he said.

"Well, if you'll just wait—" she said.

"No," he said. "Now. Give me a figure."

She was still looking: Was that it, that line there? Was that loop what she was looking for, the method of construction, the format that ran through it all?

"You tell me," she said.

He gave her a number.

"If I agree," she said, "will you give me a few minutes?"

"Five," he said. "Isn't that generous?"

"All right," she said. "You're on."

Jack watched the woman in the red suit.

Surely there had to be some order that expressed what she believed to be true: that underneath it all things made sense, and that the way they made sense, such as the neat arrangement of strands of polymers, for instance, or the shape of crystals of mica that one saw in a meteor, all implied some perfection that only needed to be understood. It was a matter of perception. So where was it? She went down one line of code and then another, just like someone shopping in a place where the items for sale were in bins that you could pick over and then discard. She came to a section that she was convinced was Briggs's work. Clean. To the point. Precise. He probably wasn't aware that he had conveyed this knowledge to her, but that was what had happened, in the same way that she knew what his most secret dreams and desires were, and what she felt now was a keen sense of intimacy. It made her feel so close to him.

The first change was the hardest, because she wasn't certain about it, not really, and she hoped it wouldn't come back to cause trouble. For instance, she didn't want to end up with the game giving her the horrors. She tried another change, tentatively at first, and as she worked through the code, feeling a sense of empathy and security, too, her impulse to take chances grew. The effort left her calm, as though what she was doing here wasn't a matter of skill, but of understanding and wisdom. She closed her eyes as she worked through the possibilities, going through the loops for the logic of the thing. And as she made the changes, the game began to do the registration over again.

"Wait a minute," Hart said.

"What?" she said. "I thought you were ready. Let's start."

"Oh shit," he said. "Wait. Wait."

His hand reached for his belt, where his suit was plugged in, but midway there he froze.

She looked into his eyes and guessed that the thing she had done was right, although if she had to do it again, she would have worked through it a little differently. She suspected she could take some other shortcuts, or find some more graceful solutions, and now she considered those other methods, which really were empathetic with the method by which she had been produced. At its heart, the game was orderly and pretty simple.

Hart said, "Oh no. Ah no. No." His voice seemed to sink. "Oh no."

HART HAD taken chances before, and often he had done so because of his love for his daughter. It was difficult to describe what she meant to him, but he could feel it when he went without so that she could have a little something extra. He wanted to give her things that made her happy: clothes, trips, anything that would give her a better chance than he had. Her name was Sally. She had freckles, red hair, and green eyes.

Hart had been in enough bad places to have learned the mental discipline to confront the most dire state of mind. He could dismiss it as delusion, just nerves, too much coffee, a mood that produced an imprecise way of seeing things. He had good reasons to feel this way, too, where the games were concerned, since he had devoted his life to their construction and their integrity. So, when he suspected a detail was off, he had something to fall back on: the discipline of facing up to distress. How many times had he come right up to the edge of panic? He couldn't even count. The important thing was to take a deep breath. Look at things clearly. Start at the top.

As he looked at Kay, though, he had the suspicion that playing with her was a mistake. So he started again, taking a deep breath, trying to be disciplined. Was everything he had ever believed nothing more than a sappy delusion, just phrases and details that he had invested with substance by repeating them in safe circumstances?

The machine did the registration a second time. This was unusual but not unheard of. The games were delicate, and there were all kinds of scales that needed to be addressed: humidity, skin chemistry, the cologne one wore, even the slight psychoactive elements that were in the skin from the bad nightmare a player had had the night before. Hart never liked registration, since it left him with the feeling of being watched. Unpleasant, but necessary.

Like any gambler, he knew the odds on all kinds of things, and the prospect of anything unpleasant came in terms of one out of a hundred or one out of a thousand or one out of a million. The probability of its not happening was the thing that made it hard for him to see what *was* happening. After all, what were the odds that the machine was doing anything more than a complicated registration? Maybe Kay had never played this version before, and the machine needed to get a good take on her. It was to his advantage, really, since if everything was hooked up as it should be, why then he would be able to do his best. What he was troubled by was the notion that ill will was the operating principle of the games, or of this one: it had a metaphysical risk that he hadn't noticed before. He tried to explain it away, like a medieval religious commentator in the days of the plague.

The game was Arctica X. It was one of the survival series, and in this one, he and his opponent would appear as people who had been dropped into the Arctic. Each player had a limited number of tools and only a little knowledge, too, such as which lichens were edible, and how one went about killing a polar bear. There were meteorological elements too, low temperatures, freezing rain, hard-packed snow, high winds, icy white-outs. But the real danger lay in bands of primitive people, all armed with spears and with the knowledge of traps, and they were out there, watching, trying to find you. Hart noticed right off that the world itself seemed to be revolted by his presence, as though he were a freak of some kind. He understood the environment not by its harshness, but by its hostility to him. He felt like some doomed creature that had fallen out of favor with the gods. He dismissed this as mere superstition, but there it was.

He started with the basics. Territory was something you wanted to control. The first thing was shelter, since if you couldn't get through the night, you couldn't do much about anything else. In this climate he had to make something out of the packed snow. The construction method was simple but beautiful. You made a circle and then you cut blocks of snow out of it and made the first layer, like bricks, but the thing that made the construction work was to cut this first row on the bias, from the surface to the top of the first brick at the end of the first row. This made the other bricks of snow spiral around, getting closer and closer to the top of a dome. The dusk was increasing: the sky in the west was turning a purple-blue, but even that was odd, since the color looked like something he had only seen as a kid, when he had found a man frozen to death in an alley, and had looked at the hue of the skin under the man's fingernails. How did the game know this color?

Hart had a piece of pressure-flaked obsidian, but when he tried to cut into the snow, it broke off at the handle. Had there been a crack he had missed? Wasn't that the first rule? Check the tools you had for imperfections. As he stood there looking at the black stump, he felt the cold seeping into his clothes, and he was certain, too, that he heard the squeak of sealskin boots on the snow. And then he could smell the stink of an animal, a polar bear, which had been eating something rotten, some dead fish it had found. He heard it, too, the sound of its breath coming with a stinky *ah-huh, ah-huh, ah-huh.*

The primitive people came over a ridge, their silhouettes black against the oddly colored dusk. Hart knew what the ornaments the primitive people wore were made out of, and one of them even held up a necklace so that he could get a good look. Behind him the animal's claws made a rattling scratch on the frozen snow. He saw some smoke, like a strand from a cigarette, which must have been from a shelter someone else had made. He guessed it was Kay's place.

He started walking in her direction, his shoes making a squeak in the snow, which he felt in his teeth. The wind blew and he had the sensation of struggling against it, as though it were almost fluid, as though it came out of a fire hose. His fingers were numb. Would she listen? Didn't she have a heart?

Then the primitive people followed. And as they did, they signaled to each other, holding up their hands. He knew he had seen them do this before, but he couldn't remember what they meant. He stopped. The wind blew. One of the primitive people was leading a young woman by the hand, and now he pulled back her hood so as to reveal her red hair, her freckles, her green eyes. How had they gotten his daughter? She stood there, watching. He called out, telling her to close her eyes, that there was nothing to be seen here.

"Close your eyes," he screamed. "Sally, don't watch what they do to me. Do not watch."

"Dad," she said. "Stop them. Why won't you stop them?"

"Don't watch. Darling. Don't watch."

One of the primitive people took out a hand-flaked knife, which didn't have any cracks and which they used with such skill.

By this time Hart was up, off of the couch, sitting back, staring at Kay.

"I'll take the money," she said.

"How did that happen?" he said.

"How?" she said. "You lost. That's what happened."

"Something was different," he said.

"Pay her the money," said Jack.

Both Kay and Hart looked up at the display at the top of the game, which showed how the wins and losses were figured. The odds were figured not on the outcome, but on the varieties of outcome, or combinations of events, like a trifecta. It was a lot of money. Other gamblers in the room stopped when the word spread that Hart had taken such a loss.

Hart didn't bother to change his clothes. He pulled on his coat, over the suit, and went to the door. And there, at the entrance, he saw the bell, the rope of it hanging down like the tail of some dead thing. As he looked at it, he could imagine that hard, poignant sound when it had been rung off the rocky coasts of South America or Africa. He could imagine the coasts, shimmering in the heat, the gray or black mountains in the distance like some humped-up, ill-meaning presence. He thought of the shrieking of the birds on those coasts, the busy conglomeration of them at once vital and yet so intent on their own existence as to leave the people who saw them with a sense of vulnerability. He tried to imagine the bell breaking the tedium of those watches, which had been observed even in those hot, dry afternoons, when everyone wanted to sleep. He stood there looking at it, thinking of the freedom that it suggested: long sea voyages, the ability to disappear from ordinary life, to get away.

Outside, when he couldn't pay what he owed, they'd probably kill him. He had always thought he would be able to stay one jump ahead of the interest, one jump ahead of the bank. He had been wrong. The Money Men were already waiting for him. At least his daughter wouldn't be there to watch.

Kay stood at the door and watched him go, pushing her wet hair away from her forehead. It was chilly outside, and she stepped back to get away from the air that came in through the open door, and as she did, she looked up at the kiosk that was inside. It was covered with gimmicks, promotional devices for other games that were about to be released. They came in different shapes and sizes. For instance, there was one like a matchbook from a survival series called Pacifica. Another looked like a fan that a coquettish woman might have used in Asia. It was constructed from red paper, folded like an accordion, between two pieces of wood that were painted gold. Kay wasn't so sure about the fan, but she picked up a gimmick from Pacifica.

"What do you want that for?" said Jack.

"Don't you want to see the South Seas sometime?" she said.

"Not particularly," he said. He looked at the women in their filmy suits. "There's plenty to occupy me here."

CHAPTER ⑧ | *March 26, 2029*

THE MEETING was scheduled for the first thing in the morning, and by seven o'clock Briggs stood in front of the brick building. People were arriving at work, but none of them spoke to him or even nodded while he stood around outside. He had hoped that one or two might greet him or be friendly, but as he stood there he realized what he was really doing: making a guess, on the basis of atmosphere, as to where he stood.

A New Wave was beginning; it had been gathering momentum during the last month or so. The younger men were wearing white shirts with round collars, and a couple of them had on red shoes. They weren't a bright red, but a cordovan. Liver-colored. Their pants were tight at the ankle, and baggy at the knee. Retro zoot-suit. Hair shaved in a strip from the collar up and allowed to grow a little so that it turned blue, like the color of Superman's hair. The whispers would soon begin for those who weren't dressed this way. The whisperers would say, "Look at his clothes. Old-hat, not hip, and just not into the way we do things now . . . " The New Waves came in cycles: their arrival brought with it a whiff of hip condescension and a tyrannical sensibility.

Briggs saw a couple of young men wearing the new shirts and the red shoes. Not a lot. One or two. The clothes still looked striking and unusual, and they had that edgy style. Briggs was still wearing the casual gray shirt and pants from the last look, the baggy jacket. Sometimes a New Wave turned out to be nothing more than a false start, and there was an ominous, odd time when everyone tried to guess whether it was going to go or not. That's what was happening now, although this New Wave looked more viable with each passing day.

A woman came up to the building and caught Briggs's eye and almost smiled, but then hesitated. He tried to remember where she worked. In budgeting? They always had a hint about what was happening. He noticed that she was wearing a new pair of red shoes. The collar of a transparent blouse showed at her neck.

The door to the stairwell seemed heavier than usual, but he was glad when it swung shut with a pneumatic hush that assured his privacy. At least for a minute or two. He went around the stairwell, going deeper into the basement. The damp concrete smelled almost fresh and clean. Almost. He put his hand on the banister, the metal one, and then let go of it. Too cold.

The room where the growing platforms had been was empty. Not a thing was left. No tubes, wires, monitors, IV stands, platforms, gauges, cutters, or the small tools that were needed from time to time; no sheets, stainless-steel shelves. It was all gone. Not only that, but there were two men applying Insta-Wall, the stuff coming out of the containers through nozzles like a vacuum cleaner's. Then the men put two electrodes into the muck and dialed for a finish, and the wall assumed the shape they had chosen: smooth, clean, new. Not a hint of what had been before. The room was ready for a new project without a sign of what had been here before—not a fleck of skin, not a piece of dandruff, not a fragment of bacteria or DNA. Nothing. It would be sprayed at the end, just to make sure, with Clorox. When they were done, it would have all the sterility of ground zero. Briggs stood there in the clean room, feeling his heart beat. Well, this was not what he had hoped for. Everything was disappearing, and where did that leave him? He thought of people going through his apartment, looking for mungo.

Upstairs, Briggs went into his office and sat there. He was early. He got up the manuals for the project, the rules and regulations, the specifications. Maybe he could come up with some technicality that would throw them off the chase. He scrolled through the pages. As he worked, he heard some New Wave music, something called Stomper Rock, although he wasn't sure whether it was coming through the floor or from down the hall. The city seemed to exist as an extension of the sound, which had its roots in retro-techno. The lyrics of a new hit were "Whatcha got goin', Whatcha got goin', Whatcha got goin' . . . ?"

He read through the small type of the appendices, where the real dirt usually was, but still he came up with nothing, and then he realized that it wasn't something in the manuals that was missing, but in himself: his sense of the future was gone.

"Find anything?" said a man who stood at the door of Briggs's office.

Briggs wiped his hands on his pants. The man at the door was wearing musk: you could smell the New Wave, which was like the ocean at low tide. He wore red shoes and a new shirt. They were beginning to wear thin ties, too. Briggs wondered what they were thinking, in terms of new changes, and how things could be organized. Who was expendable, who was old-hat, who was using slang and phrases that weren't right up to the moment? The language you spoke had a nasty way of identifying you with some old style if you weren't careful about it. If your slang was out-of-date, you were caught speaking the Language of the Dead.

"No," said Briggs.

"Uh-huh," said the man.

"I'm just looking over an old project," said Briggs.

"What's the use of that?" said the man.

Briggs nodded. The man used peppermint candies, small red ones that came out of a dispenser, and now he used the dispenser to extrude one of them into his hand. He put it in his mouth. His words came out in puffs of mint, like sweet centers in a cloud of musk.

"Say," said the man. "What unit are you in now? Is it the gaming stuff or wetware?"

"Wetware," said Briggs.

"Uh-huh," said the man. "That's good. We're interested in wetware. A lot of places it could go."

"Yeah," said Briggs.

"Who do you report to?" said the man. "Mashita?"

"Yeah," said Briggs.

Briggs looked around, through the glass walls.

"What's he like to work for?" said the man.

"It's okay," said Briggs.

"Hmpf," said the man. "Maybe we should talk it over sometime."

"Sure," said Briggs.

"Maybe he's made some mistakes. Or he has shown obvious errors of judgment. A project that wasn't working out right. Budget deficits. Wasted money. That kind of thing," said the man.

"Well, I don't know much about that," said Briggs.

The man waited there, sucking the mint. Finally, as though producing a confidence, or making an overture of friendship, he said, "Well, if anything comes to mind, call me. My name is Phillips. Here."

He held out his card.

"You might think of something," said Phillips.

Briggs looked at the card, but he didn't take it.

"I hear you're going to be transferred," said Phillips.

"Is that right?" said Briggs.

"Yeah," said Phillips. "Do you want this, or not?"

Briggs took it.

"Thanks," he said, feeling the word in his mouth like something stale.

The inquiry was in a room that had a view of the city. A large table stood in the middle of the room, with three padded chairs around it. The window showed the river and some new buildings that stuck up out of the sprawl. Mashita was wearing dark clothes, a pair of baggy pants, and an off-color, gray and crimson tie. It reminded Briggs of what organs looked like as they were forming in the growing medium. In fact, as Briggs stood there, he guessed that one of the reasons Mashita had this job was that if things got bad enough, he would probably commit suicide. Was this one of them?

Krupp sat in the room with his usual two-day growth of beard. Same close-cropped hair, although it looked a little steel-colored now. Same dark clothing too, and small glasses. Every now and then, as always, he reached up and squeezed the sides of his nose.

"Ah, Briggs," said Mashita. "Glad you could come. You've met Krupp, haven't you?"

Before Briggs could answer, Krupp looked away, out the window. So, thought Briggs, he's going to pretend he doesn't know me.

"So, shall we get started?" said Mashita.

Krupp squeezed the sides of his nose again.

"It won't take long," said Mashita. "Sit down."

Mashita moved with ceremonial delicacy.

"You remember, Briggs, how we used to talk?" said Mashita. "How we used to argue whether fate had a sense of irony?"

"I remember," said Briggs.

"I was just thinking about that this morning," said Mashita. "Tragedy is a terrible vision of life, but sometimes fate leaves a man looking as if he's sat on a wedding cake."

"I don't think this is funny," said Briggs. "Do you?"

"No," said Mashita. "The consolations of philosophy aren't that good in the heat of things. Not when you get right down to it."

"Come to the point," said Krupp.

"We're going to transfer you," said Mashita to Briggs. "That's final. There is no discussion about that."

"What am I going to be doing?" he said.

"Something a little more commercial," said Mashita.

"All right," said Briggs. "What about the last project?"

"Oh, that," said Mashita. He turned to Krupp. "What do you have to say about that?"

"Nothing," said Krupp. "It's history. As far as I'm concerned, it never existed. If there is no evidence of its existence and we forget about it, who is to say it ever happened at all? Is that understood?"

The sensation of being nauseated was a little stronger than before, and as he looked out the window, Briggs wondered just what he was being told, anyway.

"I'd like to ask a question," said Briggs.

"A what?" said Krupp.

"A question. I wonder about . . . " said Briggs, but then he stopped. He coughed. Then he looked out the window, where the river showed in a long, lead-colored S. Even from here, he could see the bright scales on it made by the wind.

"What about Kay and Jack?" he said.

Mashita shrugged.

"They took off without the medical check," said Mashita.

"I thought that was done right along," said Briggs. "You know, I had written procedures for that. Right along, the technicians were supposed to be checking."

"No," said Mashita. "We thought we could do it later, all at once. It's cheaper and better. No duplication. So they took off without it."

"Oh," said Briggs. "I thought it was the other way."

"What's the big deal?" said Krupp.

Briggs turned to the river again, the languid shape of it in the sunlight suggesting a different scale of time, more geological and infinitely slow.

"I didn't think it was going to be that way," said Briggs.

"Well, it's too late now. Tuberculosis, meningitis," said Mashita. "Encephalitis? Maybe they'll spend a little time in an airport. Do you know how easy it is to get a sore throat in an airport?"

He didn't look unhappy about this.

"So, if they are going to die anyway, what we have to do is to sit tight. That's the long and the short of it, isn't it?" said Krupp.

"I'm not so sure about that," said Briggs. "It's hard to say."

"What's hard to say?" said Mashita. "You know, Briggs, I'm asking you to be precise. So don't give me a hard time. Just tell me what you mean."

"One of the things we do, when we do the medical check right along, is to make sure they aren't producing something new. A new disease altogether. But I guess that wasn't done."

"I didn't think they were going to get away," said Mashita. "I thought we could do it all at once. You act as though we were planning to let these two go. We weren't. They were for demonstration purposes only. Why should we have spent the money on early medical checks if they were only for demonstration?"

Mashita and Briggs looked at one another.

"What's the big deal?" said Krupp. "Jesus, will someone around here just answer a fucking question?"

"They could be carrying something new. A new disease," said Briggs. "They wouldn't get it, but we might. I mean ordinary people."

"How are we going to know if that's happening?" said Krupp.

"I don't know," said Briggs. "How can you look for something you've never seen before?"

"You're not looking at this clearly. There are new diseases around all the time. You know what goes on in the alleys downtown? Jesus, don't tell me about new diseases. And as far as Jack and Kay are concerned, if they don't get sick, there are a lot of surprises out there. Believe me. So, if one thing doesn't get them, another will. We've just got to sit tight. That's my take," said Krupp. He shrugged. "If there's a problem here, it's self-liquidating."

Mashita said to Briggs, "Do you understand?"

"I guess," said Briggs.

"Briggs," said Mashita, "there isn't any room for guessing here. What we need to know from you is whether or not you understand."

Krupp looked up. No squeezing of his nose. He looked tired but alert.

"Yes," said Briggs.

"Yes, what?" said Mashita.

"Yes, I understand that it never happened and if anyone asks me about it I will deny it. There is no evidence aside from our memories."

"*Our* memories?" said Krupp. "I never saw a thing. Did you?" He turned to Mashita.

"No," said Mashita.

"See?" said Krupp. "We don't know anything. Right from the get-go. You have to look out for what you remember. You're on your own."

"What about the technicians?" said Briggs.

Mashita showed a little irritation; it was the only moment when he lost his grip.

"They've been transferred," he said.

Briggs wondered if the mungo men were already at work in the technicians' apartments.

"All right," Briggs said. "Is there anything else?"

"No," said Mashita. "That about sums it up."

"Well, then," said Briggs. "I guess I'll go down the hall and clean out my desk. When will I get my new assignment?"

"This week," said Mashita.

Briggs nodded. Then he turned and went to the door, but when he got there, Mashita said, "Briggs. For God's sake, be careful. I'm concerned about you."

"God knows why," said Krupp. "Jesus, where do you get these guys?"

"This one comes from Yale," said Mashita.

"What's the world coming to?" said Krupp.

Mashita turned back to Briggs.

"Some people here are wondering about how they knew to get away," said Mashita. "Now, I'm not saying anything about that. Not now. We're working on a need-to-know basis. Okay?"

"Yeah," said Briggs. "Sure."

"But, just to make sure we are on the same page," said Mashita, "and because I have your best interests at heart, I want to know if there is anything you should tell me. Any little irregularity with this project, anything that I should know."

Briggs looked from one of them to the other. Then he shook his head.

"No," he said.

Krupp stared at him.

"He might be lying," said Krupp. "That's the way it looks to me."

"Well," said Mashita. "Can we trust you on that?"

"Yes, sir," said Briggs.

"Sir?" said Mashita. "We aren't that formal here."

Krupp went on staring at him.

"What's eating at you?" he said.

"Nothing," Briggs said. "I guess all of this has gotten to me a little."

Krupp looked away.

"Oh," said Mashita. "There is one other thing. What was the cue for the demonstration of what these two models could do?"

"A bell," said Briggs. "They respond to the ringing of a bell."

"Is that right?" said Krupp.

"There aren't many bells anymore," said Briggs. "The telephone buzzes. The computer uses a chime. I thought a bell was pretty safe. When was the last time you heard a bell ringing?"

"It's been a while," said Krupp. He squeezed his nose. "So what happens if Jack hears a bell?"

"He gets violent. If you want to get rid of someone, all you have to do is point Jack in the right direction. The way we had planned the demonstration was with a condemned man. We'd ring the bell—"

"We?" said Krupp. "I never said I'd ring a bell. This is the first I've heard about this." Krupp looked like a man falsely accused. "And?" he said.

"Kay would direct Jack. Or he'd look around for the likely target. Of course, Kay has a series of commands too. After Jack has done his job, Kay is supposed to get rid of him."

Mashita said, "What a nasty world we live in."

"Oh, it's not so bad," said Krupp.

"Is that it?" said Briggs. "May I go?"

"What about sex?" said Krupp. "Are they going to be groping each other all the time?"

"No," said Briggs. "They're not interested in each other. They're more like brother and sister."

"All right," said Krupp. "That's it. At worst, I guess we could just send a couple of thugs out to pick them up."

"No," said Briggs. "You won't be able to find them. They've been trained along those lines. Believe me."

"I guess that speaks well for the wait-and-see approach, doesn't it?" said Krupp.

Briggs went out into the hall. The blue light from the monitors, the soothing dimness of the spaces between the cubicles, left him with the sensation of being a shadow, something that could be swept away. Of course, now that he had a moment's reflection, he knew what was happening. They had decided it was not a legal problem, but a public-relations one. He thought, *But what happens when they see it the other way around?*

He went down the hall, and as he went, he thought, *The problem is always the same. It's not what we know that can cause trouble. The problem is what we don't know. The unintended surprise.*

Briggs had gotten through some hard times, and he had done so because he had learned one of the hardest lessons of all, which was to keep his mouth shut. But if they had asked him how Kay and Jack were vulnerable, what would he have said? It was possible, he supposed, that some bacteria or perhaps a virus, like equine encephalitis, might kill them, but another dynamic would probably come into play. Since they hadn't been exposed to childhood diseases, the part of the immune system that had historically dealt with parasites would have been stimulated. This reaction would have made them susceptible to asthma, allergies, anaphylaxsis. Anyway, that's what Briggs thought was most likely, even though they still might be carrying something new.

BOOK

BRIGGS CAME down the hall from the meeting with Mashita and Krupp and started to clean out his office. He hoped a security guard wouldn't come in to make sure he took only personal items, and since there wasn't one there yet, Briggs started to pack as quickly as possible. But even as he put his manuals and catalogs into a box, he kept touching the tube he had in his pocket. It was filled with fluid from Kay's platform, and he ran his fingers over it again and again to make sure it was there. He was most concerned about the possibility that Kay and Jack could be carrying a disease, a virus or bacteria that had secretly undergone the same process of *in silica* natural selection that Kay and Jack had gone through. And of course it might not be just one, but two or more that operated together, synergistically, a benign bacteria, or a seemingly benign one, operating on another seemingly benign one to produce a new medical condition. Briggs wasn't sure what he should be looking for, but he thought he would recognize it when he saw it. A new bacteria or virus, whatever it was, only had to find a way to placate the rules for natural selection that Briggs's program had set up. After all, that was what life had been doing for billions of years. Why should it suddenly stop?

Briggs still had a pass that worked for the machines downstairs at Galapagos, but word would get around fast that he had been transferred, and soon his account wasn't going to work there anymore. When he had cleaned up his office, he touched the tube in his pocket again, the glass surface so warm as to feel almost alive. When he held it in his fist, the tube gave him the sensation that his difficulties had become concrete. He put the last of his manuals into a box, and then stood there with the tube in his hand.

His footsteps echoed in the stairwell as he descended into the depths of the building, where, at the bottom, he heard the hum of the machines and smelled the familiar dry-ice odor. Doors of a cheerful color, salmon, rose, or yellow, were spaced every thirty feet, and he opened one that was the color of a grape Popsicle.

Two technicians sat at a monitor.

"This looks like one of God's mistakes," one of them said. He pointed at the images on the screen.

"Yeah," said the other. "I guess. But it wasn't God. It was that jackass from MIT. What's his name? The one with the fat girlfriend."

"Colby?" said the first.

"Yeah, that's the one," said the other.

"You know, this reminds me of what they say in Alabama when something goes wrong."

"What's that?" said the other.

"Thank God for Mississippi. It's even worse there."

The technicians glanced up, saw Briggs, glanced down. Briggs went up to the machine that he was looking for, put a syringe into the sample he took from his pocket, and injected the lymph fluid into the rubber opening for this purpose. It made a little squeak when he put the needle in. Then he started a complete workup, not only for viruses and bacteria that were known, but for any genetic irregularity. Some of the work had to be done mechanically, which meant an actual culture, and that took time. Anyway, he would be able to keep track of it from wherever he was, or at least as long as his computer account was still valid.

The technicians looked over. One of them said, "You've got to sign in."

"Later," said Briggs. "Got a meeting."

They both looked at him as he went out, their eyes showing a blankness that was nonetheless ominous. He stood outside and put his head against the wall. He hadn't used all of the fluid, and he guessed the best place to keep the rest was in a refrigerator someplace, not here, not in the building, but at home. He reached down and touched the tube in his pocket, as though the thing were a medicine bottle, perhaps containing tranquilizers that he really didn't want to be without.

BRIGGS'S NEW job was on a commercial strip in one of the prefabricated buildings that had been put up quickly, and the geography was a sure sign that the company wanted him out of the way but still available. He couldn't tell whether or not he was reassured or alarmed by the one obvious fact of this neighborhood. Here, nothing lasted.

The building had a glass door in front, a directory behind glass, a stairwell in which some plants were growing. He stopped to look at the leaves of a plant, which were coarse and without any shine to them, and as he touched them it was as though he could feel the desolation of this place, where no one wanted to come and from which everyone was trying to get away. When he looked out the glass of the front door, he could see the rolls of razor wire, like misery itself, on top of the chain-link fences.

Mostly what they made here were souvenirs for the tourist trade, pornographic tricks, cheap illusions of one sort or another, minor animals, pets with a short half-life. His office was at the back on the second floor, at the end of a hall lined with gray metal shelves. It looked to him like a boneyard where machines were stacked that were too expensive to throw away, but were too costly to fix. He stopped here and there to see just what there was. He guessed he could work with some of it—that is, if he took the machines home at night and did the maintenance himself. This meant calling around to get some parts, and perhaps there were some people who hadn't heard about his demotion and who would still talk to him, but he knew this was just a dream: people that stupid didn't last long.

The first thing was to clean up the place where he was going to work. The machine on his desk was not so bad. He turned on the light and looked at the walls. Numbers had been written here and there, and part of a sentence that began, "Please, O Lord, in thy mercy . . . "

The first projects were pretty straightforward souvenirs, just like the junk he had done right out of school. He guessed he was in limbo, or was it purgatory? What was the difference between the two? The essence of both, he supposed, was that nothing was final yet, like the time a prisoner spent between conviction and sentence. Surely there must be a word for such a state. How about living without gravity? That was what it was like, since he had to fight to keep his feet on the ground, or to stop himself from simply vanishing into the air around him, as though he were nothing more than smoke. Then he thought, *Stop it. Stop it.*

He tried to log onto his old account at Galapagos. The prompt came up, and he put in his password and username, then he put his hand on the small screen at the side of the keyboard which read his fingerprints. The machine did its registration, and Briggs wondered what would happen if he couldn't keep track of the analysis he had started for the fluid. The machine made a little grinding sound. He was in. He scrolled through the partial results, seeing the lists of proteins and amino acids, although he didn't have a manual for the shape of each of the proteins. They could be folded a number of ways, and, of course, how they were pleated or bent determined the effect each had. The hard tests, the ones done in actual dishes with growing media, were just getting started, although he could tell that something was growing. He looked at the stains in the growing medium that showed up on his monitor. Just like mold on wallpaper. Or a small green spore on bread.

Briggs turned to the wall where the words said, "Please, O Lord, in thy mercy . . . " He supposed it was possible that he would find a disease no one had anticipated. How would he tell Mashita about it, or Krupp, when they were trying to pretend they didn't know anything about what he had done? If he discovered something, it would be precisely the news they didn't want to hear. This was a time when no one wanted things to go wrong, and that was, of course, when such things happened, just when everyone was most vulnerable. He knew about vulnerability, and he thought of the years when he had experienced it like a bruise that was still tender to the touch.

When a new car pulled up in front of this building, Briggs wondered if he had been sent for. Or when he saw a man at the end of a block, taking his measure, he wondered if a decision had been made. Then he tried to comfort himself by thinking that if they had decided to get rid of him, he'd have no warning. Was that right? Or would they play with him?

After work he stopped in the park by the river, which was swollen and dark brown with snow melt, and one afternoon there had been some freezing rain and the benches were covered with ice, like some grotesque dessert, some sugar-coated monstrosity.

Missing Kay and Jack, he assumed, was just sentimentality. After all, he had had to forget things many times before, and he knew how to do it. Change your routine. Realize that there isn't much to be done. Cut your losses. He tried to sing, "I'll be around to pick up the pieces . . . " Well, funny or not, wasn't this what he had to do? It was the grown-up course of action. He was like a divorced man who was reminded of his wife's departure again and again by opening a closet door to find her clothes gone, and nothing left but the scent of her perfume and her sweat. He could almost hear the infinitely sad *ting* of wire coat hangers knocking up against one another in such a closet.

When he tried to see where he stood, he was convinced that the silence was a bad sign. It wasn't noticeable at first, just the fact that no one called him and that there was no message from Krupp or Mashita. He hadn't thought that they would contact him right away, but still, as the days went by, he hoped that there would be some word. He knew that new projects came across their desks every day of the week, just as he knew, too, that there were few men or women who could do the code the way he did. For instance, there were effects he could produce simply by the use of style or by invoking beauty, by the fact that he had a coherent vision of what the model should look like at the end. Either you could do it or you couldn't. He wondered what kind of cheap imitation of him they were hiring.

But the really keen moment was when he woke at three o'clock in the morning and didn't know where Kay and Jack were. That was the trap of the personal. Once you started with it, you couldn't simply forget about it, since this was like forgetting yourself.

He painted his office, but he didn't white out the line that said, in a shaky hand, "Please, O Lord, in thy mercy . . . " He thought of it when he saw two obvious torpedoes, just gangsters, who came down the street toward the building where he stood behind the glass door, watching them. Briggs stood in the lobby, smelling the cheap odor of the plant that sat by the stairwell. He looked out the window. Were they coming in or not? And if they did, what would he do? Argue with them?

The men walked along next to the cars parked at the side of the street. One of them tried a door handle. The other shrugged. Then the two of them looked around like two predators who were trying to decide whether the chase was worth the joy of the kill. Just car thieves, Briggs guessed. Or was it hoped? This was the problem of trying to think clearly when he was scared: What was he really doing, thinking or just trying to reassure himself, and how could he tell the difference? Well, he knew that the first thing he was going to do was calm down. Surely that would help. He guessed. Shit.

But these things were just on the surface, the silence and people looking at cars, just the most minor varieties of fear. The real one came at night when he was in his bed, the sheets somehow uncomfortable, either too hot or too cold or damp. The clock sat on her bench, legs crossed, hands on her thighs. He stared at the ceiling, hearing the sound of her breathing, which was a little throaty. It was reassuring to hear it, and made him feel needed. As he listened, he thought, *Maybe Mashita and Krupp are just putting me through this so that when the time comes I will be more ready to crack, that I will hold nothing back.*

That was one step down. The next one was that he was getting shaky because they wanted him to get this way, and that they knew how it worked. For instance, they knew he would figure out that they were letting him twist slowly in the wind, just as they knew that when he discovered this, it would only make him feel worse. When he thought this, he said, "Well, maybe they've bitten off more than they can chew."

It made him feel better for a few minutes, but the real step down was this: He had given of himself to Kay, and he wasn't alive so much in one place as in two places, and if anything happened to her, why, then something would have happened to him, too. The clock sat there, breathing, *ah-huh, ah-huh, ah-huh.*

What would happen if they just disappeared? How would he feel then? His sense of love seemed to blend perfectly with his sense of terror, and it was right there at the boundary that he hung, like a hawk in the updraft of a thermal. Warm air as love. Gravity as terror. He hung there, thinking about Kay. Or about the risks of love. And friendship.

He had a different attachment to each of them. Jack was a friend, a man you could trust down to your last shot. And it wasn't just the physical bravery that one could depend upon, not the fact that he was smart enough not to make too many mistakes, but something else altogether, which was, for lack of a better term, spiritual strength. He was someone who could look into the terror that Briggs felt tonight, into that profound sense of exposure and the possibilities of malice and, while nodding in agreement about the scale of it and the danger of it, would also have the strength to say, "Yes. So what do we do now? We aren't going to cave in, are we? Either we take our courage with both hands or we are going to die."

He said, "Kay . . . " Then he looked around into the dark. He was pretty sure no one could hear, but these days it was hard to tell for sure. This entire process was familiar: the worse he felt, the more he tried to think of her, and as he did, the more he realized how distant she was.

He knew that she missed him too. But if she did, then why didn't she contact him? The clock's breathing came regularly, quietly, like that of a child who has a cold. Around six, the light came in from the cracks around the window, a gray dimness that appeared in long triangles across the ceiling. He thought the answer might be in the fact that she suspected his apartment was being watched, and that if she showed up here, she might be caught before she could even knock on the door. He wasn't certain she could come to this place safely, so why should she even try? For an instant he clung to the thin intimacy that they might both be thinking this same thing.

He rolled over, hearing the stale rustle of the sheets. He looked into the dark, facing away from the clock.

Of course, Kay had a cue, too. Hers was in Jack's action. After Jack did his job, she'd get rid of him. But there was yet another cue that Briggs had written in. He had thought about this for a long time.

Originally, if the project had run its natural course, the Committee on Evaluations would have seen Kay and Jack. Where had the money gone, after all? Briggs didn't want to be at the demonstration and to have her take one look at him and have her . . . recognize him. Of course, she'd try to talk to him, and, God knew, he wanted to talk to her.

Anyway, he hadn't wanted her to see him and to have her feelings unleashed just like that, in front of the people who were there to see a demonstration. In front of strangers. He wasn't sure what she would do when she recognized him, but he knew it wasn't going to be tolerated by the Committee on Evaluations, brought in by Mashita. Who knew what they would do to her? Perhaps she would catch sight of him through the transparent steel of the room where the committee sat, watching. Maybe she would come up to it, looking at him with a frank urgency. Maybe she would tap against it, desperately trying to get his attention. What was he going to do, pretend that he didn't know her, or that he didn't have a clue what she meant? Sometimes, late at night, he could hear that tapping.

When he was in the midst of adding things, he thought, *How dare you? How can you do anything to her? Leave her alone. Why can't you just leave her alone? Everything you are doing is going to get the both of you killed.*

Just as he thought, if any human being could make the person he loved, love him, what would he do? No flinching now. What would you do, if you could make the person you loved, love you?

Also, as he did this work, he had his doubts about whether anyone was capable of Kay's passionate devotion, and if anyone was, he wasn't sure she would want to be. He thought that both of them would be safer if Kay's love for him came into existence on the basis of a cue. Maybe he would set it up so that after he explained what the cue was and what it would do, she could decide whether or not to use it. It would be her decision. He would say to her, "Would you like to know what it is like to love someone more than life? Here. I will give you the power to know. You decide." It would be like Eden, only he would be the one to offer her the apple and to let her decide what to do with it.

Anyway, that was what the original idea had been.

So he had started thinking about what the cue would be. He decided that it wouldn't be something bland or bureaucratic, like Pi-16-A, like a defined variable in code, but more private. He had begun with the lists of flowers, of orchids, and he had looked at the plates of thousand of species, the petals of them pink or red, some sprayed with moisture, others speckled with the most miraculous patterns, as though the order of things were visible right here. Well, he had decided to go with the name of an orchid. *Phalaenopsis* was the variety he chose, and the specific flower was a hybrid called "Sweet Memory." *Phalaenopsis* was the cue, and the name of the hybrid, *Deventeriana X violacea,* was the safety. All three would have to be used together. How could anything go wrong with that?

KAY AND JACK walked along the river. At the bridge, they crossed over to the older part of town, where they stopped in front of a pawn-shop window. The pistols were laid out on black velvet. They were big, humped up, with a large bore showing under the burnished luster of them. The finish was just right: it wouldn't reflect light at an awkward moment. Kay looked through the glass into the dark hole of the muzzle, and when she glanced up, the pawnbroker was right there on the other side of the glass. He had a thin beard, his hair in a ponytail. He tapped on the window.

"I want to go in here," said Kay.

She put the fingers of her left hand into the palm of her right and rubbed the slight tingle. It was similar to the sensation an amputee has in the missing limb, at once haunting and irritating. She could imagine touching the handgun, as though she had spent years practicing with it.

They came into the pawnshop. Musical instruments were lined up on one wall, not arranged in any particular order, and Kay went along the trumpets, clarinets, violins, guitars, all of them looking like animals that had been killed and hung up to age. She ran her finger over the black neck of a violin that was curled at the end like a new fern.

"Over here," Jack said to her. He pointed at the case with the pistols in it.

"Can I help you?" said the pawnbroker.

"Yeah," said Jack. "I think you can."

The pawnbroker unlocked the case: they could reach through what had seemed like glass. Kay picked up a large pistol, and as she held it, seeing the fit of the handle in her palm, the pawnbroker said, "You were made for it."

"It sure feels that way," she said.

"Oh yeah," said Jack. "Oh yeah."

"I can feel the balance of it in my toes," she said.

"That's the way it's supposed to be," said Jack. "Here." He reached into the case and took one, too. It had a large bore, a magazine like a bloated cylinder, and the grip was made of textured plastic. Jack swung it up with the air of a carpenter picking up a maul. "Yeah. That's the one," he said. "We'll take these."

Kay and Jack emerged from the building and into the atmosphere of cooking pierogis, cabbage soup, newly baked bread. Kay rolled her head and put one hand up to the back of her neck. In this neighborhood, men in long, dark coats walked along, carrying books with loving devotion. Kay and Jack carried the guns in a bag.

"It's a good fit," said Jack. "I mean both felt right."

"Yeah," said Kay. "I like the grip for mine. The sights are about right. But, you know, handguns aren't really for distance work. Everyone knows that."

"Yeah," said Jack. "Do you think we need practice?"

"No," said Kay. "You never forget."

"A little tune-up wouldn't hurt."

"I don't think so," said Kay. "It'll be all right."

April 3, 2029

BRIGGS SET the table in his kitchen for one, a knife, fork, and spoon, a bowl, a glass with some water in it, a napkin. A lamb stew sat on the hot counter, the juices of it brown and fragrant, the peas appearing as small globes, fresh and not puckered with overcooking. A glass of dark beer, the head of it as rich as cream, sat on the table. He had thought that if he had an ordinary dinner he could think clearly, if only because the details of cooking and serving it would compel him to go through one task with a beginning, a middle, and an end. Now, though, he sat with the napkin in his lap and just drank the beer. But even so, he thought, someone had to see Kay and Jack when they got away. Or someone had to help them go, and who was that? They hadn't walked out naked, had they?

It was late, after two in the morning, when Briggs came up to the Galapagos building. The streetlights glowed in the fish-colored fog, and in the distance Briggs heard the unemphatic bleat of a horn, out in the harbor. He stopped in front of the black doors, above which the turtle squeaked, its mouth opening and closing, its flippers endlessly swimming, its slow breath coming as a labored *Unh, Unh.*

About six inches of cleaning mist was spread out on the floor. It swirled around like a hurricane seen from a satellite. Then the stuff disappeared into the dark vents along the bottom of the wall. Briggs waited until it had all slipped away before going up to the reception desk.

A new man was there, about forty-five years old, his gray hair in a crew cut. He had thick shoulders, and a flattened nose like that of a boxer who hadn't had the sense to know when to get out. Hair like indoor-outdoor carpet, pale skin, as though he existed on a diet of suet pudding and sausage. The man looked up, his eyes blank, and yet not without menace. How could he seem to care so little and yet still look as though he could cause you such trouble? Maybe it was just his indifference; that always looked bad when you needed something. Briggs took a deep breath, just to buy a little time, to count to ten. They hadn't even replaced Jackson with a man, but with one of the early models, a banged-up one at that.

"I was looking for Jackson," said Briggs.

"Who?" said the man.

"Jackson," said Briggs. "He used to work here on this shift."

"I don't know anything about that. People come and go. You know, people are so transient these days. I saw something on the TV just the other day. Lots of reasons for it," said the man. "I'm new here. Kind of quiet at this hour, you know?"

"Yeah," said Briggs.

"What do you want with him?" said the man.

"Who?" said Briggs.

"Jackson," said the man.

Briggs shrugged.

"I wanted to ask him something, that's all," he said. "What about Jackson's boss? What was his name? Jarrell. That's it. What about Jarrell? Is he around? Maybe he'd know where Jackson is."

"No," said the man. "Retraining seminars this week. They have them all over, now. I think Jarrell went to Hong Kong. Seemed pretty excited about it. Said there were all kinds of things to do there you couldn't do here."

Briggs waited. What now? He wanted to make it seem that all of this was of no importance, and that he was just passing the time of day. He shrugged. Well, that's the way it goes.

The new guard looked Briggs over more closely.

"Should I take your name?" said the man.

"That's all right," said Briggs. "Thanks."

"I better take your name," said the new man. "In case Jackson shows up."

"That's all right," said Briggs.

He had always liked the cool touch of fog, the mist of his breath seeming cinematic and romantic. That wasn't the way it seemed now. Now it felt cold and damp and made it hard to see. He went on walking, going into the park, knowing that it wasn't the smartest thing in the world at this hour. He sat down on one of the benches and put his head in his hands and wondered where Jackson was now. Laid off? *Well,* thought Briggs, *that's one way of putting it.*

April 4, 2029

USUALLY, AFTER Kay played, when she put the lid over the keys and made a rustling sound as she gathered up the sheet music, Stone was drained, but underneath it all, he was exhilarated too. He found that when she was playing he remembered events that seemed inconsequential, yet meant everything to him. For instance, one afternoon he thought of a young woman he had known in Venice, a musician. As she had practiced, Stone had sat near her, the music somehow mixed up with the gleam of her hair and the hawklike expression in her eyes. Once she had winked at him, as though only the two of them understood what she was doing. Stone remembered this unstated but perfect understanding with an almost tactile sensation, as though it were a cool scarf being dragged across his fingertips.

Each day when Kay finished, Stone began to anticipate the next day, just like a man who has taken a drug that leaves him with the desire for more, and who, even in the lingering effects of the last dose, makes plans for getting his hands on the next one.

Kay came to practice seven days a week. Each morning Stone awoke in his bed with its gray sheets and mismatched pillowcases in the room that was filled with slashes of light from the sides of the shades, and as he sat up, fingering the gray hair on his chest, he thought, *She must be waking up now. She must be thinking about what she is going to play. She is pulling on her clothes, and as she tucks in her shirt, as she tugs on her pants, she is thinking about the music. It is in everything: the cadence of brushing*

her hair, her walk, the swinging of her arm, or her coat as it twirls out
behind her when she puts it on.

Then Stone sat up. The sheets were damp and the pillow was
clammy. He ran his fingers over the damp cloth and wondered how
much time he had. His diabetes was getting worse, and he had pains in
his side and back. Every now and then he had angina, which he felt as a
constricting band made of something stronger than leather. There were
some new drugs, but he didn't like to take them, since he didn't feel quite
himself when he was using them, as though he were buying time by no
longer being who he was. The new drugs left him feeling that he was just
hanging in a closet like an old coat. He sighed now, and stood up. Before
Kay had come, he hadn't been so concerned about when he was going to
die. If anything, he just wanted it to be painless. But now he worried
about each moment, each second, because all he wanted was to see her
play in public. And as far as he could tell, she was almost ready, although
he didn't want to do it too fast, or to do her harm by bringing her along
too soon. He had done that once years before, and the musician, a young
woman, had hanged herself. He remembered going to her funeral and
having the musician's mother hit him, her hand open, just hitting him,
saying nothing.

The light came in not only from the side of the shade, but from the
tiny holes in it too, which he thought looked like a constellation, one he
had never seen before, maybe in some other part of the universe or in
the sky after a hundred thousand years. *A hundred thousand years,* he
thought. *I'll be lucky if I have two or three months.*

He had black coffee and a piece of black bread for breakfast,
although now he gave himself a treat, covering the bread with jam that
had whole strawberries in it, each one glistening, heart-shaped and covered with minute blonde fuzz. He held a berry in his mouth, the taste of
it perfectly melding with the memory of Kay's practicing.

At lunch he went down to the store at the end of the block and
bought caviar, of the highest grade they had, and he served it the way he
used to eat it in Russia. He buttered bread and then put on a layer of
gray-black caviar. Then he took a bite, closing his eyes. He let the taste
remind him of the years he had gone through, the rehearsal halls, the

students, those who had panned out and those who hadn't. The moment
Stone had lived for was just after a brilliant student had performed. This
was the instant when the audience seemed to hang, as though suspended
in air, between the trance of the performance and the fact of its conclu-
sion. It was a moment of emotional free-fall that ended when the audience hit their seats with a start. Then the frenzied applause began, a
hysteria that acknowledged how far the music had taken them from
their ordinary problems and the mundane aspects of life.

Stone had stopped thinking about these memories, but after he met
Kay, he started again, and now at lunch he tasted the fishy caviar and the
sweetness of the butter: this taste made it easier for him to remember his
best moments, like an old song. Now, though, as Stone sat in his office,
two flights up from the street, the place filled with those old books of
sheet music, he took another bite and luxuriated in the thrill that came
from no longer looking back, but anticipating the future.

Kay usually arrived at one. Jack was with her. They went up the rubber tread on the stairs. Kay put the key into the door and Jack pushed it
open, only to be greeted by the odor of paint and lacquer: the walls were
clean and white and the floor had been redone. Stone went in and
opened the piano, flipped open the cover over the keys, which lay like a
dessert of some kind made with layers of white and dark chocolate. He
touched one key, and the sound came into the room. Then he took his
usual place.

Jack took his, too, by the window, where he removed a striped paper
bag from his pocket and shook some crumbs out of it onto his hand.
Then he lifted the window, which made a squeak, and spread out the
crumbs. Jack looked upward, searching the sky with methodical intensity. The pigeons appeared in the distance, first as a flock, like a shimmer
of darkness, and then closer, the green luster of their breasts coming up
to the sill. There was an almost inaudible scraping of feet on the stone
sill, and a cooing, which replaced the beating of wings.

Stone liked to have the light at his back so that he could see Kay as
she bent to her work. The sun, on a bright day, allowed him to see her
hands in an almost clinical light, as though he were a doctor and she
were displaying her hands under a surgical lamp. Stone had been looking
at the hands of musicians for many years, and he had never seen any like

these: her fingers were long and somewhat delicate, but their strength and almost athletic grace were instantly obvious. Her skin was pale, and just under it lay a pattern of ivy-colored veins, not prominent so much as vital. She played hard, tired slowly, and seemed to have inexhaustible energy, although when she was finished her face had the expression of a marathon runner near the end of a race.

While she played, Jack stood by the window and looked out, watching the sky or the birds, and when she was done with one piece and before she went on to the next, he might say, "Rising barometer," or "You can see Venus, even at this hour."

Kay usually wore a T-shirt and some Spandex shorts, white socks, and running shoes. Filaments of light shone in her hair when the sun came in the window. She came in and put some sheets on the music rack. Little sounds filled the room, the squeak of her shoes, the leg of the bench screeching on the floor, the rustle of Jack's coat as he took it off and dropped it on a chair, the zipper ticking against a leg of it. Kay rolled her shoulders and put one hand to the back of her neck. She opened her hands. Then she sat down, her hands in her lap, seemingly thinking nothing, just relaxing, but Stone knew that while it was relaxation, it was something else too, a peacefulness that was a contradiction. While she was calm, she was also taut, or very much in control, and this mixture of tension and relaxation was a quality that only the best had. For instance, a violinist, one of the best, had told Stone that the key to the touch of his fingers on the strings was the way his feet, and his toes in particular, touched the floor.

He was happy with the room, which was fresh and new. Still, though, he was worried, because his experience with promising young people had been that many of them looked good, but just when you began to think they were the real thing, they showed some flaw, some reluctance to make the effort, or they had some inability, physical or emotional or spiritual, that left them looking like just another precocious kid who had fooled a lot of people. So, when Kay wasn't playing, Stone thought about her, looking for a sign, a symptom, but so far he had found nothing. In fact, he was close to giving up on this last bit of suspicion. She was out of the first drawer. Or no, not out of the first drawer, but a new one altogether.

So he listened to her, and the difficulty was that he couldn't articulate just what it was about her performance that was so striking. Just when he thought he could put it into words, she came to the end of a piece, and the certainty of what he had felt was gone. But even then he had that watery sense in his eyes and the notion that he was in the presence of something he had only felt in the most religious music, in those pieces that had been written to be played and sung in the Sistine Chapel, for instance, or music that had come out of the monasteries of Russia. Kay was able to produce these effects when she was merely "playing around," as she called it.

Every now and then she tried to perfect the music that she was writing. The power of it was like coming across some forgotten item one had put away because it was too precious to discard and yet too emotionally charged to see very often. *Oh,* Stone thought when he heard it, *Oh.* The piece she was writing progressed too, in that each time she played it she had added texture and something that Stone apprehended as her dexterity with his most keen longings and misgivings. Love, God, a sense of the essential part of being human: diminishing time.

These were the moments Stone recalled when he ate his butter and caviar and considered the future. He thought about what she was writing and how audiences would react when they heard *that*. It made him chuckle. Sometimes, though, he didn't do anything but remember the hours when he sat in the studio with the heat of the sunlight on the back of his head and shoulders. Kay played. The shadows of the birds slid across the floor. Jack stood silently at the window.

Once, when she had finished, and the flecks of dust in the air had flashed as a reminder of individual notes, he had said, "Kay, can you tell me something?"

She had looked up, as though noticing him for the first time.

"Yes," she said. "What do you want?"

"What are you thinking when you do that, when you allow the feeling to come into what you are playing?"

"Oh, that," she said.

"Yes," he said. "That."

"I'm thinking of someone I miss," she said.

"Who's that?" said Stone.

She shrugged.

"What's the difference?" she said.

"Is it important?" said Stone. "Could it get in the way of your playing?"

She shrugged again.

"I don't know," she said.

"Let's go," said Jack. "We'll come back tomorrow."

Kay got up and came over to Stone and put a hand on his shoulder.

"I'm sorry," she said. "I didn't mean to be abrupt."

"No. Be abrupt. Be anything you want. But be back here tomorrow," said Stone.

She and Jack walked to the door.

"Wait," said Stone. "I'll come with you."

"Why?" said Jack.

"Why? I do my best thinking when I'm walking around. We've got to decide when you should begin to play in public. When you should make your debut."

"When will that be?" said Kay.

"Now, now," said Stone. "Soon. It will be all right. We don't want to rush it. We want to take our time."

"Who says?" said Jack.

"I do," said Stone.

Jack looked at him.

"You know, maybe we aren't communicating," said Jack.

"You are trying to communicate with me?" said Stone. "About what?"

"Time," said Jack.

"Time?" said Stone.

"Yeah," said Jack. He stepped a little closer. "Like maybe we haven't got a lot of time."

"Jack," said Kay.

"What?" said Jack.

He took another step toward Stone, his hand reaching up to take the lapel of Stone's jacket.

"Look, we're all tired. It's been a long day. All right?" she said.

"I'm not tired," he said. He turned to Stone. "Now, there's two ways we can do this, the easy way and the hard way."

"I don't think I like this," said Stone.

"Jack," said Kay. "Forget it."

Jack rolled his shoulders and then his neck, like a boxer. It took a moment, but then he smiled. It was one of the most charming smiles she had ever seen.

"If you say so," he said. He smiled again. "How's that?"

"Better," she said.

"Come on," said Stone. "We all need some fresh air."

They went down the stairs with the brown rubber tread, Kay and Jack going first, Stone moving his weight from side to side and carefully putting his hand on the chipped paint of the banister. Kay put a hand to her head. She sneezed.

"Gesundheit," said Stone. "You look a little flushed."

"I'm just tired," she said.

"Your eyes are swollen," said Stone. "You should take care of yourself."

She stopped in the dusty air behind the front door. In the distance they heard the sound of someone practicing.

"Come on," she said. "Let's get outside."

"You should eat," said Stone. "Are you eating?"

"I'm not hungry," said Kay.

"Listen to me," said Stone. "Take care of yourself."

Kay turned to look at him.

"Okay," she said.

They walked outside, passing the shops where the skinned animals hung, and they passed the walls where handbills in Ukrainian had been put up: dances, a new furniture store, a place where you could get fresh pierogi. Over these someone had plastered posters for the Marshall Competition. The Marshall was an important one for pianists, and Kay, Jack, and Stone stood in the street and looked at a poster. It had a typeface like that of a stock offering in the financial papers. Kay said, "I think I'm ready for that, don't you?"

Stone said, "Yes. I do."

"So?" she said.

"There is an audition," he said.

"Can you arrange it?" she said.

"Yes," he said. He nodded. "They will take my word for it."

She nodded.

"Good," said Jack.

"Tell me," said Kay. "Who comes to the competition?"

"Important people," said Stone.

"What kind of important people," said Jack.

"Oh, senators, congressmen," said Stone.

"They're just politicians," said Jack. He shrugged.

"Well, the chairman of the banking board comes too. I think he is one of the few of them who understands music."

"That's Wendell Blaine, isn't it?" she said.

"Yes, yes," said Stone. "He is on the committee for the audition."

"Good," she said. "I'm glad to hear that."

They walked a little farther.

"Does he ever come backstage, after a performance?" she said.

"Who? Blaine? Wild horses couldn't keep him away," said Stone. "He has been very helpful in the past. He has opened doors. He is an important man, and don't you forget it."

"We've got good memories," said Jack.

 April 5, 2029

JACKSON'S NAME was in the telephone directory, and when Briggs looked it up, he saw that Jackson lived in the older part of town. All of the back streets there were named for trees, Apple, Oak, Birch, Pine, Spruce, Elm, Pear, Orange, Lemon, Ash. Some of them were short alleys, culs-de-sacs in which brownstones still stood, three and maybe four stories, with steps that went up the front. Briggs supposed that there were small gardens in the back. People who lived here kept gardens for flowers and vegetables, and one of the ways to get a tomato, a real one, was to come here in September. Eating one with vinegar, oil, and a little salt and pepper was like being in another age. Jackson had a green thumb, and he had brought Briggs a tomato from time to time.

Jackson's name was missing from the list of tenants next to the buzzers by the outside door, but there was only one name gone, so Briggs knew which apartment must have been his. Even from downstairs Briggs could hear the sound: the Mungo Men were already at work.

He leaned against the wall downstairs, hearing the sound. Briggs supposed that Jackson hadn't known where Kay and Jack had gone; maybe he had just helped them get away and that was all he knew. Briggs tapped his head against the wall. Then he turned and started climbing, taking the steps one at a time.

The door of the apartment hung by the top hinge. The bottom one had been torn from the frame. The lock had been smashed. The Mungo Men communicated by grunts of disbelief that anyone could care about something as worthless as the object one of them had just found, or they used another sound, a guttural exclamation of curiosity or the interrogatory. *Augh. Unh?* Briggs pushed the door open.

Three of them were at work. Their clothes were mismatched, worn, picked up here and there in the apartments they ransacked. One of them had a scarf around his head and wore a coat made from fur that looked as though it came from an animal that had been killed for a bounty. The place had the smell of the cheap beer and brandy they drank.

One of the men went through the sofa with a knife, his stabbing a slow yet oddly insane motion, like a lunatic who was taking his time in killing someone. The stuffing of the cushions was on the floor. Briggs realized that the way in which the room was being attacked wasn't as chaotic as it seemed; if you watched for a moment, you saw that they had divided the room into one-foot cubes, and that they were going to look through each one, completely, even if some object happened to be in it.

An older man, whose beard was a mixture of gray and black, was smashing things in Jackson's bathroom. He stopped when he discovered Jackson's dentures, which had been sitting in a glass on a shelf next to the medicine cabinet. The man made a grunt of excitement *(Unh)* and picked them up and put them into his toothless mouth. He grinned at himself in the mirror, the teeth too large for him but probably workable, and when he turned to look at Briggs, his expression was something like Jackson's. Briggs looked at the smile and thought, *Jackson didn't even have time to get his teeth.*

The apartment was only one room, a studio, and in it were a bed, a sofa, a desk, a table, and a chair, which had been moved to the center. The place was distinguished, even in its dismantling, by a paucity of emotional life. A lamp with a bent shade suggested how a drunken woman would wear a hat.

The Mungo Man came out of the bathroom, still satisfied with the teeth. He opened and closed his mouth, like a man who has peanut butter stuck on his palate, and as he stood there, his jaw working like a fish, he found a Hawaiian shirt. He stripped off his coat and put the thing on. Then he turned to Jackson's desk, where he opened a drawer and found some letters that Jackson had saved. The Mungo Man went through them, scanning them, looking for numbers of accounts, details that could be turned into cash, and, finding none, moved on to the next item.

Briggs reached into the mess on the floor. It looked as if everything in the apartment had been suspended in the air, in free fall, and that it had suddenly stopped and everything had collected on the floor.

"We were here first," said the Mungo Man with the teeth. "So don't get cute."

"I don't want anything," said Briggs.

"Bullshit," said the Mungo Man. "Everybody wants something."

"Well, maybe," said Briggs.

"So, what is it?" said the Mungo Man.

"I don't know," said Briggs. "I just thought I'd look around. Maybe I'd see something."

It was like talking to someone on an exercise machine: the man didn't break stride. He opened the next drawer and used the edge of his hand to sweep the things in it from side to side. Photos, a birth certificate, a high school diploma, a book of pornographic pictures, which the Mungo Man looked at once and then dropped, and said, "Sex. Every one of these jackasses is into it. They like this or that. I could make a list." He opened the next drawer, pulled it out, and turned it over, the things in it instantly changing from possessions to junk by the time they had hit the floor. The Mungo Man spread these items out. One good look was enough. No booze, no money, nothing to wear, no drugs. Fuck.

One of the Mungo Men had finished with the furniture and turned to a print on the wall. He broke the frame into small sections and looked at each one. They went about their work, grunting now and then, rodentlike, repetitive, their mouths opening and closing with the effort, with anticipation that seemed endless, no matter how disappointed.

They finished and turned to the pile of things they had made in the middle of the room to divide up: one took something and someone else grabbed it, and then the one who had grabbed something first kicked another object at the man who had objected, like kicking a dog to an alligator. One man got a half-empty bottle of brandy, a shirt, a couple of pairs of cotton underwear. Another man got the chair, a blanket, and what looked like some new razor blades. The last man got the teeth and some sheets. He looked quite happy. They kicked through the junk one last time, making sure they had missed nothing before giving Briggs a look of weary hostility. There really hadn't been much here. The furniture, aside from the chair, had been too heavy to carry, given what it was worth. The credit cards were worthless. What they really wanted was a chance to hit someone's apartment before word was on the street. Maybe even with a woman still there.

They left. Briggs sat down on the broken sofa. Sunlight slanted into the room. Somehow the disorder of the place was more upsetting than any abstract idea about Jackson. Here, at least, one could feel the certainty of life coming to an end. Briggs wished he had taken on one of the Mungo Men and had . . . had what? It was like saying you wanted to take hold of fate so as to stop it from being ugly. Then he felt his eyes filling for the briefest instant, just a little moisture, the arrival of it coming as a warning. He swallowed and stopped it, but didn't feel any better.

He didn't go. He was still sitting there when the Mungo Man with Jackson's teeth came back, kicking through the things on the floor.

"So?" said the Mungo Man.

"I thought maybe he had stolen stuff from work," said Briggs.

"What the fuck," said the Mungo Man. His eyes darted back to Briggs, though, suspicious, furious, penetrating. What was it Briggs wanted? Had to be something.

"There's nothing here," said the Mungo Man. "Nothing but shit. Look."

He kicked the trash.

"I'm telling you," he said. "That's it."

The man stepped a little closer, bringing with him the ammonia smell of piss.

"I was here earlier," said the Mungo Man. "Before the crew. Where did you say you worked?"

"Galapagos," said Briggs.

"Oh, yeah," said the Mungo Man. "They've got that turtle up there above the door. I've seen it. And they've got a picture of it on some blue cases, don't they? Got diskettes in them, don't they?"

The man took his hand out of his pocket, bringing out a blue handkerchief, with which he blew his nose. He did so while keeping his eyes on Briggs, although the man gave his nose a terrific side-to-side twist. Then he looked into the middle of his handkerchief before making a ball of it and stuffing it into the recesses of the coat.

The Mungo Man turned and abruptly moved away from the wall. After a couple of steps, though, he said over his shoulder, "So, are you coming or not?"

"Have you got the case?" said Briggs. "Did you find something earlier?"

"A blue case. Had a turtle on it," said the Mungo Man. "Do you think he was stealing stuff? Heh?"

"I don't know," said Briggs.

In the street, the Mungo Man's limp was more pronounced, and his gait gave Briggs the sensation of being on a platform of a merry-go-round and having a horse go up and down next to him. Their progress was steady and pretty fast, too, although Briggs had the feeling not so much of advancing horizontally as of descending. The sidewalk was cracked, with grass pushing up through it, and they went by two-story buildings that had obviously been put up in commercial haste which segued into an almost immediate decay. The fronts of many of them were covered with posters, which had been painted over with the graffito, "Whatcha got goin'?"

Needles and drug paraphernalia made the insidious glitter on the sidewalk, as though on this spot dreams had been so utterly consumed as to leave nothing more than this bright grit. The front of one building was like a warehouse, and on it were signs for ragpickers and junkmen, for product "liquidators," and many of the names were written in Asian scripts he couldn't read.

"Where are we going?" said Briggs.

"Down to the dump."

The Mungo Man proceeded with that up-and-down gait. He put his hand into his pocket and brought out a sheet of newspaper in which he had wrapped a piece of smoked fish and a crust of bread. He took a bite, still going up and down, his jaw working in time to his walking, and when there was just a piece of skin with a shine on it, he held it out to Briggs.

"Here," he said. "Eat."

"That's all right," said Briggs.

"Are you too good to eat with me?" said the Mungo Man. "Ah, I could see it right off."

Briggs reached over and picked up the skin. He put it in his mouth.

"I just don't want anyone getting snotty with me," said the Mungo Man. The Mungo Man rolled up the piece of brown paper and put it back into his pocket, like someone folding up a pocketknife.

Briggs looked into the distance, where the buildings became increasingly shoddy until it was hard to tell where the buildings ended and the junk began. The backside of the city, beyond the commercial part of it, was a moraine of shacks, a detritus of the most desperate souls who lived at the boundary of the dump. It was an open pit.

The surface was uneven, like waves, and each one seemed to be covered with a flotsam of only partially recognizable bits, shiny metal that could be part of a machine or just some packaging, a clutter of paper, old checks, more wrappers, something that could have been shattered glass, the edges of it giving off a spectral light. All of it stretched away to the horizon, shiny here and there in the way that only something worthless can be shiny, which is to say filled with false promise that had so correctly come to nothing. Overall, it gave the impression of a green-brown sea, sparkling here and there in the pale sunlight, uneasy, with some bad weather working in the distance.

They turned in at the gate. Briggs and the Mungo Man walked over the surface, which had been pushed around and compacted by a huge bulldozer. Every now and then they came across a canister of something that had broken and was oozing. Many broken lightbulbs. Shiny wrappers for toner. Briggs heard a dog's two-tone woofing.

A hut stood at the side of the parking lot for the heavy equipment, the walls of the structure made from aluminum torn from truck trailers, the sections of it covered over with foil that looked as though it had been obtained from a space suit. A little smoke came from the roof, out of a heating duct that had been made into a stovepipe. The barking got louder.

"In here," said the Mungo Man.

The dog was a brown animal, with a red tongue and the thick fur of something that had been manufactured rather than born. It had eyes like marbles and its movements were smooth, although repetitive. Briggs glanced at it once and then sat down at the side of the place, on a bench made from a plank and two engine blocks. He could still taste the fish.

A man was playing with the dog, cuffing the side of its face, on its jowls, knocking it one way and then the other. The dog jumped up, wagged its tail, and came in for more. The man cuffed it again, knocking it over. The dog jumped up and did it again. The man cuffed it. The two of them went about this like creatures at work, as though they were digging post holes. Briggs put his head back against the wall and closed his eyes. What he heard was the watery, saliva-muffled slap of the man's hand as it hit the dog, but after a minute or two the barking and the slapping stopped.

"Hey, what's happened to your mutt?" said the Mungo Man. "Hey, Frank, I'm talking to you."

The dog had rolled over on its side and now lay still. Frank pushed its rank fur with his toe.

"I don't know," he said. "It was all right."

"Maybe you shouldn't hit it that way," said the Mungo Man.

"He likes it," said Frank. "He always came back for more."

"Well," said the Mungo Man. "The mutt doesn't look too good."

Frank stood there, looking down.

"I used to like to play with 'im," said Frank.

"You aren't going to start bawling, are you?" said the Mungo Man.

"He was a good dog," said Frank.

"Ah, Jesus," said the Mungo Man.

Frank sat down and put his head in his hands. He was whimpering now.

"Ah, Jesus. Stop it. You make me sick," said the Mungo Man.

Frank sobbed harder.

"We used to sit here and have a game," he said. "His fur was a little rough. But that was the only thing wrong with him."

Briggs got up and looked at the dog. He turned it over and looked at the seam, which was a rough one, ridged, red. He wondered how anyone could do work like that. He guessed it was being done in Taiwan, or maybe Siberia. He had his tools in his pocket, and he took them out now and opened the seam. Frank stopped crying. The Mungo Man watched too. Briggs reached in and found the works, which sat in a bath of slime, a variety of impact-absorbing compound that looked like jelled mineral oil.

"Have you got a machine?" said Briggs.

"Over here," said the Mungo Man.

Briggs turned it on, smelling the slime as he did. He set up the works from the dog and started scrolling through it. Clunky. Right from the beginning. He looked for the right spot and then broke in. There was the problem, the Trauma Factor, which anyone could see would make the animal not last any time at all. Briggs guessed it was set up that way so that just when a child, who was playing with the dog, got used to it, the thing would break and they would have to go out and buy another. He made the change. He guessed it would be good for about a week more. Then he put the works back in, used the sealer, and reached down to pat the thing on the head. It looked up.

Frank stared at Briggs. Then he put out his hand and called the dog, which jumped up and went to him, the motion absolutely the same as before. He cuffed it, his eyes still damp, although now he was laughing too, as before.

"Hey," said Frank. "Look at him, will you, frisky as ever. Hey." He cuffed the dog, which barked. Frank said, "Oh, I love you, you big, ugly thing. Yeah. I do. I love you."

The Mungo Man looked at Briggs.

"Happy as can be, those two are," the Mungo Man said to Briggs. "Just look at them." Although he didn't. He kept looking at Briggs.

They sat and listened to the sound of the man playing with the dog. The room was warm from the fire, although what they were burning had a chemical stink. The Mungo Man went to a file cabinet at the back of the place, and pulled out a couple of shirts, a fur coat, a thermos from which he poured a stream of shattered, mirrorlike flakes.

He said, "Here. This is what you were looking for, isn't it?"

He held out the blue disk cases.

"Yes," said Briggs. He gave them a little shake. Disks were inside.

"What are they?" said the Mungo Man. "I couldn't make head or tail of them."

"Just a job that got canceled," said Briggs.

The Mungo Man stared at Briggs. Then he looked over at the dog and Frank. The dog barked, its head out, sides heaving with the effort.

"All right," said the Mungo Man. "You got what you wanted, now get out of here."

Briggs stood up.

"Let me tell you something," said the Mungo Man. "You sure are lucky you fixed that thing. Oh yeah."

KAY AND JACK walked across the bridge into the haze of lights, and up to a window in which the mannequins moved, their clothes changing, and behind them the weather of the window turned from a clear day in spring to a snowy one in winter, short skirts and sleeveless tops morphing into coats and boots that were worn in the midst of a storm of perfect flakes.

Kay took in every detail of the store's luxury: the polished metal, the wooden banisters, the brass plates that had small, graceful lettering, all imbued with an opulent mixture of sizing, furniture polish, and the lingering ozone that came from the work of machines that cleaned the carpets. She picked out underwear, which she tried on in front of a mirror, and then in front of Jack, who tried to say just what it was that each article did for her, or didn't. Peach or gray? Red? Black net? He liked the sheer things she stood in, garter belt, brassiere, stockings. She picked out silk dresses, and some made from other materials, too, that hung from her shoulders and hips, breasts, over her arm in such a way that suggested fluid grace and a perfection of figure. She didn't know how she knew a line of poetry, but she did, and she said out loud, "Wherever Julia goes I see the quiet liquefaction of her clothes . . . "

"Herbert," said Jack. "Or is it Crashaw?"

"I thought it was Lovelace," said Kay.

"Naw," said Jack. "Not Lovelace. Lovelace is a dog."

"Well, who's good, if you know so much?" said Kay.

"Yeats," said Jack. "Hardy. Eliot."

She bought some skirts, blouses, a sweater, and an overcoat. When she tried on the coat, she put her hand into one of its pockets a couple of times to see how fast she could do it

Upstairs in the hotel, the bags from the stores seemed to exist as a cloud of tissue paper and a miasma from the cosmetics counters. Kay held up one thing and then another, looking at herself in the mirror, letting a skirt fall across her legs. Then she went into the bathroom and ran the water, the steam filling the room like white smoke. She got into the tub and let the water creep up her sides. Jack came in and sat on the toilet seat. She shaved her legs and underarms. Then he said, "So, are you going to go out?"

"Just for a little," she said.

"Oh," he said. "Do you want me to come along?"

"No," she said.

He sat there.

"You want to be careful," he said.

"Sure," she said. "I know that."

"Maybe I should come along," he said.

She shook her head.

"Hand me a towel, will you?" she said.

He handed her a towel, which she wrapped around herself. In the other room he sat and watched as she tried on some of the clothes she had bought. Then she put on her trench coat, and as she stood by the door, Jack said, "You better take this."

He held out the pistol, which she put in her pocket.

After walking for about twenty minutes, she stood at the beginning of Briggs's street. It was a little more stark than she had supposed, although she could see in the scraggly trees, which looked like something from an autopsy photograph of nerve cells, that there were buds on them, too, just small black shapes that were about to explode into leaves. She guessed the thing to do would be to walk down the street on the opposite side of the building, to see if there was anyone in a car, in an alley, or who just seemed out of place. Perhaps she could take a look at the back of the building by going in the alley. She put her hand in her pocket and walked along like someone who was out for a stroll.

She didn't see anything, but to be sure, she went away for a half hour, and then came back and did it again, going over the neighborhood from another direction. She didn't see anything the second time, either.

Kay went up the steps to the glass door of Briggs's building and looked in at the tiled floor, the green walls, the banister that went up into a place that she couldn't see from the door. Then she turned back to see if anyone was behind her. She knew that the best place to make a fight was in the middle of the street, where she could move around, rather than being trapped against a wall. She knew, too, that she wasn't going to waste ammunition. Hold, aim, breathe, put it where you want. It was surprising how much time you really had if you didn't get shaky. She looked in through the glass. Then she pushed a couple of buttons next to the names of the tenants, and when she heard a buzzing sound, she opened the door.

Fourth floor. She knew that anyway. She started climbing, going around the stairs, putting one hand on the banister, which was polished by years of people touching it. How often had Briggs gone down these stairs, she wondered. Plenty, she guessed. She tried to imagine the atmosphere here when he had come home. She reached out for the banister and touched it, and then she thought, *Don't be sentimental.*

The tile on Briggs's floor was made of small hexagons, white ones around a black one. Someone was taking a shower and she could hear the hot water in the walls, a high-pitched shriek like a small animal caught in a trap. She couldn't hear any sounds from down below. Briggs's door was painted green, the color of pea soup, and in the middle of it was a little brass peephole. She stood in front of it so he could see her face. Her knuckles made a slight, imploring tapping on the door. He would know the chance she had taken, and that would surely count for something, wouldn't it? She waited.

Then she turned and leaned against the door. All she could smell was the dust in the hallway, and the odor of cooking cabbage. She had never tasted cabbage. Then she thought, *Why not take a look inside? Won't that tell me something? All I want is to feel close to him for a moment.*

The door didn't look as if it had much of a lock, and she wondered why Briggs didn't have a better one. She guessed it was because he knew he wouldn't be able to stop anyone who wanted to come in, and so he didn't make a big deal about it. A plastic card would do the trick, and she reached into her pocket to take the one she had from the hotel, which worked as a key. All she had to do was lean against the door, push the card against the latch, and the door swung open and she stood inside.

The first thing she did was to close the door. In front of her was a sofa and a low table. A couple of lamps. A rug. The sofa was large and looked comfortable, and there were a couple of paintings on the wall. A Wolf Kahn. Greens, blues, and yellows, all vital and alive and suggesting life that she felt as a variety of ache. Then she touched the books in the shelves, the papers on his desk that were next to the keyboard for the machine he had at home. She leaned forward and put the tip of her tongue against one of the letters.

In the kitchen she looked at the pots and pans he used to cook food, and she imagined sitting down opposite him. Maybe they would just have a snack, some cheese and bread. A glass of wine. They could make chitchat. Nothing too serious. Then she closed the cupboard and went into the bathroom, where she picked up his shaving brush. She ran it across her face, smelled it: soapy badger. She began to wish she hadn't come in, and yet she didn't want to leave, either, since it was as though they had spent some time together here and that if she left, it would come to an end.

She went into the bedroom and saw the clock.

"Who are you?" said the clock.

Kay stood there with her hand in her pocket. The short blond hair of the clock, the freckles, the Midwestern voice were irritating, like a noisy alarm.

"No one," she said.

"Uh-huh," said the clock. "You're lucky that Briggs made a change. Usually I'm supposed to call the police if someone comes in, but he told me not to, particularly if a woman should show up here."

"No kidding," said Kay.

The clock smiled.

"No kidding," she said.

Kay smelled the powder the clock wore, which was fresh, like a spring day in a field filled with daisies. Maybe there would be clouds in the sky, big white fluffs with gray undersides. Kay leaned forward and put her nose into the clock's hair, and as she did so, she thought of the things the clock knew, the moments she had shared with Briggs, the sheer accumulation of hours that they had been together. How would Kay ever be able to build that up, or to have even a part of what the clock took for granted. The clock's skin was white with a dusting of powder. Its eyes were blue.

"You just sit here?" said Kay.

"Pretty much," said the clock.

"That's all?" Kay said.

"Oh," said the clock, "I think about doing things for Briggs. Trying to understand. Trying to be there when he needs someone."

"No kidding," said Kay. "Is that all you do?"

"Oh no," said the clock. "Oh, not at all."

"So what else is there?" said Kay.

"I like being here," she said. "You've got to be on the dime. I'm with the program. See? There's more than one way to skin a cat."

Kay looked at the clock.

"No kidding?" Kay said. Kay reached in, under the clock's Spandex top at the back. The skin was smooth and warm to Kay's touch.

"What are you doing?" said the clock.

"It will be all right," said Kay.

Kay found the power switch.

"Please," said the clock. "I don't like that. The darkness."

"I'm sorry," said Kay.

"Wait. I won't tell anyone you were here," said the clock. "Promise. This is just between us."

As Kay felt the clock's warm skin, she wanted to knock it off its perch, to break it like some romantic souvenir that Briggs had kept. Then Kay thought, *For shame. Would you take vengeance on a dumb creature, shower fury on this inanimate object, on this* thing *as though it had done something cunning or malicious? It's nothing more than a dumb brute. There are times, though,* she thought, *when malice molds its intent in ordinary objects, and if you are alert enough to the essential horror, you can see it for what it is. How innocent all of this must have seemed at one time.*

She was sweating again. Surely these were the thoughts one had in the midst of disease, weren't they? Or was it worse than that? Was she hovering at the edge of insanity? *Perhaps,* she thought, *my state is how I perceive being alone and without my love. The world seems ill-meaning when you are denied that. And what ill-meaning god has cheated me out of the time to show my devotion, my passion, my desire to please, and the possibility of blending with another human being? It is like a sting, a lash, an unexpected slap, the thing that makes it hard to breathe. Is there any bitterness I will be spared?*

The clock sat there in a trance.

The bed was behind Kay, a double one with a blue blanket on it. It was a soft material, like merino wool, and Kay ran a finger across it. Then she pulled back the covers and slipped her hand under the cool sheet. The pillow was a large one, comfortable, and she put her hand on it. Outside in the hall, she heard the sound of someone walking on the hard tiles, a *click, clock, click, clock,* and she put her hand in her pocket. She thought, *I should get out of here. Right now.*

Instead, though, she sat down on the edge of the bed. The sheets rustled behind her. After all, she was tired. She had taken a lot of chances in coming here, and they had left her exhausted. She reached down and slipped off her shoes. Then she stood and removed her skirt and blouse and put them on top of her trench coat, which was on a chair by the head of the bed.

The sheets were still cool, and she pulled them and the blanket over herself. The pillow made a rustle under her head, a domestic hush that pierced her. She closed her eyes, and concentrated on the odor of the pillow: she could smell his hair, his skin, the miasma of many almost impossibly delicate fragrances that validated his existence. What she wanted to do was empty her mind completely, try to become as calm as possible, so as to absorb what it was like to be there. As she tried to do so, she started sweating. She was nauseated too, but against it she had the rustle of these covers where his presence could be detected. The warmth under the comforter permeated every aspect of her, working its reassuring heat into every bit of her, right into her eyes. Then she hovered there, trying to think nothing so as to appreciate the warmth. Why wasn't he here?

After a while she got up and dressed. She looked at the bed and thought, *Some other time.*

April 5, 2029

BRIGGS STOOD at the threshold of his apartment and noticed a change. He couldn't say just what the difference was, not a sound, not an object out of place, but nevertheless something was different. He had the impulse to call out, but didn't want to admit that he was uneasy. Instead he lingered at the threshold of the living room, looking around, thinking that he really had to get control of himself, although when he did, his relief was indistinguishable from exhaustion.

The diskette he had gotten at the dump had the surface of a CD, although the thing was an inch thick, and as Briggs held it under the light, the surface of the diskette was streaked with a band of light. Briggs watched the streak swing back and forth, its colors as spectral as an oil slick, as he reached out and put the diskette into the machine. In an instant he saw that it was a complete record of Kay and Jack's development, the log of an almost infinite number of small details that determined how and what they were.

The search tools showed him where the tampering had been done, just as it showed the origin of the code in which the changes had been added. A lot of the really basic construction for this project was prefabricated, and it had been purchased from contractors on the outside. He went down to the notes beyond the slashes where the names of the vendors were listed. Bingo. A small software company on the other side of the river. A contract outfit. Just like that.

Briggs went into the bedroom, took off his clothes, and threw back the sheets.

"Hard day?" said the clock.

He glanced at her face, her short hair, her impossibly cheerful smile.

"On a scale of one to ten?" he said.

"Yeah," she said. "That's as good a way as any other."

The sheets rustled as he got under them and turned on his side. The clock dimmed the lights and Briggs closed his eyes.

"Are you wearing new perfume?" said Briggs.

"No," said the clock.

One of his pillows had the nutty-sweet scent of skin, and in his fatigue he wondered what it was like, and after a moment, he thought, *Well, like intimacy itself.* Then he put his nose against one pillow and then the other: they weren't the same.

"Did anyone come here today?" said Briggs.

"No," said the clock.

"Are you sure?" said Briggs.

"Well, I think so," said the clock.

"You think so?" said Briggs. "Do me a favor, will you? Turn around."

"What's this all about?" said the clock.

He pulled down her Spandex pants and ran his finger over the scar, like an appendectomy, that ran on one side, just above her hip. Then he got his tools from his pocket, the ones he had used to fix the dog, and used the Med-Liner to open the pink scar and take out the chip and the board inside. The clock sat there, not moving, not saying a word. He attached the board to the chip and plugged them into the machine on his desk. It took a couple of minutes, and during this time the clock sat there with the fatuous expression one associates with coma or death.

He came back and put the chip and the board and the coded material back in, and used the Med-Liner to close it up. You couldn't even tell. Not a scratch. One of the things he had always had was a light hand and good technique.

He sat down opposite her again.

"So," he said. "Is that better?"

"I'm not so sure," she said. She blushed.

"I didn't think you could lie," he said.

"Well, you know something, the world is full of nasty surprises," she said.

"Un-huh," he said. "Who was here?"

"A woman. She said her name was Kay," said the clock. "She came in here like she owned everything. Like she was pushing me out of here. What do you have to know about her for? What's she to you? We get along all right, don't we?"

"Yes," he said. "We do."

"That's what I thought," she said, as though vindicated.

"Is this the first time you've lied?" said Briggs.

"I didn't like her," said the clock.

"That's not what I'm asking," said Briggs.

"You and I get along fine. That's what I am trying to say. I don't need any women coming in here and, you know, breaking up a good thing . . . "

She blushed again.

"I understand," said Briggs. "But I asked you if you had told any other lies."

She nodded.

"Yeah," she said.

"Well?" said Briggs.

"Your boss and some guy who needed a shave came here. They fixed me so I would tell them where you went," said the clock. "You aren't mad at me, are you?"

"No," he said. "Does your back hurt?"

"No," she said. "Everything's fine now. We'll tell the truth to each other from now on, all right?"

The odor of Kay's hair seemed to be fading, but he guessed this was a matter of his sense of smell being fatigued. He tried to sleep, but the warmth under the sheets was so close to the heat of her actually being here that it was impossible to sit still. He got up, nude, and started walking around the apartment. In the living room he looked at the manuals and diskettes, the catalogs from the discount houses which he had started using again for the new job. Then he tried to imagine where Kay had stood, the items that her fingers had touched, and as he moved around the room, in and out of the shadows, he felt the planes of light as they slipped over his shoulders or across his legs with the maddening hint of almost being touched by her. He wondered what she had left behind, or how a room was changed by the presence of another human being. When someone left, was there any lingering presence? Or was it that when someone departed from a room, there was nothing left at all, and the emptiness one felt at such a separation was a hint of mortality?

He stood there, straining after the smallest detail that could suggest her. He tried to imagine the rustle of her going from one room to another. What he was left with was not so much the discovery of any residue here as the awareness of his own longing. And yet, as he walked around, touching anything that she might have picked up, he realized that she had put her life in danger to come here. Didn't this leave something in the room he could depend upon? He felt an impossibly delicate miasma, something that might have been only imaginary, but still seemed to be a matter of his longing combining with hers so as to suggest promise. *How like her,* he thought, *to let me feel that promise, to let me sense it in such an unstated and yet overwhelming way.* This moment, he was sure, was one of those things that only the two of them understood, and he moved into a slash of light where he felt her presence like a caress, a promise to be made good later.

He got into bed, and as he began to fall asleep, he thought, *If Kay were a carrier of some new disease, would the aerosolized material of her hair be one of the vectors?*

C H A P T E R   ❽

April 12, 2029

KAY, STONE, and Jack stood backstage, waiting for the audition committee to assemble in the otherwise empty seats. Kay looked at the cables and pulleys that worked the curtain, at the catwalk above, the rails for lights, all of it seeming not dramatic but industrial, as though these things were the levers and gears and ladders of a small foundry rather than an auditorium. It was dusty, too. Beyond the curtain she heard the door at the rear of the auditorium open and then the padded footsteps of someone who came down the carpeted aisle to a row of seats very close to the stage. She heard the squeak of a seat as another member of the committee sat down. There were ten or so. The committee members spoke quietly, which was odd, since no one else was in the theater, and they could have talked as loudly as they wanted, but the silence and dark gloom of the place were more intimidating than if it had been filled with people.

Kay and Stone had discussed what she should wear, and Stone had said, "Keep it simple. The trick here is to make your playing seem entirely unstudied and innocent. That way they will be even more surprised when they hear the music. We want to set them up for it." She wore tight blue jeans, a blouse, and a pair of running shoes. A little powder to make her skin look pale.

Now Stone walked back and forth, stopping to look out between the dusty curtains. Kay waited in the shadows, taking a deep breath every now and then. She had decided to play the final version of the music she had been writing, although she guessed that she wouldn't really know if it worked until she had played it.

"Don't be nervous," said Stone.

"I'm not nervous," said Kay.

"Why should she be nervous?" said Jack. "You think she's pretty good, don't you?"

"Yes, yes," said Stone. "I know what is good and what is in a new realm. I know." He looked out between the curtains. "The question is, do they know?"

Almost all of the committee was there, the women with gray hair, although two of them were younger and richer and had had plastic surgery and had their hair fixed, too. The men had small pot bellies and a couple of them were bald, their heads showing as bullet-shaped objects in the enormous space of the empty theater. They turned their heads, craned their necks, looked toward the back of the theater.

"Is Wendell Blaine coming?" Kay asked.

"He is a busy man," said Stone. "But I told the committee that he would want to hear you. That he would not believe his ears."

"What about seeing?" said Jack. "He will probably want to see her too, don't you think?"

"I guess," said Stone.

"Maybe you're the one who shouldn't be nervous," said Kay.

"I know what I know," said Stone. "But what if I'm getting old, what if I'm somehow imagining what I think I'm hearing? That is the thing that is making me worry."

"It's all right," said Kay. "I promise. I'll play something nice."

"Nice?" said Stone. "You've got to be kidding. This is not the moment for nice. This is the occasion for . . . for . . . " He gestured with a hand, going around and around, the movements vague but somehow still suggesting something large.

"You don't have to worry," said Kay.

"I want to explain something. If I ever made a mistake," said Stone, "if I ever said that someone was brilliant, that someone was the real thing, or more than that, and it didn't work out, they would never believe me again."

"She said don't worry," said Jack. "So don't worry. If they don't see the light, maybe I can explain it to them."

"Don't you dare," said Stone.

He opened the curtain.

"There he is," said Stone. "He came."

He pulled back the heavy curtain, and Kay stepped up so that she could see too. Coming down the aisle was a tall man in a dark suit. He moved with all the assurance of someone who knew that his word, or even his expression, could affect world markets. He had gray hair combed straight back, and his eyes were blue. He was perfectly shaved. His suit fit him in a way that made him look five years younger than he was. The other members of the committee turned to look and then looked away. A woman with blond hair and a long neck said to another committee member, a man with a bald head, "This really better be something. Or there will be hell to pay. Whose idea was it to call for a special meeting anyway?"

"Stone's," said the man with the bald head.

"Stone?" said the woman. "That old has-been? Oh Jesus."

Kay stepped next to the curtain, the light that came from over the stage cutting across her face like a primitive decoration, a slash of gold that ran from her hair across her brow, leaving a gold film in one eye. Blaine came in and took a seat, just behind the other members of the committee, almost as though to keep an eye on them. The women in the group, even the older ones, squirmed in a frankly excited way. His suit fit him beautifully, and his tie showed as a silky luminescence.

"Good afternoon, Mr. Blaine," said one of them.

"Good afternoon," Blaine said.

"Some people are a little worried about, you know . . . " said a woman. "Share prices."

Blaine nodded. It was obvious that he was thinking about it and that he wasn't going to say a word.

"It is a beautiful afternoon," said another, a man with a bald head who seemed to think that having said this was one of the most idiotic things he had ever done.

"Yes," said Blaine. "I noticed."

"We are supposed to be hearing a very talented musician today," said another committee member. "Gifted."

"We'll see," said Blaine. "Won't we?"

"And how are things in the world of finance?" said a woman at the end, who wore bright red lipstick and carried a red handbag and who wore red high-heeled shoes.

Blaine hesitated for the briefest instant, and said, "As expected."

"But really talented," said a woman on the end, who had been waiting to say something and now took the plunge. "That's what we have been told. The musician is supposed to be really talented."

Blaine turned his head the slightest amount, in the direction of the woman who had spoken.

"By whose standards?" said Blaine.

"I don't understand what you mean," said the woman who had taken the chance and was now regretting it.

"By my standards or yours?" said Blaine.

The other members of the committee tittered, and Blaine turned back toward the stage.

"Well?" he said. "What are we waiting for?"

"You, my dear," said the woman who had the most style in the group. "Or have you lost your sense of importance?"

"Me?" said Blaine. He smiled now. "Important? Surely you are joking. I am just a cog in a big machine."

It was obvious that the ceremony of his arrival had been handled in a way that met his approval. The other members sighed. Thank god they had gotten through it all right.

Kay let the curtain swing shut, and the light vanished from her face. She pushed her hair back. The silence of the backstage area seemed overwhelming, like a gas, although here and there she heard a small squeak as the upper regions, where she could only barely see, warmed or cooled.

"What are you waiting for?" said Stone.

"I'm just thinking," she said.

"This is no time for that. This is the time to play," said Stone. He put a hand to his head.

"What do you think he weighs?" said Jack.

"Who? Blaine? How can you ask something like that now?" said Stone. He gave Kay a little push. "My darling, just go and play. Just as we planned."

"I thought I'd play something I've been toying with," she said.

"Oh, my dear," Stone said. "Please. Don't take any chances. Please."

He held back the curtain. She walked out of the darkness of the backstage into the pool of light in which stood a piano, its top gleaming, the keys looking like some code in black and white. She walked directly to it, her carriage upright, her shoulders back, and as Stone watched, he realized he had never seen anyone move with such sultry grace. In the darkness of the auditorium there was nothing aside from an occasional flash of eyes. Beyond the members of the committee, the tops of the seat backs, curved like fingernails, seemed to stretch into a dark infinity. She sat down and pulled the bench forward; it squeaked like a small cry of surprise.

Jack sat down on a chair backstage. Stone stood just behind the curtain. He breathed quickly, putting one hand to his chest. Then he went over to Jack and said, "Sometimes I don't think she realizes what a chance this is."

"She knows," said Jack.

Kay started to play. The objects in the gloom around Stone seemed instantly frozen, as though seen in a photograph taken of this moment. Even the flecks of dust in the air around the piano seemed to stop their sluggish transit, and to hang without movement. This was the first sensation he had of the music. The next was that he didn't care about anything around him, as though the clear, certain, perfectly phrased notes obliterated everything.

That was the first effect. The experience was distinguished by a momentary recognition of his most chaotic and previously hidden sense of longing, which he now apprehended clearly for the first time. It was as though Kay had understood every missed chance, every regret, and had somehow been able to imbue each of these with a sense of infinite beauty and vitality. It was not that Stone had time to tell himself he would not weep. Instead he found himself weeping, not out of unhappiness, but from the joy of finally understanding the power and beauty of his own experience, which now, at this moment, appeared to be more significant than he had ever suspected. Then he abandoned words and gave in to the sound, and as he did, he found that he put one finger against the heavy curtain so as to open it just a little, just enough to see her. Her eyes were open, her shoulders square. At this moment she seemed to fill the auditorium completely. It didn't seem empty and large, but barely able to contain her presence.

The committee sat as though facing a breeze. Three or four of them cried without shame, without even caring about the tears running down their cheeks. The woman with the red lipstick cried the hardest, as though her endless follies were apparent to her at last, and she had finally realized the gift of being alive. She closed her eyes in shame at not having understood before, and at the small and tawdry pursuits she had indulged herself in and which, she now realized, had been nothing more than tedious distractions. The lovers who didn't care for her and for whom she had a secret contempt, the rank materialism of her life, even the clothes she wore, now seemed to her to be the worst excesses of someone whose lack of imagination was equaled only by the presence of far too much money.

The member of the committee who had been a musician closed his eyes, and slowly shook his head from side to side, not with disbelief, but with acknowledgment that needed this gesture to begin to express it. I don't believe it, he seemed to be saying, I don't believe it, I don't believe it . . .

Wendell Blaine seemed to have the best control, although this was probably a matter of his practice in hiding what he thought, but even he sat without moving, hardly appearing to breathe, his expression having changed from keen and suspicious scrutiny to one of frank disbelief.

She stopped.

For an instant the hall resonated with the last few notes. The committee strained after that lingering vibration, its disappearance coming as an echo of the end of her playing, which had left them sitting there in the empty space. It made them feel again, in diminished form, the first loss of the end of her playing. Nothing could be heard but their crying. The committee sat there, none moving aside from the odd, back and forth motion of their sobbing. None tried to say anything. A couple of them shook their heads, or lifted a hand in utter incapacity. The tears, the wet eyes, the rills of water in the creases of old faces, all had a moist radiance in the light from the stage. Kay sat with her hands in her lap.

The members of the committee stood and began to file out, none of them caring about their bureaucratic responsibilities as members of the Marshall Competition, or about any responsibilities at all, aside from the most serious and personal matters of their own lives. They needed a little while to think. They picked up their coats and went up the aisles, their feet padding on the thick pile of the carpet, some of them bumping up against a seat in their serial disorientation, which arrived with each successive memory of the feelings the music had stirred up. They went out, bent at the waist, quiet, looking for privacy. They disappeared, the old doors squeaking behind them.

Only Blaine and the member who had been a musician still sat in the auditorium. Blaine said, without looking at the musician, "What is her name?"

"I don't know," said the musician. "Excuse me. I . . . I . . . " Then he stood up and went out, past the empty rows of seat backs.

CHAPTER 9

April 12, 2029

IN A café not far from the auditorium, Jack picked up a newspaper on the table next to where he and Kay sat. The front page had a picture of some men in stylish suits beneath a headline that said, SPIKE HEEL GANG CRASHES. The men in the photo had the stylized bravado of rich South Americans who thought they operated according to special rules of physics. The Spike Heel Gang were traders in São Paulo who had tried to corner the future markets in copper, and while it had originally seemed to be nothing more than the usual scandal, the damage from it was spreading in a way that showed weaknesses in the financial institutions far away from South America. They were called the Spike Heel Gang because when things were booming, they drank champagne out of a woman's spike-heeled shoe. Jack read of suicides of bankers in Tokyo and Paris. What was one to make of this? Were these suicides a matter of money, or some private concern? And if it was personal, why were the suicides coming in a cluster?

Jack tried to imagine a Brazilian nightclub: women in sequined dresses, the movement of sleek hips under the red and blue shimmer, a leg extended with a shoe dangling from the toe as a dare, the shiny bubbles rising from a dark green bottle . . .

He held the paper out.

"You think this is the one we're waiting for?" said Jack.

Kay glanced at it.

"I don't know," said Kay. "It's got possibilities. First it will have to spread into Asia, or maybe Russia. A week or two, I guess."

A waiter brought some ice cream in metal bowls covered with a frosty, silver condensation as bright as the quicksilver of a mirage. Kay idly put her fingers into the spots the waiter made where he touched the bowl. Then she picked up the spoon and dipped it into the white ice cream.

"Well, I'll tell you one thing," said Jack. "You wowed them. Wowed them."

"I thought I played all right," said Kay. "Some of it still gets away from me, though."

"Well, it didn't get away from them," said Jack.

He looked at the paper again. The faces of the men appeared, in the moment, like a fad that is the latest thing and is about to be replaced by yet another quickly changing style. Dated, but not yet knowing it. Jack stared at their faces and said, "Yeah. It was just a matter of time, I guess. What do those economists you've been reading have to say about something like this?"

"A good kick in the right place and it all collapses," she said. "That is, if the circumstances are there."

She looked down at the paper.

"What's the right place?" he said.

"Credit," she said.

"Oh yeah," said Jack. "Well, speak of the devil. He's out there watching you. What did I tell you? Wild horses couldn't keep him away."

BLAINE STOOD in the street and looked in the window of the café. Kay dipped the tip of the spoon into the ice cream and put it into her mouth. Then she closed her eyes and slowly withdrew the spoon, leaving a little ice cream on the tip of it. Jack sat opposite her, his back to Blaine. Blaine had left his coat at the auditorium, and he shivered a little in the breeze. The glass of the front of the restaurant seemed familiar to him, but he couldn't say why until it occurred to him that the reflection of the blue sky in it reminded him of the sheen of a soap bubble that he had blown, as a child, with a toy that his father had given him. He hadn't thought about such a thing for years, and the recollection of innocence added to his impatience, his confusion, and his desire to spend a moment with Kay. As he saw her lips and skin, the movement of her long fingers as they held a spoon, the pursing of her lips over the cool ice cream, he thought of the music she had played, the phrasing that seemed to express so perfectly his own longings and chaotic desires and a sense of beauty he had never known existed. His newly remembered innocence, the impact of the music, and her sultry presence left him trembling in the cold, not knowing whether it was the cool air of spring or the fact that he was compelled, in a way he didn't really understand, to stand here looking at a young woman eating ice cream.

Kay came out first, then Jack. When they walked out to the sidewalk, Jack looked one way and then another, but his eyes stopped on Blaine's face. Kay smiled.

"Hi," she said. "You were at the audition, weren't you?"

Even now Blaine didn't trust his voice. He ran his hand over his face, and he was repulsed by his appearance, the way he had aged, the creases in his face. It was evidence of how he had wasted time. He realized with a kind of self-loathing that he had earned the face he now had, and yet he was almost hysterical in his desire to get rid of it, to start again. This was one of the qualities of the music that Kay had played, maybe not the ability to start over so much as the promise of understanding. In a way, they were almost the same thing. And if he was going to start over (which, he realized, was part of Kay's attractiveness), how in God's name could he get rid of the appearance of his face, which so obviously revealed the days he had spent pursuing order, precision, stability. It was as though he had been rotting from the outside in.

Kay went on smiling. Blaine swallowed.

"You know," said Jack, as though he had seen what he wanted, "I've got to see someone."

"Do you, Jack?" she said. She turned her eyes on him.

"You don't mind, do you?" he said. "Do you want me to hang around for a while?"

"No," she said. "That's okay. Go on. Go do your errand."

Jack looked at her carefully. Was she sure about this?

"Go on," she said. "I'm all right. Mr. Blaine and I want to talk. You do want to talk to me, don't you?"

Blaine nodded.

"Okay," said Jack. "Nice to meet you, Mr. Blaine."

Jack put out his hand as though he were a courier who had delivered something and was going on his way. Blaine turned his eyes from Kay to Jack. Was something being offered here, or, better, conveyed or given? Blaine looked back at Kay, who smiled. Jack shook Blaine's hand and went up the street, not turning around, doing nothing but going away with his frank, athletic way of walking, not swaggering, but confident, certain.

"Where do you live?" said Kay. "Is it far?"

She seemed more frank in the street, and without the window between the two of them, her presence seemed more real. He looked at the color of her eyes, which he hadn't been able to see before. Gray, with a pupil of exquisite darkness. She seemed to invite him to look at her.

"Not too far," said Blaine.

"Shall we walk?" she said.

"No," said Blaine. "I . . . My car and driver are up there, at the end of the block."

"All right," she said. "Come on. I've been waiting to talk to you."

"Have you?" said Blaine.

"Yes," she said. "The moment I saw you in the auditorium. It's strange to think that one can be so curious at a distance."

She looked at him as though trying to determine whether she had been right, and her consideration left Blaine wondering what it would be like to have the current atmosphere between them, which was one of almost infinite possibility, evaporate because she had decided that she had made a mistake. He flinched.

"Is something wrong?" she said.

"No," he said. "Maybe not."

When they came to the car, Jimmy got out and opened the door, and Blaine said, "We want to go home."

In the car, she slid across the seat, not right against him, but close. He tried to concentrate on being polite or charming, or somehow to make sense of having her here, right next to him, but instead he felt her presence in such a way as to leave him overwhelmed by a scent, a caress in the air, a change in what being alive felt like that was so keen as to be almost alarming. She hummed a little something, a bit of music that he didn't recognize. He tried to say to himself, *There's no fool like an old fool,* but he instantly dismissed this, or just put the consequences of it off, knowing instinctively that he would gladly pay the price later. That is, if there was going to be anything to pay for.

They came into Blaine's apartment and went down the hall with its brown shadows and gilt-framed pictures, Blaine's footfalls suggesting an almost staggering exhaustion. At the end, through the doorway of the library, they saw the luster of the piano, the black and white keys, the pedals at the floor curved and antiquated like the levers of a clarinet.

The housekeeper came in, her apron in her hands. Blaine's schedule never varied, and the slightest deviation was, as far as she was concerned, evidence of a certifiable emergency.

"Mr. Blaine?" she said.

"I'm going to have a guest," said Blaine.

"A guest?" she said. She blinked. Mostly Blaine did not have unexpected guests. "Well, there's plenty," she said with the voice of someone who has been filling a refrigerator with left-over food for years on end. She went out, stopping once in the hall to turn and look back into the room. In the hall, a clock with roman numerals on its face and with a pendulum swinging beneath it made a steady tick, tock, tick, tock, the sounds as definite as someone dropping washers into a metal bucket.

Kay sat next to the piano. She held one of her knees with both hands. Blaine was still shaky from the afternoon—*off guard* was the way he put it to himself, and he blushed when she glanced at him in a such a way as to make him think she could read his mind. Then he thought, *Who the hell cares if I blush or not?* It was as though every bit of discipline, every moment when he had had to go without something he had craved, had produced a sum, and he was suddenly aware of the scale of the amount and the interest he had had to pay on it, too, the instant Kay looked at him with that expression of exquisite frankness.

Now, though, when Blaine tried to speak, he stopped and swallowed, trying to get control of both his feelings and the obvious signs of them, too. He put the shaking tips of his fingers together.

Of course he wanted to ask the obvious questions, such as where she had studied. Also, he wanted to know what the piece of music had been at the audition. How could she have been playing anywhere in the world and not be known? Where had she lived? As he sat there, it occurred to him that there was a more obvious explanation: maybe she had had a nervous breakdown, as young musicians often did, and had been tucked away in some psychiatric hospital. This seemed quite possible, yet when he looked at her, when she smiled and flashed her eyes at him, he had the impression of succulent vitality, at once youthful and fertile, and while he detected emotional turmoil of some kind, it only made the strength of her spirit that much more obvious.

The aroma of dinner came into the room, and it made the shadows in the library seem warm and domestic. Blaine tried to think clearly. He wondered if he was losing his mind. He considered the possibility that it was happening so suddenly as to leave him with no way to confront the fact, no time to come up with a theory, a strategy, some illuminating notion that would get him through it. So he sat there, looking into the golden light of the library, at Kay. She had a vein in her forehead, hard to see, but there. It made her more striking, as though the vein were an indication of passionate intensity.

She picked up one of his hands. He felt the touch of it so keenly as to have the sensation that he couldn't tell where he stopped and she began. She looked around the room. "You live alone, don't you?"

"Yes," he said.

"I wonder why," she said. "This place, the comfort of it, seems made to have someone else here."

"My work," said Blaine. "It takes up a lot of time."

"Oh?" she said. "Well, that's too bad, isn't it?"

Blaine swallowed.

"But I guess someone has to be responsible. Did you see the paper today? Something about men in South America drinking champagne out of a woman's shoe," she said.

"It's not the champagne that's the problem," said Blaine.

"No," she said. "I guess not."

She reached down and took off one of her shoes.

"Would you like me to play?" she said, gesturing to the piano.

Kay had been working on another piece, and she began to play, her shoulders square and her head up. Blaine saw her profile, her short hair against the lights of the city, although now, as she played, the lights had an order that he hadn't noticed before. They appeared bright and filled with his most secret longings. She was the element that allowed him to forgive himself, and God knew he wanted to be forgiven for his failures. He thought of the look his wife gave him as she waited for him to die. After a moment or two, he stopped thinking altogether. He only knew that he wanted to spend some time with Kay.

She came to the end. When Blaine got up to look into the dining room, he found the housekeeper on a chair behind the door, listening, so distracted that she trembled and picked at a strand of her hair. He put his arm around her, the first time they had ever touched in this manner, and pulled her against him.

"My God," said the housekeeper. "Oh my God."

They sat for a while. Then the housekeeper got up and said, "Here. It is on the table. It will be getting cold. What could I have been thinking?"

Kay and Blaine sat down.

She talked about many subjects: butterflies, mountain climbing, rare fish, mushrooms. Then she went on to the history of coins. Did he know where the first coin had been minted? After each new subject was introduced, she watched. Was he interested in one rather than another? He spoke now, not in his usually dry and viciously witty way, but slowly, with some hesitation.

She described a method of tracking financial indices and cross-checking them so as to predict the markets, and while it was abstract, having only to do with numerical trends, it had always intrigued Blaine. Of course he knew the work and he'd thought he understood it, but Kay made some small adjustments in the way these theories were applied, and then spoke of the history of panics, from tulips onward through the IBM sell-off, and as she went through each one, she explained it according to the revised theory. Then he turned his head to one side, as though he had heard something at once true and at odds with what he believed.

"I hadn't thought of it that way," he said.

"Of course," she said. "It's just an idea I had . . . " She shrugged. "We can talk about it some other time," she said.

"Maybe what you say is true," said Blaine. He put a hand to his head.

"Think about it," said Kay. She shrugged. "It might be useful sometime. In a panic."

They finished and sat in the quiet room. Kay got up and stood next to Blaine and then knelt next to him. Her hand reached out for the napkin that was in his lap and slowly drew it away, and as it slipped from his hands like some worry that was simply being forgotten, he felt the touch of her lips against his face, and the pressure of her breath as she said, "Come into the other room for a minute. Can't you humor me? I get so tired of practice, of work. That's why I wanted to come here, to be someplace where I can be safe and where I can relax. Won't you help me?"

He stood up and came after her, going into the room with a view of the city and where the enormous bed, in which he had been conceived, stood between two windows. Blaine wanted to do the right thing, to think clearly, and he tried to do so, but what got in the way was an enormous fatigue which manifested as a restraint. As she touched his hand, or rubbed a smooth cheek against him, the fatigue seemed to evaporate. He sat next to her as she took off his tie and opened his shirt. She took off his shoes and then stepped out of her jeans, wearing just her underwear, and then the two of them lay back, into the heavy goosedown of the pillows.

"Please," she said. "Just let me lie down with you here. Put your arm around me. Just like that. I promise you there will be other times, but now just lie next to me."

Blaine felt the heat of the two of them together, which seemed to be indistinguishable from the fragrance of her hair. More than anything else, what he wanted was to live in the moment, but instead he found that all he could do was to keep thinking, over and over again, of the puzzle of good fortune and of his mystification that he could have been so wrong about so much for so long. Now he could see his errors clearly, or at least he could feel them dissipate in the warmth between them, in the touch of her skin, in the memory of her playing. He had never felt so close to another human being. She hummed something, and as he felt the slight vibration of her lips against the skin of his neck, he wondered for an instant whether or not actually sleeping with her might kill him, and as he put his hand under the elastic of her underwear, feeling the softness of the skin of her hip, he stopped. She wanted to lie like this, and he didn't want to do anything to interfere with the delicious intimacy of the moment. He hovered there in the warmth of their mutual touch, in the scent of her hair and skin, the soap that she had used to wash her hands, all of it validated or made real by the almost infinitely small sounds of the room: the rustle of her blouse, the hush of one of her bare legs crossing another, the small, wet drawing of her breath, the almost audible sound her tongue made as it touched her lips. She put her lips against his ear and hummed, the vibration seeming to somehow be the one detail that he knew he would remember, the diminutive buzz seeming to linger like the memory of a bee on some languid, hot afternoon. More than anything else, he wanted to go on hanging there in the touch and sound of her, since for a short time, anyway, he found that he was only giving thanks for this opportunity, for which he realized he had been waiting for years. She sat up a little sleepily, dragging her short hair down the side of his face, and said, "I so needed to be able to trust you like this. You can't understand what it means."

"Oh," he said, "but I can."

"I'll come back another time," she said. "I'll make you feel so good."

"But you already do," he said.

"You know what I mean," she said.

She got up and pulled on her jeans and then went out to the dining room to find her shoes. She came back and sat down next to him and put them on. He felt her weight on the bed next to him.

"I've got to practice," she said. "But I'll be back."

Blaine sat up and began to speak, but he confronted so many new possibilities while so many of the usual items in his life seemed to be vanishing that he sat there, working his jaw like a man who has had a stroke and cannot speak.

He followed her into the hall and then waited for the elevator. He reached out and touched her arm. He still didn't know what to say. The elevator creaked as it came up, as though rising from depths with all the power of a secret making itself apparent. She leaned closer to him, her breast compressing lightly against his arm, to kiss him good night, and as she did, he said, "It's hard for me to trust people."

"You can trust me," she said.

"Do you promise?" said Blaine. "Look at me. Will you come back?"

"Oh yes," she said.

"You won't make me send people to find you, the police, a detective, my own staff . . . "

"I'll come back," she said.

"All right," said Blaine.

She got into the cage. The elevator door squeaked shut and the cage descended, leaving Blaine in the hall. Then he turned and went inside. There he walked through the apartment that had been so reassuring for so many years and that now appeared to him to be something he had used up and no longer needed. What had he been doing all these years, anyway? Playing the fool? He sat down in the library and looked at the polished surface of the piano. Then he put his head on the keys. They made a sound that was nonsensical, as ugly as everything random and yet ill-meaning, and Blaine sat there listening to it, wondering if it revealed just how shallow he had been all these years.

THE DECORATIONS of the subway station were stylized arches and aluminum reliefs, muscular men and woman with slabs of hair. Intense faces, not necessarily happy, but all having a purpose. Briggs got into the train, where the lighting was at once golden and filled with brown shadows. The train ran into the darkness beyond the station, and Briggs saw all the passengers, himself included, reflected in the windows. It all looked so ordinary and dull, just men and women sitting on benches, their clothes brown and gray, their eyes hidden in the shadows of their brows as they went into the darkness of the tunnel.

The train came into the station and Briggs smelled roses and orange blossoms, orchids. A florist had a shop underground, and Briggs saw the petals, stems, and slick leaves, the flowers that trembled now with the rumble of the departing train. Briggs reached down and put his nose into a rose. He thought of Kay.

Small manufacturers had originally put up loft buildings in this neighborhood, and while these brick and mortar structures still looked the same from the outside, inside they were filled with new enterprises. It was like being in a new country where one's own language is spoken. Briggs was reminded, as he walked down the street, of the first time he had been to England. Everything seemed all right on the surface, but what barely suspected and incomprehensible activity took place beyond what he had been able to see?

Briggs stopped in front of the contract outfit that had done a lot of the work on Kay and Jack. While it was housed in what seemed to be just another old loft building with glass-and-wood doors, brass hinges, and an antiquated doorknob, it nevertheless had the air of being intensely modern. Narrow venetian blinds, a brass plate with logo, an intensity of maintenance that would have been unthinkable when the building was new. Beyond the door, the light had a green tint, as though filtered through leaves in springtime. Fresh and clean. He opened the door and went in.

The receptionist's hair was cut into a flat top and dyed purple. She wore a red latex dress and shiny boots.

"May I help you?" she said.

Her smile wasn't warm.

"This isn't a sales call, is it?" she said.

"No," he said. "It's not a sales call." Beyond her he saw a hall with a hardwood floor. White walls with framed prints and posters. "No. I wanted to talk to someone about some trouble I'm having."

"What firm are you with?" she said.

"Well, right now I'm working out on the strip," he said.

"Is that right?" she said.

At the end of the hall, the light looked as though it came through an old Coke bottle.

The receptionist went down the hall, her feet clicking on the hard floor, her back and hips in shiny latex. She came back and said, "Down there."

Briggs went into an office with that same greenish light. Venetian blinds. The usual machine on the desk.

"Briggs?" said the man. "Haven't we met somewhere? Maybe at Galapagos?"

"Maybe," said Briggs.

"Well, my name is Strick," said the man. "This is Leslie Carr."

Briggs turned and saw a woman in a black dress on the sofa behind him.

"Hey, Briggs. How are you?" she said.

"All right," he said. "It's been a while, hasn't it?"

"Oh, time flies. But, yeah, it's been a couple of years," she said. "This is where I landed."

"No kidding," he said.

"Perhaps he wants some tea," said Strick. "I like a nice cup of tea at this hour."

"He doesn't want tea," said Carr.

"No?" said Strick.

"He wants something stronger than that," she said. "Don't you?"

"Yes," Briggs said.

"How did you know?" said Strick.

"Intuition," she said.

Carr went to the pantry at the rear of the office. A cupboard opened and closed, and Briggs heard the hard *thunk* of a glass on a counter, the *thock* of a cork being pulled from a bottle. The trickle as it was poured. He thought how ordinary the sound of a man being given his dinner on a tray sounds, and yet how filled with dread it must be if this is the sound of a last meal being given to a condemned man. Carr came back, her hips swaying a little under the clingy material, and gave him the drink. Their fingers touched.

"Thanks," said Briggs.

"Don't mention it," she said.

"I guess you've been keeping busy," he said.

"Yes," she said. "I have. And then I have a couple of small projects I've been working on. Private items. You know about them, don't you? I mean, you've done a couple of private things, haven't you?"

Briggs took a sip.

"Yeah," he said.

"That's what I thought," she said. "In fact, I seem to remember your doing a little of that kind of work a few years ago. Didn't you?"

"If you say so," he said.

"Sure," she said. "Did you like it? Did you get anything out of it?"

Briggs shrugged.

"Come on," said Carr. "You're among friends here."

"Don't bank on it," said Strick.

"His bark is worse than his bite," said Carr, gesturing to Strick. "Tell me, did you get anything out of what you did? I mean, has it worked out the way you wanted?"

"Not exactly," he said.

"See?" she said. "Just when things are going the way you hoped, something comes along and causes trouble. I feel sorry for you."

Briggs concentrated on the heat of the liquor in his mouth.

"Come to the point," said Strick. "What's wrong with the product we sold you?"

Carr sat down in a chair opposite Briggs. Without looking at Strick, she said, "I think I'm the one he wants to talk to."

"How do you know?" said Strick.

"Just a lucky guess," she said. "Look at him. He's desperate to ask a question. Can't you tell?"

Strick looked at him.

"I don't know," said Strick. He turned to Briggs. "Do you want to ask a question?"

Carr smiled, and then sat back and crossed her legs, bouncing one foot up and down.

"Yes," said Briggs. "I'd like to ask Carr a question."

"So?" said Strick. "Ask."

"It's private," said Briggs. He looked right at her. "Isn't it?"

She bounced her ankle up and down, smiling at him.

"That's right," she said. She turned to Strick. "I'll take him someplace and find out what he wants."

"Fine," said Strick. "You do that. I've got better things to do than to sit around like this."

They went out to the street, into the cool air, Carr walking with a businesslike stride, looking straight ahead. Briggs felt not warmth from the liquor, but disorientation. Some birds flew down the street, just above their shadows, their wings beating with a repeated snap, like sheets on a clothesline in the wind.

"In here," she said.

The place was a coffee shop with venetian blinds, and they sat down in the slats of light that lay in bright strips across the table. Carr slid over, making a little squeak on the seat of the booth. She lighted a cigarette and then spoke puffs of words.

"What did you add?" he said.

"Just like that," said Carr. "You come out and ask. You are a direct man and I like that. No beating around the bush, no trying to trick me into saying something I didn't intend to say, no expressions of false friendship."

"Would you go for that?" he said.

"No," she said.

She sat there smoking her cigarette.

"I learned a lot from you. I really did," she said.

He looked across the table, the slats of light falling across her nose and cheeks. It made her lips seem very red.

"You really do nice work," she said. "It took me a long time to see that you had such a delicate touch. You remember those parts about innocence? About devotion? About recognition of another human being? Of delighting in life? Of the thrill of the moment just before orgasm, when one human being really knows, without any doubt, that this is the true test of being alive. That if you love someone enough, matters of right and wrong become a part of one's attempt to be worthy of someone else's love."

"Yes," he said. "I remember."

She bit her lips, shifted her weight in her seat. The slats of light made her skin radiant, her hair a mass of filaments.

"I guess you didn't add anything like that?" he said.

She shook her head.

The waitress came over and they both asked for black coffee, which came in heavy cups, the black circles of the liquid swinging back and forth. Carr put her lips to the cup and tasted the bitter coffee.

"You didn't answer me," said Briggs.

"No," she said. She looked right at him. "I didn't add anything like that. I don't care about things like that."

"No?" he said.

"I had my weak moments," she said. "And you know what happens to you if you have a weak moment? You aren't the same as you were before you made the mistake. You see things differently. It's amazing how things can get turned inside out, love turned into fury, beauty into ugliness, order into the attractions of chaos. And make no mistake, chaos has its own attraction. You've got to see that."

"Carr, Carr," he said. "We used to be friends."

"We were never friends," she said.

She smoked her cigarette, letting the clouds rise above them with a slow, swirling motion.

"I hope you like surprises," she said.

"No," he said. "I don't."

She took a sip of coffee.

"You've been devious," he said.

"You're scarcely one to talk about that," she said. "But then you would probably say that in the service of the good and the beautiful, you can afford to be devious. Isn't that the way you think? It all starts so innocently, right? Well, let me tell you it doesn't always work out so nicely. You think it's going to. What can be wrong when you let yourself feel the best of what humans can feel? Well, plenty. One day you aren't the same person anymore."

She gave him a look of contempt.

"You haven't told me what you added," said Briggs.

"Well, let's just say it wasn't what you added."

Her hands were shaking.

"How did you do it?" he said.

"I contacted Jackson," she said. "He wasn't making much money and he wanted to have a little something extra, and he liked the idea of doing something antagonistic to those people who made him sit there at night and smell the stink of the stuff they used to clean the floors. I gave him code to add."

"But Jackson was a guard," Briggs said. "What did he know about it?"

"I wrote some applets that did the work. They searched through your code to find the right place to put things. All Jackson had to do was to load it in. Nothing to it."

"Oh," Briggs said.

"That's the way it is," Carr said. "So it's going to come down to you or me. Is she going to do what I want, or what you want?"

"Time will tell," he said.

"But not much time," she said.

"Maybe she has ideas of her own," Briggs said.

"I doubt it," she said. "I really do. She's angry. And that's something you can depend on."

In the street, Briggs felt the last irritating effect of the drink, which left him at once restless and tired. He walked through the blue shadows of evening that fell into the alleys and doorways where the gloom was even darker yet, and as he glanced into these entrances and back lanes, he had the desire to step into one and sit down, just for a moment, to rest. But he was afraid of giving in, and so he went up to the subway station and down into the noise of the arriving trains and the perfume from the underground florist's shop.

CHAPTER 12

April 14, 2029

BRIGGS SAT down at the machine in his apartment. Surely Kay was using the networks. This must have been one of the things she would try, since she understood machines, or thinking machines, better than anyone did. After all, there was a lot she didn't know, and yet she would learn very fast. All she needed was information, and God knew the networks were a good place for that.

Briggs had been stealing software from work, and while he hadn't sold it, which was far too risky, he had nevertheless used it. He had a library of utilities right there at his fingertips, and he picked up the first one, which was a hacker's bible. The first thing was to get a list of all new accounts that had been set up on the East Coast in the last week or two. Mostly, of course, these would be kids, since almost everyone was assigned an account when they were twelve, and then they kept it, like a social security number, until they died. It was an odd thing for an adult to set up an account for the first time.

He guessed it would be pretty easy to sift through the new accounts and decide which was which. For instance, while without a password he couldn't see precisely what the new accounts were looking at, he could still find out what the general pattern was. Sex manuals, pictures of women with no clothes on or those that showed them in various acts, and a record of various sports teams: obviously this would be a boy. The girls did a similar thing, although instead of sports it was Calvin Klein and pages that dealt with skin care. So it was easy. He put together these patterns and worked through the new accounts again, setting up the search so that these patterns were eliminated. The numbers fell. Almost all the accounts had gone for sex. The few that were left could be looked at in one glance: thirty-five or so.

He guessed that a lot of these might be from immigrants, although mostly people kept their old accounts, since using them didn't require being in any particular country. Citizenship, in a lot of ways, didn't matter quite the way it used to. The New Waves hit every place with the same intensity, and you couldn't hide just by being in Switzerland rather than South Africa. So he went through this handful of accounts. Maybe some of them were people who had had amnesia or had been in prison, or in some other way had been out of the loop for a while. Surely a large number of the new accounts read the news, and he supposed this might be explained by amnesia. There was only one account that had accessed a library.

This was the one that intrigued him, and he brought it up and started to work on it. He had another utility to help with a password, but this just ground through an endless number of possibilities, and even with a high-end machine like his, it could take a couple of hours. If he was onto the right one, he should be able to guess the password. So he tried Kay1, and Kay2, then Remilard1, then Portman, Portman1. He went through the date when they had gotten away. Nothing. He tried running their names backwards, combinations of both of their names. He supposed they were in the older part of town someplace, although he wasn't sure about this. For all he knew, they were in Europe by now, or Australia, but he didn't think that so. So he tried the names of some of the streets in the old neighborhoods. Nothing. He tried *Phalaenopsis,* the species of orchid that he had chosen. Nothing. Then the name of the hybrid, *Deventeriana X violacea.* Nothing. Often the variety of an orchid was referred to by the contraction of *Phalaenopsis* to *Phal,* and he tried Phal Kay, Phal Jack, Phal Briggs. Bingo.

He thought, *No. This is something I might have picked, not her. She wasn't supposed to know anything about the names of the flowers.*

He swallowed and looked around. Outside he heard a siren as a fire engine went by. Well, maybe she just knew one of the words and had chosen it out of random association. Something unconscious. After all, if he was going to choose something at random, wouldn't it be a word with associations that he couldn't articulate? He guessed that was it.

Phal Briggs. He was in. There was a list of the items she had accessed. She had used the local directory, and had gotten his address. There were other items she had searched for too, such as repositories of sheet music and a number of titles of books. These were in the library.

Of course, the Gutenberg Project had gotten a lot of the books copied onto a machine, but after a while it became apparent that this was wasted effort. No one read them. It was easy to erase them from a computer, but harder to get them out of the libraries. Although there had been some agitation, as part of one of the New Waves, to get rid of the books in the library, the idea had been resisted: the argument had been that the books were like rare plants that needed to be protected, not because they were beautiful, but because they might produce something practical, just as a rare plant might produce a cure for an emerging disease. Who knew what was squirreled away on those dusty shelves?

All Briggs had were the call numbers of the books she had tried to get. He printed them on a slip of paper and put it in his pocket. Then he turned off the machine.

The clock said, "Briggs."

"What?" said Briggs.

"You haven't been sleeping much," she said. "Early to bed, early to rise makes a man healthy, wealthy, and wise."

"Uh-huh," said Briggs. "Do you know where my library card is?"

"What's a library card?" she said.

"It's a . . . " he said, but then he stopped. The top drawer of his desk slid open on the air-brackets, silent as a snake. Briggs moved the stuff in there from side to side, a couple of old letters, a picture of him at school as a member of the crew, all of the young men with their hair short, looking out at the water where a race was about to begin. Underneath he found the card, green with a spectral hologram.

THE NEXT evening, Briggs stood in a darkened aisle between the stacks. Even in the gloom he could see the gleam of a few titles, which had an exotic quality, like gold jewelry on the arm of a woman who stood in musky shadows. The overall impression, though, of the shelves of books, one opposite another, was of narrow walls and a low ceiling, with only a couple of bare bulbs that stretched away to a brick wall. Briggs reached up and touched a piece of string that hung there in the darkness and that had a little bell-shaped piece of metal on the end. The light went on. He turned to look at the books.

A lot of them hadn't been touched for years. The shelves were brown metal, and the ceiling was brown too, although the paint was curling away. The silence existed here with a hint of the serene, and as Briggs luxuriated in it, he looked up at the gilt titles suspended in the gloom. He put a finger onto the cool shelf. He was sure the silence here was different from that in a room, in which, say, old legal records were kept, receipts, checks, leases, contracts, motions to dismiss or to charge, to annul or to reinstate, to appeal or to cancel. The atmosphere here came from the record of what people had seen or done, wanted or imagined, known or desired. It had been built up one word at a time, through a ridiculous effort that couldn't be explained and yet was filled, too, with an instinct for beauty. But still, the books had been abandoned in this place to wait for fate, like every other object. *Beauty,* he thought. *Why can't I just forget it? Why do I have to keep coming back to it like . . .* Well, he didn't want to say. He thought of the aroma of opium as it rose from the doorways in those alleys. He went along the books, checking back to the number on the slip of paper he had in his hand.

He found the first one. It was heavy and printed on shiny paper. The publisher was Harvard University Press. He walked between the rows of books to a desk that sat under the window at the end of the shelves. It had an oak chair, with shadows falling away from its legs like sheets of black rubber. Outside, the pigeons flew up to the window, their wings spread as they came to the sill, the shape of them falling over the pages of the open book. The reading lamp above him had a round knob, textured so as to be easy to grasp, but when he turned it, nothing happened. He guessed the window provided enough light to read by, anyway. He opened the book, titled *A Clinical Account of Obsession.* The table of contents showed chapters having to do with theory, both historic and speculative. Then there was a list of cases. Briggs ran his fingers down them, the name of each one having a clinical, bureaucratic style, having to do with the notation of when the patient first appeared: Jun-fem-3. A female who asked for help on June third. Just the way Galapagos named its projects. Feb-Ma-8. Man on February eighth.

. . . The subject was first seen by the examiners on May 14, [May-Fem-14, thought Briggs, what was wrong with these guys?]. She was then a woman of twenty-three, of medium height, with red hair and blue eyes. Physical examination revealed no scars or marks, no signs of disease, no lasting effects from any infection. Her scores on the California Personality Inventory and other diagnostic inventories, including the Benet-Richardson scales, were normal, or above normal.

Her account was that when she had been twenty, she had gone with some friends to have a picnic by the river, and that as she sat there, laughing and eating a sandwich, a man came along. She can still recall the effect he had on her. She often refers to this moment as having a "light," or a presence that seemed to "sweep" through her with a quality that she found hard to describe, but which nevertheless made her at once very happy, even ecstatic, and yet very fearful too, since it was so strong and so sudden. The man who produced this effect was about six feet tall, with dark hair and blue eyes, and he stopped and smiled. She smiled back and stood up. He introduced himself as Robert Berlin, and he said that he was a student at the university. She reached out and took his hand, and as she touched him she felt again that sense of keen "recognition" which nonetheless had a warmth which seemed to spread through her with the sense of making her seem, for the moment, separated from the bank on which she stood, or from her friends, the woods around them, even the sounds of the birds, which flitted from tree to tree and which made a repeated call. In her interview at the Institute, she insisted on imitating this call, which was a small chirping with increasing intensity. When she did this, she smiled, as though recalling something of exquisite pleasure.

On a personal note, this interviewer, who has been in practice for forty-five years, has never seen anything that can compare with the intensity of feeling this subject revealed when she tried to describe certain details and sensations. And, no matter what happened or how extreme her circumstances became, she maintained that the intensity of the experience was such that she would do it again, on a moment's notice, no matter how often she pledged not to, and no matter what penalty she was facing. Upon more-penetrating questioning, she became quite serene, and seemed to be certain that either the interviewer could understand what had happened to her or he couldn't. Frankly, this interviewer finds it very difficult indeed to understand just what it was, although he can attest to the fact that it must have been exceedingly pleasant, at least in the beginning. Or perhaps there is another explanation, which is that as the experience became more intense, as she had to sacrifice more to continue, this only added to the intensity of that original feeling of pleasing warmth and recognition.

Without a moment's hesitation, and without the least embarrassment, she asked if she could see Berlin again. They agreed to meet the next morning at a coffee shop near the university. She said that she was there waiting for him, and what she recalled was a collection of details (typical of hysteria) that seemed to linger with photographic recall: she could remember the texture of the white tablecloth, over which she ran her hand, feeling the texture of the white threads against her fingertips. A blue vase, in which were four daffodils, the stems as green as celery, stood on the table, and across from her was a brown chair, which she described as being one like those used by lion tamers. The light from the window fell across the table in trapezoids, and she heard the voices behind her and could smell the cinnamon that the coffee shop used in baking sweets. As she waited, she imagined that she was imprisoned and that Berlin came to visit her. All that was between them was a sheet of glass, floor to ceiling, and that they were both nude and she tried to touch him, putting her hand against his face or chest, or putting it down opposite the space between his legs. She tried to press herself against this transparent surface, or to put her cheek against it. Then she imagined another visit, a little later, when there was only a screen between them, and then she could put her fingers against it, and almost but not quite feel his skin, his face, his chest. She put her tongue against it, trying to taste his skin, which she could, but which was tainted by the metal taste of the wire . . .

He was late for the meeting in the coffee shop. She was agitated, but when he arrived she felt that same warmth and penetration, which she described, smiling, as a moment of revelation and certainty such as she had felt at no other time. They had tea in brown cups with white interiors, and she watched as he put honey into his, drawing the spoon out of the pot, the strands hanging from it as he looked at her and smiled. Everything about this moment, the texture of the honey, the shape of his hands, the look in his eyes as he smiled, the light, the shadow of the birds that flew down the street and passed by the window, all seemed to be part of that warmth and recognition. She thought of how she would like to pursue this feeling, not knowing definitely what this would be, but nevertheless feeling a predisposition not toward the sexual so much as toward abandoning who and what she was for this moment, and if sex would help with that, all the better. She maintained that even in the most extreme moments, this was never, strictly speaking, a sexual infatuation or obsession, but something more profound and illuminating. Sex, she maintained, was not the purpose or the goal, but the mere expression of that warmth she had first felt by the river and seen again in the coffee shop, with the honey streaming from a spoon and the scent of cinnamon mingling with the sight of daffodils.

Of course, later, when he did not have the time for her that he once had, when he tried to make excuses, she became frantic. This, she said with a smile, as though she had found a solution to her difficulties, was the moment she "bitched him up in earnest." She had found the place of entry, the secrets he had kept to himself, but which she discovered and used to great effect. After that, she said, "nothing could stop us . . . " What wouldn't they sacrifice for a few hours together, when the innocent and sweet pleasure was invoked through such acts as are described in appendices

3–110a. . . . Of course, it is hard to believe in the stamina, in the sheer vitality needed to pursue such activities, day after day, until each of them was certain they were right at the edge of dissolution of self, which, if properly exploited, as they discovered, could be used to such sensual advantage. . . .

Briggs closed the book, feeling a little whoosh of air that came out of the heavy pages. Then he looked out the window at the brick wall on the other side. Silence behind him. Well, he thought, he didn't want to get to the end of this one, and he guessed it was best not to look too carefully at the appendices. He was curious about what the man's secrets had been, but he guessed, in a way, that he already knew.

What man doesn't know just what it is that he would give anything for? Or what the moment would be like if a woman knew what this was, even better than he did, and that one day she sprung this knowledge on him, with a gasp of joy? And a shiver of excitement? He had always known that Kay had enormous power over him, but until this moment such considerations had been abstract. He looked up and saw the pigeons, their wings sawtoothed at the window ledge as they used them to brake just on the other side of the glass.

He looked down the dark aisle. Then outside again. He thought about Berlin. At some point this man must have realized that he was in the midst of an attraction that had its own imperative, and that the confusing thing about it was that as it advanced, as it consumed everything in his life, it became that much more pleasurable.

Kay had been interested in some other books too, and now he went looking for them. She wanted essays by Nobel Prize–winning economists. She was particularly interested in economic metrics. Indices. Movement of capital. Above everything else, she was interested in those theories having to do with establishing market trends. Briggs flipped through these things. It wasn't his realm of expertise, and he guessed that she was smart enough to want to be clever about the money she must have gotten her hands on. Surely she was living on something. She would open an account someplace and use the money in some clever way. He nodded to himself as he held the book in his hand. She was practical. She would manage the money in a way that made sense.

The last book she had wanted was an account of a slave revolt in Rome. This was in another section, and he went toward it, through the maze of shelves, going along the titles, finger up, like a man testing the wind. The books were pleasant to touch, the cloth of the bindings soft to his finger. He stopped. Here it was.

The book was a collection of speeches, records, invoices from an itinerant executioner, all of it assembled with the order of sediment in a cross-section of geological strata, laid one on top of another in the order that they had been produced. Briggs stood in the brown dimness, holding the book. He realized that he would discover which of these accounts she responded to by his own feelings. She had looked as he did, if not here in this place, then in another library, and surely she had read what he did.

Of course, he was interested in revolt too. What wouldn't he like to say about the people who controlled his life, who decided which project he would be allowed to do, when he would be paid, the people who often decided, for the most tedious reasons, that he would be shipped out to some strip, downgraded to the second rate? How often had he fought back from this stigma, picked up the pieces, and continued? He was still doing it now. Or what he would like to say about the way he lived, or the way everyone lived, when the future arrived as a bullying rumor, a part of which would come true?

He stopped at a speech by Tacitala, the leader of a revolt in Sicily in the second century. The words had been recorded by one of the men who had survived and who, as a secretary to a landowner, had been taught to write. And to remember, too, by the Roman method: the first thing to do was memorize the architecture of a building and then, when committing something to memory (a speech, for instance), to assign various parts of it to the rooms of the house. When the speech was recalled, one imagined going through the architecture: What was in the first room downstairs, what was in the second?

Tacitala spoke from a few rocks on a hillside in the afternoon, and around him stood olive trees, the silver-white of their undersides flickering in the breeze. He spoke to five thousand slaves who knew that the Roman legions were about to arrive. The air was thick with smoke from the campfires, where the men had prepared a last meal, which they had eaten, slowly, with deliberation, and then they had stood before the hillside where Tacitala spoke.

"My friends," he said, "the Romans are just over the hill. You can see the dust from their approach. And with the dust there are vultures, who are clever enough to know what that dust means. There is not much time, but I wanted to speak to you from the heart. If I do not speak in this manner now, why, when should I do so? From the grave or from the cross where some of us are going to be hung in a few hours? No. I think the time to speak is now, with the dust in the air, when you can almost hear the sounds of the Romans as they march. Some of you worked on ranches, on the *latifundia* in chains, and some of you, as I did, in the mines. We know things that no other men know, and this knowledge binds us together. Let us be thankful for that closeness, for the fact of our unity. It is the one thing we have. We can depend upon it in the most trying circumstances. Surely this is one of them. I would not dare to tell you otherwise.

"I want to speak honestly as well, because if this is not the time for honesty, then what is? In a few hours from now? No. The time for honesty is this instant. With vultures approaching in the train of the Romans. The first thing is to address the facts. It appears as though the gods love us less than others. This is what eats at my heart even more than the things we have all endured: Why should we be so shunned? I would cry if it wasn't a futile waste. And, under these circumstances, what do I have to offer? Let us make a pact. Let us agree that when the Romans come, as they will soon, they will know that they fought human beings. Not some reduced creatures, not some fearful children, but us, informed of the circumstances as they are, as the universe really is, and that we have chosen to be remembered by this moment. You could call it defiance if you have to have a word, but we know what it is. By any word you want to use.

"The Romans will stand on the ridge of the hill and make a war cry. But we are more practically minded. After all, we have had to work in places most people only see in nightmares. As a practical man I am going to do a practical thing. I am going to reach down and pick up a stone. Like this one. And I am going to use it to sharpen my sword. You hear? That scraping sound as the edge comes true? When the Romans come up the hill, when we see their dust as it streams up, every one of us will use a stone to work on his sword. Let us try it now. Yes. And again. Yes. Again. That is the sound they will hear from us when they first approach. Then we will be in a position to leave our mark and to show these men, brave men I am sure, that we were men, too."

The book made a little sliding sound as he pushed it back onto the shelf, and then he turned off the light and stood in the darkness.

CHAPTER 13

April 15, 2029

I N T H E evening, Kay sat up on the side of the bed and looked out the window at sky. Jack slept on the bed, and his pale legs, the marblelike definition of the muscles in his chest, the corded veins in his arms, the angle of his hips made him look like Renaissance sculpture. She touched his chest, the hair under one arm, ran a finger around one of his nipples. The pistol was on the nightstand and she picked it up, reassured by the heft of it. In the mirror she appeared in white and shadow with the pistol on the bed next to her.

Kay got up and walked around, the pistol hanging by her thigh, which seemed to make her feel more naked. In the bathroom, the radiators clinked and the pistol made a clanking sound, a counterpoint to the radiators, as she put it down on the porcelain tank of the toilet. She turned on the shower and stepped into it like someone walking into a tropical rainstorm. She thought, *It's just nerves.* Finally she took the small, cheap towel that the hotel left in the bathroom and began to dry off.

She had gotten lucky when she had gone to Briggs's apartment without being caught. But what good was luck once you had used it? She didn't think it was a good idea to go back, and yet she didn't know what else to do. Then she thought of Jackson. Jackson might help.

Certainly, Jackson had helped them before. He had found them in the hall of Galapagos when they were trying to get away. He could have sounded an alarm, but he hadn't. In fact, he'd looked as if he had been waiting for them. But no matter what he'd been thinking, he had said, "Don't be afraid. I'm not going to hurt you. Come on. Don't worry. Jack.

Don't worry." He had given them the jumpsuits and some money. On the night they had escaped, he'd taken them to his apartment for a couple of hours.

Jackson had been nice to her. And something else too. He had been polite. She hadn't had any experience, but she had liked his politeness. He'd asked her what she wanted to eat or drink and he hadn't made her feel embarrassed because she didn't understand something. Jackson knew that she might be awkward, but he seemed to be certain that this wouldn't last long. At the heart of his treatment had been respect, and she realized now how lovely it had been. He had given her a cup of tea and watched her drink it. Given her a cookie. Told her to be careful about ever coming back to this apartment. He had liked her, and she had experienced this as warmth that she could almost feel. He had spoken to her like an adult, right from the beginning. Anyway, he had told her not to come back to his apartment, ever.

She tried to comfort herself. Maybe in the blinding will of revolt, she would really be alive and capable of love. Not just the obsessive love she felt now, but a conscious, gladly given passion. Both eyes open. She sat there in the bathroom, feeling the pistol warm on her thighs.

Oh, let it rest, she thought. *Can't I just have a little pleasure? Isn't a girl even allowed that?* Who was to say it was obsessive? Fuck them. The people who used this word had never had a moment like this, when they were crazy to have just the touch, the whiff, the hint of someone . . . And yet, with each passing hour, she became panicky with the desire to break away, to be defiant. What if Briggs wasn't what she wanted after all? What would she do about that? She sat there, trembling.

She went to the dressing table and looked through the junk there, cosmetics she had bought, and in the clutter of powder and brushes she picked up the promotional key chain for a game called Pacifica XII. It was the one she had put in her pocket when she had been in the gaming parlor. The gimmick wasn't much, really, about the size of a matchbook, but if you opened it up, a single eye inside winked at you, lascivious, beckoning. If you took the thing to a gaming parlor, it let you have a look around in a new game. If you held the gimmick in your hand, it took a quick registration of your pheromones and then adjusted the game so as to reflect just what your ideas of romance really were.

Jack was still sleeping. The light from the setting sun outside lay over him like an aureate dust, the shadows of the muscles of his chest looking dark, almost the color of coal against the gold film. His chest rose and fell. She held the gimmick up and let it swing back and forth, and then she ran it across her lips. Well, she guessed it had possibilities.

The cheap computer with the cigarette-burned lid made a little squeak as she turned it on. The trouble was that the machine only had one adapter, and it didn't fit the promotional gimmick. She went into the bathroom, looked through the medicine chest, in the closet, but there was nothing there, just some crumpled-up tissue. She found the nail file in the drawer next to the bed, and she used it on the adapter: she did the job carefully, counting the strokes, rotating the plug even more precisely than it could have been done on a lathe. One stroke, turn. Keep the pressure the same. Then she clipped the key chain onto it, the connection to the computer making a diminutive and reassuring snap. The power came on. She looked at the guts of the key chain, scrolling through the code. *Hmmm,* she said, *hmmm. Look. That's where I could do a little work. Right there. If you did it right, you could turn it into a place to leave a message.*

She added new lines, inserted new uses, and then she took a piece of paper and wrote in her neat, Palmer method script, "You might use this sometime." She put the promotional gimmick and the note into an envelope she found in the drawer of the nightstand. No name on it, but not clean, either, with a round circle where someone had put a wet glass.

After a while she put her hand to her neck and rubbed it, and then she got up and put on her new coat, with nothing underneath. She buttoned it up and put the pistol into the pocket before she went out into the last of the sunset, which lay on the walls like a pink dust. She didn't want to sleep, since she had become frightened of dreaming: her dreams were filled with such longing. Jack slept while the door clicked shut.

She walked through the city, and as she went, she looked at each shadow, listened to each small sound, the almost inaudible pad of a cat's foot on the pavement of an alley, the plink of a drop of water from a flower box, all of it being examined, thought about, put into context. She didn't think anyone would try to stop her. It was late when she stood in front of the post office, her hand in the pocket of her coat. *I'll be waiting for you,* she thought. Then she dropped the envelope in the mail.

CHAPTER ⑭ | *April 16, 2029*

IN AN older part of town, the neon signs tinted the fog with colors that reminded Briggs of Popsicles. Cherry, lime, strawberry. How long had it been since he had eaten a Popsicle? Years. They had gone out of business when he was a kid. Briggs tried to remember the taste of them, a little artificially sweet, frost forming on the brightly colored ice in the heat of an August afternoon.

The dive he walked into had some models above the bar, old twentieth-century passenger liners, black-hulled, with white upper decks and cabins marked by a row of lights. A couple of the small bulbs were burned out, and the effect was of something that didn't have all its teeth. Briggs asked for a small glass of scotch, which he held to his nose so he could smell the fragrance. The liquor was made from malted grain, which meant that it had started to grow before it was put into a vat to cook.

"Hey, Briggs," said Mashita.

Krupp stood in the dim light, too, and he looked about the same, unshaven, a little tired, but still looking around, sizing things up. Mashita was wearing good clothes, and his hair had been cut, short like a brush, just as his goatee had been trimmed. Pressed pants. New jacket. He looked like a million dollars.

"Is that any good?" said Krupp, making a motion toward the scotch on the table.

"Yes," said Briggs.

Krupp looked around the bar.

"I'll have one of those," he said to the bartender. He pointed at the small glass on Briggs's table. Then he turned to Mashita. "What about you?"

"Hot saki," said Mashita to the bartender. "In a little pitcher. And a porcelain cup."

"Let's go over there," said Krupp. He pointed at a booth. It was made of wood, and the table had some scratches on it, like white hieroglyphics on a brown wall.

"How did you find me here?" said Briggs.

"Does it make any difference?" said Krupp.

"I guess not," said Briggs.

"There it is," said Krupp. "Guessing. We asked around. You're not hard to find."

Mashita and Krupp sat down. Krupp slumped over in the corner in his overcoat, the collar of it turned up against the chill of the street, his eyes not seeming to look at much. Mashita sat straight up, his hands folded. The combination of these two postures left a charge in the air, as palpable as ozone.

The bartender brought the saki in a porcelain pitcher and with it a small cup. Mashita poured himself a small amount and lifted the saki to his lips.

"This is good," he said, but it was obvious he couldn't really taste it.

Krupp rubbed his beard and had a sip. Briggs thought, *Keep your mouth shut. Listen.*

"I'm going to come to the point," said Krupp.

"All right," said Briggs.

"I'm glad to hear you're receptive," said Krupp. "That's going to make it easier."

Briggs took a drink.

"Now, we thought we had a problem that was going to go away all by itself. What the fuck did we know about it?"

"At worst it was public relations," said Mashita. "That was my take."

"So we agreed," said Krupp. "No one knew a thing. Right? It was all going to disappear. Isn't that right?"

"That's what I was hoping," said Briggs.

"Fuck hope," said Krupp. "I'm not paid to hope."

Briggs took another sip and wondered just what it was he was paid to do.

"Things have taken an unfortunate turn," said Mashita.

"That's one way of putting it," said Krupp.

Keep your mouth shut, thought Briggs.

"Let's talk for a moment about integrity," said Krupp. "Now, you may not know it, but integrity is at the heart of our business. It is important for us to be believed. For instance, what do you think the worldwide revenues for gaming are? Consider for a moment that there are gaming parlors in every city worth the name, and in some of them, like Hong Kong and Monaco and London, there are hundreds if not thousands of them. We receive something not only from the sale of the games, both hardware and software, but then, as part of the licensing agreement, we get something of the handle."

"Twenty percent," said Mashita. "That was one of the things I am most proud of. It used to be fifteen percent, but I was able negotiate an agreement, worldwide, that made it twenty. Of course, we had to give up a little short-term, but my thinking was that soon we would start nibbling at what we gave away, and by the end it would be a straight twenty."

"Now, the reason we are able to do this kind of thing is integrity," said Krupp. "The games must be tamper-proof. Do you realize how much we put into making them so that no one, and I mean no one, can play around with them?"

"I do," said Briggs. He thought it was odd to say this, as though he was getting married. "I worked on a lot of it."

"That's the way I understood it," said Krupp. "That's right. And now, we hear reports that there are some changes being made in the games and that they are being made by people on the outside. That is, the people who are playing them. Now where does that leave us?"

"And worldwide revenues?" said Mashita.

"At twenty percent?" said Krupp. "Now, we are talking twenty percent of the worldwide gaming handle. Do you have any idea what that comes to?"

"It is in the same league as Microsoft," said Mashita. "Very close."

"So I'm going to put it to you straight. Just what did you do?" said Krupp.

Briggs swallowed. Was there anyone out there in the street, waiting until this was over? The bartender kept an eye on the door. He had taken off his apron and was standing at the back now.

"Briggs," said Mashita, "how often have I given you advice?"

"Not very often," said Briggs.

"Was it good advice?" said Mashita.

"Yes," said Briggs. He was telling the truth. It had always been excellent advice.

"Tell the truth now," said Mashita.

Krupp waited.

"I guess there are a lot of things that could have gone wrong," said Briggs.

"Don't guess. I hate guessing," said Krupp. "I am not paid to guess and I am not paid to hope."

"When I was working on the project," said Briggs, "I included personal things. Desires of my own. The ability to think and feel. Dreams. Romance. The ability to love."

Mashita closed his eyes.

"You did this?" said Krupp.

Briggs nodded. Krupp looked away, outside to the street, then he turned his eyes, not to Briggs, but to Mashita.

"Briggs, there are laws—" said Mashita.

"Fuck the laws," said Krupp. "Do you think I give a shit about the laws? I am worried about twenty percent of the worldwide gaming revenues."

Krupp turned back to Briggs.

"Maybe I can work something out," said Briggs. "I guess there's something I could do."

"What did I tell you about that word?" said Krupp.

Mashita finished the last of his saki.

"Listen," said Krupp. "Aren't Kay and Jack supposed to get sick and, you know, die?"

"I never said that," said Briggs. "That's what you were hoping. What I said was that they might be carrying a new disease. They might not get it but other people would."

"Have you been checking about this?" said Krupp.

"I've been keeping an eye on the medical reports," said Briggs. "Nothing."

Or nothing yet, he thought.

Mashita nodded. Krupp refused to look at him.

"I think we should talk about honor," said Mashita.

"In a minute," said Krupp. He went on looking at Briggs. He said, "Is there anything else?"

Briggs turned up the last of the liquor in his glass, and through the bottom he saw the world as through a melting icicle: the colors stretched and the lights looked blond, wet.

"Yes," said Briggs.

"What is it?" said Mashita.

"She can have a child," said Briggs.

Krupp closed his eyes for a moment.

"I'm not hearing this," said Krupp. "I'm really not."

"You know," said Mashita to Briggs, "I protected you. There were a lot of times when people wanted to get rid of you—"

"I still need a little protection," said Briggs.

"You think he's in a position to give it?" said Krupp.

They sat without saying anything.

"And just to make sure we understand how things are," said Krupp. "Are the qualities of these creatures, you know, the violence, the cues, the ability to be told what to do—all of these things that make them like insects . . . "

"Insects," said Mashita with repugnance. "Insects."

"Are these qualities set up as a matter of personal behavior for them, or are they genetic?" said Krupp.

"Genetic," said Briggs.

Krupp played around with his empty glass. Pushed it one way and then another.

"We've got to come to terms with the reality of the situation," said Krupp.

He pushed the glass back and forth, as though he were playing with a hockey puck. He glanced at Mashita. Mashita blinked, then took out a handkerchief and ran it across his forehead.

Briggs wanted to say that there were other matters too, but he couldn't be precise about them. He wanted to say that his notion of the ideal had gotten away from him, not only because of Carr, but by the possibility that his own worst impulses, the vilest instincts of his heart, the desires that made him ashamed, had somehow gotten into the code too. His sudden, irritated impulse toward brutality, for instance. Or the pleasure, before he had a chance to get a grip on himself, when he heard of someone he disliked getting killed. Of course, he had always tried to behave well. But beyond actions he had thoughts, desires, half-stifled impulses, instincts toward the cruel, all of which seemed to exist right on the edge of thought. He looked at Krupp. No, Krupp didn't want to hear about things like that. Briggs turned up his glass to get the last of the liquor in it, which ran down to his tongue in a jagged rill.

Krupp said, "Have you seen those new shirts?"

"Yeah," said Mashita.

"All this cutting-edge stuff," said Krupp. He put his hand up to his neck and his collar. It looked a little dated. "The look has pizzazz, you know, an attitude. It's like it's restrained and yet strong. It's got ideas."

"I've seen these things fizzle out," said Mashita. "A lot of people jump on the bandwagon too soon. Then they end up looking like a guy in a hula hoop."

"Hmpf," said Krupp. "Tell me. What do you think these guys with the new look would do if they found out about . . . " Then he stopped. He gestured to Briggs. "His troubles."

Mashita and Krupp were silent. They finished their drinks. Krupp and Mashita both sat there for a minute.

"You didn't answer," said Krupp.

"What's to say?" said Mashita. He shrugged. "We'd be finished."

Krupp nodded.

"If we keep our mouths shut, if we hang together, maybe we can get through this in one piece," said Mashita. His voice had a pleading quality that Briggs had never heard before.

"Yeah. One piece," said Krupp.

He looked at Mashita.

"What it boils down to is this. To do anything about his"—Krupp tipped his empty glass at Briggs—"troubles, we've got to rat on ourselves." He put his hand to the collar of his shirt. "This is no time to rat yourself out."

Mashita wiped his forehead again. Then he licked his lips.

"That's right," said Mashita.

Krupp rubbed his chin and looked toward the door.

"Have either of you heard anything about the markets today?" he said.

"Yeah," said Mashita.

"And?" said Krupp.

"It's down some more," said Mashita. "A percent."

"Do you think it's going to get any worse?" said Krupp.

"I don't know," said Mashita. "My advisers tell me it's a standard correction."

"Yeah? Well, if this gets any worse, I'm going to face a margin call," said Krupp. "Is that a standard correction? Why the fuck isn't someone doing something?"

"Like what?" said Mashita.

"Guarantees of liquidity," said Krupp. "Credit, for Christ's sake. What the fuck is keeping them from doing something? Someone should get on the phone to Wendell Blaine and tell him to get off his ass."

Krupp stopped and sat there, looking at his hands.

"Well, we've got other fish to fry," he said, glancing up at Mashita. Then he stood up. Mashita did too.

"Keep your nose clean," said Krupp to Briggs. "I'll be in touch."

They didn't say good-bye or good night or anything. They just turned and went down the bar, one polite and graceful and scared, the other disordered and swaggering, furious, and then they disappeared into the red and yellow gleam that came off the damp streets.

Briggs went out too, and walked along the river. The water was very dark, like dirty oil, and the only thing lively about it was the smear of lights from the buildings on the other side: banks, insurance companies, some very expensive stores, all of them seeming to exist in a haze of lights. Briggs kept walking. He went along, seeing a dark snag in the water, which was the crown of a tree that had the shape of antlers. What he thought was, Krupp didn't say "we'll be in touch," but "I'll be in touch." That was the giveaway. Mashita was going to be sold down the river. That would leave just the two of them, Krupp and Briggs. He walked along, hands in his pockets.

CHAPTER 15

Midnight, April 16, 2029

BLAINE SAT up at night, a phone on the table next to him, and when he looked at it, the clear, plastic instrument appeared like all the malignant and contrary things that defied him and that he didn't understand. Why, in God's name, wouldn't it ring? Kay said she would call, and now he was left like this. He rubbed a hand over his cheeks, feeling the stubble on his face, which just reminded him of how he was getting older. If he had any sense at all, he would realize that this was his last chance, and if he wasn't smart enough to take it, why, then he deserved what he would get. And what, thought Blaine as he looked into the shadows of his study, was that? More of this silence. He stood with his head cocked, listening to it, and it seemed to him to have a hissing quality, as though he could hear the searing, frying quality of his isolation and his loneliness. The more he heard this background noise, or imagined that it was a noise, the more he found himself staring at the phone. He told himself he wasn't panicky. Not really.

He recalled Kay's warmth when she had taken off some of her clothes and had him lie down with her. Now, as he stood in his library, like some ridiculous imitation of the man he used to be, he imagined that this heat had some other quality, a mellowness or soothing quality. It was like hot perfume. Not just temperature, but something else, too. He thought that he should have kissed her when he had the chance, touched her, put his hand against her back or side, pulled her against him. But she had been so certain about wanting to rest. And what did Blaine know about women? Had she wanted him to be more direct, more persuasive? Maybe he had failed with her, too.

He sat down and stared into the distance, and when he answered the phone and heard her voice, the sensation of it changed the room completely: the silence vanished, not just the lack of noise, but the bleak implications of it.

"Hi," she said. "It's me."

"Kay," he said. "My God. Where are you?"

"Out for a walk," she said. "I'm not waking you up, am I?"

He shook his head.

"No," he said. "Where are you?"

"Not far," she said. "At the telephone at the end of the street. Would you like to meet me?"

"Yes," he said. "Wait. I'll be there."

He was wearing his slippers, and as he kicked them off, he thought what a fuddy-duddy man he had become, sitting in his library with his slippers on his ugly feet. How could he have let this happen? As he pulled on his shoes, forgetting his socks, her voice seemed to linger in his ear like the buzz of an insect on a summer day. And as he waited for the elevator, not even bothering to take his coat, he realized the difference between the time he had been waiting for her and now: one was a matter of being only partially alive and the other was a vitality that can only be experienced by a man who has lived for a long time and been disappointed.

She was waiting at the end of the street, her hands in the pockets of her trench coat. Beyond her was a small park in which a path wound through some grass and trees, the benches along it sitting in pools of luminescence from the street lamps that were spaced every fifty feet. Blaine was shivering when he came up to her.

"Hi," she said. She looked away. "I've been thinking about you."

"Oh, Kay, me too," he said.

"I want to tell you something," she said.

"What?" said Blaine.

"Come into the park," she said. "Let's walk together. Here. Let me take your arm."

Blaine instantly felt the warmth of her as she slipped her hand under his arm and pulled him against her. The scent of her hair rose toward him. Blaine closed his eyes.

"You're cold," she said.

"Not anymore," he said. "I'm fine."

They walked along. She put her head against his shoulder.

"I keep thinking about you," she said. "About the touch of you against my skin. I can hardly sleep. But that's just desire. There's more than that at stake here."

"Yes," said Blaine. "I know."

"It's that I don't feel quite myself anymore," she said, looking up at him. "Do you know what I mean?"

"I do," said Blaine. "I can't sleep. I can't think."

"How can that be?" she said.

"I don't know," said Blaine.

"But I want you to know you've got me, that is, if you want me," she said.

He started shivering again.

"Here," she said. "Let's sit down. I'm so tired, just thinking about it."

They sat on the park bench, and she leaned against him. She moved her head from side to side, as though trying to find a way to get closer. In front of them, the fog drifted by in long shreds of mist, not so much ominous as vaguely false, like something you might see in a theater. Kay put her fingers inside the front of his shirt and ran them along his chest. The tips of them were warm and gentle. She reached up and kissed him on the cheek, the neck.

"You see," she said. "It's not just desire, although there is plenty of that. I am thinking of dropping everything, of letting go. Of coming to you just the way I am or the way I always wanted to be. So, it is not just a matter of climbing into your bed. I just want to be certain of you. All right?"

"Yes," he said.

"And you will do the same?" she said. "You will make the same commitment?"

"I've already made it," he said. "I can't think of anything else."

"I just wanted to make sure," she said.

Her fingers worked further down, along his stomach.

"So, you will wait a little longer?" she said.

"Yes," he said.

She put her lips against his ear and spoke in warm, hot puffs. "You won't regret it. Oh, I can promise you that."

"Would you like to come home now?" he said.

"Yes," she said. "I'm dying to come. I can't think of anything else. But, I just wanted to be sure I wasn't going to be lost, or used, or that you were insincere."

"Oh, no," said Blaine. "No."

She nodded.

"All right," she said. "Let's sit here for a minute. Then I'll walk up the block with you and say good night. But soon, I'll bring my things. I'll bring them to your apartment. Is that all right?"

"Of course," said Blaine.

"And you won't change your mind?" she said. "You won't discard me when I have given everything?"

"No," said Blaine.

"I've been such a fool," she said. "How could I have wasted so much time?"

"I know," said Blaine. "I couldn't see it until now."

CHAPTER 16

April 17, 2029

BRIGGS RECOGNIZED the handwriting immediately, and when he opened the envelope he found the promotional gimmick. It was pink and green, like leaves in springtime, and the touch of it suggested the succulent texture of new growth. The thing was supposed to be a key chain, and it looked like ordinary promotional junk. The come-on was that you could take it to a gaming parlor, and, without charge, you could have a look around in the world of the game that was being promoted. If you wanted to play, or to investigate further, you could get a discount for the first couple of sessions.

Briggs stood in the street in front of the gaming parlor with the promotional gimmick in his hand, and as he looked around, he thought, *Will I be able to resist her?*

A ship's bell hung just inside the door, and it gave the place a little atmosphere, as though this were a gentleman's club from decades ago.

"Can I help you?" said the attendant at the door.

"I'd like to try this out," said Briggs.

He held up the matchbook-sized object.

"Over there," said the attendant.

He pointed at one of the booths near the front of the parlor.

"A lot of people like it," he said.

An introductory look at a game only used a cuff, like the ones that were used to take blood pressure. Briggs put the key into a slot, and then his arm into the cuff. It grasped him with a firmness that surprised him; its speed and strength suggested a trap being sprung. The registration began, once and then again, the cool chill on his arm occurring twice, as though the machine were trying to be sure about something. He pulled the curtain of the cubicle shut, and then lay back on the sofa and closed his eyes.

It was like falling asleep. But as he relaxed, the sensation grew, not like a dream, but like waking up. He heard a man swearing in the main room, but the sound diminished. He breathed deeply. The chill washed over his arm.

Pacifica XII took place on an island in the south seas. He guessed it was one of the extreme adventure series and that it would involve the basics: typhoons, natives who were cannibals, the Robinson Crusoe routine, sharks in the water, pirates, native women, and so on. The beach appeared to him as a long stretch of sand, and the edge of it, where the waves washed up and slipped away, looked like a mirrored plane, although in the distance the gray mirror disappeared in the shimmer of heat, the wet sheen of it blending perfectly with the liquid and mercury-like mirage. He could see, in this fluid heat, the reflection of someone, the gentle swaying of hips matching the undulation of the heat. Who-ever it was appeared to be waist-deep in the heat, and as Briggs stood there, his hand over his brow, the image went across the sand and into the jungle. He turned that way too.

The jungle was like a wall of leaves, and the shadows underneath them appeared in shades of green on green. He saw little stars in the shade, which he supposed was an aftereffect of the bright light on the beach. The sand squeaked under his feet as he hurried into the green shade, where orchids hung in scarlet and white chains, the petals open and wet. Above him a parrot preened, its blue and red feathers opening like a hand of cards. The jungle buzzed around him, a million insects at work. A moth with pink wings hung on a trunk, and some red ants made a chain into the heart of a flower, which was filled with a sweet fluid. It was cool here, out of the sun, as refreshing as walking into a florist's cold chest. Butterflies floated here and there like blue checks. Water formed bright pendants, the color of mercury, as it dripped.

Kay stood behind a screen of ferns, the fronds of which opened like a fan. Behind her a cascade of orchids hung from the vegetation, the ver-milion petals fitting together like the scales in an armored suit. Briggs reached out to push the fronds aside, like green jalousies, but they wouldn't budge until she stepped back.

"This way," she said.

He stepped into the place where she had stood. The light on the floor of the jungle lay like scattered pieces of a green and gold jigsaw puzzle. The light flickered over her back and head as she went, although after she had gone a few steps she stopped.

"What are these flowers?" she asked. "Are they orchids? *Phalaenopsis?* Is that the variety?"

"What?" he said.

"Sweet Memory. Isn't that *Deventeriana X violacea?* A hybrid."

"Yes. I think that's the variety," he said.

"You didn't think I knew that, did you?" she said.

He swallowed.

"No," he said.

He looked around. The shades of green, one on top of another, seemed to pile up with an endless sense of variety. And depth. He swallowed. The leaves were shiny, firm, and when he tried to push them away to touch her, he found that he couldn't. When his finger was just a fraction of an inch away, it stopped: he guessed this was the limit of the promotion. He knew one thing for sure: he had lost control.

"Don't look so surprised," she said.

"How did you know that?" he said.

"Oh," she said. "I know you. It's why I love you so. You are like an open book to me."

He looked right at her.

"For instance," she said. "Who are you worried about?"

"A man," said Briggs.

"What's his name?" she said.

"Krupp," he said. "He works at Galapagos. He's someone to worry about."

She shrugged.

"You want me to take care of the problem?" she said. "I'm good at that kind of thing."

She smiled.

"Kay," he said. "Look . . . "

"Darling," she said. "Do you think I could stand by while someone did something to you?"

"Kay," he said.

"The heat is so brutal," she said. "Come over here."

She went through the leaves, the petals of the orchids breaking away and falling in a mass, like butterflies all landing at the same moment. The trees rose above her hundreds of feet, and at their bottom the trunks had enormous supports, like rocket fins, to keep them upright. Parrots preened and screeched.

The house she went into had a thatched roof and a veranda and it had been built at the edge of a small clearing. The interior shade was a brownish green. In the main room he saw a bed with mosquito netting, which she pushed aside and climbed under. She was wearing Spandex shorts and a T-shirt.

She put her head on a pillow and pulled the netting shut. He sat next to her and looked through the sheer netting at the shape of the veins in her skin, the angle of her hip as she tried to get comfortable. Outside, in the jungle, he heard the buzzing of the insects. From time to time a bird screeched, not plaintive so much as imploring, as though its voice weren't responding to fear, but to desire.

She put her hand to her head.

"I've wanted to see you," she said. "I even took a chance coming to your apartment. That was stupid."

"Yes," he said. "I knew you had been there, though."

"How did you know?" she said.

"I could tell," he said.

He put his hand against the sheer netting, but he couldn't get any closer.

"Has anyone around you gotten sick?" said Briggs.

She looked at him through the netting.

"No," she said.

"Where are you staying?"

"Come on. Don't be that way," she said. "You've got to trust me. That's all I'm asking for. Is that such a big thing?"

He went on looking at her. What was hidden in that glance, in that flirtatious smile?

"I just need a little time," she said.

"What's it for?" he said.

"Oh, I've got a little chore to do," she said.

"Like what?" he said.

"Wouldn't you like to know?" she said, turning a full, pink-lipped smile on him. Then she put her lips against the netting, the threads crossing them in squares. "Put your lips close," she said.

"Look," he said.

"No," she said. "Trust me. When I'm done, I'll find you. Isn't that enough? Do you think a promise from me is worthless?"

In the air around them, a mosquito flew through a series of figure-eights. It made a slight buzzing too. The lazy and repeated pattern the insect described almost put Briggs to sleep, and when he lowered his eyes he found that she was looking into them.

"Well?" she said. "Do you think I don't keep my word?"

"That's what I'm afraid of," he said. "I don't know what you're planning, what you are thinking of, what you want . . . "

"Now you are asking me to be indiscreet, too," she said. "Oh, I wouldn't do that. Put your ear against the netting here. Right there . . . I want to tell you what I have been dreaming of." She whispered, the words coming through the netting in small puffs. "And you didn't think I could bitch you up, did you?"

"What is the chore?" he said.

Through the netting he saw her skin flush, the anger coming over her with a sudden, pink tint.

She sat up and put her mouth against the netting. "You know what I think? Bravery has a practical benefit," she said. "It keeps you from dying like some sniveling coward. See?"

Briggs waited, watching her.

She sighed and looked around. Just like that, the anger vanished. She kept her eyes on his as she spoke. What wouldn't she do to make sure he cared for her in the same way she cared for him? It wasn't physical so much as a way of finding access to how they both felt: what she wanted was a trance, a buzzing communion that revealed how much they were perfect for one another. As she spoke the same words over and over, they were like liturgical phrases. Briggs could almost see a figure swaying back and forth in the incense smoke and golden highlights of a church or shrine, the words repeated until their meaning had been absorbed in the hypnosis of faith. That is how she felt about him. Did he understand?

She pulled off her T-shirt, the muscles along her stomach contracting as she did so. The Spandex of her shorts made a little tearing sound as she pulled them off.

"It's so hot," she said.

She put a pillow under her head.

"Will you take me out for ice cream?" she said. "I want to go out in the heat of the afternoon and eat vanilla ice cream."

"All right," he said. "Let's make a date."

She smiled.

"Oh," she said. "You think you are clever, don't you?" She smiled. "I'll contact you."

"Kay," he said. "I'll worry about Krupp. Leave him to me."

She winked.

"Are you going to let me love you or not?" she said.

The parrots squawked outside, and in the distance he heard the sound of the surf, the susurrus of it adding to the languid nature of the heat and the afternoon.

Kay turned on her side and slept. He sat next to the netting and watched the expansion of her ribs, the way the muscles stretched over them, the line of small bones that ran down the middle of her back, the shape of one hip, tilted, as she lay on the thin, tropical mattress. She murmured in her sleep, and rolled over, one arm falling languidly over her head. Outside, in the sunlight, bits of insects, nothing more than golden filaments, moved through the air.

He went through the decisions he had made that had brought him to this moment, each one small and seemingly minor, but all of them adding up, the calculus of them leaving him with the sense of being able to see who and what he really was. In the distance, when he looked out the door and across the veranda, he saw a rainbow as the sunlight shone through the vapor that came from a wave breaking over the reef. How could he do the right thing?

"My darling," she said, waking up now, her voice sleepy.

My darling . . .

In that same sleepy voice, she said, "You know I keep thinking about having a child. But, Briggs, would you protect the child?"

"Kay," he said. "That's a long way off . . . "

"Is it?" she said. "Well. Tell me. Theoretically speaking?"

"What do you think?" he said.

"I have my hopes," she said. "That you won't fail me."

She got up from the bed and pulled on her shorts and shirt and went out, into the veranda, and when she turned, all that was left was the rainbow over the reef. She vanished into the flowers and the shade, the shapes of the parrot's feathers opening and closing.

The weave of the mosquito netting interfered with itself where it hung in folds around the bed. After a while he stood up, the tropical flooring giving under his feet. Then he went down the steps and into the shade where the parrots preened their head feathers, their black beaks searching along a wing for a spot that itched. Briggs walked through the jungle and emerged onto the light and heat of the beach. Then he opened his eyes and heard the voices in the gaming parlor, angry and insistent, despairing or triumphant.

"How did you like it?" asked an attendant.

"It was all right," said Briggs.

"Oh, it was better than that," said the attendant. "You'll be back. I can always tell. This one is going to be a hit."

"I don't know," said Briggs. "It depends."

BOOK

THE FIRST names started to appear on the walls. They were written in the New Wave script, which was wavy, the letters drifting into each other, and done in such a way as to suggest three dimensions. Something like subway graffiti, but more intricate, harder to do just right. Of course, a lot of people tried to settle old scores by just putting names on the wall, but they couldn't get the script right. The lame or the uncool tried, but it never looked right. You could tell they weren't authentic.

Briggs stood in front of a wall. The script looked right.

Once your name was up, you could start waiting for the piss and fishy odor of a Mungo Man, who reached out for you in the hallway of your building, the cold touch of his fingers, the stink of his breath all showing that, as far as the New Wave was concerned, you had been found wanting. Were your clothes right? Your slang? Or were you out-of-date and speaking the Language of the Dead? One night you smelled the fishy odor and felt the surprising bump, just like being punched, but that's the way the ice pick felt. After that, they went through your apartment for what was left.

This is why a sniff of disdain about one's style was so ominous: you could be on the way out. The New Waves were cool, and who didn't want to be cool? Of course, when one came, it was used to get rid of people who were in the way.

Briggs recognized two of the names. One was an impossibly dowdy woman who worked at Galapagos. She left used Kleenex around, and her blouses had sweat stains on them. She picked her teeth with a matchbook.

But Briggs had always liked her. She did her work and never said anything stupid. Briggs put his head against the wall. Mashita was the other name.

That leaves just the two of us, me and Krupp, he thought.

Everything was quiet, but then he heard a shuffling as a man came along on the pavement. The footfalls seemed erratic, as though someone who kept a dog to beat was dragging the thing along the pavement. Then the Mungo Man stooped and looked up at the script on the wall. He wore a gray coat that, even in the darkness, had the sheen of a fly. He took a stump of pencil and a piece of brown paper out of his pocket, spreading the paper on the wall. Then the Mungo Man looked up, moving his lips as he read the names. The flylike sheen on his coat was exotic, like a peacock feather, and yet deadly too, as though the color were associated with a serious medical condition. Gangrene, for instance. The man smelled of sweat, food, piss. He wrote slowly, checking the names, the work done one letter at a time with the cadence of a grave digger who has learned that the way to get through the work is with a steady, deceptively slow pace. The Mungo Man's eyes went back and forth, between the paper and the wall, and then he turned and looked at Briggs.

"Your name here?" said the Mungo Man.

"No," said Briggs.

"Sure?" said the Mungo Man.

"Yes," said Briggs.

"Then what are you hanging around for?" said the Mungo Man. He stepped closer to Briggs.

"There's no law against standing here," said Briggs.

"You're going to talk to me about law?" said the Mungo Man. "Say, what's your name?"

"That's all right," said Briggs.

The Mungo Man took a step closer, his nose almost up to Briggs's. The brown paper made a crinkling sound as it was folded up and stuck in a pocket of the man's coat. The Mungo Man nodded to himself, then he stood back, glanced once at the enormous, stylish script on the wall. The mist seemed to be absolutely still, fish-colored, and it smelled of the ocean. The Mungo Man turned and walked away, his gait irregular but still having purpose. He jerked his gimpy leg, grunted at the effort, and disappeared into the mist.

| *April 19, 2029*

BRIGGS TUGGED at the button on his coat that was about to fall off. He pulled at it just hard enough to feel that it was loose, but not hard enough to break the thread. He twisted it one way and then the other while he scrolled through the results of the tests he had ordered for Kay's fluid. The lists of proteins went from the bottom of the monitor to the top, but he didn't have a diagram of the shape of each one, and it was this architecture that determined the practical impact a protein would have. In the midst of it, in a bright orange band, he saw one that was labeled PATHOGEN. He stopped, highlighted the protein that had set off the alarm, and asked for a library search on it. It took a minute or two, but then he understood why so much time had been used: the library had no papers, no information at all. It was something new. He asked for clinical tests with animal models. He got another prompt that said, INSUFFICIENT PARAMETERS. ENTER PROTEIN INFORMATION. He ripped the button off and sat there with the small, useless thing in his hand. A couple of black threads stuck out of his jacket where the button had been, and he picked at them, hoping that this way he could disguise the fact that the button was gone.

A materials salesman came in, smoking a cigar and looking around, trying to figure out just what kind of budget Briggs had to work with. The salesman, whose name was White, glanced at the button in Briggs's hand, then at the shelves in the office, most of them filled with broken equipment. He sighed. White's shirt was an old-fashioned one with pointed collars.

"You're new here, aren't you?" said White.

"Yes," said Briggs.

"I hate it when that happens," said White. "When I lose a button."

Briggs put it in his pocket.

"I'll sew it on tonight," Briggs said.

White didn't look convinced, but he nodded as though that was the right thing to do. He glanced around again and said, "You know, I figure you in for ten percent of the order."

"What?" said Briggs.

Briggs turned around and saw that the word PATHOGEN was still there in bright orange. Then he closed it up. White was rolling his shoulder as though he had a cramp in his neck.

"Your order," said White. "You're going to need materials."

"Oh," said Briggs. "Sure. Materials. I get a lot of stuff from a discount house."

White looked as though he had eaten something that didn't agree with him.

"A discount house doesn't figure you in for ten percent," said White. "Do you see what I'm saying?"

White said he could get Briggs good polymers and he would make sure they arrived when they were needed, and of course he could make sure there wasn't any mismatching of colors, which happened with the cheap discount places, always mixing different batches, taking just the dregs of what was left over and making it seem that it was all one batch. It wasn't. Sometimes it was three. That's why it was discounted.

"You're offering me a kickback," said Briggs. "Is that it?"

White looked a little sour.

"I didn't say kickback," said White. "I just said ten percent of the deal. It isn't like it comes out of my pocket. And it doesn't come out of yours. So who gives a shit? You just increase the bill by ten percent, and then we split it. What could be better?"

Briggs reached into his pocket and picked up the button again and fingered it while he thought about the orange band that had run through the monitor, rising like a spirit released from the depths. The same color as a Halloween pumpkin.

White said that his competitors mixed batches of texture too, and this caused problems you wouldn't believe. His expression was that of a man who had seen real trouble.

"I can imagine," said Briggs. He stared at the wall where someone had written, "Please, O Lord, in thy mercy . . . " Briggs squeezed the button.

White said, "All right. Fifteen percent. That's as high as I can go. See? That's seven and a half for you and seven and a half for me. It's like free money. If the orders go up, why, great. I use my share to keep a little place downtown . . . "

"I'm sorry," said Briggs. "What did you say?"

"If that's the way you want to be," said White. He shrugged. "No skin off my nose."

White stood and picked up his case, zipped it up, hiked up his pants. Then he stood at the door.

"All right," said White. "Ten for you and five for me. Now I can't do better than that. You know that."

White looked around to see if anyone was listening.

"I mean, you don't want me to take less than that, do you, for Christ's sake?" said White. He began to flush a little.

Briggs looked down at the button again.

"Maybe we can work it out," said Briggs.

"Yeah," said White. He was still insulted. "Like how?"

"Can you get me antibiotics?" said Briggs.

"What do you need stuff like that for?" said White. "In a junk outfit like this? Come on. Who are you kidding?"

His eyes flitted around the room, trying to figure out what to do.

"I've got another project," said Briggs.

"Yeah?" said White.

Briggs nodded.

"In a place like this?" said White. He looked around again, as though he were seeing it all through the haze of a fever. He blinked.

"I'll need stuff for all stains. Red, purple, yellow. The works."

"Sure," said White. "I could do that. Fifty-fifty split for the fifteen-percent increase. Right?"

"Okay," said Briggs.

"Say, what are you working on out here?" said White. "This isn't some dummy outfit, is it? You didn't come out here to do something you want a little privacy for, did you? Because if that's the way it is, you can count on me."

Briggs stared at the scrawled line on the wall. *Mercy.* Then he looked back at White.

"See what I'm telling you?" said White. "Don't go out to Dow or Borg or any of those big outfits. I can do just as well. With a good order, I can play with the big boys."

"I'll remember," said Briggs. "I'll need all stains. Can you get them?"

"Don't be silly," said White. "I can get almost anything. Didn't I just say you could count on me?" He glanced around the office again with a commercial disbelief, and then back at Briggs. "Say, you don't look so good. Have you got a fever?"

"No," said Briggs. *Not yet.*

"Well, there's something always going around," said White. "You got to eat right. You got to lose weight. I got to lose thirty pounds. I want to be light on my feet."

White put his hands in the small of his back, and from somewhere in his body Briggs heard a small, definite crack. Then White put his cigar in his mouth and blew out little puffs of smoke. He sighed. Then he made his way down the hall, mumbling to himself, the keys and change in his pocket jingling as he hitched up his pants and sighed again. Briggs looked at the smoke that hung in malignant puffs, like exhaust from an engine that was burning oil. He took out the button and fingered it. He looked at the phrase on the wall, and then, as though it were too painful to read, he glanced around the room filled with broken equipment. The accumulation of things that no longer worked added a muted presence to the room. It was keenly silent, but filled with a minor dread that could be felt in every junkyard in the world.

FROM THE front, the hotel's fire escapes resembled a series of enormous black Z's, one on top of another. Kay and Jack stood underneath them and looked up the street, where some buildings made a broken-toothed clutter against the sky. Kay waited for a moment, testing the wind, since she knew that the neighborhood had two contradictory aspects. It was like a man who was nice when sober, but nasty at night when he was drunk, although there was a peaceful, even angelic period of transition. And when Kay and Jack came out of the hotel, it was the angelic hour of the afternoon when such a man went into a bar where a waiter, with a fatigued wariness, put down the man's first diamond-clear martini.

"You know, I'd like to have a little fun," Jack said.

"Okay," she said. "What do you want to do?"

He blushed. Then he looked down the street. On the front of one of the buildings he saw a marquee that said, ICE SKATING. FREE SKATE EVERY AFTERNOON. Jack gestured toward the sign. "I'd like to go down there."

"All right," she said.

They started walking, and as they went, she said, "Are you carrying it?"

"Carrying what?" he said.

"Don't be cute," she said.

She reached over and touched his jacket pocket. The pistol was there.

"You can never tell," said Jack. "Everything is fine now, but wait until dark."

The lobby of the rink was like a motion picture theater, and they bought their tickets from a booth. Inside, they heard the music that the rink played, old songs and waltzes. A sign said, RENTALS INSIDE. Beyond it they saw the ice, a white oval, opalescent and obviously cold under the theatrical lights. A dozen skaters went around and around, looking as though they were dressed in cloaks torn from a black flag. One skater had both his arms out as he tried to keep his balance. The music was from a long time ago, and it gave the place a retro feeling.

The counter where they rented skates was covered with green linoleum that had been worn down to a white around the edges. Jack ran his finger over it, trying to guess how old it was, perhaps a hundred years, maybe more. They both rented a pair of skates and went over to a line of chairs to put them on. Kay giggled when she stood up. Jack laughed too.

"You walk like a penguin," he said.

"Oh yeah? Well, what do you think you look like, Mr. Big-Time Skater?" she said.

They managed to get out to the ice. Kay pushed off and began to skate, putting her weight on one blade and then the other. Jack caught up with her and took her hand. They went around together, and then Jack said, "Watch." He turned on his skates and started going backwards, right next to her. She laughed and said, "Oh, Jack. I didn't think you could do that."

"Here," he said.

He put out his hands and invited her to dance, old-style dancing like one saw in movies. What did they call it? Ballroom dancing. She kept her eyes on his and then reached out, putting one hand on his shoulder and taking the other hand. The sound system played a waltz, and they went around, Jack looking into her eyes every now and then, leading her, turning her from time to time. They came to a stop in a spray of ice shavings.

"Come on," he said. "You aren't going to stop now, are you?"

They waited at the side of the rink for more music. Kay's breath came in heaves and she leaned back, her cheeks red with the cold, her eyes bright. One of her skates made a chipping sound as she tapped in time to the music.

"Just let me catch my breath," she said.

On the other side of the ice, a woman came out through the door in the waist-high enclosure of the rink. She wore a white short skirt, and a white blouse, white tights, and white skates. The woman shoved off, her hips moving with the thrust of skating, the blades flashing as she went around in time to the music. Jack watched.

"I'm going to take a turn while you rest," he said. "Do you mind?"

"No," she said.

She suddenly felt the coldness of the room penetrate the heat of the skating. No, she didn't mind. Not really. She wanted him to have a good time. Mostly all he did was sit around the hotel or go to practice with her. Her sense of loneliness came over her with a sudden heaviness. "No," she said. "Go on. Have a good time."

"Are you sure?" he said.

"Yes," she said. She tried to smile. "Go on. I'll watch for a moment."

She leaned back against the rail. Jack went out, seeming to slide around the rink, his hands clasped behind his back, his skates swinging out in short, stylish strokes. He gained on the woman in the white skirt, who glanced over her shoulder once and smiled. She went a little faster, putting her weight into it now, and yet Jack came up beside her, with a speed that was hardly imaginable. They went along, the skates silent on the ice. The music changed. Kay could almost recognize it: something from a previous age, but still having a sweetness to it that she was ashamed she responded to, and as she did, that sense of surprised loneliness came over her again. Well, she didn't want Jack to stop. She guessed. Jack reached over and took the woman's arms and then they went around together, blades of the skates flashing together. Jack bent closer and whispered something and the woman laughed, and when he spoke again she put her fingers to her mouth, pleasantly shocked. They went on skating with each other. The woman's cheeks were red now, her eyes turning every now and then to Jack, as though she couldn't believe her good luck.

Kay guessed she felt something like homesickness. She realized that another human being could give her a sense of warmth, and not just in the moment, but deeper than that, as though her existence could be hotter, lighter. In fact, she felt being alone as lack of heat, as though her cold toes, the sting on her cheeks, were the manifestation of separation. Why had Briggs done this to her, left her on the ice, facing such a vista? Cold, harshly lighted, indifferent. What could she do about being made to exist like this, isolated, frozen, as though this place were the expression of the emotional landscape she had been condemned to?

On the ice now were some other people, men mostly, who were wearing shirts with round collars and pants that were tight at the ankle. As the men skated, they kept coming closer to Kay, one of them glancing over his shoulder at her. He said to one of his pals, "Hey, look at that, will you?"

"Oh yeah," he said. "All alone."

"Not for long," said one of the others.

Kay shoved off, back onto the ice. Up ahead, in the swirl of skaters, in the rush of them, she lost sight of Jack and the woman. She guessed it would be all right. She went around once, listening to the music. She turned around on her skates, went backwards, and saw the men in the tight pants and white shirts.

"Say," said one of them to Kay, "how come I haven't seen you around?"

Kay went on skating.

"It's my first time," she said.

"Oh, the first time. Say," he said to the others. "Her first time. Well. Isn't that something?"

The others couldn't think of anything to say, so they just kept on skating on the ice, like a dark squadron.

"You know there's a first-time tax," said the one who had spoken. He turned to the others. "Isn't that right?"

"Oh yes. The first time. The tax," said one of the ones who skated in a group. The others just went along grimly, blinking into the wind. She wished they would say something, anything, which was better than dumb and stupid silence.

"I'm just trying to have a good time," said Kay. "All right?"

"Well, that's what I mean about the tax," said the first. "Say, my name is Freddy. What's yours?"

"Kay," she said.

"Isn't that nice," he said. "Kay."

He said it as though he was trying it on for size.

"Well, Kay, let me tell you about the tax," he said.

"That's okay," she said.

"I'm the tax collector and you've got to give me a kiss," he said. "See, we go back under the stands there and you give me a kiss."

Kay went over the ice. Why had they come here, anyway? She looked up ahead, but Jack wasn't there. More people had come onto the ice, and the accumulation of them all moving, some of them falling down, contributed to Kay's sense of disorientation, which now came to her not just with the sense of being alone or abandoned, but with a general apprehension. She was in the wrong place and she knew it.

"Just one," said Freddy.

He pointed.

"Over there," he said. "At the end of the grandstand. See? Right there under the speaker."

"You can't hear nothing because of the music," said one of them from the pack. "It's noisy, but it's kind of private for all that."

Kay started counting. One, two, three, four, five . . . Then she looked up ahead, but didn't see Jack. Now his absence seemed like a betrayal of some kind, although she knew that this wasn't his fault. He was just trying to flirt a little with that pretty woman, but now she wished he hadn't. She wanted to go back to the hotel. Tomorrow she'd have to go to practice again.

"Over there, see?" said Freddy.

The others, the ones behind him, spread out a little, and as she went one way they herded her like sheepdogs, pushing her toward the door of the rink closest to the grandstand. As they went toward it the music seemed louder, since they were getting closer to the speaker. The cone of it had a black and shiny membrane.

"Don't you like my shirt?" Freddy said.

"Sure," said Kay. She looked around at the others. They didn't smile, didn't smirk, didn't do anything but force her in the direction she didn't want to go.

"Well, I'm glad you like it," he said. "That shows you have good sense."

"It's a pretty cool shirt," said one of the young men at the back of the pack.

"You got to be cunning," said Freddy. "Now, that is the first thing you've got to remember. Like a wolf."

One of the men put back his head and yowled, and the others laughed now. Then they yowled, too. They all came up to the door of the rink, and the inertia of their speed helped them jump over the small lip there onto a rubber mat beyond it. The mat was like a piece of licorice the size of a flag.

"Just one kiss," said Freddy. "That's all. Come on."

The others stood there, blank-faced.

"Only Freddy will have one," they said. "See?"

"Sure," said another. "Just one. That's all."

They moved between her and the ice, but it was so bright that the men seemed like shadows in front of it. She had been trained for this, but that sense of weighted isolation got in the way. She felt her need, even her hopes, as nothing more than fatigue. She even thought for a moment of whether she should just go and give the jackass a kiss and be done with it. Who cared? But she knew it wasn't going to be taken care of that easily. She looked at their necks, at the vulnerable spot.

"So," said Jack, as he stepped over the lip of the door. He was taller than the others. "I see you made some friends."

"They aren't friends," said Kay.

"No?" said Jack. "Then what are they doing here?"

"Who are you?" said Freddy.

"You'll get out of here if you know what's good for you," said another.

"Look at his shirt," said one.

"What's wrong with my shirt?" said Jack.

The others just smiled. The music was very loud as they stood underneath the speaker. The black material of it looked like the ocean under moonlight.

"We're just going to take Kay back in here for a minute," they said.

"Oh yeah?" said Jack.

"They have a tax or something," said Kay. "A kiss."

"Just to get things started," said Freddy.

"A kiss?" said Jack.

"That's right," said Freddy.

"Come back with me," said Jack. "I want to tell you something. Back in here. Under the bleachers."

The four men in the tight pants stood on their skates, looking at each other.

"Okay," said Freddy. "Let's go back in there."

The woman in the white skirt came by, and as she did, she glanced over at Jack. She smiled and waved. Her arm rose and the hand came up and wagged from side to side, the entire gesture having about it an air of a pretty girl on the deck of a sailboat, waving to a friend. It was as though every summer, every warm day and blue sky, every bit of youth and cheerfulness and sweet desire came down to this open hand and the smile of those vermilion lips against the ice.

The young woman reached into her pocket and brought out a black band, which had a small piece of metal attached to it. She reached up and put the band on, the velvet strap making her neck seem longer, whiter. Then she skated off. She made the first turn and went along the far side of the rink, her speed increasing, as though she just wanted to come back again, so she could wave at Jack. And so he would see her velvet strap, which made her neck look so long and white. She seemed to know how cheerful and seductive her wave was. But as she came to the end of the straight part of the rink, Kay strained to see what it was on the black velvet ribbon. Even from a distance, Kay saw that it was made of silver, a pendant of some kind, like a drop. She heard the sound of it, too. She was reminded of Russia, of something specific: the sound of a troika, of three horses, with bells on them, pulling a sleigh through the snow. She had never seen this, and yet it seemed to be right there as though she had: the horses blowing plumes of steam, the harness black and brutal as it went across the horses' backs, the lines of bells on the harness, silver and tinkling in the snow. It announced the horses' arrival, the sound carrying so perfectly on the subzero air. Kay stared at the young woman, and in the flash of the blades of the skaters, in the clutter of their movement through the spray of ice, she heard the bell, still diminutive, but all the more piercing for that. Jack turned to listen.

"Jack," she said.

"What?" he said. His voice was matter-of-fact.

"Jack," she said. "Let's get out of here."

"No," said Jack. "Wait."

Overhead the speaker played "Summertime, when the living is easy . . ." The young woman came along this side now, smiling, shaking her curly hair, her neck up, the bell tinkling. She waved again, the quick movement of it just like before: sunny days, sails, water, a blue lake, puffs of white clouds . . .

Freddy and the others went first, and Jack followed.

"Oh, Jack," Kay said. "Please listen . . . "

"Later," he said. "I've got business."

He turned and went back into the shadows under the bleachers. The dark clothes of the men were absorbed there, and their awkward locomotion as they walked on skates only added to the clutter of the space under the stands, where the cross supports made of black wood could barely be seen in the shadows. The men receded into this black, angular conglomeration, awkwardly to be sure, like men in black who walked on frozen feet. The music got louder. Kay went around to the front, so she could see under the seats, but the space there was impenetrable, nothing more than darkness on darkness. She heard a scuffle, and one short cry, and some other sounds, clunky, heavy ones, like sacks of wheat being dropped from a loading platform onto the ground. She sat down. How did she ever get to be so tired, and yet so alert to her own state of mind?

The woman in the white dress passed by, her legs pink in the tights, her hips moving under the short skirt, her eyes flashing in the lights over the ice. Kay wanted to be like that: just skating along, flirting with someone, without a care. The woman came around, close to the rail, her eyes searching Jack out. Then she stopped, skates scraping, coming up to Kay in a shower of ice.

"Where's Jack?" said the woman, her curls bouncing.

"Jack?" said Kay. "Oh, he'll be back in a minute. Can I see that?"

She reached out for the velvet strap and the bell.

"This?" said the woman. She reached up to her neck and undid it. "It's just some old thing I found in an antique shop."

"Really?" said Kay.

The woman dropped it into her hand. Kay closed her fingers around it.

"Do you like it?" said the woman. Her voice was just what Kay had imagined it to be, one that went along with the wave and the red lips, the blue skies and white clouds. Kay couldn't believe her luck. The girl was going to give it to her.

"Yes," said Kay.

"Keep it," said the girl, with an air of frank generosity. Then she looked around. "I'll catch up with him later."

"Okay," said Kay. "Good. I'll tell him."

The young woman skated into the sound of that old music. Kay watched her glide away, skates flashing, hips driving, and as the young woman went, Kay turned back to the darkness under the bleachers. It held a fascination for her, like some forbidden pleasure that she always tried to pretend held no attraction for her, but was actually something she lived for. Then she felt the cool air of the ice. It occurred to her that she didn't have the pistol, and how was she going to take care of this if she didn't have that? She guessed that she could borrow Jack's, since he wouldn't suspect anything. He didn't know that she had a cue, too, did he? Kay started shaking. She put her hand to her hair, tried to think clearly, but instead what came to mind was the most profound irritation, as though she couldn't restrain herself for a moment more and all she wanted to do was to slap Jack, but she knew it wasn't just a slap she was thinking about.

Beyond her, in the black clutter of the bleachers, she saw some movement, slashes of dark on dark that seemed to be someone not only falling down, but to one side too, as though being thrown.

"Jack," said Kay. She raised her voice. "Jack. Please . . . Ah, Jack, don't do this . . . "

The music seemed to get louder. Kay walked to the end of the bleachers where she could get inside, or underneath, and from the end she saw the regular supports, which from there looked like the latticework of an oil derrick. Up ahead she still saw that movement, downward and to the side, and as much as she hurried, it was difficult, since the beams and dark wood were close together and anchored to the floor by four-by-fours that had been fastened to the concrete. She guessed that men in the bleachers who had been here for hockey games had urinated into the dark space below, since here it had the smell of an overflowing toilet, and as she went through it, the stink seemed to make it harder to work her way around the gussets and beams. When she turned toward the rink she saw the ice between the seats, the surface of it impossibly white, and for an instant she was transfixed by the diamondlike spray of chips from the blade of a skate, and the sleek movement of women in pink and white tights. Then she came up to Jack.

He stood so still that she recognized him by the whites of his eyes, which were filled with the luminescence of the ice. On the ground she saw the dead men, all of them lined up, side by side, like some display of desperadoes who had been killed and laid out for people to see. He glanced down to the men on the ground, and as he did, Kay shook her head, as though she had come to a point of such bleak comprehension as to give her the sensation, at once horrifying and claustrophobic, that the darkness here was simply absorbing her. It seemed to her that no one would ever be able to comfort her. The skin of the men seemed white, although there were some stains, like black silk, that ran out from their noses, hair, ears, mouths. Jack looked from them to her and said, "We better get out of here."

"Yeah," said Kay. "We should go. Someplace private."

He nodded.

"I can tell you one thing," he said. "They aren't going to give anyone any trouble."

"I guess not," said Kay.

"They were asking for it," said Jack. "That's all there is to it."

The two of them came out from under the bleachers, and as they emerged into the light, Kay had the sensation that she couldn't quite shake the darkness there. They sat down in front of the rental counter and took off their skates. The music was "Buffalo girls won't you come out tonight, and dance by the light of the moon . . ." Kay took her feet out of the skates and put on her shoes. She looked over at him.

"Hurry," said Jack.

Then he picked up her skates and his, and put them on the counter. They turned and went through the entrance, out to the front, emerging from under the marquee into the light of the street, which was bright and left them blinking. On the sidewalk was a trash can, and into it Kay dropped the velvet ribbon and the bell; they fell into the darkness without a sound.

She knew what she was supposed to do, but as she stood there, she felt the deepest sense of dissonance, of wanting two things at the same time. She had responsibilities here, in this moment. She should get rid of him and she knew it. But she thought of those times when they had spent time together or used the language for the first time as though they were naming things; she thought of his dependability, his quiet trust, as he slept next to her each night. Could she just dismiss this as though it didn't matter at all?

"Let me have it," she said.

"What?" he said.

She reached over and touched his pocket.

"Oh," he said. "That."

He looked around. There was no one else on the street. Then Kay closed her eyes.

"Here," he said. He took it out and offered it, the thing looking enormous on the street.

She shook her head.

"Don't you want it?"

"No. You keep it," she said.

"Hey, don't look so worried," he said. "You'd be surprised what people get away with."

"Would I?" she said.

"Sure," said Jack. "Who's going to say boo?"

CHAPTER 4 | *April 21, 2029*

WENDELL BLAINE'S chauffeur, Jimmy, woke up and looked at the cracked ceiling. Sometimes, when he was feeling bad, the cracks looked like a map of the Amazon, and through his feelings of discomfort, he would imagine black canoes paddled by men with bones in their noses, or with bright feathers on their arms, the whites of their eyes bloodshot with the effect of a drug they took when it was time for war. That was how the ceiling appeared this morning. The cracks forked off and curved around, going upstream into a realm that was all green and brown shadows, animated by creatures that the vegetation concealed perfectly. Then he closed his eyes and tried to concentrate. What did he know about stock, or economics?

There was a pool of warmth next to him where his wife had been, and now he put his hand into it. He opened his fingers to feel it a little better. Outside, in the kitchen, he heard the lonely sounds as his wife put a cheap spoon, which rang like a tin bell, on the table along with a cup of coffee and a piece of toast that had been made out of stale bread. His wife didn't know anything about stocks and bonds, either, and her one economic strategy was an ironclad thrift, which became more intense with each passing year.

In the bedroom he put on his blue suit and noticed that the seat and the elbows were a little shiny, although his cap was new, and the bill of the visor was shiny. He tied his blue tie, shoved up the knot until it was tight around his neck. His collar was a little looser than usual. He was losing weight.

He got the car out and drove to Blaine's apartment building. Usually, Blaine would be right behind the door of the lobby, and as soon as Jimmy pulled up, he'd come out, under the awning, and then Jimmy would come around and open the door, saying, "Good morning, Mr. Blaine."

Blaine didn't always answer this greeting, but Jimmy could distinguish the varieties of silence. Sometimes it was amused, other times it was preoccupied, as though he couldn't be bothered. Sometimes Jimmy would say it was the reticence of a hangover. Now, though, he pulled up in the car and waited. Blaine was late.

It was raining, and Jimmy watched the windshield wipers swinging back and forth, obliterating the small, crown-shaped splashes where the drops hit. The wipers made a little sound, a *flip, flip, flip,* that he had always found reassuring, but this morning all he heard was the sound, nothing more. It wasn't reassuring so much as hypnotically gloomy. Before Jimmy had a chance to get out and open the door, Blaine had stepped away from the awning, in the rain, and had jerked on the handle and gotten into the backseat.

"I'm sorry, Mr. Blaine," said Jimmy. "I don't know what I was thinking. Just sitting here."

"It's all right," said Blaine.

"Did you get wet?" said Jimmy.

"No," said Blaine.

Jimmy pulled away from the curb. Through the gray rain, the lights of the other cars looked bright and serious. In the rearview mirror Jimmy saw that Blaine hadn't shaved very well, and his shirt didn't look clean. At a signal, a boy came along with a morning paper, under plastic, the headline right there for everyone to see. The plastic was covered with drops that looked like wax from a candle that was as clear as water. They both looked at the headline: PANIC SPREADS.

"Push on through," said Blaine.

"The light's against us," said Jimmy.

"Push on," said Blaine.

"The light," said Jimmy. He pointed upward, through the hypnotic movement of the windshield wiper.

"Oh?" said Blaine. "Well. All right."

"Some traffic this morning," said Jimmy.

"What? Oh yes," said Blaine. "Terrible."

Jimmy gripped the wheel and looked in the rearview mirror. The rain fell with that quick and irritating tempo. He thought about his hand in the warm spot that his wife had left in the bed; he had put his hand in the warmth for many years. He had always been able to depend on it, like sunlight, or her kiss on his cheek. This kiss had never been perfunctory, and as the years had gone by, he realized that she had always meant it. Warm, slightly damp, constant. He thought about the heat under the sheets, like a hen's warmth around an egg. Blaine was watching him through the mirror.

"My wife says I should talk to you," said Jimmy.

"Your wife?" said Blaine. "I didn't know you were married."

"Twenty-five years," said Jimmy.

"Twenty-five years," said Blaine. He nodded. It was as though he was weighing regret parceled out in years. Or decades. It all added up.

"Yes," said Jimmy. "She says the papers say you aren't doing anything, and it's going to cause trouble."

"And did she say anything else?" said Blaine.

"Just that," he said.

"And what about you?" said Blaine. "What do you think?"

"Me? I don't know. My wife is pretty upset. That's all."

Blaine looked out the window. The rain came along in lines, like pieces of silver wire, all lined up in the same direction.

"I know I should do something, but I don't know what."

"You've lost your nerve?" said Jimmy.

"You could call it that. That's as good a way of putting it as another," said Blaine.

"Oh," said Jimmy. "Well."

The black windshield wipers thumped back and forth, looking as though they were made of licorice. The water on the windows ran down in rivulets that had a little texture to them and in which the colors of the street, the reds and yellows, seemed to run, too. Blaine looked through them.

"Twenty-five years," said Blaine. "That's a long time, isn't it?"

"It goes by pretty fast," said Jimmy.

They worked their way through traffic, going over the film of light on the moist pavement. The rain had pushed some gulls in from the ocean, and their wings tottered from side to side as they landed on the sidewalk and started pecking at crumbs of something there. White birds with orange beaks. Jimmy looked at their feet as they landed: splayed out, like tines on a garden tool.

Blaine sat back, not looking one way or another.

"Right in front?" said Jimmy.

"Yes," said Blaine. "Right in front. Just as always."

CHAPTER 5

April 22, 2029

"HI, REMEMBER me?" said Jack as she came out of the skating rink. Her cheeks were bright with the exercise, and she had her workout clothes in a bag, her skates tied together with their laces and slung over her shoulder. She emerged from the lobby into the lines of rain. It was right there, when she hesitated, that Jack came up to her.

"Yes," she said. "How could I forget someone who skates like you, Jack? Hi."

She looked one way and then another. Good, no one to meet her.

"I've been thinking about you," said Jack.

"And what have you been thinking?" she said. She smiled now, and looked around again to make sure.

"Oh, this and that," said Jack. "What's your name?"

"Gloria," she said. "Will you just look at this rain? How am I going to get home in it?"

Then she glanced back at Jack.

"Where's your friend?" she said.

"Friend?" said Jack.

"You know, the woman. The one you were with at the skating rink?" she said.

"Kay?" said Jack. "Well, she had something to do."

Gloria kept looking up at him, her eyes moving back and forth across his face, from one of his eyes to the other.

"You know all I do is practice," she said.

"I know," said Jack. "No one ever lets you do anything."

"Yeah. That's the way it is," she said.

"But you can work a little fun in. You know what I mean?" said Jack. She looked around, then reached under her coat to scratch.

"I've never just gone off this way, with a stranger," said Gloria.

"Who are you kidding?" said Jack. "Anyway, I'm not a stranger. We went skating together just the other day."

"My mother would kill me," she said. "If she knew."

"You'll be a little late," said Jack. "So what?"

The rain fell around them all, the puddles looking like insects were hatching from them. From the street came the sounds of horns and engines, and a man rolled down his window and yelled at the car ahead of him, "Why don't you hire a hall, you idiot."

"Maybe they'll get out and have a fight," she said.

"Maybe," said Jack. He took a look at the man who had yelled. Then he said, "But I don't think so."

"What makes you such an expert?" she said.

"You can tell," he said. Jack went on looking at the driver, and when he turned back to Gloria, his lips brushed her hair, her ear under it. She looked up, her eyes on his. She blushed and then reached out and took his arm. "You don't think badly of me for going off like this, do you?"

"Me?" said Jack.

"Well, I'd just like to know," she said.

"I like a girl with spunk," said Jack. "Why, everyone around here is like some kind of gloomy bird . . . "

"It's a goony bird," she said. She laughed. "You don't even know that it's a goony bird . . . " She stepped away from him and put out her arms, and waddled like a penguin. "See, that's a goony bird."

She took his arm and he felt the slight bounce and tug of her as she laughed against his side.

"Yeah, well," he said. "So long as it isn't gloomy. I get so sick of hanging around and never living or anything."

"I know," she said. "What do they think we're made out of, anyway?"

He stopped and leaned down and kissed her, the heat of their mouths touching in the slippery instant. She leaned forward, and when he turned back, up the street, she said, "You shouldn't do that out here, where everyone can see."

"Let them look," said Jack.

She giggled, but then said, "Let's be a little more private next time."

They stepped into a retro pinball parlor, and in the damp heat of the place the machines made that bing, bang, bing. Jack started to play, making the flippers work, and then he got her to play, putting his hand over hers, guiding her fingers and pushing them at the right moment. She put her lips against his ear and said, "You've got good reflexes."

"Well, I guess," he said. He paused for a moment. Then he went back to the game. She moved impatiently from one hip to another.

"Jack," she said.

"What?" he said.

"Where are we going to go from here?" she said.

"A hotel," he said.

"I've never been to a hotel," she said.

She looked at him in the heat of the room.

"Boy, am I going to get in trouble."

She giggled.

"I wouldn't be here if you weren't such a good skater."

They went out into the street, into the rain, and as they hurried along, her skates thumped against her shoulder like the beating of an anxious heart. When she looked up, she had to turn her face into the rain, and her wet hair, which was plastered to the sides of her face, made her skin seem pale.

They came to the steps of the hotel. The street was more deserted here, nothing but gray light and reflections off the windows. The lobby had a marble floor and a couple of sofas, which were empty. The elevator was in the back, and they walked toward it, Gloria taking his arm and putting her damp face against his shoulder.

They got into the elevator.

"I've never done anything like this," she said. "I'm shaking in my knees."

"Me too," he said.

He put his arm around her.

"Oh darling," he said. "I wanted you to come up here with me the minute I saw you, you know that?"

"Did you?" she said.

"Yes," he said.

"And you don't think badly of me for coming with you?" she said.

"No," he said.

They stepped out into the hall and up to the door, which Jack opened. Inside she put down her skates and took off her shoes and her coat. Then she looked around the room. A double bed, a mirror at the dressing table, some of Kay's things hung up on the door. Gloria went over to them and ran her finger over them.

"If my friends could see me now," she said.

He stood next to her, in the slight odor of her skin from skating. She said, "Well, I guess we better sit down, don't you think?"

T H E Y   L A Y under the sheet with their legs drawn up, so that their knees made four white peaks. She kept the cloth around her waist, beneath her belly button, and a slight golden curl showed around the edge of the sheet. Her arm was behind her head. Outside, in the street, occasionally they heard the sound of a horn.

"I like it when you . . . " she said. "When you put your tongue . . . " She turned toward him.

"I thought so," he said. "I like it too. That was my first time."

"Oh, come on," she said. "You say that to all the girls."

"No," he said.

"Well, you might get some of them to believe it, but not me."

"Okay," he said.

"How can you say such a thing?" she said.

He shrugged.

"You've got to realize that I don't lie," he said.

"Oh, sure," she said. She rustled around in the sheets. "When are we going to see each other again?"

"I don't know," he said.

"What does that mean?" she said. "You aren't going to disappear on me?"

"No," he said. "I'll try not to do that. I'll come by the place where you skate."

"When?" she said.

"Soon," he said.

She turned toward him.

"Can I depend on that?"

"Yes," he said.

She turned on her side and put one arm under her chin so she could see him. Then she glanced around the room. It was cluttered, but it seemed to her to be a place where only transients stayed.

"What are you doing here, Jack?" she said.

"Just visiting," he said. "You know, looking around, seeing the sights . . . "

He slid his hand along her thigh under the sheets.

"And how are the sights so far?" she said.

"So pretty," he said.

She blushed.

"And do you have any friends, Jack?" she said.

"Sure," said Jack.

"Like who?" she said.

"Well, I've got friends. You know, people I could go to for help," he said.

"Oh yeah?" she said.

"Sure," said Jack.

"Oh, Jack," she said. "Just don't tell me any lies, okay? When can I see you again?"

"In a couple of days," said Jack.

She looked at him, from one eye to the other, trying to decide if she could trust him, and as she was doing this, Kay came into the room. She stood there with the door open, just looking for a moment, her raincoat open and her hand lingering on the doorknob. Then she came in and closed the door.

"Hi, Jack," she said.

"Hi," said Jack, "This is Gloria."

"Yeah, I guess that's right," said Kay.

Kay sat down at the dressing table, although she could see in the mirror that Gloria had gotten up out of bed and slowly and deliberately started getting dressed, bending down and pulling on her underwear, putting on a brassiere, fastening it beneath her breasts and then turning it around so that the clasp was at her back. Gloria went into the bathroom and then they heard the sound of the toilet flushing. Kay sat without moving, eyes down. Gloria came out, although she didn't say anything until she had gotten her shoes on, and then she picked up her skates and stood by the door.

"Well, I better be going," she said.

"I'll come to see you," said Jack.

"Okay," she said. "I'll see you later. 'Bye." She turned to Kay and said, "'Bye."

Then she went out the door.

Jack didn't have any clothes on and he came around and sat behind Kay on the edge of the bed. His image was in the mirror in front of her, and she leaned forward, and with a quick, damp exhalation, she made the cool surface of the mirror cloud over. Jack disappeared into it.

"How come everyone except me has someone?" she said.

"You'll get your chance," he said.

"Yeah, well," she said.

"You aren't upset, are you?" he said.

"What's it to you?" she said.

She put her head down on the mirrored surface of the dressing table.

"Oh, Jack," she said. "What was it like?"

"It was real nice," he said.

She looked at his reflection in the mirror.

"Like how?" she said.

"Oh," said Jack. "It's hard to say. You'll have to see for yourself."

She sat there, looking down.

"I've got to warn you, though," said Jack. "It isn't something you just want to do once. It's not like you get your curiosity satisfied and that's it. It's more like you want to keep at it. And there's something else."

"What's that?" she said.

"It might change you," he said.

She looked up at the mirror, and into her eyes.

"Maybe that wouldn't be such a bad thing," she said. "I'm tired of being this way."

"What way is that?" said Jack.

"So alone," she said.

He reached out and touched her. She was sweating and laboring as she breathed. She put a hand to her head.

"It's just the flu," she said.

"Yeah," he said. "I guess."

BOOK

CHAPTER *April 23, 2029*

BRIGGS SUBSCRIBED to a newsletter of the Artificial Life Association. A lot of the stories in it were filled with lousy reporting, mistakes, and suggestions of problems that didn't really exist. The editors were interested in sensation, and Briggs took this into account. It had a listing of jobs and a who's-who section that gave the lineup of the people who were in the business now. It also had a registry of what were called "wild diseases," new ones that turned up without a perfect etiology.

He scrolled through lists of medical calls now, dismissing one and then another as obvious reporting errors or lousy lab work, or just a mild flu that some college student had hatched up for a prank. He stopped, though, at an entry that had just been posted. The woman who called in the case said that a clerk in a hotel, a fleabag of a place, had gotten sick. There was nothing unusual about that. In that part of town there were all kinds of things. For instance, there were new strains of sexually transmitted malaria. Hard to treat, but not impossible. But what got Briggs's attention was that the clerk's eyes were itchy and his lids looked dark, as though he were wearing mascara. The lining of his mouth had been black, and his lips had been black too. A medical technician had been dispatched to take a look, but aside from the color, there wasn't much else to go on. That was it. Briggs had been uncertain what amount of time a new disease would require for an incubation period, but he guessed it would be more than three weeks and less than six. Kay and Jack had been missing since almost the end of March, and it was now close to the end of April. Say four weeks.

Briggs went out and looked for a cab. When he got into the backseat, the driver said, "Where to?"

The hotel wasn't much to look at. The usual old ironwork, the gray stone façade, fire escapes, a neon sign that buzzed like a hive of insects getting ready to sting an intruder. Briggs got out, paid the cabbie, and looked one way and then another, a gesture that he found himself making more and more these days. Then he went in.

Not much of a lobby, just a couple of sofas, some ashtrays filled with cigarette butts and silver paper, a floor of black and white tiles. A young man, just a kid, sat at a desk at the back. He gave Briggs a quick glance. Briggs had the impulse to hold his breath, but this was stupid. It wasn't going to do any good, and he knew it.

"How are you feeling?" said Briggs.

"Me?" said the kid. "Never better. Why do you ask?"

The kid had acne and a slack chin and neck. His skin was a little greasy and pale.

"We had a report about someone being sick here," said Briggs.

"Oh," said the kid. "That? They had a wrong number."

"Is that right?" said Briggs.

"Uh-huh," said the kid. "You want a room?"

"No," said Briggs.

"Well," said the kid. "So?"

Briggs stood there for a while, counting slowly.

"I was just wondering if you were the one who was sick," said Briggs.

"Do I look sick?" said the kid.

Briggs shrugged.

"Well, I'm not," said the kid.

"Then who was?" said Briggs.

"Look," said the kid. "I explained it all before to the technician. I had a little cold, but that was it. And let me tell you, sometimes some people here have more than a cold. Oh yeah."

"So then a technician came here?" said Briggs.

"Yeah," said the kid. "I told you. Someone turned in a report, and it was just some kind of stupid rumor. One of the women who uses this place was cutting up, you know, getting mad because we wouldn't give her credit. Happens all the time."

"Uh-huh," said Briggs.

"So the technician had a wrong number," said the kid.

Briggs looked at the door behind the desk. The kid licked his lips.

"But you weren't the one who was really sick, though, right?" said Briggs. "That was someone else, wasn't it?"

"What's the big deal?" said the kid.

"How's he doing?" said Briggs.

"Who?" said the kid.

"Come on," said Briggs. "How sick is he?"

"I don't know what you're talking about," said the kid. He didn't sound convinced.

"No?" said Briggs. He looked around, thinking that the technician who had come here had probably been tired and worried about a lot of things, not just one isolated report of a clerk with a strange skin condition. The technician saw stuff every day that put a strange skin condition a bit lower than the top of the list.

"Look," said the kid. "We don't need anyone butting in here, or anything like that. No quarantine. Nothing like that. We get all kinds of people here."

"I see," said Briggs. "Who was sick?"

The kid stared at Briggs.

"Are you a cop?" said the kid.

"No," said Briggs. He thought, *Worse than that.*

"Ah, shit," said the kid. "I don't know."

Briggs waited. He looked around.

"He's in there," said the kid. He pointed at the door behind the desk.

Briggs tapped on the door behind the desk and pushed it open. The room had the feverish atmosphere of a sickroom: damp, and the air felt intimate, as warm as a toilet seat that someone has just sat on. Briggs looked at the posters on the walls, which came from model airplane conventions: the wings set in dihedrals, the fuselages visible under the Japanese silk, the beauty of the designs. Beneath them, on the sofa, lay the clerk. He panted a little. Every now and then he reached up and scratched his eyes with the back of his hand, and it left a dark smudge. His lips were black.

"Ah, Jesus," said the clerk.

Briggs leaned a little closer so he could look at the man's eyes. The lining of the eyelids was dark, and it sloughed off in flecks when the man blinked. He did so repeatedly.

"It's coming off more than it used to. Bigger pieces, like."

"Uh-huh," said Briggs.

Briggs watched the man's mouth. The clerk looked as if he were swallowing something unpleasant. Briggs guessed that the lining of the man's mouth and the surface of his tongue might be sloughing off.

"I got to go pee," said the clerk. His voice was a little sibilant.

"You want help getting into the bathroom?" said Briggs. He was holding his breath again. Then he tried to stop it, but it was still hard to fill his lungs with the air in this room, so he stood there, taking shallow breaths.

The clerk spit into his handkerchief, but he didn't look at it. Briggs saw it, though, and then he swallowed. It wouldn't do to get sick here.

"Come on," said Briggs. "I'll give you a hand."

The clerk shook his head.

"No," he said. "I'll wait."

The clerk blinked, and then puckered his chin. When the tears came out of the sides of his eyes, they were gray. Briggs thought they were this color from small pieces of the lining of the eyelid.

"I don't want to," said the clerk.

"Why not?" said Briggs. "If you have to use the bathroom, you have to. Right?"

The clerk shook his head.

"No," he said. "Something happens when I do it."

"Oh?" said Briggs.

"Yeah," said the clerk. "So I'd rather just sit here."

"What happens?" said Briggs.

"I don't know," said the clerk. "Oh shit. Oh fuck."

The clerk put out his hand, asking for comfort. He just put it out, and Briggs stood there. Then he put out his hand and took it. The clerk puckered up his chin and said, "It comes out inky. Like something from an octopus."

The kidneys, thought Briggs. *That's probably what it is.* He thought of the early attempts to make creatures, and how some of these had gone wrong: they had turned black from the esophagus and lungs inward. Briggs recalled, with a flinch, the expressions on the faces of the technicians when this had happened.

"I don't know what to do," said the clerk. "I don't know what to do. Doctors always scared me, but maybe I need one. What do you think?"

Briggs held the clerk's hand.

"We've got to call a doctor," said Briggs.

"Uh-huh," said the clerk. "That's what the others said."

"Which others?" said Briggs.

"A man and a woman," said the clerk.

"Oh?" said Briggs. "How old?"

"They were in their twenties, but they seemed fresher than that. Not younger, just cleaner. Yeah. That's it. They seemed *clean.*"

"Did the woman have short hair? Pale skin?" said Briggs. "Did the man look like a runner?"

"Yeah," said the clerk. "They were nice. A little goofy."

"Uh-huh," said Briggs.

"She had white skin. She carried sheet music around," said the clerk.

"Where are they now?" he said.

"Jack and Kay?" said the clerk.

"Yeah," said Briggs. "Kay and Jack."

"I don't know," said the clerk, with a kind of infinite finality. "They checked out."

The clerk coughed. Briggs tried not to look away, but he had to when he saw what the clerk had coughed up. The clerk breathed through his mouth, exhausted, and he had the blinking, vacuous expression of an animal that has been stunned, like a steer under a sledgehammer, just the instant before it collapses in a heap. Briggs looked at the clerk's lips and chin and went into the bathroom to get a towel, but the ones on the floor were already stained black. He picked up the cleanest one and took it out to the clerk.

Briggs picked up the phone and dialed the emergency number and gave the address. He sat down for a moment and looked at the airplanes on the posters. The wings seemed long and delicate, and the airplanes were so self-contained, so perfectly designed for one thing: flight. He looked back at the clerk's eyelids.

"It won't be long," said Briggs.

"Oh, yeah?" said the clerk. "Well, that's good. I guess." He blinked. "Itches."

The clerk sat back, his face smeared. A stain, with a sweet odor, spread from the crotch of his pants. Briggs saw that the clerk's head was leaning to one side and that his mouth was open, slack, rubbery. Briggs let go of his hand. Then he stood up and looked around, not sure what he was trying to find, but then he realized this was just a tic, just aimlessness. He didn't know what to do, and so he moved from one side of the room to the other, trying to come up with some idea. He guessed the only good thing was that with an unknown like this, the medical crew would treat it as infectious, which it probably was.

Outside, in front of the desk, the clerk said, "How's he doing?"

Briggs shook his head.

"He's dead," said Briggs.

"Gee," said the kid. "I knew he wasn't feeling good, but I didn't think it was . . . you know . . . "

"If you get sick, go to the doctor right away. Don't wait around," said Briggs.

"Me?" said the clerk. "I don't want any trouble. No one's going to pin anything on me. That's a promise."

Briggs heard the sound of the medical crew in the street, and when he got outside and was walking away, he tried to imagine something that was the opposite of chaos—a hard, shiny point, like a diamond—but as he did, all he could think of was the infinities of the sky. Down the avenue the flat land spread away into the clutter of lights, and around him, on both sides of the street, Briggs saw buildings that were getting ready to be torn down, junk wrappers blowing along the gutters, cars that left black exhaust in the air like the first appearance of a genie that offered no wishes at all.

CHAPTER 2 | *April 24, 2029*

BLAINE WENT through the lobby of his office building. Above him, in the dome, the stern angels reached out for one another in an attempt to make contact. The blue sky, with puffs of gold-tinted clouds, stretched into the infinities of the horizon. The atmosphere of the lobby was one of putative calm, although it was so mannered as to suggest an electric, thinly disguised hysteria. Blaine waited for the elevator to open, and when it did, he stepped in. It shut behind him with a sigh and a thud.

From his office, Blaine looked out at the city. The river made a mirrorlike S, and in the distance he saw the smoke rising from a section where they still did some manufacturing. It was allowed here because Blaine liked to see it and to be reminded of the fact that economic activity had, at its heart, the work of making something. Now, though, he sat down and stared. He couldn't really remember what it was like to make decisions. All he knew was the ability to do so was gone.

No one came into his office. This was usually the case when the markets were tense. No one wanted to come in and ask a question and be exposed to those languid, appalling eyes as they looked up from a report to answer what he thought was a stupid question. Usually, though, he sent out requests for information, for interest rates in various cities in the world, Berlin, Paris, Moscow, Tokyo, Rio, the answers to his requests coming on small slips of paper that he had had printed for this purpose. Of course, this was antiquated, but he had a notion that information that was not written down by hand or that just appeared on a monitor was imprecise and numb. He wanted to have the sense that a human being had prepared a report for him.

Shares were falling now in earnest, and they fell with more than ordinary volatility. What was the correct attitude? How, for instance, would wheat futures be affected when the disruption had gotten into the oil markets? He looked at the reports and guessed that people were on the verge of dismissing each other and had started to look out for themselves. That was the true test of a panic: the common good was the first casualty.

"Mr. Blaine," said a secretary who came into the room. The secretary was a tall, slender man with black hair. He looked like a mortician's assistant, and when he spoke, he glanced away from Blaine's eyes. "You have a call."

Blaine held up his hand. He didn't want to take any calls.

"It's Evelyn Black," said the secretary. "From the board of overseers . . ."

Blaine went on looking out the window for a moment and then said, "All right."

He picked up the phone.

"Well, Wendell," said Evelyn Black. "You're a hard man to reach these days."

"I've been busy," said Blaine.

"Have you?" said Evelyn Black. "Well, I'm glad to hear that. What the fuck have you been doing?"

"Evelyn," said Blaine.

"Evelyn what?" she said.

"I'm doing my best, as I'm sure you know," Blaine said.

Evelyn Black was quiet on the other end.

"All right, Wendell," she said. "We've known each other for a lot of years. I wanted to say that the board of directors is going to release a statement today saying that we have complete faith in you. And your decisions."

"I appreciate that," said Blaine.

"Do you, Wendell?" said Evelyn Black. "Well, that's great. What are you going to do?"

"I have a plan," said Blaine.

"Well, Wendell, it better fucking work," she said.

Blaine put a hand to his head. Evelyn Black waited, her breathing rough and wet, like a child with asthma.

"So," she said. "Is that all you have to say?"

"Evelyn, we've been friends . . . " he said.

"Wendell, this isn't a friendly call," she said. "Do I have to spell it out for you?"

"No," he said. "I'll think of something."

"Well, you better do it fast," she said. "That's the message. Am I making myself clear?"

Downstairs, the people in the lobby looked at their watches. Soon, they thought, Blaine would make the announcement that quieted the markets, that gave people here something to talk about at lunch, and, of course, at dinner in London, Berlin, Rio, Paris, Moscow, Tokyo. Maybe Blaine wanted this to go on a little longer, but what was the point of that? Billions were getting ready to disappear into failed shares. Could that be good for anyone? If so, who? People looked at one another and tried to smile, but it didn't do much good. Mostly these smiles looked like those of people who had had minor surgery and were going to work anyway.

Blaine went home in the afternoon without saying a word. In the lobby downstairs, the people turned to look at him. He went through them without a glance, and got into his car outside, and then he sat in the back of the car, saying nothing.

Blaine went to sleep without eating, and in the morning he sat at the side of the bed, looking at his ugly feet coming out of the cuffs of his green silk pajamas. His toes were long, and he sat there thinking of all the mornings he had looked at his ugly feet and started the day with the first effort to pretend that he was getting everything he needed. He knew this brooding was not a good sign, and he struggled against it, but as he went in to shave, as he took his bath, as he picked out the shirt that smelled of starch, he kept stopping short. Then, holding his razor, or his toothbrush, like a figure in a wax museum, he came up against the same wild impulse, which was insufficiently put into words, but which came out now as one word. "Kay."

He tied his tie, looked in the mirror, and told himself that this torment and distraction was for other people. It was precisely what he had spent years trying to avoid. He said to himself that there was no fool like an old fool, that he was besotted with a young woman, but then he realized that this was just another way of trying to hide from himself how he really felt, and above everything else, the last weeks had shown him that he was tired of lying.

A little later he got into the car and told Jimmy to go to the part of town where Stone's studio was, and they went down the forlorn streets, passing the Chinese and Turkistan restaurants, the garish storefronts. They pulled up in front of Stone's building, and Blaine sat in the back, looking out the window.

"Doesn't look like much," said Jimmy.

Blaine got out and opened the door, and then looked at the directory on the wall, like a man examining poisonous insects under glass. He found the name and climbed the stairs and then knocked on the door, once, and then again, harder.

"Mr. Blaine," said Stone as he opened the door. He was wearing a silk dressing gown with food stains on it, and he brushed the crumbs off it. "To think that Wendell Blaine would come here." He looked over his shoulder, into his apartment. "You will have to forgive my rooms. I don't keep house the way I used to, but then I used to have help. You know, in Vienna? But come in, please, would you like a cup of tea?"

"Tea?" said Blaine. "I . . . no, thank you. I don't think . . . "

"Of course, you are a busy man," said Stone. "How could I think that a busy man has time for tea? Well, what can I do? You must be looking for Kay. Do you think she will get a chance at the Marshall?"

"Yes," said Blaine. "But I need to talk with her."

Stone shrugged.

"I don't know what to say. It may not do you any good," he said. "She is not an easy listener. You can't just ask her a question right out. She is slippery."

"No," said Blaine. "I mean, where can I find her?"

"She hasn't been coming to practice lately," said Stone.

"Don't you have her address?" said Blaine.

"No," said Stone.

"Can you get a message to her?" said Blaine. "Can you ask her to come to see me?"

"Of course, I can try. If she comes. If she doesn't . . . " Stone shrugged.

Blaine closed his eyes.

"Of course, you are busy," said Stone. "But even in a time like this, one thinks of Kay. Do you remember when she was playing at the audition? I have been thinking about a certain phrase. Piercing . . . "

"Yes," said Blaine. "I remember."

"Well," said Stone. "How can one explain that? I have tried, but I can't. And even now, in the midst of worries, I can see you are still thinking about it."

"Worries?" said Blaine.

"The panic," said Stone.

"What?" said Blaine. "Oh that. I guess." Blaine closed his eyes. "Yes. You are right about it being piercing. Please give her the message, will you?"

"If I get a chance," said Stone. "Good day, Mr. Blaine. It was a pleasure to see you."

Blaine took a step and then turned back.

"She admires you, doesn't she?" said Blaine.

"Sometimes," said Stone. "Yes."

Blaine nodded, looking at Stone carefully.

"You know, people have dismissed you as washed up," said Blaine.

"I know what people say about an old man," said Stone. "But that is the beauty of being old. You don't care so much."

Blaine went on staring.

"Well, I wanted to tell you they are wrong," said Blaine. "For what it's worth. Good afternoon, Mr. Stone."

CHAPTER ③

April 24, 2029

THE SALESMAN drew on his cigar, and under the ash at the tip, the dull coal came alive for an instant and then faded away. A stream of smoke leaked from his lips and curled in the air. Then the salesman flipped up the lid of his briefcase, reached inside, and brought out the shrink-wrapped materials. Briggs watched them rise, as though they were levitating, and as he reached out for them, he was already in his mind turning them over to see the batch number and the expiration date, which he supposed couldn't be faked. But the salesman pulled them back a little. He looked at Briggs and said, "We've got an understanding, right? If you are up to something that you can't talk about, that's fine. But if it gets funded, big time, then you are going to put an order in through me, right?"

"Yes," said Briggs.

The salesman drew on the cigar, the coal glowing like some living thing.

"Here," said the salesman. "From Sandoz, no less. You see that?"

Briggs nodded.

"It looks good," he said.

"Well, that's what I was trying to tell you, you moron. I've got the goods. See?"

"Thanks," said Briggs.

"Well, it's not like you won the lottery or something, for Christ sakes."

Briggs put them in the pocket of his jacket.

"It's hard to say about that," said Briggs.

The salesman lipped the wet end of the cigar, which had the color and shine of a stuffed grape leaf.

"No kidding?" said the salesman.

"In a manner of speaking," said Briggs.

"No kidding," said the salesman. "Well, all right. Just remember me when the time comes. When you can put in a big order."

The salesman got up and left, leaving a long strand of smoke behind him. Briggs looked at the materials again, turned them over, and glanced at the expiration date. Still good. He got up the original analysis and started searching through it until he came to the pathogen prompt. He put these proteins aside and went on searching. There was no reason why there would only be one new disease, and if there were many, he was going to have to have more biotic materials. He waited while the machine searched, and when it was done he looked at the pathogen, and then turned to the manuals.

He went downstairs, into the basement of the building. It had the sharp fragrance of peat moss, as in a potting shed, and the walls were moldy. He guessed he could do it here. Sterilize the place, get some antibacterial lights set up, order some basic stuff. Put a lock on the door. Then he sat down on the floor, his back against the wall. He guessed he'd have to start tonight.

April 25, 2029

KAY SAT in front of the mirror of the dressing table. She put a hand to her hair, and as she did, she thought, *What if Briggs has another girl, someone he likes and is seeing every night, right now? Maybe she comes to his apartment and he fucks her.* Then she tossed her head, as though to get rid of this idea, but it came back. She wished she hadn't thought of this, since she couldn't shake it, and mere mental repetition of such a notion seemed to imply its validity. She put a little makeup on, not much. You couldn't see it unless you were very close, and even then you couldn't be sure. Kay thought, *I wonder what she smells like, after she has spent the night with him? Does he like it? Well, let me find the little bitch there sometime.* She put on a silk blouse, and as she did, she thought of another possibility: What if Briggs told Kay to go away, that he wasn't interested, that he had changed his mind and that he didn't want her anymore? That she was just a freak, a mistake, a monster? Kay put her hand to her forehead as she felt the first hot, damp blush of nausea. This was another one of those ideas that she kept springing on herself. She imagined his voice as he spoke this way, the two of them standing in the street someplace. Maybe she would cry. That would be the best of it. The worst would be after she stopped crying and didn't know what to do. Maybe the girl Briggs saw was a cheap blondie, like Jack's friend.

She tried to make a fist, but it was impossible. The knuckles of her right hand were swelling. Her breathing was damp and wheezing, although she tried to pretend it wasn't important. Jack rubbed one hand with another, going over the swollen knuckles. They had made a tacit agreement: if she didn't bother him about it, he wouldn't bother her. She hoped that they would get better, and if ignoring it was how they were going to fight it, why, then that was what she would do. Maybe it was arthritis.

"I thought I might go out for a while," said Jack. "I got something I've got to do."

"What's that?" said Kay.

"Oh," said Jack. "Wouldn't you like to know?"

"Yes," she said. She turned her back on him, and her silk blouse swung around in a shimmer of light. "It's that blondie from the skating rink, isn't it?"

"I thought I'd take her out for a cup of coffee or a drink or something," said Jack.

Kay stood up and put on her skirt. Stepped into her high-heeled shoes and turned to look at herself, running a hand over her hip to smooth out the skirt.

"Do you object?" said Jack.

"No," said Kay.

"Then why are you being so stiff about it?" he said.

"I'm not stiff," she said.

"Well, you could have fooled me," he said.

"I'm not stiff about it," said Kay.

"What's the problem?" said Jack.

"I don't know," said Kay.

"Ah, shit," said Jack. "You are getting soft."

"It's easy for you," said Kay. "You've got your . . . "

"My what?" said Jack.

"You know what I mean," said Kay.

"My what?" said Jack. "Are you afraid to say it?"

"You know what I mean," said Kay.

"My *slut?*" said Jack. "Is that what you are trying to use? I didn't think you were a coward. Go on. Say it."

"I didn't say that," she said.

"But it's what you think," said Jack. "Isn't it?"

"You don't have to stick up for her," said Kay. "You don't have to justify anything."

"I'm not justifying anything," he said. "Do you think I have to justify anything to you? Or that I have to apologize for her?"

She shrugged.

"I don't know what I think," she said.

"You and I could split up," he said. "If you are so troubled about it." She turned and looked at him.

"Maybe," she said.

She sat down on the edge of the chair in front of him. Their knees almost touched, like two people sitting opposite each other in a train compartment. They looked right at each other for awhile.

"Oh, Jack," she said. "We were always good friends, weren't we, Jack?"

"Yes," said Jack. "No one was ever a better friend than me."

"And do you remember when we got to that first hotel? I found some lipstick in the bureau. Do you remember? I put it under my arms."

"I remember," said Jack.

"And the stockings. I found those too. Ah, well," she said.

"You know," he said. "I always knew this moment was coming. When we were going to face up to things."

"Did you, Jack?" she said.

"Yeah," he said. "I'm on borrowed time with you. Oh, I know it."

Then he stood up and went over to the closet and opened it up. There in the shadows, he took out a dark violin case. He held it up and said, "Let's go over to the rehearsal hall."

Jack turned his head as though he had a crick in his neck. He rolled his shoulders. Kay put on her coat, and the room was filled with the soft hush of the coat lining sliding over her blouse. In the mirror, through the open panels, she saw the shape of a nipple under the silk, and as she drew the coat together and tied the sash, she thought of being pregnant, of the vital weight of it. Then she thought of the cheap little blondie who was probably seeing Briggs. Maybe she had a tattoo, or a sluttish piercing . . .

"What are you thinking?" she said.

He shrugged, remembering the rules for handling a firearm. If you want to make a good shot, squeeze the trigger between your heartbeats. You had to feel your heart. These were the kinds of things he really knew, and now he found them so insufficient, so bald. What good were they when he wanted to try to talk about the mystery of loyalty, for instance, and how caring about another human being felt good.

"Come on," he said, picking up the case. "Let's go. I want to show you something."

They went out into the hall and up to the elevator, which arrived with a squeak, and then trembled as it went down. Kay could feel the depths below, the length of the shaft, and over her head she could feel the dark cables and pulleys, and the electric motor that sat at the top of the shaft, like some mechanical gargoyle from another age. As they went, one floor passing another, the elevator squeaked. In one corner there was a small red box, with a sign that said, IN CASE OF EMERGENCY, PULL SWITCH. They came out, Jack carrying the violin case, Kay with her hands in her pockets.

A kid was in the street, freckle-faced, his shirt dirty and his pants having a hole in them, but he looked up at Jack with a cheerful enthusiasm and said, "Hey. Whatcha got in there? In the case? Yah? Whatcha got. A gun?"

The kid held his hands like a gangster in an old movie and made a *rat-tat-tat-tat-tat* sound.

Jack stopped to look at him.

"You got me," he said.

"Then why don't you fall down?" said the kid.

"Maybe later," said Jack.

Jack hesitated, standing there with the case in his hand, like a child on his way to a lesson. Down the block a siren began. The kid still held his hands as though he was carrying a gun. Jack stood there, brow wrinkled, staring into the distance. He closed his eyes for an instant. Then he opened them and looked at the kid.

"Rat-tat-tat-tat-tat . . . " said the kid.

Jack slumped against the wall. Then he sat down on the pavement, one hand on his stomach. In the other he held the case. Jack breathed hard, and he made a sound in his throat, a bubbling, wet respiration as though he were trying to lift an enormous weight but couldn't really get his breath.

The kid came closer.

"Bang," he said.

Jack snapped his head back.

"Jack," said Kay. "Jack."

Kay put a hand to her mouth and then turned and leaned against the wall. She closed her eyes and tapped her head against the brick.

"Hey," the kid said, "I didn't mean anything."

"I know," said Jack. "It's fine. Here." He reached into his pocket and took out a bill. "Here. Go get yourself a pop. Go on."

He held it out. The kid stood there, looking at Jack.

"I didn't mean nothing," said the kid.

"It's okay," said Jack. He turned to Kay. "Tell him it's all right."

"It's fine," said Kay. "It was just a game."

"Go get a pop," said Jack.

The kid reached out and took the bill, and then turned and ran down the street.

"Kids," said Jack. "What do they know?"

They walked together for a while, knowing the way perfectly, since they had taken it so often. There weren't many people on the street, and here and there they walked across shattered glass, which lay on the sidewalk as though an icicle had fallen from the roof. It crunched under Jack's heel.

"Jack," said Kay, "do you think it was worth it? You know, getting away and doing this?"

"Oh yes," said Jack.

"What did you like best?" she said.

"Gloria," said Jack.

"Uh-huh," said Kay. "I understand."

"Do you?" said Jack. "Well."

They went along for a while.

"There are other things," said Jack. "I liked the equations, you know, the ones that describe all kinds of things. And then I liked going shopping with you."

"No, you didn't," she said.

"Sure I did," he said. "When you tried all that stuff on. I liked sitting there, saying, 'Yeah, that one, no, not that one.' You looked good. So good."

"Do you think so?" said Kay.

"Yeah," he said.

They came up the stairs and into the room where the piano was. Jack took off his jacket and draped it over a chair, just like always, the zipper clicking against the leg. Kay sat down at the piano. The pigeons flew up to the window and spread their wings to stop on the sill, their shadows sweeping through the room. The cleanliness of the room, the pure light that came from the window, the new plaster, the wax on the floor made the room seem ordered and safe.

Jack opened the case, where the violin lay in a red velvet bed, the colors of the instrument like the wood of a racing single. The neck had a gray-black look to it, and the head curved like a fern in springtime. He picked it up and fingered the strings in the moving shadows of the birds. Kay knew what he was doing: feeling the floor with the tips of his toes and trying to maintain a lightness of touch, both on the floor and in the tips of his fingers: a relaxation that was at once complete and perfectly controlled.

They began to play. The shadows slid down the opened lid of the piano. They played Mozart's Sonata for Violin and Piano in E-flat Major, K. 380. Jack looked at her from time to time, as though saying, "It was worth it. You know that, don't you?" She played, allowing herself the luxury of enjoying it, not thinking of anything at all, really, aside from the music, waiting for the phrasing to be done in a way that left her certain, and that let her know he was right there with her. When Jack and Kay stopped playing, they heard the pop-pop-pop of the wings of the pigeons as they flew up to the windowsill.

"Well," he said. "Do you like that?"

"Yes," she said. Kay rubbed the swollen fingers of one hand with the fingers of the other.

"Do you want to play some more?" she said.

He looked at her hands.

"How badly does that hurt?" he said.

"What do you think?" she said.

"I think it hurts," he said.

He rubbed his fingers together.

"Mine aren't so good, either," he said.

"Do you want to play some more?" she said.

"No," said Jack. "I think that does it."

He put on his coat, and Kay put on hers, too. They went to the door and Kay said, "Aren't you going to take your violin?"

"No," said Jack. "I think I'm done with it."

CHAPTER 5

April 27, 2029

THE PEOPLE who worked with Briggs now did what was required of them: they tried to be innocuous, and to suggest that they were only having setbacks in otherwise ordinary careers. They reminded Briggs of people at an AA meeting: a little ashamed, hoping for the best, but certain that the worst had already happened. Perhaps Briggs had this idea because of the odor of the stale, reheated coffee everyone drank here, but he doubted it. And, moreover, the people he worked with had no curiosity. They had no interest in anything that didn't affect them personally. No one went downstairs into the cellar where there was a locked door, and if someone did, it wouldn't have made any difference. Who cared about a locked door in a hall that was dark, where the rats scratched and where the cockroaches skittered away when a light came on?

In the hall of the cellar, Briggs walked through the caress of a spiderweb. Everything about the adhesive tug of the filaments left him with a dry chill. He pushed the key into the lock and put his shoulder against the door. It swung into the blue light of the room.

The room smelled like a swimming pool dressing room from the Clorox he had used here. The apparatus, which sat on a bench, appeared to be simple: stainless-steel tubes, a central processing section, receptacles for the biotic materials he had managed to get his hands on. He had discovered a hundred or so viruses and bacteria in this room, no matter how hard he had tried to keep it sterile, but none of them were a serious contaminant. Or so he hoped. That was the terror of winging it. No tests with animals, no follow-up studies, nothing like that at all. Soon he would be in a position of trying it or not.

He watched a drop of the silver vaccine form, and on the surface of it he saw the blue shine of the lights behind him and his own shape, as in a wide-angle lens. What he thought was, *It is all in the shape of the proteins.* He thought of the mistakes he had made in school under conditions that were far better than this, but then he hoped his early mistakes had been those of an immature sensibility, rather than of technique. And, anyway, his technique had gotten better over the years. Then he looked up at the mold stains on the ceiling. They looked like a fossil of some kind that had been dead for millions of years.

The waiting left him tired, and he was glad to get away for a few hours. He took the subway home. It passed into the darkness of the tunnel between stations, and there he looked up at the faces that came out of the yellow gloom of the lighting, and while cheeks and lips were streaked with shadows, they still had an air of vitality, the women with their cheap makeup, the men in their tight jeans and shirts. In the onward shaking and rush of the car, Briggs was mildly comforted by their resilience. You did what you had to, and that was that. A woman at the end of a bench, in a black dress, flirted with a boy in a cheap coat. He nuzzled her neck briefly, his lips against her neck under her brown hair.

Briggs came up the stairs of the underground and walked to the end of the block, where names had been put up on a brick wall.

They had been done in the new script. A few Mungo Men were copying from the wall onto scraps of paper with a piece of crayon that had come out of a child's room. One of the new names was

H
A
L

B
R
I
G
G
S

One of the Mungo Men had false teeth that were too large. Underneath the coat he had on a flannel shirt for which he had made buttons out of chicken bones. He hadn't shaved, and his beard showed as white lines, which suggested the chaotic way in which it grew. A cowlick, a kind of turbulence where the hair of his neck mixed with the stubble on his jaw. He had a piece of bread in his pocket, which he took out and started to chew, and then he turned to Briggs and said, "Slim pickings tonight, but, shit, what can you do?"

CHAPTER **6** | *May 1, 2029*

IN THE blue light of the basement room, Briggs watched as the fluid dropped into the vial, one silver pendant at a time. He had a pneumatic syringe with him, a portable one that still had good power and was capable of shooting a large dose through his skin. But now he put it down and watched the accumulation of the vaccine. The first thing to do was to print the formula, to make notes about it, and to make sure those notes were available to anyone who wanted to see what he had done if things didn't work out. He made a hard copy, and then stored the formula on a number of machines, mailing it to himself at home, to the machine upstairs. All shipshape and orderly.

Over the years he had learned to have confidence, not of a bragging kind, but of a kind that suggested that if he had enough time, he could do good work. This had gotten him through a lot of bad spots. The difficulty now was that there hadn't been a lot of time, and he had had to do quickly things that usually were done with all the attention to detail that hard-learned procedures required.

He didn't like to think about the specific possibilities, but what he wanted didn't have much sway when he loaded the pneumatic syringe. It had a stainless-steel body and a piston in which Briggs put the vaccine. Even the dose was a matter of conjecture, although he had used the models of other vaccines, and he supposed he was pretty close. But it wasn't the dose, so much as the effect. He thought about mucus membranes turning black, the lining of his nose, for instance, or other, more intimate orifices. Or the lining of the esophagus sloughing off in black tubes. And these were the best of possibilities if things went sour. What if the lining of the brain were affected? The world would seem toxic, stinging. He would perceive every surface, every wall, as poisonous to the touch. And of course there was the possibility, under these circumstances, that he would simply cease to exist as he had always had, and that while he would be gone, the almost infinite misery of living without a sense of self would be the method by which he knew that he was still alive. So, he picked up the pneumatic syringe and cocked it and held it against his arm. *Well,* he thought, *do you believe in yourself or not?*

"Ah, shit," he said.

The syringe made a little *pfft!* He felt the cool sensation of the injection on his forearm, and then rinsed out the syringe with the cleaning solution that came with it, and turned it upside down to dry. Didn't hurt much. He ran his finger over the red spot, which looked like an insect bite. A little swelling was all right, he guessed, but he wasn't so sure about more than that. His finger lingered on the stinging itch as he tried to abandon the impulse toward brooding about the possibilities this bump suggested. There was nothing to be done now. Still, this was a moment when the short-term comforts of fatalism were obvious. Fatalism helps with the jump, but not the fall.

May 1, 2029

"PSSSST," SAID one of the Mungo Men. "Hey. You."

In the shadows, their plumes of breath spewed into the air like bubbles coming out of an Aqua-Lung. Briggs looked around, not expecting help, but still taking an inventory of possibilities. The moon above the rooftops was so large and clearly visible that Briggs could distinguish white mountains and lunar seas and the accumulated debris of endless impact.

"Not now," said Briggs.

"Not now?" said one of the Mungo Men. "You hear that? That's what they all say. One way or another."

Up ahead Briggs made out the steps of his building, but he didn't think it was a good idea to go there. All he had was a list of things that were bad ideas. The evening dew gave every surface a gleam as though it were covered with freezing rain. He looked around and realized that he was in the last refuge of the hunted: no plans, just the habit of what he had been doing last.

The lights in the brownstones were impossibly promising, and as he looked at them he tried to imagine the smell of soup, of chops broiling. Maybe soap and the slight domestic reminder of bacon that had been cooked for dinner. In the living rooms men sat reading newspapers or listening to music. Behind him, the limping shapes came out of the space between the buildings, the shadows falling away like capes.

Briggs stopped. He turned to face them.

He stood at the entrance to an alley, and a sound came from the back of it, a sigh of some kind, a slight intake of breath. He had guessed that under those circumstances the best thing was to be absolutely still: it was what an animal did when cornered. He heard light footfalls in the shadows, and when he glanced that way, he saw movement, like moonlight on a black scarf.

"Briggs," said Kay.

She wore a raincoat, her hand in one pocket, and as he turned to her, the men in the street came along, limping, dragging their feet, drawn forward with determination. Kay took a step closer to him, her breath trailing over her shoulder. She opened and closed her raincoat to tie the sash more tightly, and when she did so, he saw that she wasn't wearing anything underneath it.

"I think what we need to do is to walk away from here as though we haven't got a care in the world," she said. "Letting them know you are afraid brings out the worst."

She had put her lips against his ear to whisper, and her words came as warm, insistent puffs.

"Come on. Let's just walk away. I'm going to take your arm. Is that all right?"

The street was lighted by a few neon signs, reds and greens that were so bright as to suggest a taste, like cherry or mint. Kay pulled on his arm a little, trying to steady herself. When they walked together, the cadence of their steps was perfectly matched.

One of the Mungo Men had a knife, which he scraped along the metal rods of a fence, and when he came up to the wall of a building, he ran it across the bricks. Kay pulled Briggs's arm against her side, and turned a little so that she could briefly hug it against her chest.

"I never thought it would be like that," he said.

"What?" she said

"Being able to touch you," he said.

She took his hand and put it under her coat, against the warm skin of her side, his fingers feeling the texture of her ribs.

"You're not going to leave me, are you?" she said. "After I took a chance to find you? Do you know how long I waited in the cold?"

The men behind them whistled to each other, as though arranging themselves in some preconceived pattern to cut off avenues of escape. Briggs thought of the details that were reported about people the Mungo

Men had caught: the small, deep puncture wounds, the disfiguring slashes, the bones that had been pulverized into wet grit. The papers tried to suggest what tools might have been used, a bat, a pipe, a home-made weapon of some kind. He looked back.

"I'm not going to leave you," he said.

She hugged his arm against her. At the end of the street there was a lamp, and in the light of it he looked at her hair, her eyes, touched her skin.

The all-night café had windows all the way around, and the light from the place fell onto the sidewalk in trapezoids. Inside it had a counter, some chrome coffee urns, and a man in a white shirt with a white hat bent over a sink, washing dishes. At the counter, one man had spread out a newspaper, which he read, one sentence at a time. Then a bite of a doughnut. A sip of coffee. The next sentence.

The diner smelled of coffee and Danish, home-fried potatoes and toast and jam, the heavy atmosphere of the roast-beef special with mashed potatoes, peas, and gravy. The man who was washing dishes looked up briefly when Briggs and Kay walked to the back, where there was a booth. The men in the gray coats came in too, their beards showing as black and white sand, their eyebrows bushy. The man behind the counter was about to say something to them, but then thought better of it. He stood up, drying his hands on a gray towel, looking around. Then he came over to Kay and Briggs.

"What's it going to be?" he said. He wore a white cap and a white apron. He glanced over his shoulder, just once.

"Ice cream," she said. "Vanilla."

It came in small stainless-steel cups, which reflected the green table-top and Briggs's and Kay's hands as they picked up their spoons and began to eat. Kay kept her eyes down when she took her first bite, hold-ing the sweet ice cream in her mouth. The Mungo Men milled around in the front, shoving each other, sitting down, standing up. One of them licked a palm and poured sugar on it and then put it into his mouth.

Kay put a spoonful of ice cream into her mouth and drew it out, the surface of the ice cream grooved by the texture of her lips. She left a point of vanilla, almost like the curve of an ice skate, at the tip of the spoon.

"It burns my mouth," she said. "It's so good."

He ate his, too. She finished, scraping the small bowl all the way around so as to get all of it. Then she put the tip of her tongue into the cup and licked the edge. She got up and came to his side of the booth and took his hand, which she put under her coat, the warmth of her side coming as a smoothness of temperature, of air almost more than skin.

"Where are we going to go?" he said.

"Are you sure you want to come with me?" she said.

"Yes," he said, "but where?"

"We could go into the bathroom and lock the door," she said.

He looked around.

"I'd like something else, though," she said. "My hotel isn't far away. Are you willing to try to get there? It would mean going back out on the street."

"All right," he said.

"Don't be afraid," she said.

"No," he said. "I won't." He looked up at the front of the diner. "Come on."

They got up and walked up to the counter, where there was a line of stools on chrome posts. The cash register was chrome too, and polished. Along the top of the counter was a sign that said, HAM AND EGGS, HOME FRIES, POTATOES, $36.00. The counterman wrote on his pad, tore off a small green slip, and passed it over. Briggs paid him and the man made change, and when he passed it over, he said, "Are those guys after you?"

Briggs nodded.

"Well, that's too bad, isn't it?" said the man. Then he glanced once at the men behind Kay and Briggs.

"Good night," said Kay.

"Yeah," said the man. "Good night."

In the street Kay said, "The hotel is up here."

In the storefront windows they saw distorted images of themselves. Briggs thought the red lights of the hotel were far away. Kay walked with her head up, shoulders back, the heavy object in her pocket swinging back and forth, bumping against her thigh.

They came up to the front of the hotel, into the lobby, the men in gray coats behind them. At the back of the lobby, Kay pushed the button for the elevator. The men behind them stopped at the desk and said to the clerk there, "What room is she in?"

"Her?" said the clerk. He glanced from one of them to another. "Five-oh-six."

"A couple of you take the stairs," said one of the men.

The elevator creaked down and stopped. Kay and Briggs got in, and she pulled the gate shut, the dark geometry of it swinging out with a squeak and then a bang. The cage had antiquated bars with spear-shaped points at the top, and above them, around the entire car, was a pattern of iron leaves and vines, which, against the dim light of the lobby, looked like black lace on white skin. Kay put her hand on Briggs's face, one finger just tapping his lips and then running back and forth over them, her touch at once gentle and yet shaking. The elevator went up the center of the spiral staircase, where it was enclosed in a wire mesh.

She breathed with an asthmatic panting. The elevator rose in its erratic ascent, jerking a little, trembling, squeaking in the pulleys up above. In the stairwell beyond the mesh, they heard the pounding of steps, the gasping of men who were out of shape, shouting to one another not in words, but in exhausted syllables.

Kay hit the emergency button. The lights went out and the elevator was filled with the gray luminescence that came from the floor above as it hung there, suspended in the iron mesh that surrounded the cage. The touch of Kay's tongue in his ear overwhelmed the dim light, the sound of the men pounding on the walls, their cries of distress and anger. She looked into his face, put her hand on his belt and unbuckled it. She said, with her lips against his ear, the words almost inaudible, "Shhhh. Now, you look at me, just at me. That's right. That's good. Oh."

"Wait," he said. "Wait."

"For what?" said Kay. "We don't have time . . . "

She opened her coat, her skin white in the dim light. Her hands went along the small of his back, pushing his trousers down, her fingers slipping under the band of his underwear.

"You're going to tell me you don't want to? Look at me and tell me you don't want this . . . "

"What about a child?" he said. "About getting pregnant . . . "

"Oh, that," she said. "Don't worry. Don't be afraid. We don't have to worry about a child. Is that what you are worried about?"

In the hall, one of the Mungo Men said "Fee, Fi, Fo, Fum . . . "

"What?" said the other. "What did you say?"

"Just something from when I was a kid," said the Mungo Man. "'I smell the blood of an Englishman.' Did you ever hear that?"

"Naw," said the other Mungo Man. "We didn't talk much at my house."

She went on looking at him, pursing her lips, sucking his fingers, her skin white in the dim light of the car. Above her he saw the scrollwork at the top of the cage like the shadows of a tree on a sunny day, at once lacy and intricate. She held his face so that he couldn't look away, and she whispered, telling him that she forgave him, and that all she wanted was a little time. Wouldn't he give her that? He slumped down on the floor, and she sat over his naked legs, the front panels of her coat opening so that she could press her sweaty skin against him.

"You know what I want," she said. "Don't you?"

"Yes," he said.

"Well, won't you let me have that?" she said.

He saw that she was crying, the paths of her tears running from the side of her eyes and down her face as she heaved, still shaking her head, still saying, or seeming to say, *Don't make a sound.* Not a sound. As she heaved, he felt her contractions, the tightening grip of them.

She put her lips against his and said, with a pant, a shudder of excitement, "You thought you could say, No . . . didn't you? Didn't you?"

"No," he said. "I knew I never would."

She pulled his face against her, put his lips against the tears. She whispered that she was crying, not out of sorrow, but happiness, delight. Did he understand that? Outside, the Mungo Men shouted, banged on the wall. She put her head against his, the hardness of the bones coming through the caress of her hair. Her lips were warm and slippery, insistent.

"Have you ever wanted something, waited for it, dreamed of it, tasted it in your imagination, needed it? And when you got it was it everything you wanted, hoped for . . . ? That's what this is, even on the floor in this rundown elevator. Can you understand that?"

She put her hands on the bars just above him, and when she pulled against them, the panels of the coat opened, the texture of her skin brushing against his cheek, his forehead. She strained as she grasped the black bars, shaking them a little, her breath asthmatic.

"Trust me," she said.

"I trust you," he said.

"Do you? Show me. Come in me." She looked at his face. "Yes. Like that. Oh, just like that."

In the darkness the men stamped, whistled, hammered on the mesh of the cage.

She stood up. He did too, trying to pull himself together as she tied the belt of her coat, and then she reached over and kissed him, nicely, innocently, like a kid. She reached over and hit the red button and the elevator lurched upward. He put his lips next to her ear and said, "Oh, Kay, Kay . . . "

She put her head against him and said, "My room is just down the hall."

He listened to the men around them, pounding the walls.

"I'll grind his bones to make my bread . . . " said one of them.

The elevator stopped. The door creaked open. Briggs looked up at the antiquated floor counter, the arrow of it pointing to 5. As they stepped out, Briggs squinting a little, already recoiling a little from the first blow, he saw that Jack was standing there at the top of the stairwell, looking down. Then he turned to Kay and said, "Are these guys bothering you?"

The Mungo Men stood there, just on the threshold, the mass of them coming up from the dark clutter, the mesh like fishnet stockings, the banister made of black metal and supported by those same wrought-iron vines and leaves. They looked up and hesitated and then one of them looked at Briggs and said, "We haven't forgotten. Don't you worry. Some other time."

They filed downward, the sounds of their departure going around and around in a spiral until they vanished in the depths below. Kay looked at Briggs and said, "See? Nothing to worry about."

"Uh-huh," said Briggs. He put a hand to his head.

"Hey, Briggs," said Jack. "Good to see you." He listened as the last sounds died in the stairwell. Down below they heard the squeak and slam of the street door. "Well," said Jack, still looking down, "I guess they've gone."

"They'll be back," said Briggs.

He turned and saw Kay watching him.

"Hey, Jack," said Kay. "Do you want to take a walk?"

"Sure," he said. "I've been inside all day. Dying to get out."

He started into the depths, his shape disappearing into the darkness of the stairwell.

"Let's go in," she said to Briggs.

She undid the sash of the raincoat.

"Come on," she said. "Don't you want to?"

AS THEY lay in the warmth of the bed, they heard the water dripping in the bathroom. Kay put her lips against his ear and said, "That's nice. Just to be here. Almost as good as the other."

Briggs said, "Well, they both have their advantages."

Kay touched his shoulder with her finger, tapping it in time to the dripping in the bathroom, and as she did so, she said, "Whenever you hear that sound, you'll think of me, won't you?"

"Yes," he said. "Sure. And what about you?"

"Me?" she said. She shrugged. "I don't know. Maybe. That doesn't seem like much, really, a drop of water. But it is. I could hear it when we were . . . well, a little earlier."

"Was it nice?" he said.

"It was so loud I could hardly breathe," she said.

"Still, it would be nice to have something more than that," he said.

"Like what?" she said.

He shrugged and threw back the sheets. He got up and stood there, looking for his clothes. Then he found his shirt and put it on. "You aren't leaving, are you?" she said. "I mean, just like that?"

"No," he said.

They got dressed and went out into the hall, and then took the elevator down to the lobby. Outside, on the street, they saw some smoke in the distance where people had set cars on fire and where some windows were broken, the glass spread in the street as though someone had dropped a block of ice.

She took his arm and they went toward the burning cars, the smoke rising into the lights of the buildings.

"So, what are you going to show me?" she said.

"In here," he said.

They went into the smoky atmosphere of a gaming parlor where men and women walked in a chiaroscuro haze, and while they appeared in silhouette, they were still sleek and muscular in the suits they wore. The booths where people played were lined up around the walls, and above each of them a small marquee stuck out, making it resemble a diminutive movie theater. The name of each game was displayed in stylized type on the marquee. In the back of the room, near the changing room, Briggs smelled the scent of opium and saw people in a nimbus of smoke. He wondered if it was being smoked by someone who was celebrating or consoling himself. He had always felt a moral certainty when smoking it, and he looked around and thought, *Yes. It would be nice to have a little certainty now.*

The small marquees made the room appear like a miniature strip where movie theaters were lined up, and in the middle, men and women loitered at a bar, drinking slowly, killing time, not quite flirting, but not totally uninterested, either, all of them looking for the next mark.

Briggs picked up a promotional gimmick, a collapsible fan, for a game called Bangkok. The fan was made of paper, creased like an accordion, and the wooden ends were painted gold. He showed it to the manager of the place and told him that he wanted to take a look around in the game. What was new in Bangkok? The manager had black, slicked-back hair and a small mustache, and he gave the impression of a croupier. He didn't say a word, but just motioned to a booth along the wall.

Inside, Briggs and Kay sat on padded benches that were opposite each other, the gimmick dangling from Briggs's hand.

"So," said Kay. "What now?"

Briggs looked at her and said, "I'm going to hot-wire this thing. So that means we are not going to stay long, all right?"

"I guess," she said.

"Oh," he said, "there's no guessing about this. All right? We'll leave when I say?"

"Okay," she said. "What is this, a cheap date?"

He thought of the chance he was taking by using the game to show her what he was thinking.

"You tell me," he said.

At the back of the booth was a panel that felt like flesh, like the inside of a woman's thigh, and Briggs took the tools from his pocket and opened it up. Inside were a chip and a keyboard; the keyboard was used by the maintenance people, and now Briggs took it out and made some changes, doing so quickly, adding a line here or there, and as he worked, he heard the hilarity and drunken laughter of the people outside. The fluid from the slit that Briggs had made dripped onto the floor, clear, like a lubricant of some kind, and it fell with a steady, repeated cadence. Kay listened to it.

"What are you thinking about?" said Briggs.

"Oh, the sound," she said. "It reminds me of the hotel. Of those moments when you came in me. I can still feel it." She watched him work. "You know, when I made changes, I didn't do it like that."

"Oh?" he said. "Well, it's done now. It should last for a little bit." He turned to listen. He supposed it was possible to set off an alarm doing this, but years ago he had done some of the security code, and what he didn't know he guessed at.

"Here," he said. "Put this on."

She slipped the cuff over her arm. Then she sat back.

Briggs put the cuff over his forearm and lay back, feeling the thrill of the registration, just as if his arm had been sprayed with rubbing alcohol. Then he put his head back and let his sense of the machine wash over him.

"Close your eyes," he said.

She went on staring at him.

"No. Trust me. Don't be difficult," he said. "We don't have a lot of time."

"If anyone comes," she said, "they'll wish they hadn't."

"Maybe we can avoid that," he said. "Just close your eyes."

"Where are we going?" she said.

"Close your eyes," he said.

The noise of the room, the scent of opium became indistinct before they vanished, and for an instant Kay felt that she was descending, slipping into a cool and restful darkness. Then she woke up. She looked around and saw that she was in a city she had never seen before. She stood in a square with a fountain, and in it were muscular men and women, the water playing over them in enormous sheets tinted with the colors of a rainbow, and when she and Briggs walked up to the marble figures, the air was immediately filled with the wild beating of wings. Pigeons rose around them.

It was just evening, and the Mediterranean light played on the walls of buildings that were only three stories high and had wooden shutters, but the remarkable thing, as far as Kay was concerned, was the way the setting sun played over the pastel wash of the walls. The wash was a tangerine color that glowed in the sun, although Kay noticed something else too, which was that the combination of light and color had an emotional quality, a warmth that seemed to spread through her. She couldn't tell where the warmth of the colors ended and where she began, or where she ended and the skin of Briggs's hand began.

"I thought you'd like Rome," he said.

They went through the piazza and up to the corner, to Largo Argentina, and there they got on a tram, a green one, which moved along in a sparking locomotion as it got electricity from the overhead wires. The Romans sat in the grinding hum of the engine, the women elegant and sultry and the men flirting with them, and as the car went past more of those walls with that glowing wash, Kay felt Briggs next to her, and when she turned to him, he flirted with her, just like the Romans, winking at her and smiling.

They got off the tram and went into a restaurant, where they ate marinated lobster, potatoes, onions, and tomatoes out of a silver bowl, and they drank wine and had fresh berries for dessert. After lunch they walked along the bank of the river, and she tried to articulate to herself just what was wonderful about the temperature of the air. The caress of it and the warmth was indistinguishable from the sensation of being loved. They came up to the Ponte Garibaldi and walked out into the middle of the bridge. They stopped to lean on the stone balustrade and listen to the sound of the water and feel the temperature of the air. Kay tried to put the certainty of the moment into words, if only to be able to remember it, but when she tried to do so, it eluded her, and when she was afraid it was gone forever, she felt the warm certainty of his kiss, which was indistinguishable from the temperature of the air. The warmth of the kiss coalesced into the memory of their lovemaking and the possibility of having a child.

They walked back toward Largo Argentina and then out toward the Coliseum, the thing snaggletoothed and broken here and there. But no matter where they went, she kept turning to the salmon-colored light, which left her warm and that much more able to understand her attachment to Briggs, or maybe it was better to say that here, where he had brought her, she didn't have to think about this attachment so much as to feel it on her skin or to have that sensation of existing with him in that haunting, illuminating light. She wanted to thank him for bringing her here, but words seemed so useless and at odds with the warmth, the physical sensation that was so oddly a matter of understanding, too.

She heard the harsh noises of the gaming parlor. Briggs sat up, turning to listen to what was going on outside, and said, "I think we should go. I'm not too sure about how long . . . "

"No," she said. "Just wait."

"We agreed," he said.

"Just wait. Close your eyes. It won't take long," she said.

He looked out and saw a policeman who had come into the room. The policeman spoke to the manager.

"Kay," he said.

"Close your eyes," she said. "Please."

Briggs lay back, forgetting the sounds in the room and the policeman, and he instantly saw a night sky, and as he looked at it, he noticed that the distances didn't seem cold or intimidating, although they hadn't lost their scale. Instead, as the distances became more obvious, as he saw a nebula in the shape of a horse's head, the masses of stars of it so thick they looked like mist, he felt a hot sense of belonging and an increasing scale that would have scared him if he hadn't been certain of Kay's presence. It had been a long time since he cried, but as he gave in to his impulse to do so, as a complete abandonment of restraint, he had the sensation of rising into a cloud, like the mist of a star-speckled nebula, which was made up of Kay's warmth. For an instant he was about to cry out, but he was soothed by the fragrance of her skin, her smile, and the reassuring touch of one finger. As he opened his eyes, he felt her breath against his ear.

B R I G G S   L E F T Kay at the hotel. He hadn't worn a coat, and when he had walked a short way, the chills began. They started as a vague discomfort and a sense of being a little seasick. He went down to the avenue and walked up to the corner, to the subway, but up ahead he saw some people in the street, a couple of hundred of them, and they were looking up at a man who was standing on a ledge. Briggs walked farther up and stepped into the crowd, glad he was with a lot of people, but when he felt the roll of chills, he stepped back away from them.

The man on the ledge didn't look down, and his demeanor had the false serenity that comes from facing the worst, but in fact he was waiting for a moment of clarity. Briggs looked up like the rest of the people, and then realized the man had lost everything—money, security, his sense of who he was. The markets were getting worse. Briggs wondered how many other people were standing behind windows and thinking about climbing out on a ledge. Up above, in the cold air, the man stared into the distance.

Briggs turned and walked away. He didn't want to see the man jump, and it probably wasn't a good idea, he guessed, to be close to other people. He supposed it was possible that he was going to have a slight case of the disease, but what was a slight case? And then he wasn't certain that this was just a reaction to the vaccine, since he might have missed some other pathogen altogether. That was one of the problems of working alone. It was easy to make a mistake, and no one was there to check up on you. The nausea came in earnest. He put his hand to his mouth and turned into an alley, not wanting to be seen vomiting on the street. Black fire escapes, trash cans, the skittering of rats, if that's what they were, maybe just cats, and, here and there, old newspapers that seemed to stir in the late-night air like creatures that had only been half-killed and still wanted to live. He moved into the alley and leaned against the wall. The fever came too, with pains in the joints and a sense of disorientation. *Oh no,* he thought. *Not like this.*

Well, he had learned one thing, which was that where Kay was concerned, he wasn't able to resist her, but then how would he ever have been able to do that? She knew everything about him, what was exciting, what was mysterious, what left him with a sense of terror. She understood him. Now, as he sat against the damp wall, certain that the fever was getting worse, he didn't know what left him more mystified: that he might have made a mistake with the vaccine, or that he had been unable to resist Kay. Didn't his beliefs amount to anything? Or, he told himself, maybe it was the other way around, maybe he had gone with her because of his beliefs. Loyalty, beauty, the strength of a human being when things were bad. Didn't she have all of those qualities? *It's like looking in a hall of mirrors,* he thought. *How am I ever going to see what is happening to me? It is as though I am living in a world where my best impulses are leading to a moment like this. And how am I going to make sense of that? If you can't trust your best qualities, or your most fervent hopes, then what have you got?*

He turned and vomited slowly against the wall. The stink of his own sickness made him ill again and he tried to get away, first standing and putting his head against the brick of the wall. His face was dirty and he could still smell the sour odor. The alley had puddles of water in potholes here and there, and he walked over to one and knelt next to it. He took his handkerchief from his pocket and put it into the water. It was cool to his fingers, and he was glad to have it against his forehead and around his mouth, and while he wasn't happy about where the water had come from, he felt a little better, not so much clean as differently dirty.

He stood up and went to the end of the alley. The chills came and went in a way he had never experienced, since the wave was comprised of individual points that were so distinct he could almost count them. Or he could have counted them if they weren't moving so fast across his shoulders and into his hair. The sensation was like being naked and having someone spray him with rubbing alcohol, and the chill was made up of individual droplets. He rolled his shoulders and stood there.

A bar was at the end of the street. As he looked at the pink and green neon sign of the place, he realized that he had to urinate. His eyes itched a little, and when he rubbed them, he saw that the back of his hand had a black streak on it. Had he picked up something when he had washed his face, some soot? Some grease that had been in the puddle? Was that it? He thought of the clerk in the hotel, the dark stains on his face, the flecks of black skin around the man's mouth, the inky stains that appeared on the man's pants.

Briggs went up the street, but the fever made it seem as though he were walking through wind that blew from one side. Then he stood in front of the frosted glass of the door. He guessed that he could get something to drink, a glass of water, but then that might just make him have to urinate more, and he didn't want that. He looked around, seeing the late-night fog roll in from the river in a bank that obliterated everything.

The bar was wooden, scarred here and there where people had scratched into it with a key or a knife, but those words or names had been cut into the bar a long time ago, and now they didn't seem like vandalism, but the reminder of people who had existed a long time ago. Time had made the scratches on the bar into something quaint. The bartender looked at him and said, "What do you want? A drink? Or, do you want something to eat?"

Briggs shook his head and put his hand to his mouth.

"Scotch," he said. "And a glass of water."

"Hey," said the bartender. "Are you all right?"

"Sure," said Briggs. He tried to smile, but he was pretty sure it came out as a grimace. "Fine. Just a drink."

The bartender poured the drink and brought over the water, putting both down as though he had second thoughts about the entire thing. Briggs reached into his pocket for some money, and put a large bill on the wood in front of the bartender. Briggs rolled the liquor around in his mouth. A mirror was hung behind the bar, and through the collection of bottles Briggs tried to see the smudge on his face. It could have been dirt.

"Have you got a bathroom?" he said.

"Back there," said the bartender, gesturing to the rear of the place.

Briggs finished the drink and staggered down the line of chrome stools with red leather seats. He thought he could call Kay. Maybe she would know what to do, but then how could she? If he had something new, what could she do about it? He swallowed and turned into the bathroom. Maybe he had misread some of the specifications for dosage and concentration, or maybe he had been confused about the way the vehicle he had chosen conveyed the vaccine.

The light here was fluorescent, and he stood in front of the mirror. He opened his mouth, but the light was directly above him, and all he saw was the rictus formed by his own barely recognizable lips. Then he went into a stall and stood in front of the urinal. He was so frightened of what he would see, the inky urine that came from the dead lining of his kidneys, that when he produced nothing more than a clear stream, he started shaking. Maybe the fever would pass. He swallowed and then stood in front of the sink, where he washed his face with soap that smelled like the stuff that had been in the bathrooms of the schools he had gone to when he had been a kid.

KAY WASN'T hungry, exactly, but nevertheless she had a craving that left her a little agitated, and while she tried to think what it might be, she knew that someone had done this to her. Not Briggs. She was pretty sure of that. However much she knew this craving was artificial, she wanted to satisfy it. Whatever it was, she hoped she would recognize it when she saw it, but how to find it, or to get herself in a place where such recognition could take place? For a while she assumed that it was something she wanted to eat—French fries with ketchup, a crumb doughnut, a steak with onions, pasta with sun-dried tomatoes and garlic, chocolate cake— but as she went through the list, the craving grew.

She looked out the window of the hotel. The thin clouds covered the sun like a photographer's umbrella. Some birds flew against it, and they coasted after each wingbeat, making an up-and-down pattern like the sagging of telephone wires between poles. Was that it? she thought. The desire to fly? To get away?

On the street she didn't go in any particular direction, although she noticed that she wanted to see plants and flowers, and she walked toward the trees at the end of the block and stood in the green tinted shade. It was refreshing, but it didn't do that much good, really, and soon she was so restless again that she continued searching. In this part of town she saw some food carts on the street, and she stopped in front of some, but it was useless. It wasn't food. She passed a church, and while she was tempted by the dark and empty shadows, the remote and diminishing odor of incense, she only hesitated and then moved on, hearing the flap of wings and seeing the shape of the birds against that bright, lumines-cent sky.

The Botanical Garden was at the end of a long avenue, and after Kay passed it, she stopped and turned back. The building was made of marble with a Greek Revival front, and on both sides of it, behind black bars that were topped with spikes, formal gardens stretched into the dis-tance. Even from here she heard the plash of a fountain, and she saw a marble figure standing in a pool of water, a woman with full hips, her hands holding a fish, from the mouth of which green-tinted water flowed.

She bought a ticket and went in to the marble-floored lobby, where her shoes made a clicking echo. Directly in front of her was a greenhouse with a glass roof, and in the soft air and the soothing light she saw a chaos of fronds and palms, mosses, creepers, small flowers that weren't much bigger than a pinhead. The fronds were neatly arrayed, like jalousies. She went in.

She sat on a bench next to a woman in a dark dress who wore very red lipstick. Everything about her seemed familiar, and the damp, warm air of the greenhouse, the mixture of leaves and flowers, the sight of chains of red ants, all contributed to a sense of comfort.

"Kay," said Carr.

Carr had a bag of lemon sweets. The paper made a diminutive, sad crinkle when she opened it.

"May I have one of those?" said Kay.

Kay reached out for one, and then glanced back at the tropical tree trunks, which had the color of an elephant's skin, and against the bark the orchids hung in a cascade of petals. The moment in the elevator came back to her when the wetness ran along her leg, the stuff getting everywhere, on her hands, the lining of her coat. The petals had a ridged texture, the raised lines reminding her of the pattern on the vanilla ice cream when she had drawn the spoon between her lips. She closed her eyes to recall the taste. Finally she put the lemon candy in her mouth: that was what she had craved. The instant she tasted it, she knew she had been sent for.

"What do you want?" Kay said.

"Oh, such a sharp tongue," said Carr. "Well, that will come in handy."

The room had a hush that came from so much vegetation crowded into the enclosed space.

"I guess," said Kay.

"My," said Carr, "you sulk beautifully. So tell me, have you broken any hearts recently?"

"And what is it to you?" said Kay.

"To me?" said Carr. "Why, it is everything to me."

Carr carefully looked into Kay's eyes.

"And what gives you the right to feel that way?" said Kay.

"How dare you speak to me like that?" said Carr. She raised her hand as though to strike, but then she stopped and sat back. She looked around, seemingly hoping that she could draw something from the leaves and flowers. Then she looked back at Kay and said, "I am sure you know, if you would just give it a moment's thought. Haven't you ever been discarded? And when you are discarded, my sweet, you learn something about self-loathing," said Carr. She made that small, sad laugh. "And self-loathing is the sister of revenge."

"I guess," said Kay.

"Oh, sulk like that," said Carr. "I love to see it. So tell me, are you going to see Blaine?"

"Soon," said Kay.

Carr swallowed as though she had been thinking about something that she craved. "I'll want to know if he cried, if he begged. I want the words he says, flecks of gold, each one." She came closer to Kay. "You and I will gather them up. We will hammer them into some beautiful thing to wear."

Kay looked at the fronds, which were so like green venetian blinds.

"But it's not enough to break his heart. Not really. What we want is to make sure he loses his sense of who he is. He likes to think he is competent. Well, we will fix that, won't we?"

"We will?" said Kay.

"Of course, my sweet," said Carr. "But of course. Can't you feel the impulse?"

Kay looked down.

"Yes," she said. "I can feel it."

"And?" said Carr.

"It's so bitter," said Kay.

"Yes," said Carr. "And who is more bitter, you or me?"

Kay swallowed.

"I don't know," she said.

Carr took Kay's hand and held it in her own.

"Listen to me," she said. "Confuse him. Give him bad advice. Let him make mistakes that only a fool would make. He won't even know who he is anymore."

Carr got up and kissed Kay on the forehead.

"You are so lovely," she said.

She held out the bag.

"Would you like another?" she said. She opened the bag up, displaying the jumble of lemon balls.

Kay had the feeling that if she could resist the craving, if she could simply swallow and forget it, she would be able to do what she wanted.

"Here," said Carr.

Kay reached into the bag, her fingers going over the candies. She put one into her mouth and sat there, sucking it.

"Bittersweet," said Carr, "isn't it?"

Carr walked into the greenish light of the place, passing the small fountain where a spout gurgled, and in which people had thrown coins as they had made a wish. The coins lay in a clutter on the bottom. Kay thought of Rome, of the fountains there, the light that covered all the walls like dust. She wished that she had a piece of paper and a pencil so she could write to Briggs, just a few words, and while she was sure they would be imperfect and imprecise, she hoped that in the imperfection of what she wrote, he would see something of her, some quality that could only be conveyed by awkwardness, which, at certain moments, might have a beauty of its own. Then she stood up and walked out through the open fans of the ferns, the cascades of flowers, as though a handful of bright red scraps of paper had been dropped from a height and now fell through the green-on-green shadows here. She went out into the street.

"DID KAY call?" Blaine said to his housekeeper.

"No," she said.

"And she hasn't come here? Hasn't left a note?"

She shook her head.

"I'm sorry, Mr. Blaine," she said.

Blaine's housekeeper put an early dinner on the table, and later she saw that he was sitting there in front of the roast, the spinach soufflé, the wild rice, all of it uneaten. Blaine sat there alone, looking at the food as though the things there were an indictment of him for never being able to ask for what he needed. Or for not understanding what he required. This was what appalled him: his inability to know what he needed, and how important the ordinary really was. He imagined his wife as she had sat opposite him at their lunches, waiting for him to die. Surely this was the saddest pleasure, waiting for someone you hated to die.

When he was certain that he wouldn't be able to eat, he went back into the library, where, on a card table, he stared at the jigsaw puzzle he had worked on for the last few days. The pieces lay there with a mysterious incoherence, a refusal to be put together. He stood there, a tall shape in dark clothes in the yellow light of the library, and in the shadows he picked up the box the puzzle had come in and swept it in. He thought, *Yes, my son is waiting for me to die, too.*

He sat down and looked out the window. Now, at eight, a few lights burned, and he saw the stars beyond the roofs and towers, their shapes mocking, since a few days before the stars had seemed to be part of an order, a pattern, which made sense and had been studied and understood, but which now just looked like flecks of senseless blue light. The buildings appeared as usual, although their luminescence seemed frail, like a flashlight bulb when the battery is running down.

He wanted to put a label on what he had gotten from Kay. He tried to do this by saying to himself that she had given him a sense of sweetness, like the aroma in a Vermont sugarhouse in the spring, when the clouds of steam were like a sweet fog that he could feel on his skin and taste on the tip of his tongue. But the odd thing was that this sensation wasn't physical, but mental. Along with it he had the certainty that she understood him. She forgave. She made him feel that his coldness had been a vicious artifice, and that if he was lucky, she might give him a second chance.

He hadn't shaved, brushed his hair, or changed his shirt. He knew that soon people from the office would be coming for him, but he didn't care. He waited for Kay to arrive. He was certain that if he could spend some time with her, he would know what to do. She might play for him. Afterwards they might . . . They might what? She might kiss him. Could he really be so far gone as to want just a kiss? Well, maybe more than that, when he got down to cases, but a kiss was what he craved. Then he thought of what it would be like to sleep with her, to be in that sweet, damp caress, at once physical, as though inhaling the dulcet fog of the sugarhouse, and yet mental too, as though his thoughts were part of that same enveloping mist.

The housekeeper came in and said, "She's here," and then turned and went out, her red, pink-soled shoes squeaking on the floor. Kay came into the room in the wake of the housekeeper's departure.

"Ah, Kay," he said. "Kay."

He moved forward on his chair.

"Don't get up," said Kay. "Don't. You look tired."

"Do I?" he said. "Well. Here I am. The great man himself. Just look!"

She sat down opposite him.

"And how did I come to this?" Blaine said.

"You'll feel better in a little while," she said.

"Oh, that's where you're wrong. Wrong," he said. "I can't think clearly."

He put his head in his hands.

"Don't you have to make a decision about what to do?" she said. "About the markets?"

"Yes," he said. "I guess . . . "

Kay looked around the room. Then she turned to Blaine. How reduced he was, nothing more than a bundle of nerves. He had brought himself to this by throwing away the things she had craved: children, family, a regular life. She even thought of him standing on the rail of his terrace, looking down, hair in disarray, the birds swirling around him, making him dizzy as he thought of stepping off: this would be the moment when he realized that he was a failure as a bureaucrat and as a man, too. She could already see his stricken expression.

"Kay," he said. "Won't you play a little something?"

She got up and went to the piano, lifting the cover from the keys. The line of them, in black and white, stretched away into the darkness at the end of the keyboard. She put her coat on a chair behind her and sat down. Then she pulled up the bench and worked one of the pedals, which made a squeak. She kept looking at Blaine, at the room, and as she looked around, she wanted to get away. She didn't have time for this. She had other things to do.

"Well?" he said. "What are you waiting for? Are you sick?"

"Shhh," she said. "Please."

"Please what?" he said.

"Please be quiet. I don't want to hear your voice."

"My voice?" he said.

She reached out to the lid of the piano and slammed it shut, and then again, the humming, discordant sound of the piano coming once and then again, and then a third time when the lid cracked at the hinges and hung like some drunken thing.

"Kay," he said. "Kay!"

"What did I tell you?" she said.

She thought, *Now. Now is the moment.* She stood up and walked over to him, her hip next to his face. Outside, the city lights shimmered in blues and yellows, and for a moment she couldn't determine whether they looked like that because of the air or because of her fury.

"Will you do something for me?" she said.

"Yes," he said. "Kay. Anything."

She sat down in the chair opposite him.

"What? Tell me," he said.

She closed her eyes. For a moment she remembered the elevator in the dim light, the sweat, the touch of the bars as she reached out with one hand to steady herself.

"I was supposed to get you to do something stupid," she said.

"Were you?" he said.

"Yes," she said. "I was going to bitch you up and give you some bad advice. I've already started. Didn't those things I told you about Indices Tracking sound good?"

"Yes," he said.

"That was just something to establish a little credibility. I had some other ideas."

He watched her.

"My advice would have sounded good," she said. "But it wasn't worth much."

"And you had planned on doing this?" he said. "From the beginning?"

"Yes," she said.

He looked at her, his eyes bloodshot, his face hanging in tired jowls.

"And why would you have done that?" he said.

She shrugged.

"Anger," she said. "Bitterness."

"Yes," he said. "Bitterness. That's something I understand. At least now."

He sat opposite her, looking at her face, her hands.

"And why didn't you go through with it?"

"I wanted to be at my best," she said.

"Oh?" he said.

She nodded. Out the window, over the jagged tops of the buildings, the stars had emerged as yellow points in the pink-gray sky. The effect of them was soothing, and she sat there puzzled by their effect. Then she considered those moments when she had imagined that shade of pink, in the heart of the first leaves of spring, when the new growth had appeared like the open mouths of birds, their flesh just as pink as the first blush of the leaves they resembled. What, after all, is at the heart of a color, or the implication of it? Hope. It was so tied up with wanting to be at one's best for another human being. To be trusted. And admired.

"I fell in love," she said. "That's the short answer. You want to be at your best then, don't you?"

"I wouldn't know," said Blaine, a little sadly. "Tell me, whom did you fall in love with?"

He looked up with a delirious hope.

"No," she said. "Not you."

"Oh," said Blaine. "Well."

He stood up, into the shadows, then he put his hand out, into her hair.

"My darling," he said.

She sat there, letting him touch her, head down.

"Go on," she said. "Make a decision."

"I don't know," he said. "I'm tired. A little fuzzy."

"Take a bath," she said.

"Maybe," he said. "I don't know."

"And shave," she said. "You'll feel better."

"Will I?" he said. "Kay?"

"Do me a favor," she said.

"And what is that?" he said. "I'd do anything for you. Kay, you must know that."

"Do what you know how to do. Make a decision," she said. "Be a . . . "

"A what? A man? Is that what you mean?" he said.

She shrugged.

"Yes," she said. "You could put it that way."

"Perhaps. I've got to change my shirt. Put on a tie."

"That's right," said Kay.

"Then I can go downtown," he said. "Jimmy will take me."

"Yes," said Kay. "Jimmy will take you."

She stood up and kissed him once on the lips, and turned and went through the shadows and out to the door. Blaine watched her go. Then he said, "Kay, please. Wait."

She shook her head.

"No," she said.

"But wait," he said.

"I've got something to do," she said. "I'm in a hurry."

"Kay, Kay," he said. "Where are you going?"

"I've got to meet someone," she said. "Do you know a man by the name of Krupp?"

"No," said Blaine.

Kay shrugged.

"It shouldn't take long," she said. "I'm going to do a favor for a friend."

"Who's that?" said Blaine.

"Just a friend," she said.

BRIGGS HEARD the upward, steady, insistent clicking as someone came up the stairs of his apartment building. The footfalls had a cadence, and he imagined the shape of the stairs from the side, the **Z** of the steps as they went up to a landing, then switched back again, up to the next landing: the sound suggested this shape, a tap, tap, tap, tap, then a shuffle, and the tapping began again. Briggs thought of those times when he had come home in the afternoon, when the beveled glass doors had filled the hall with flecks of spectral light. He tried to remember what it had reminded him of. An old dance hall. The weight of a woman's hair across his face, the movement of hips under a sequined dress, the smell of cigarettes and champagne, all of it leaving him with a sense of yearning. Then the tapping started again, and almost immediately someone starting pounding on his door, not with a closed fist, but with an open hand. He tried for an instant to remember the tug of a woman's hand's on his shoulder, or the pleasant drag of her on his chest and shoulders as she reached up, her eyes closed, to kiss him. He was amazed that he could take comfort in such a notion, but he did, and he sat there, clinging to it for a moment. Surely they had come for him.

He opened the door.

"Briggs," said Kay. She looked right at him. "Come on. Let's go."

"But where?" he said.

"Not here," she said. "It can't be safe here, can it? Come on."

She was wearing her raincoat over a blouse and a pair of jeans. Both of her hands were in her pockets. Her hair had been brushed, and she was wearing lipstick and athletic shoes.

"Are you going to listen to me?" she said, stepping forward. She walked across the threshold, her eyes on his. She reached up to give him a moist, warm kiss. Then she took his arm and gave him a tug, at first gentle and even a little seductive, as though drawing him to her.

"I'll get my coat," he said.

She didn't like this, but she nodded.

"Be quick about it," she said.

"Okay," he said. "What's the rush?"

"Wouldn't you like to know?" she said.

He took his coat from the hook behind the door and put it on. Then they went down the stairs, going around, the tapping sound doubled now. At the landing downstairs, she stopped and looked one way and then another, and they went out into the street. She hesitated there, but it was quiet. At the end of the block he saw the warm, yellow light of the apartments where families lived. The light from these apartments, particularly at night, had always left him with an odd sense of gravitation, as though if he could just get into the light, his desire for warmth or the touch of another human being or, better yet, a sense of being understood by someone else would be realized, although at the same time this ache was made all the stronger by the notion of the impossibility of doing more than just looking.

"Where's Jack?" said Briggs.

"Jack," she said. "Ah, Jack."

She shook her head and then looked down at the ground. Then she seemed to snap out of it, squared her shoulders, put her head up.

"Jack's dead," she said.

"Is he?" said Briggs.

She reached over and took Briggs's hand. Then she put an arm around his, walking next to him.

"I feel cold," she said.

"What about Jack?" he said.

She looked down again.

"What's to tell?" she said. "I did what I was supposed to do. Isn't that what you want to hear?"

"Kay," he said.

"Kay, Kay," she said. "Kay, what? Kay, tell me you didn't do it? Kay, tell me we can start over? Kay, tell me you love me? Kay, what? Kay, have we all got what we wanted from you now?"

She looked up at him now, her eyes looking from one of his to the other. Then she jerked his arm.

"Come on," she said.

"You know I care about you," he said.

"Well, I care about you, too," she said. "I'll tell you another thing. You don't have to worry about Krupp. You hear me? I did that for you. He stepped out of his building, and I got Jack to do him, and then I got rid of Jack. By the book. You know what he tried to do?"

"Who?" said Briggs.

"Krupp," said Kay.

"He probably tried to offer you something, money, something," said Briggs.

"That's right," she said. "That's absolutely right."

She jerked his arm.

"Well, it didn't work," she said.

She trembled under her coat.

"Like I said," she said, "I'm cold. We've got to get off of the street for a while."

They went up the gray steps of an art museum, which was in a building with columns that supported a large marble triangle, like the front of a temple or a court. It had heavy brass-and-glass doors, through which they saw the lobby, filled with white, brightly lighted marble. The doors, which must have weighed a thousand pounds, swung open with a metallic sigh of their hinges, and Kay and Briggs stepped into the main room. The lush silence of the paintings swept over them.

"That's it," said Kay, pointing into another room. "There."

They sat down on a bench in front of a piece of marble sculpture in which Leda and a swan embraced. Leda's leg was thrown over the swan's back, her lips at the swan's bill, her eyes closed. One of her hands was draped over the bird's neck. The entire portrayal was of lust frozen in marble. The swan's head was beneath Leda's lips, tilted upward, at once demanding and supplicant. Kay got up and ran her fingers over Leda's neck and shoulders, across the muscled calf, the carefully done hair. She spread her fingers over Leda's stomach, feeling the cool touch of marble skin and muscles. Briggs sat on the bench, and when Kay touched the swan, he saw that one of her hands was bloodstained. She looked at him and then back again.

She touched the swan, her hand on the swan's neck. She caressed it, running her fingers up to the beak, the eyes, the slight opening in the bill. She tapped her finger against the marble, the tip-tip-tip coming as a kind of impatience.

"Didn't you ever think I was going to get angry?" she said to Briggs without looking at him.

"Yes," he said. "But I kept thinking it would be later, some other time."

"Well, the time has come," she said. "And what do you have to say to me, now that I am angry?"

"Kay," he said.

"Kay, Kay, Kay," she said. "What makes you think I want to hear you say that?"

She looked at the shape of Leda's thighs and arm, at the swan's bill, at Leda's obvious shudder.

"I love you," he said.

"Oh, darling, do you?"

Reassured by Leda's muscled sides, she tapped the marble with a fingernail, and then leaned her cheek close to the marble, running it along the beak. The stains on her fingers made the marble seem very pale.

"Here," she said. "Take my hand. Are you ashamed to touch me?"

"No," he said.

He took her hand.

"Oh, darling," she said. Then she pulled him up. "I'm the only one left now. And you know what? I'm not finished with you. I'm really not."

They went through the room, which smelled of plaster and old marble, and then out the heavy door, Kay leading the way. Outside, where it was dark, Kay jerked his arm, grabbed the front of his coat, and then reached up and gave him a hard, hot kiss, the heat of which left him instinctively reaching up for his mouth, and as he did so he felt the pistol in her pocket as it swung against him. She watched his eyes as he felt it, and then she took it out and used it to tap against the center of his chest. She took his arm again and they started walking, although their gait was erratic, since she jerked him and said, "Come on, come on, you bastard, you son of a bitch, you sweet darling, my love . . . " She shivered as she pulled him against her, then shoved him in front of her.

"Where are we going?" he said.

"You'll see, my darling," she said.

They went down the street, passing the signs in Russian and Bulgarian, the old bookstores with the windows boarded up, and stopped in front of Stone's building. She had the key, and after she had unlocked the door, she shoved it open and it banged against the inside wall, a little puff of plaster dust rising from the hole the doorknob made in the wall. The two of them climbed the stairs, Kay shoving him with the muzzle of the pistol, and then stopping, taking his hand with an exquisite tenderness that only lasted for a moment and seemed to make her angry again. At the door to the practice room, she took out another key and shoved this door open, too. They went in and she slammed the door. The boom reverberated through the upstairs practice rooms. She took off her coat and threw it on the floor.

The piano bench was in front of the window, and she sat on it and pushed him to a chair just opposite her. Beyond her, through the window, he saw some buildings and above them the moon in the night sky.

"Don't you dare say anything," said Kay.

"Why not?" said Briggs. "I have some things to say."

"What did I tell you?" said Kay.

"I want what's best," said Briggs. "You know that."

"I warned you," said Kay. "Didn't I warn you? What's talk? What's that? Just a bunch of words."

She unzipped her jeans, pulled them down, pushed them around her ankles, and, in a moment of fury, started to unlace her shoes, but then ripped them off and threw them against the wall. She pulled her feet out of the legs of the jeans and kicked them away, standing in the sheer underwear she had bought, her legs white in the light that came in from the window. She unbuttoned her blouse with both hands, still holding the pistol, and when this became too exasperating, she ripped the blouse. In the moment, which Briggs saw with an unnatural clarity, the white buttons described an arc through the air. They hit the floor with a click. Briggs said, "Kay, Kay . . . "

Her hands reached out for him, grabbed his hair, pulled him against her chest, and as she did, the pistol making a hard tap against his skull, she said, "Darling, oh, my darling . . . " She let him feel the soft heave of her breast, the powdery touch of her skin, pushed him into the warm and sweaty perfume of her underarms. She brushed her breasts across his face, her flesh flattening against his cheek, his brow, his nose. Then she shoved him away and brought the pistol up and put the barrel against his head.

"Kay," he said.

"I warned you. Didn't I warn you?" she said.

She looked into his eyes, her pupils like black marble under a film of moisture. She took the pistol from his head and swung it up to her own, the muzzle passing his face, then she swung it back and put it against his brow. She hummed a snatch of music, something that she had always wanted to write, but which only came to her now. Then she sang, "When you wake, you shall have, hush-a-bye don't you cry, blacks and bays, dapples and grays, coach and six white horses . . . "

"Kay," he said.

"Have you ever thought about the children we will never have?" she said. "Would it help if we gave them names? What shall we call them? Give me a name for the boy we never had . . . "

"Kay," he said.

"Kay, what?" she said. "Well?"

"I've thought about the children we'll never have," he said.

She put her head against his and gently tapped the hard bones of her skull against his.

"Oh, me, too. At night I wake and hear them mewling, but it's just a phantom, just some sound that comes from my imagination. Ah," she said, moving the pistol back toward her temple, where she tapped it, thinking it over, watching him. She leaned forward and kissed him with that sudden, impulsive hot and wet touch, lingering against him.

"Come here. Right now. I want you to kiss me. I want you to tell me you would die for me. That you would do anything, anything, that you would do what I have done for you . . . "

She leaned over him, dragging a firm nipple across his beard. She kissed his closed eyes, pushed his head downward to her stomach, the navel seeming small and cool, the threads of her underwear against his cheekbones, the insides of her legs smooth.

"You still want me, even now?" she said. "Hold out your hand. Let me see the fingers . . . "

He held out his fingers. They were trembling. She kept her eyes on his.

"Is that desire or fear?" she said.

"I don't know," he said. "I can't tell. All I know is that I love you."

She pushed her underwear down and stepped out of it, and then leaned close, a light brush of hair on his cheek as she pulled him against her lower belly.

"I am going to miss ordinary things, like waking up in the morning and finding you there. Your warmth next to me under the sheets. I wanted to have coffee together and talk about the weather. A dream. A little gossip about the neighbors. Don't you think I wanted that?"

"I wanted it too," he said.

"But don't you see?" she said. "We're never going to get that. Never. Do you know what 'never' means?" She put the pistol against his head now. "Do you want to find out?"

She took his head with both hands now and pulled it against her, saying, "Oh, forgive me."

He reached up and put his hands into the small of her back and then pulled her down onto the bench beside him. She put her head against his shoulder, but even so she bounced the pistol up and down.

Stone came in, wearing a silk dressing gown, his breathing harsh, loud, his shape round there in the light from the hall. He came in and stood by the piano, the door still open. The pistol seemed enormous in her hand as it lay there on her thigh. His eyes went from it to the segments of muscle along Kay's stomach, the definition of her rib cage, her chest and neck, the bones in her shoulders, his glance betraying the frank, intimate impulse that he hadn't felt for years. But the shock of it, the heat on his face, the sudden rush of interest, only made him more disoriented and uncertain.

"What is this?" said Stone. "What is the meaning of this?"

Kay looked up at him and said, "And you."

"What about me?" said Stone.

"All you can hear is music, but you can't feel anything any other way. All you know is technique. Not the person playing it. And what do I think of that?"

"Kay," he said. "Please."

"Please what?" she said. "Please pretend that you felt something you didn't? That you cared for me as much as what I played?"

"My little one," he said.

"Shhhh," said Kay. "Quiet. I'm giving you good advice. Just be quiet."

"Kay," said Briggs, "let's go home, to my place. Let's talk things over."

"Did you say 'home,'?" she said. "Home? Home?" She looked around with disbelief. "We haven't got a home."

"Kay," Briggs said.

"Can't you see?" she said. "We're never going to have a home."

"I—" he said.

"You what?" she said. She stood up, right next to him, her hip against his face. "No. Shhhh. There's nothing more to say." she said. She looked around and said, "Ah, well," and then put the pistol to her head. Briggs felt the jerky shock in her hip, and when she fell away, the night sky was visible beyond where she had stood. He saw the moon, the ridges of mountains there, the Sea of Tranquillity, the debris that had come from endless impact, and as the sound filled the room, as Stone stood back, his face blank now, as though in the midst of the first instant of a practical joke, the moon appeared to undergo a transformation, the shadows becoming more distinct, darker, like a black stain on a sheet.

May 3, dawn

BRIGGS'S EARS were still ringing when he stood on the bridge that connected the two parts of town. The air was cold, but even so he waited in the middle of the bridge, feeling the rumble of the cars that went by as he leaned over the metal railing and looked at the water. The air here was damp, and everything about it suggested the promise of night. It was hard to say just how the temperature, the breeze, and the dampness combined to make him uneasy, but the effect of them was nevertheless to leave him feeling vulnerable and exposed. He tried to recall the touch of Kay's breath, her voice, her glance, but it only added to his sense of the breeze as being cold. He turned away, pulling up his collar, but even so he kept looking at the surface of the river, as though he could, by effort, by concentration bring back the sense of warmth he had had on the Ponte Garibaldi. Now the surface of the river, dark and streaked, left him with the certainty that he was alone. He stood up and started walking, trying to remember that tangerine glow that came off the walls in Rome, and the emotional certainty it suggested, but it was useless. What he saw was the road, the dark cars crossing the bridge. He put his hands in his pockets and started walking, ears ringing, looking up to the sky, but it was cloudy and smoky, and after a while he simply went on walking. The fever seemed to be diminishing, and as it slipped away, as the points of the chill became less distinct, he found that his relief was indistinguishable from a sense of loss. He walked across the bridge to get away from the sound of the water as it broke against the pilings below.

At home, the clock said, "Well, no use crying over spilt milk." She waited for a moment. "And there's something else. I hear they've taken your name down from the walls. How about them apples? It never rains but it pours."

BRIGGS SAT in his office, which was down the hall from the one he used to have. It was much better, on the corner, with windows on two sides. Much better than when he had been a contract worker. The light was soothing. When he looked out through the walls of the glass cubicle, he noticed that while people wore white shirts, they were letting their hair grow again. Not so many red shoes.

He had been hired again after Phillips came to see him about a problem, a new disease that had been showing up in the less reputable parts of town, in flophouses and cheap hotels, among prostitutes and hustlers. It started like the flu, but soon the linings of the eyes, the mouth, the lips, and other intimate places started to turn black and itch. Phillips had come up to Briggs's apartment and described the condition, and Briggs had said, "Yeah. I've been watching the medical reports."

"Do you think you could do something with it?"

"Yeah," said Briggs. "I think so."

"When?" he said.

"Pretty fast," said Briggs. "Almost right away."

"No kidding?" said Phillips. "Well, that's good. Why don't you come back to work? I think there's a place for you. Particularly if you can come up with something fast. Do you think it will work—I mean, what you can come up with?"

"Yes," said Briggs.

"No kidding?" said Phillips. "And fast, too. Hmpf."

Now Briggs worked on machines that were self-replicating, just as von Neumann had imagined. Other planets, other worlds. Often, late at night, when he was lonely, he had the impulse to add something, but he resisted it, and instead he worked on a method to make sure no one could tamper with the machines, but as he did so he realized he was up against the fact that nothing was ever won by being defensive: all wars had been won by offense and by new technology. So, while he did the best he could, he was aware that someone would start working soon to find a way around the things he did.

Leslie Carr called one night. She asked Briggs how he was doing, and he said he was all right. How about her? She was quiet on her end. After a while, she said, "I've been better." He nodded. Well, that was to be expected. Could he ask her a question? Who had made her so bitter? Who had seduced her in such a way as to make her so angry? She was silent again. Then she said, "Wendell Blaine."

"The banker?" said Briggs.

"The ex-banker," said Carr. "Did you see that he resigned?"

"Yes. I was curious about that," said Briggs.

"Yeah, well, I guess he got his," said Carr. There was a plaintive hope in her voice.

"Do you think so?" said Briggs.

"That's one of the reasons I called. I was wondering if you knew anything about it?" said Carr.

"Me?" said Briggs.

"Well," said Carr. "It was just a thought."

Carr was quiet on her end.

"Carr?" he said.

"I was wondering if Kay told you something," said Carr. "Anything. Maybe she mentioned something about Blaine . . . "

"All I know is what I read in the papers," said Briggs.

"Well," said Carr. "I just thought I'd call."

Briggs looked for news of Blaine, although there wasn't much. Blaine spent a lot of time looking for young musicians, now that he was retired. He traveled often. There were rumors that he had made a fool of himself over a young woman, a pianist, in Brazil.

So Briggs did his work. He made some money. At night the clock listened to his breathing, and from time to time, when he rolled over, he saw the radiance of her Spandex outfit, the gleam in her short blond hair, her cheerful expression, her Midwestern freckles and large teeth. Then he tried to go back to sleep, but still the hours between midnight and dawn often ran slower than at other times, as though dragging something: memory, old desires, hopes that had come to nothing. Finally he got rid of the clock, although the peacefulness of the apartment didn't bring relief so much as it increased the intensity of an undefined longing.

At work, the sounds of the old mill building had a reassuring quality, and when he stood in the hall, he could look down on what had been the floor of the machine shop, although now it was filled with the blue glow from the monitors that lined the room from one side to another. At the end of the floor were a coffee machine and a pool table where people took breaks.

From down below, Briggs heard a shout. It was keen, sudden, a sound that came from an argument. He guessed that it was bound to happen as more and more men and women paired off, and he supposed that couples would argue, even at work. He got up and went into the hall. From here he saw the black floor of the lobby, and the black, horseshoe-shaped desk where a guard sat. Some people were standing around the guard, who spoke to a woman. She was trying to get past him, and when he questioned her, all she said was that her name was Gloria. Gloria, she said. She was wearing a red dress, a short one. Even from a distance, Briggs noticed that she had a glow, a quality that was hard to be precise about, but was still obvious. The guard shook his head at her and she started yelling, trying to push by, and when he stood up and put out his hand, she broke free.

Phillips came out of his office, too. He carried some papers, which he had been reading when he'd heard the noise from below. Other people came out of their offices, too, drawn toward the commotion. Down below, the woman came across the floor, her stomach swelling under the red dress. Briggs guessed she wasn't more than six or seven months pregnant, her belly firm and high. As she came, she yelled some garbled words, which she repeated, and each time she went through it again, she shouted louder. She came to the metal stairway and started climbing, still looking upward, searching the faces that stood along the upper walkway, all of them peering down with a curiosity perfectly imbued with alarm. She called out, "Briggs. Briggs. Where is Briggs?"

"Stop her," said the guard. "For Christ's sake, will someone grab her?"

She turned up the stairs, one hand on the banister, her face turned up. She was carrying a shopping bag, and she held it as though it were the only thing she had in the world.

"My name's Gloria," she said as she came up the stairs. "Gloria. Does that mean anything to you?"

The woman kept climbing, her feet hitting the metal mesh of the steps, her eyes going from one face to another.

"Are you Briggs?" she asked one man.

"No," said the man, but he didn't offer to point him out.

"Up here," said Briggs. "What can I do for you?"

"Are you Briggs?" she said.

She stopped now, panting on the landing as she held her sides.

"I'm Briggs," he said. "What can I do for you?"

"Oh," she said. "Thank God. They wouldn't let me in. He said you would help me. If I ended up like this. Look."

She put her hands on her firm stomach.

"Can you see this?"

"Yes," said Briggs.

"He said if I needed anything to contact you," she said. "You know, Jack. You know Jack, don't you?"

She looked right at him.

"Well," she said. "Are you going to help?"

"What's this?" said Phillips.

"He said you'd help," said Gloria. "If I had trouble or needed money, I should come to you. That's why I'm here."

She took the next couple of steps up to the top.

"Well?" she said.

Briggs looked out the window. At the end of summer, the river was slick and green. He saw that some dark, yet still compelling thing was floating against the bank. Briggs knew it was there by the birds that funneled over it like black checks. A dead dog, perhaps, or maybe something larger. At the horizon, long pennants drifted away from smokestacks, and through the yellowish smoke, birds appeared and disappeared. He tried to watch them as they dipped and turned on his side of the smoke, and he found it hard to explain why their disappearance left him straining. He guessed it was because they reminded him of something that he had always depended upon, but that was nevertheless slipping away. He went on staring out the window, trying to make sense of the landscape, but all he could think was, *Jack. Jack.*

"Can you handle this?" said Phillips.

Briggs swallowed. The men and women who had come out to the top of the stairs now turned away, although many wished they could stay.

"What?" said Briggs.

"Can you handle this?" said Philips. "Do you want some help? Someone to show this young woman out?"

"No," said Briggs.

"They better not push me around," said Gloria. "I'm tired of that. They push me this way. They push me that way."

"Briggs?" said Phillips.

"I don't think you can help," said Briggs.

Phillips shrugged.

"Well, okay," he said. Then he glanced down at the papers in his hand and turned away, back toward his office, although he looked over his shoulder.

"You don't mind my coming here, do you?" said Gloria.

"I think you better come in," said Briggs.

C H A P T E R **⑮** | *October 1, 2029, afternoon*

GLORIA'S SHOPPING bag had moving images on it, two rainbow trout that swam from one side of the bag to the other, where, at the end, as though it were the side of an aquarium, they peacefully turned to glide back the other way. Rainbow trout with a bright red streak on the side. Briggs and Gloria went down the street, and he kept looking at the fish on the surface of her bag. Every now and then a mayfly nymph rose from the bottom of the image and tried to make it to the surface, but one of the trout picked it off. Briggs watched with subdued fascination, since it was one predictable action he could count on. Everything else left him afraid. As he watched the transit of the fish, he thought of something else that scared him each time they turned, as though they described the path of his own thoughts.

Briggs knew he was obligated to go to the police. Women weren't supposed to get pregnant in this way, and if one did, it was a capital offense. He imagined them arresting her, binding her wrists, pushing her down on a chair in one of those dreary halls of a holding pen. The worst would be the process from there, the administrative hearing, the genetic testing, the rest. And then, finally, sooner or later, she would realize where all of it was going. He knew that long, desperate legal procedures ground people down, and at the end she would be left with nothing more than the overwhelming fatigue in which a human being obeys the last brief orders. Sit down. Put out your arm.

They went on walking in the air of fall. The smokiness of it, while mildly claustrophobic, still carried a lingering warmth from the summer months, and something else too, which he guessed was the promise of harvest, of fields that were stripped of what they had produced and then were burned over. Maybe that was what made the smoky afternoons of fall so complicated, a mixture of fruitfulness and scorched earth. Up ahead he saw the illuminated globes that stood in front of the police station.

Concrete steps led up to a frosted-glass door with black letters on it. Scrap paper blew along the street, and a woman paced back and forth in front of the steps, obviously determined to take some action but equally afraid to do so. Above her, by the door, stood two officers. They leaned against the walls of the entrance, uniforms wrinkled, faces unshaved. They looked as if they were working long shifts, twelve, fourteen hours. Maybe more. They glanced toward the horizon, and then their eyes swept back to the pacing woman, not so much with curiosity as with a variety of emotional gravity. Soon they'd have to go down there and ask her what the problem was.

Gloria said, "Ouch. Wait. I've got a stitch."

She touched Briggs's hand. He looked up at the police.

"It kicks sometime," said Gloria. "It's such a funny feeling. Ow. There it is."

She didn't smile, though.

"Here," she said. She reached out for his hand. "Do you want to feel?"

"Look," he said. "Let's just sit down here until you feel better, all right?"

They sat down. Her shopping bag wrinkled as she put it next to her, but then she moved it because it was between them. The policemen came down the steps, and the light-textured soles of their boots made a fatigued *hush, hush, hush.*

"What's the trouble?" said one.

"Do you need help?" said the other.

"I think we're okay," said Briggs.

"I didn't ask you," said the first. "I asked her. You aren't pregnant, are you?"

"No," said Briggs.

"Well?" said the first.

"It's just a stitch," said Gloria.

The policeman shrugged.

"When are you due?" he said.

"Two months. Maybe more."

They both looked away, not actually suspicious so much as habitually used to not believing anything that was said to them.

"All right," said the first.

"Are you the father?" said the other to Briggs.

"He's a friend of the father," said Gloria.

"Where's the father?" said the other.

"I don't know," said Gloria.

"Christ," said the first cop. "Hey. You." He pointed at the woman who was walking back and forth. "Yeah, you. What's the trouble?"

"Me?" said the woman.

"Christ," said the first cop to the other. "I'm going across the street for a cup of coffee. You coming or not?"

Briggs watched them go, both in black, swinging from side to side as they went. In the park at the end of the street he saw the trees. They had lost their leaves early this year, and so the prospect before him was one of the yellow horizontal line of the river, the silver clutter of the trees, and then the yellow sky. As he watched those fish swim back and forth in the advertisement on the side of Gloria's bag, he thought of the next thing that left him afraid: that more than two people had been adding things to Kay and Jack.

Any number could have been adding things. He had been vain, he guessed, in his ability to discover one of them, and this vanity had stopped him from considering whether or not there were others. Someone totally unknown, a technician, a disgruntled employee, anyone with a bone to pick. It was almost pointless to try to discover who it had been, since his quandary wasn't so much who they were as what he was going to do about the young woman who was sitting next to him, panting in the fall air.

Gloria's skin had a moist glow to it.

"I didn't want to have this baby," she said. "The instant I found out, I went to the pharmacy and got something." She took Briggs's hand. "It didn't work."

"What do you mean?" said Briggs.

She looked at him as though he was being dense.

"I told you," she said. "Then I went to see a doctor. And you know what she said? She even showed me the pictures. The baby is attached to me, inside, in a way that would start bleeding, a lot of bleeding, if they got rid of it. No one wants to risk that kind of bleeding. See? She said it was one in a million."

"One in a million," he said. "Was there anything else unusual?"

"I don't know," she said. "That's all they told me."

He sat there, trying to feel a little of the afternoon sunlight on his face, but the shadow of the building had swept over them, and all he felt was the approach of the cold months. Even now, in the gray-purple shadow, he sensed the worst nights of January, when everything had a kind of arctic stasis. Then he thought that he should contact Gloria's doctor, but he knew from his own work that the doctor would only be able to tell him what had happened, not why. In the shadow, the trout on Gloria's bag seemed clearer, more perfectly colored. The mayfly nymphs were gray, with the texture of silk.

"Come on," he said.

"Where are we going?" she said.

"My place," he said. "It's not so bad."

"Are you sure?" she said.

He picked up the bag, where the fish finned back and forth, waiting for the next mayfly.

"Yes," he said. "I'm sure."

"Do you have a lot of room?"

"No," he said. "Just a living room and a bedroom."

"Where am I going to sleep?" she said.

"In the bedroom," he said. "I'll sleep on the sofa."

BRIGGS OFTEN came home and heard Gloria taking a bath. The apartment was scented with the soap she used, and as she sat in the tub she let hot water trickle in to keep the temperature constant. She sat in the early-fall light that came in the window, her belly seeming to float in the soapy foam like a firm island. When she heard the door open, she said, "Briggs. Don't you want to see? Look."

The water made a plash as she moved, trying to get comfortable, or when the baby kicked. He stood in the doorway.

"Briggs?" she said.

"Yes," he said.

The light made her skin seem not pale so much as white and glowing, and under the soap her growing nipples were the color of dark cherries.

"Will you wash my back?" she said.

"Sure," he said.

"Don't be shy," she said.

"I'm not shy," he said.

"Yes, you are," she said. "You can look at me. I want you to look at me. See? That way we're in it together. Not a lot, but a little bit."

He picked up the soap and ran it across her back, going over the muscles there, up the crease in the middle of her neck, down to the water, where her skin disappeared into the damp and shiny swelling of her hips.

"Hmmm," she said. "That's good. You'd think that after this, I wouldn't be interested in sex at all, but I think about it all the time."

She stood up, the water rushing over her white skin in sheets, and as she dripped he handed her a towel. He dried her back, too, helped her out of the tub. She stretched out on the bed and he rubbed her stomach and legs, her breasts with oil. He did it slowly, watching the light from the window fall across her skin. In the slick warmth of the oil he had the sensation of not being able to tell where she ended and where he began. Then he put on her shoes for her, kneeling in front of her bare legs and stomach.

On the bulletin board in the kitchen was a list of basic food groups. He wanted to make something good, since the best part of the day was when they put food on the table in the small kitchen and she ate with good appetite. They talked about how much weight she had gained, how much exercise she was getting, how she was sleeping. She didn't sleep very well.

She often went to bed early, and then Briggs sat down in the living room to do chores he had brought home from work. He set up a problem and started going through it, although from time to time he heard her moan or cry out, and then he went to stand at the foot of the bed until she slept quietly again. Still, there were times when he felt her come up behind him. She asked how he was doing and started to rub his back. He closed his eyes and felt her affection for him in the touch of her hands. And then the certainty of her pregnancy had a soothing effect. It was something he could concentrate on. She squirmed against him when she rubbed his back.

"Is that better?" she said.

"Yeah," he said. "Thanks."

"You know," she said. "I didn't really care about Jack. I was just looking to have a little excitement. That's all there was to it."

He helped her into bed again and sat there while she fell asleep. At these moments he felt how much the apartment was improved by having her here, or, to be more precise, how much he had been improved by having her here. And when he looked up from his work and tried to say why this was the case, he supposed that one of the reasons was her frankness. He depended on it. He missed her when he was at work. He brought flowers home and she was delighted by them. She rubbed petals on the skin behind her ears and asked him to smell the fragrance.

One night, when he had been working for a while and she had been sleeping, she woke up and came into the living room.

"Hey, Briggs," she said. "Have you got a minute?"

"Sure," he said. "What's the trouble?"

"I'm scared," she said.

"There's nothing to worry about," said Briggs.

She shrugged.

"It's not like a thing I am worrying about," she said. "Like about having the baby. It's not that kind of scared. It's a more general kind. Like when you're afraid of the dark. You don't know why you're scared, or what you're scared of, you just are."

"It will be all right," he said.

"That's easy to say," she said. "Do me a favor, will you? Lie down with me until I fall asleep."

She got back into bed, and he lay down behind her. The walls glowed with a soft luminescence from the light outside. She took one of his hands and slipped it under the covers, under her breast, so that he could feel the heat. It was like touching a hot water bottle. She whispered, "Have you ever felt anything like that?"

"No," he said. He closed his eyes.

"Get under the covers, will you?" she said. "I'm scared."

He got under the covers and she took his hand again.

"Feel that?" she said.

"Yes," he said.

"It's nice, isn't it?" she said.

"Uh-huh," he said.

"Open your shirt, will you?" she said. "Take off your pants. Don't you ever get lonely?"

"Sometimes," he said.

"Just sometimes?" she said.

He took off his clothes and lay next to her under the sheet. She turned toward him, the smooth heat pushing against his skin.

"Oh," he said.

"That's better," she said. "Don't you think so?"

"Yes," said Briggs.

"I don't want to be scared," she said.

"Me neither," he said.

"You don't have to be," she said.

"I'm not so sure about that," he said.

"When I first came to see you, you looked scared. Were you?"

I still am, he thought.

"Yes," he said.

"About what?" she said.

"You think one thing is going to happen, but then it turns out another way."

"Like what?" she said.

"Oh, I guess it's the kind of thing any pregnant woman worries about. She worries about having a monster. Or she worries about deformities. I guess I worry about things like that."

"But you have to get over that, don't you?" she said.

"Yes," he said. "You do. You really do."

She put her head against his, the strands of her hair tickling his face.

"Tell me," she said. "Do you think we can work things out?"

"I hope so," he said.

"Yes," she said. "It would be nice, wouldn't it?" She turned to face him. "And we don't have to worry about monsters. Do we?"

"No," he said. "No monsters."

ABOUT THE AUTHOR

CRAIG NOVA is the author of nine novels. He has received an Award in Literature from the American Academy and Institute of Arts and Letters and is a recipient of a Guggenheim Fellowship. He lives in Vermont.